By The Light Of A Darkened Forest

By The Light Of A Darkened Forest

J.W. Goodwin

Published 2016 by Creativia
Paperback design by Creativia (www.creativia.org)
Cover art by Creative Paramita
Edited by Elizabeth N. Love

To Sherry,
If not for you, Garlandon would truly be lost.

Contents

Prologue

A devastating battle had just ensued in a once peaceful land. Only a few war-riors remained out of the once large armies. The lives that were lost that day were surely in the hundreds, if not thousands. It was unsettling to any of the survivors. Sure enough, the god of war would have been pleased by the amount of blood that was spilt that day.

Many of the bodies were seen littered among the dead horses, swords and ar-mor. A sea of blood formed under the discarded bodies. As they walked through it, one could hear the sloshing and feel the warmth of the liquid seep into the leather boots. It was a horrid sight. Many of the dead were friends, brothers, sis-ters, fathers, mothers, uncles, aunts and grandparents. Every one of the fallen was close to any one of the survivors.

Those that had died were from both sides of the battle. They all lived in the same village. They were split apart by a newcomer. He had twisted the fate of those caught in his lies. He promised a better life for those who served him. The only thing he asked for was their souls and unwavering loyalty to his cause, no matter how gruesome or hard their lives were at first. It twisted his followers into something unforgivable. They were a peaceful race, and that man changed them for war.

A soldier clad in dark iron slowly walked forward to the opposing line. He avoided and tried to step over the fallen that sprawled out before him. He stopped and knelt down to one of the bodies. He recognized it to be a relative, one that he cared for deeply, as the one next to it was of council. He frowned knowing that they all had worked together once for the sake of unity and peace. How little did they know that they had changed the future, one filled with pain and grief.

He looked to the opposing line. Their eyes were soulless as he knew the magic that held them. They followed their leader and sold their souls to the evil in their hearts. He removed his helmet slowly and allowed his sweat-drenched, long, blond hair be caught in the wind. His deep forest green eyes filled with tears of rage and pain. A growl rose in his throat and escaped his thin lips.

He stood and gripped harder on the handle of his sword. The opposing people didn't have anything more to lose. He knew that soon they would turn into creatures far more horrifying and deadly than any carnivore. They would go after his village, and his family would be in danger. They gave up everything for one man's lies. That one man who was corrupted by the evil buried in the world and sent to the past to rule everything.

"Is this the battle you wanted?" He yelled angrily at the opposing force. His mid-tone voice was harsh as he had been yelling orders throughout the battle. "Did you wish for your brothers' and sisters' deaths? What was the purpose of this act of violence besides following a madman's desires?" The opposing warriors marched towards the lone soldier. No response was given to the questions he had asked. They marched on without a word, without consequence.

The soldier looked behind him as the remainder of his army stood at the ready. One of them walked forward to join him. He was soon followed by the others. They took their stance by his side. They would stand their ground till the very end. Swords drawn, they were ready for the final fight.

The soldier returned his helmet to his head. It was the final fight that he could commit to. He knew from that point forward if he were to fight again, his son would no longer have a father. His wife would lose her husband and he would lose his soul. He had more than them to protect. He had to defend his best friend who had warned them of the intruder. He who was of pure spirit had risked his life and family to warn him. He who was unaware of the war beyond his backyard would now be tending to his cows.

"This is the beginning of a new age and the unfortunate end of peace," he told his comrades. "The prophecy has begun, and we are the first to feel the evil that has come. Let us stand our ground and try our best at being rid of the illness that will surely spread. We will protect our loved ones before this day is done; that I promise you. Now let's get Baltazar!"

They cheered as they raced forward to meet the enemy. A soft voice could be heard from across the field as the swords clashed for the last time. "I have foretold long before the coming of man that the evil will come, as it tried to taint my creation. Its corruption will travel to a time forgotten and change the destiny of Garlandon. Only those chosen by my hand will save us, and the cycle will begin and repeat until time's end. This is Creanni's prophecy and the destiny of the Gates of Life."

Chapter 1

Footprints in the Snow

"Hurry up, slow poke," happily teased a young woman. "We need to make it to the first marker before dark."

A second woman walked slowly behind her and breathed heavily. "Where are you getting all this energy from," she questioned breathlessly. "Usually you're the one who follows me. Why do you want to be the leader all of a sudden?"

The first woman shrugged her shoulders as she stood on a snow covered stump. Her bright aquamarine eyes looked around, making sure there were no signs of danger. Her lively, shoulder-length dark brown hair stuck out from under her black toque. Her high cheeks glowed red from the winter chill while her thin, pink lips held a smile. Her red winter coat, black ski pants and black boots kept her average build warm. She adjusted her large pack as her thick, black gloves covered her hands.

The second woman caught up with her. Her copper red hair was seen from under her dark blue toque. Her deep blue eyes watched her friend intently. She crossed her arms which caused creases in her coat. She also wore black ski pants and boots and carried a large pack with her.

"I'm usually waiting for you to catch up. What has you so hyped up," she inquired. She giggled and breathed the crisp winter air deeply. She was one of Evelyn's only friends and she was her best. She would have done anything to keep her safe. "Sorry, Paige, I'm just excited to be out with you. It's been forever since we've spent time together," she explained. She shook her head as she walked ahead of her. "I know. You've been so busy with work and me out on the weekends. It's nice to have more than just a coffee with you."

Evelyn's heart warmed as she agreed wholeheartedly. "Yes it is. We haven't done something like this since we were in high school." She nodded back. Last time they went hiking was in the summer and both nearly had heat stroke. "You know what, Evelyn, let's quicken the pace. Get a work out from this trip."

She growled at the mention of her full first name. "It's Eve ok, not Evelyn."

Paige nodded after shrugging her shoulders and they walked faster.

They continued through the winter wonderland of the Lost Lorne Forest. It was a warmer winter day than what was experienced so far that year. The trees were frosted with the cold of the night, but it melted with the hot sun. The snow sparkled and filled with glitter. The forest itself was silent. The animals were all hibernating or would keep their distance.

Snowshoes left a trail of where they had travelled. A good marker in case they got lost. The crunch of their prints and their breathing were the only things to be heard. She breathed out heavily from the exercise. The moisture hung in the air as miniature clouds. It also sparkled in the sunlight like the snow. She slowed and reached out to touch it. Through the haze of her breath, Paige was getting ahead of her. She hurried to catch up.

The sun had begun to set behind the mountains that could just be seen over the tree tops. They found the first marker and set up camp. The small clearing was made by Evelyn's grandfather. A large portion of the forest was part of her grandfather's property. Trails covered the woods along with a few camp grounds. It was all made for her to explore the place she loved so much.

Once a fire was created, they shared stories about their lives while waiting for their supper to cook. Their conversation continued as they ate. It had been too long since their last good chat. When the meal was finished, they cleaned their dishes and packed them away again. They played a card game to pass the time until sleep was near. Soon they tired, and Paige entered the tent to change.

Evelyn wasn't being completely honest with her friend. She only wanted company while she got away from her routine of work and sleep. It didn't matter who travelled with her so long as she wasn't alone. The boredom of routine tortured her and needed a change of pace. She also wanted an escape from her increasing nightmares. They would haunt her during the winter and normally would last one or two nights. This year they were constant. It started off with once a week and then progressed to every time she slept. She would awake feeling that the dream was reality and the waking world was a lie. It would make her sick and she'd cry out for help.

Her gaze was drawn to the night sky. It had started snowing and the flakes rested lightly on her exposed cheeks. Their tracks would be covered by morning. She dug out her small roll of florescent pink marker and long hunting knife. She tied it to a branch that led to the path they wanted. Getting lost was dangerous, especially with the recent kidnappings and lost bodies.

While tying off her marker, a shadow behind one of the trees caught her attention. She stared at it as she knew it to belong to a human. No one had permission to be back there. Her grandfather's land was marked well with trespassing signs, and the roads were blocked by fencing. If anyone were there, they would have broken the fence. It was no secret that the forest within the property held excellent hunting. She couldn't stand those who hunted for sport and not food.

She started to make her way forward with her sharp hunting knife positioned to attack when the tent zipper came undone. She called out to say she was finished. She turned back to where the shadow was, but it was gone. What had possessed her to imagine a person there? She shook her head and drowned the fire's flames.

After changing, she relaxed in her sleeping bag. The sound of the night wind whistling through the trees was soft. It was calming compared to the snoring that soon ensued from her companion. She sighed tiredly knowing that she needed her sleep, even though it would be a restless one. She rolled onto her side before closing her eyes and allowing her uneasy sleep to take her.

Sounds of panic woke her from her deep slumber. She groggily opened her eyes to find that it was morning. Her stomach churned as she gagged. That was a sign that a nightmare had begun to form in her mind when her friend's voice interrupted it. She hurriedly pulled on her boots and coat before leaving the confines of the warm tent.

"There you are, Eve," angrily exclaimed Paige. Her fury was strange for so early in the morning. Evelyn's eyes wandered but found calm. Nothing was taken or out of place. There was no reason for her outburst. Paige hugged herself as a fear was seen in her eyes. "Someone tried to get into our tent last night." She straightened a little and looked again. Again everything was normal. "Try looking down, genius."

Evelyn looked to her feet. Still groggy from sleep, she knelt to observe the footprints. Their prints were scattered everywhere. It took a while, but a new set tangled with theirs. They led to the tent, then back to the trees. They were a bit larger than her own feet. Unlike their boots, those prints didn't contain groves; they were smooth.

She stood, filled with her own worry. "Definitely not one of our own," she mumbled. She placed her hands on her hips.

"No really? I thought that you were walking around out here in your socks to scare me," she scoffed.

Evelyn wasn't impressed with her remark. Being woken by a scream didn't give her time to fully waken. "Well, sorry for trying figure this out. Not like I have anything better to do, right.?"

Evelyn crawled back into the tent. She hated when people judged her thought processes. She talked to herself to try to assess a situation and, being her friend, Paige should know that. As she changed and readied for another day, she thought about the prints. Most modern footwear had some sort of pattern on the sole. The only ones that didn't were ballerina slippers, and no one in their right mind would wear those outside in the dead of winter.

Exiting the tent was met with an icy glare. She sighed and began to cook breakfast. That was her friend's normal behavior towards her when she ignored an argument. "Look, Paige, whoever it was is gone now. If there are any crazy people out here, I have my knife, so we won't be unprotected. Just relax, this is supposed to be fun remember." She snorted and went to change. She rolled her eyes. She wondered if she should have left Paige behind.

They ate breakfast in silence. Evelyn was not pleased. Paige should trust that she knows how to survive in the woods. She's always prepared when they go hiking. The only thing that she didn't have was a gun, but they shouldn't need that at all. It was winter. Nothing of great danger was out there except for the snow. It was also private property, no one was supposed to be out there but them.

Once they finished their meal, they packed up the site in silence. She was still angry with Paige. The longer the silence, the longer Evelyn wished she would have done the trip alone. Before leaving the small clearing, she took off the small band of marking on the tree. She didn't want to be followed by whoever was at their tent in the night. She wanted to make sure it was hard as possible to be followed.

They began to talk to each other again closer to sunset, but it was a quiet discussion and the tension could be felt. The sound of wind picking up through the trees made her shiver slightly. It was going to be a cold night. She carried the forecast of what it should have been for their trip. It was supposed to be warm and sunny. She had a feeling that it had changed.

They set up camp at the next check point. It was done carefully, and they packed some snow on the sides of it. She wanted to make sure they were warm and safe in case anything happened. The fire was warm as it cooked their supper. The mood lightened and they began to laugh again. It had been a long time since she enjoyed herself. Her smile continued to grow the longer they joked.

Paige entered the tent to change first. Evelyn tied her pink marker to mark the next path. She looked out to the night. It was a lonely sight as the darkness swallowed the trees. It was hard to see past the gloom. The moon hidden by the clouds offered no light. She felt like the moment represented how she felt. She felt lonely amongst the city of people she worked in. Still single, she didn't date much. Not like men approached her anyways. She was the quiet girl who lived in the country. Nothing interesting there.

A shadow moved and her eyes darted to it. It was hard to distinguish, but a figure of a person stood next to a tree. She blinked a few times but it remained there. It couldn't have been her imagination. It just couldn't be at that point. No sane person would envision the same thing two days in a row. She took a step forward when the tent unzipped. Paige watched her curiously. Evelyn waved her hand and told Paige nothing was wrong. Looking back, the shadow had gone.

The next morning came too soon. The deeper they travelled into the forest, the more her anxiety grew. She felt like something big was going to happen, but it wasn't going to be a pleasant experience. This led her to have a light sleep. Any noise that was made by the outside made her startle awake. By the time dawn came, she felt more exhausted and knew that sleep would not find her.

She readied quietly. If she could nap while sitting in the light, she may have more of a chance to make up some sleep. She realized noon marked that their trip was half over. They were to spend three days out there. Time went by so quickly. She shook her head as those thoughts only worsened her mood. It would be best if she waited outside for her friend.

Morning was bright as the sun's rays penetrated the thick branches. She started the fire again for breakfast. The wind rattled through the trees. The light reflected off of the falling snow. It was calming. She felt a smile pull at her lips. She always enjoyed the snow. Winter was her favorite season as it held many happy memories for her.

She filled a small pot with snow when she noticed that the footprints from the morning before were there. She growled as she put the pot over the fire. They led her into the forest. They were gathered to where the shadow was the night before. The person had been pacing; the footprints crossed each other countless times. A closer look around proved that no one was there. She must have been losing it. People told her that loving the snow would drive people insane. She never believed it until then.

She returned to the fireside. The snow had melted but had not reached a boil. Oatmeal was that morning's breakfast, and she looked forward to it. It kept her fuller than any other meal. The ability to change the flavor was always a bonus.

Once they packed the camp, they headed off again. The day itself was boring to her. The sky was bright and clear, just as the weatherman predicted. There were no conversations between them, not even a question if they were on the right path. There was nothing thrilling to see; it was just the trees and snow. Not even creatures greeted them. It was simply just walking in the cold. Her mind didn't even wander that day, which was odd. Normally she would day dream if something was boring.

Once camp was set up, they had their supper. It was the final meal of the trip, one that brought sadness that it was ending. They talked about how they felt free after the hiking. They mentioned the snow and how everything was so peaceful. Throughout it all, never once were the mysterious footprints mentioned. Evelyn didn't even bring up what she had seen that morning.

Paige entered the tent first as Evelyn tended to the site. As usual supper needed to be stored and the fire extinguished. Her final step was tying the pink marker when a rustling came from the path ahead. It startled her and her body tensed. She looked around tentatively and found the shadow once again. "I'm tired of you following us. You are on private property and I am not afraid to kill you," she shouted at the shadow. It didn't move. It was more than unsettling. Normal people would have fled; then again, stalkers were not normal.

The tent unzipped and Paige crawled out. She was frightened by Evelyn's outburst. "Who are you talking to?" She whispered.

Evelyn ignored her and returned to watch the shadow. Unlike before, it still lingered. "There's been a shadow of a person watching us every night. Each morning after I see the shadow, we have those footprints. I've had enough of them following us."

She quickly retrieved a flashlight from her pack. She had had it with being frightened. It was her property and there should have been no one but them. The shadow was still there but altered somehow. Her heartbeat quickened the closer she got. In her other hand was the hunting knife. If it was someone dangerous, she would be ready for them.

She aimed the beam at her target. An old, white cloth was blowing in the wind. The ground below it didn't hold any footprints. Her eyebrows furrowed. The cloth shouldn't have been there. Her grandfather didn't have anything like that and it was too small for a sheet. She put her knife away and wiggled it free from the tree. It was big enough to be a cloak as she noticed a clasp that was undone. The material was thick and rough.

She returned with the cloth in hand. She sighed and packed it with the rest. Maybe she had been hallucinating the shadow the entire time, but the new object couldn't have just appeared on its own. Perhaps it was left by a trespasser long ago as it was aged by time. Her friend was horrified with the expression still apparent on her face. "It's alright Paige, it's just an old cloth. Knowing grandpa, he may have lost it. Though I've honestly never seen it before."

Paige's shoulders lowered as she breathed out slowly. "Thank goodness, at least it's taken care of. Come and get some sleep. We should get up early so we can get home sooner. I hope your grandma has some cookies left."

Evelyn agreed. She looked forward to being home again. She could sleep in her warm bed and bake cookies for her and her grandfather. Her cheeks warmed at the thought as she dumped large piles of snow onto the fire. When the embers were out, she crawled into the sleeping bag. She was hoping for a good sleep as she felt like she was running on fumes. Soon sleep over took her and she sailed off to dreamland.

* * *

"Death to all who oppose me," shouted an enraged deep voice. It was dark and filled with malice. It made her tremble with fear. She wanted to run. She needed to find safety. She felt like the voice was going to take everything that she held dear. It was going to kill everyone. Suddenly, another sound reached her ears. *Click. Click. Click.* She felt her fear increase to terror. That sound brought death. It was in the legends and told as warnings to never stray from the spirits. "Bugs everywhere! Run boy, save yourself," yelled a closer male voice. Sadness filled her soul from the sound. That voice was familiar, and she wanted to know whose it was. They were important to her. She always felt safe with him. He would protect her. She couldn't leave him. "But I can't, if I leave you here you'll die." Her lips reacted on their own. It was her yet not her.

Click. Click. Click. Her body trembled from the fear. She wished she could see what have happening. She might be able to figure out how to save that man. She wished she could save him. If anyone was out there, they had to save him. "Leave boy, before they find you," ordered the voice. He was scared too as his voice quivered. He was never afraid. He was brave and strong. She wanted to cry. "No, I won't leave you."

Click. Click. Click. She heard a maniacal cackle. She wanted the other voice to reach out to her and hold her close. She was always safe with him. He was smart and could always come out of things. He would always say the same thing of her. "Join me and we shall conquer this world and its future," offered the evil one. She shuddered but felt defiant. "No! If I help you, you'll kill him."

Click. Click. Click. Unbearable sadness and helplessness filled her. She knew she couldn't protect that man. She was useless and weak. What could someone so small do? He gave her so much but she couldn't give anything in return. She couldn't even save him. "Leave him alone," she cried out. The evil snorted. "A sacrifice must be made for my domination. You know the prophecy. You of all people should know it."

Click. Click. SCREECH!! Reality left her. Trembling, she let out a long cry. "Daddy!"

Chapter 2

Shadow of Insects

Evelyn woke up damp from sweat and cold from tearing apart the sleeping bag. Tears soaked her cheeks and her body trembled from the fear. Those nightmares have haunted her since the night her parents died. It was so long ago, she couldn't remember them. All she had was the terror. Every time would be a reminder of the emotions and pain. She curled into a ball, holding onto her pillow. *It was only a nightmare; it wasn't real.* That was a mantra a psychologist suggested. It didn't always work but it was better than nothing.

As always, it took too long to settle down. The tent was glowing pale yellow from the morning rays. It was always a welcomed sight when panic had settled in. She sighed tiredly as she rolled over. Her body and mind had no rest from the night; it was if she had never gone to sleep. She wiped the sweat from her face. It was if she had been swimming all night instead of sleeping. Paige slept soundly. Her terror had thankfully not woken her.

It wasn't long for the soft boot prints to be obvious. She grumbled and rolled her eyes. They were fresh as snow was heavy in the air that morning. It was so thick that their trail had disappeared. Obviously her threat didn't mean anything to whomever followed them. It was strange as usually people were threatened by sharp knives.

She followed the prints past the tree line. Their presence made her burn with fury. Out in the trees, nothing was found. It was like every other time. She had had enough of it. "Alright, stalker, kindly show yourself or else the cops will be called," she warned. No answer. The woods remained silent. She growled menacingly. A break from her boring reality was what she wanted, but she never wanted danger. She only wished for a change of pace. "Fine, be that way."

The rest of the vegetables, potatoes and stewing beef out of her pack would be their breakfast. It would be a quick stew and the flavors wouldn't meld but it was better than nothing. While it cooked, she organized her pack and enjoyed the silence. The sounds of the forest always sung to her soul. There was a deep connection she couldn't deny, but she hid it from others. No one understood the song that was silently sung. The woods crumbled from their conquest, their music gone forever.

A rattle came from the tent. She quickly spun around as red hair flared from the opening. Paige seemed groggy. Evelyn was thankful that she would have her company. She needed a better distraction after her terror. A friendly face with bright smiles made everything better. It was the light in the world.

Paige slowly made her way over and slouched on the stump.

"You looked tired this morning," Evelyn observed cheerily.

Pagie snorted, keeping her attention on the fire. "I should be considering all of your screaming last night. Something about bugs."

So she had disturbed her friend. "Sorry about that. I thought I had a handle on them."

Paige shook her head and yawned. "You have a handle on those things, yeah right. I've known you since we were kids, Eve, and those nightmares don't change. I should learn to sleep with earplugs."

The mood became very grim. It was the last day. After they returned to her grandparents, they would split ways. They wouldn't see each other for a long time, and it would only be for coffee, if they were lucky. She knew that her friend, who she considered a sister, would go back to her life and she would to hers. They may pass each other on the street, but that was nothing compared to the quality time they used to spend together. Whatever time that they had, it would be short.

They started hiking again. There was no point delaying the inevitable. They pushed through the usual break as the snow became more and more in the sky. The clouds darkened to black as they emptied their loads. There were no forecasts of storms; it was supposed to be nice. It wasn't long when they lost sight of the path. She should have stopped and waited it out, quickly set up the tent for some shelter. Paige urged them forward. She expressed that the storm brought bad feelings of despair and she wanted to be home. Evelyn shook her head, knowing they couldn't separate.

The blizzard raged on. Evelyn yelled out to stop. They needed shelter; to travel any farther wasn't safe. The other turned around, looking defiant. She motioned around them. The glare she received chilled her. Her friend wanted to press forward and make it home. Evelyn wanted the same, but there was no point in risking their lives for it. It was difficult to see past the closest tree. It was hard to make out the difference between tree and rock.

She began to close the gap between them when a shadowy figure landed, interrupting her. All she saw was a blur of green and brown as it hit Paige and then dashed into the forest. This ignited her rage and her instincts to protect her friend. She recognized the shape of the person and took off after it without hesitation. How dare that stalker hurt her.

"No, Eve!" she faintly heard Paige call out. "You'll get lost in the darkness."

Her friend's cries were lost as she sped on faster. That intruder needed to be caught. There were not supposed to be people in the forest. No one had permission to enter the woods behind the highway. It was all her grandparent's land and most was untamable forest. There had been rumors about how the forest would protect animals from hunters, how they were grabbed by roots or stabbed by branches. There were stories how the land would protect the family in the farm house in the same way. The shadow's presence caused her a great deal of grief and fear. How did a person make it so far without injury?

Her voice echoed through her mind as she slowed. The storm had worsened considerably since her flight. There wasn't anything but snow, even then it was bright enough to nearly blind her. Any sight of trees or rocks was gone. She was in the middle of a whiteout with no direction to head into. Her gut sank as the realization came over her. She was lost during the middle of the worst storm she had ever seen with no shelter for protection. Chances of survival had just plummeted to most likely not.

She felt panic creep in and settle where her instincts used to be. She was going to freeze. If she wouldn't freeze she would starve. If neither of those, she would be eaten by a hungry bear that she would probably disturb. That was her luck lately. She fell to her buttocks and stared blankly at the snow. She had been stupid. She had done the one thing her grandfather forbade her to do. She ran off the trail.

Even through the howling wind, she heard a sound that chilled her to her bones. *Click. Click. Click.* Her eyes widened as she looked around frantically. She was not sleeping. She was sure she wasn't sleeping. There was no transition from alertness to sleep. There could be no way that her nightmares were real. They were creations of her sleeping mind and nothing more. They could never be real. Nothing so horrible could be real. It just couldn't be.

Click. Click. Click. Once again rang out the sound of them coming. Fear reared its ugly head as the sound shattered any courage she had left. The feelings of her nightmares flooded back to her. The helplessness of fighting the lethal unknown. A small sensation from the back of her mind told her that the creatures attached were terrifying. She should be running and defending herself, it warned. She remained in the snow, knowing that nothing she'd do would stop them. Not even the knife she carried would be enough.

Click. Click. Click. The sound grew louder as they approached. She hoped to find something or someone to save her. There was nothing but white space, she should have known better. The world was made up of nothing but snow. As she stared at the white fluff she felt a calm drowning her soul. Whatever would happen would come in an instant and her pain would be over. No more nightmare. No more repetition and ignorant people. No more fighting.

Click. Click. Click. She curled into a ball against the snow drift that was forming. Just as in the dreams, the next set would be her last. It had always been so. It was the one constant thing she could depend on in her nightmares. The clicking always signaled the end. She would have never imagined it was foreshadowing hers.

Click. She breathed in deeply and prepared for the coming pain. She closed her eyes as she didn't want to see what was going to kill her. The sounds were enough. *Click.* At least Paige would make it out alright and go on with her life. She wouldn't go on the dangerous adventures anymore. She would be safe and happy at home.

She waited for what felt like eternity for the final screech. After a while, a small glimmer of curiosity bubbled. She opened her eyes slowly. The storm had died down to just a light flurry. It had changed quickly, which was strange. She had never heard of such a thing. There was nothing there except trees and boulders. The forest was back to its winter calm again.

It was strange and out of place that the storm had just stopped. It was as if someone had turned off the weather. What was worse was the disappearance of the clicking. They never left their prey behind. That's what her dreams ensured. They always went for the kill. They never stopped. They swallowed everything they could find. Then another thought occurred.

"Is anyone out there?" She stood from the snow and looked around. She couldn't shake the feeling that she wasn't alone, which made a tangled ball of worry gag her. Only a skilled soldier would have a chance at killing the monsters. It was what the nightmares have shown. Perhaps it was the stalker, perhaps they were lost in the woods and were afraid to approach a civilian. Then again most from the Redgate army would not hide in the shadows if that were the case. They were a proud bunch and liked to be seen doing their heroics.

"Hello? I know there has to be at least one other person out here. I don't chase just anything," she called out again. The whistling wind responded, but it was not what she was expecting. She frowned. It made no sense why there was no response. There should have been crunching snow from someone walking or running away. Out there was nothing but the sounds she made.

Out of nowhere, a hand grabbed her shoulder causing her to shriek. She spun around and pushed the person hard. A green shirt stumbled backwards only to fall next to a tree. She recognized the colour instantly as well as the build. It was their stalker, and she would set them straight. She lunged at them and wrestled them face-first in the snow. They didn't fight back once buried under her.

Long, light brown hair spilled on the snow while free strands blew with the wind. A long green scarf was wrapped around their neck twice and tucked into the shirt. The prominent, old green tunic felt thick in her mitts and must have been as effective as a winter coat. The thick brown pants were the same. Leather gloves covered their hands as they struggled to get free of her grasp. A white cloak made out of a dense cotton waved lazily in the strong wind. Their feet were covered by leather boots that were a bit larger than her own and left smooth tracks in the snow.

"What are you doing out here? This is private property and I have all rights to turn you over to the authorities," Evelyn raged. The person beneath her tried to answer, but the snow muffled the mid-tone grunts. The stalker was definitely male from what was observed, which made her more suspicious. She pulled on his hair to lift his face from the snow. "Try that again."

He spat and coughed before breathing in deeply. "I am no stalker. Is this any way to treat your savior," he questioned angrily.

His voice was heavy with an unrecognizable accent. Its sound made her heart flutter, which was not needed. It was strange but she loved the sound of his voice, though the one attached infuriated her. "You say following us this whole time is not stalker qualification?"

"If I told you that those insects were following you and your friend, would you still say the same thing?"

She lost her grip as the forest closed in around her. Her nightmares couldn't be real. Nothing like that existed. No one knew of them besides her grandparents, Paige and the psychologist she used to see. "Those insects..." she started. Fear crawled from her stomach and choked her. The terrors from her dreams were following them, and she couldn't even tell they were there. "How do you know about those," she asked tearfully.

He shook his head as he crawled from under her. "The white insects, Zakulnea, crawl through this forest incessantly. One dies and ten replace it. It has always been this way in the Lost Lorne Forest. Though..." he paused. His back was still to her as he remained silent and still. Once he turned, she felt her breath catch in the depths of her lungs. His eyes were fierce, reminding her of an eagle's stare, and were the colour of dark, gray stone. His skin was fair, and his high cheeks and slender nose were rosy from the cold yet looked so soft and warm. His slender jaw gave off a docile presence, though the scowl on his lips portrayed otherwise. What surprised her most were his long, slender ears that peeked through his hair. He reminded her of elves from fairy tales that she loved to hear in her youth.

He avoided her stare as he rested his hands on the sword at his side. It was a plain iron sword whose sheath was held by a long leather belt around his waist. He watched her intently, and she felt him scrutinize her. He had no grounds to judge her, as he was the one who looked to have stepped out of a twisted history book. "How does an Engardonian know of the insects?"

She stood and dusted the snow from her clothes. His terminology was different and confused her. "An En-gar... what?" She had never heard the term before; she doubt anyone else had.

"Never mind what I said, your kind doesn't remember the old ways." He turned and started to make his way into the trees.

"Hey, wait," she called to him. He looked back and waited. He was definitely not a soldier lost in the woods. He knew more, his confidence was proof of that. Another worry began to bother her. "Is Paige going to be alright? I mean, those bugs were after her too, right."

He shook his head, almost as if she were a mere child. "No, they just wanted you. I don't know why though, your friend feels like she has more magic than you do. They usually prefer those with larger souls, not wimps like you."

A lump caught in her throat. Why would they be after her if she was so unimportant? If she was the target, then she had put her closest friend in harm's way. She could have been killed, and all they would have needed to do was turn around on the first day. Hot tears filled her eyes and stuck to her chilled cheeks. She couldn't believe that she was so careless. She should have known better. People were more prone to go missing during the winter. One winter, the army forbade anyone from entering the woods and travelers were made to stick to the roads. She felt her scarf stick to her face from the frozen tears. She pulled it away gently but felt more fall. She covered her face with it instead.

"Don't want to interrupt your pain or anything, but..." he paused and sighed.

She glared at him with blurry vision. How dare he speak to her?! He could have warned them the first night they were out there. He could have saved them from being separated and hunted by those monsters. He could have done so much to prevent the fear they had felt.

"Once darkness falls, they multiply. I know a small shack very close to here that will keep us safe. Once we have a fire going, they will leave us be. I don't know why, but they are not fans of fire."

She shook her head angrily. Why would he think she would follow him any further than she had? She needed to find the trail and get back home. She could do that on her own.

She took her compass out from around her neck. Happy memories of her grandfather teaching her how to use it came to her. Those were fun times, and he had given her his old compass when she passed his test. She held it still and waited for it to set. It wouldn't stop waving back and forth and spinning.

He looked at the tool in her hand. "Smart, but the magnetic field around here is too strong. It's the only reason I created a beacon for my soul to follow so I can get home. If it wasn't for that, I'd have one of those too," he educated her.

It didn't make sense. It always worked when she was out there. As Evelyn looked around, she realized things had changed. None of the trees were familiar. They were much larger than those that she was used to as they towered high above them. She had never seen pine trees so big, let alone the others types that were sprinkled between the needles. She looked back down to her compass. It was her faithful companion during her forest walks. It had never betrayed her before. At that time, it was like it was teasing her. "I need to get home," she whispered. Deep inside, whispers warned her to go home. It was dangerous out there, and she needed to get to safety.

He was silent for a time. He was not sure what to make of her. "I know the way to that place, but..." he paused again. She didn't like it when he paused. She always thought he was thinking of some lie. She despised liars. "I only know how to find it when I leave my village." Something wasn't right and instincts told her to back off. "Honestly there is a path from my village to that place beyond the woods. It has overgrown here, but I can still tell where it is. I've been there many times, since it's so different from anything I've seen. I've seen you there once, I think, coming out of that machine."

She looked back at her compass before putting it back in her coat. She had no choice but to follow him. It bothered her that he didn't know what a farm or car was and the talk about the pulling of his soul was even stranger. Everyone knew what those were, even children. How come he didn't? It troubled her that her only choices were follow the stranger or wander lost in the forest. It would lead to trouble; but, either way, there were chances she was going to die. She preferred to take the chance that had the least amount of death involved.

"I will follow, but only if I know your name. If you won't tell me, then I'll take my chances with the forest." He was taken aback at her words. He stared at her as his eyes looked her over. She had always been normal and never a threat. Her knife was more for show than anything and for food preparation. His caution was uncalled for.

"I can tell you are definitely different from the others who get lost in here." He pondered her offer as he looked to the ground and held his chin. Was it so strange for someone to ask his name? She believed any sane person would ask. "My name is Darrow."

She stared at him for a moment. It was a strange name, as she had never heard of it before. It made him sound even more from fantasy, and she wondered if she had passed out in the blizzard.

"It's not a hard name to understand. You only have to say arrow with a 'd.'"

She snorted. "I got it. I'm not stupid. It's just different, I've never heard it before."

He turned around and walked off into the forest. They wouldn't get along, she was sure of that. He kept insulting her and talking about things that she didn't understand. Her lack of knowledge insulted him, as his tone was harsher when she would question him. People like that were a waste of life to her, since they caused unnecessary conflict. She had dealt with too many stuck up jerks in her lifetime and wouldn't take the abuse again. She followed him none the less but was not impressed by this 'hero' that she had acquired.

Their walk tired her and she began to nod off. The storm had picked up again and blew against them. It was cold and harsh and nothing like the whiteout before. A little voice was urging her that it was the wrong way to go, that dangers would flood her if she were to follow. She knew she couldn't stop, as he was the only way home. Her only means of direction were gone, and she wouldn't dare explore if even the trees were strangers. She had so much to lose but no choice to choose. It was infuriating but she had to continue. She had made her situation by chasing him blindly. She would have to suffer the consequences.

She stopped near a tree and rested against it. She couldn't tell the time, as clouds and snow darkened the sky. The cold sapped her strength, causing her legs to refuse orders to continue further. She was about to call out to her lead, but he had already gone. She looked tiredly at the falling snow. It was beautiful as the flakes danced down to her. If only the sun were out, then each would glimmer in their spotlight. Her trance was broken by the cold dampness of her clothes. The howling wind was a reminder of her situation and her blatant stupidity.

As Evelyn sat she felt her mind play tricks on her. Snow swirled into images of Paige and her voice was giving her a lecture for not thinking again. She did it frequently, and she wouldn't have been surprised if it was just a playback from another time. She saw her relatives gathering at her grandparents with search dogs and police to find out where she had gone. She could see her grandmother crying as her granddaughter was lost in the forest where normally people are never found. They were lost to the trees and the thickness of the bushes.

Worse of them all was she could see her ex-boyfriend shrugging it off saying it was bound to happen. How she was lousy at following instructions. How she could never be a good mother or wife due to her thoughtlessness. How she was worthless and the world was better off without her. Each vision made her cries deeper. She wished for her pleasant memories. They were what comforted her on the worst days, and it felt like it was becoming the worst day of her life.

Her weariness brought her into a deep sleep. She drank hot chocolate with her family as they all laughed while playing games. Her old dog cuddled with her as she combed through his long, thick fur with her fingers. It was so silky and healthy, she would never let go. He rested on her bed as she snuggled into her thick blankets. It was something she had forgotten, sleep without nightmares. The dream changed into a hazy vision of a young man who had been kind to her in her youth. He had helped her with something. His smell was one of the pines that covered the land. She could drown in the smell and sleep peacefully.

She was snatched away from peace as something shook her violently. She didn't want to be dragged away. She wanted to feel the safety again. She didn't want to forget that person who she had somehow lost. She begged to not have him taken away. She moaned and rolled over. When she was shaken again, her eyes snapped open and she glared at the intruder.

"What the hell are you doing?"

Darrow snorted and looked unimpressed. "If you continue to sleep here, you will die." His eyes were cold and uncaring, the complete opposite of his words.

At first she felt confused, as she was in bed with her pet. Her eyes showed her the truth as the blizzard continued to howl loudly in her ears. The world spun before she closed her eyes tightly. She couldn't have that now, she had to go forward. "Sorry, I wanted to tell you I stopped, but you were gone. Let's keep going." Her weariness had increased, but they needed shelter before rest. He didn't offer a response and kept walking. Any kindness from before was lost. She was right in being cautious around him. He couldn't be trusted.

Why would he return for her? His tone made her sound like a nuisance, and it wasn't like she was special to him or anything. She was just a lost girl. She wasn't the prettiest or the thinnest. She definitely didn't have anything to give as anything of value was at home. The more she thought about it, the more it didn't make sense. What was his goal in guiding her? Why was he in the forest to begin with?

After a while she noticed a small wooden shack built within a close group of trees. The wood was old and rotting. An old brown cloth covered the door which was poorly made. It was as if the building was thrown together as a last thought. She felt uneasy about it. The snow on the roof was thick, and she could see it caving in at any moment.

He led her to it and walked inside. She stare at it. It wasn't safe, but she had to choose between the protection from the wind or being buried in snow. She could always build snow walls and hide there. She shook her head. She wouldn't go in. Something bad would happen if any more weight were to be added to the roof.

He looked back out and spotted her. His expression remained cold and un-caring. "You going to come in, or is it a custom to sleep in the snow?" The sarcasm was not lost on her. She felt her face contort into one of her more angry expressions. For someone who volunteered to guide her home, he sure wasn't being inviting. The way he was treating her was inexcusable.

He backed behind the cloth, away from her glare. He was concerned and he should be. She would not tolerate the sarcasm or the tone. If he was leading her somewhere, he would have to work for it. If he wanted her cooperation, he would have to treat her better. She would not be goaded somewhere by that attitude. She had been treated that way before, and she had learned since she deserved better. She decided a tree and snow walls would suit her just fine. She didn't trust him or his shack, and she would rather take her chances with the monsters.

She found a tree with large roots that would hide most of her from the wind. She built walls and a partial roof with the snow around her. She cuddled inside and felt the warmth of the walls. "As a matter of fact, I love sleeping in the snow. It's very refreshing and lets me remember why I'm lucky to have a home with heat," she spat.

She heard him snort but then heard incredulousness in his voice. "Well, if you get cold, you can come in. It's not like I can lock it."

She didn't like how smug he was or how calm he always was even when he was insulting her. What twisted person would act like that? She closed her eyes as she knew that sleep would soon come. Thoughts of his attitude circled in her mind, making it nearly impossible for her to sleep. She never knew she could dislike someone so much, though she still harbored ill feelings towards her ex. She didn't like the preppy girls back in high school because they always teased her, and the same with the athletic boys. The anger she had for him was something different and scary. It was not like her despise someone.

After a while she opened her eyes, curious to why the howling wind had stopped. The storm had calmed again to a light flurry. She might have a chance to be warm if the snow didn't swirl inside. She felt her limbs freeze and her body began to shiver. She pulled her arms out of her sleeves and felt them warm up within her fleece sweater. She loved the feeling of the sweater as she pet it. It reminded her of her dog. How she missed it and wished she could find another as comforting as it.

She closed her eyes again. She felt them sag and her mind began to lose consciousness. It wasn't long before she was startled awake from the sounds of insects approaching. Their clicking caused her to tremble. They couldn't find her in there. She was hidden from the world. She dug a little under the root just in case. She didn't want to be killed, not by them. She would take anything else but them. She curled close to the center of the tree hoping for protection. Her eyes closed again and soon her mind left.

Chapter 3

First Taste

Images of snow surrounded her. Icicles formed from leaves still clinging tightly to the ends of branches. It all twinkled in the sunlight, offering a mystical scene. It wasn't cold like it should have been. The snow falling was warm like a summer's rain. It was refreshing as it caressed her bare cheeks. It was strange and it confused her senses. Her memory told her it should be cold and that she should be shivering. Her sense of touch told her that she would be fine to strip her winter gear.

She sat up. She was still in the forest, the one that was unknown to her. Its abnormally large trees were green with life. Flowers covered the base as moss climbed up the trunks. Through it all, snow fell and stayed on the ground below. She knew she had never seen such a thing before, yet a small part of her knew that place. It was that small part she wondered if it was ever hers.

She took off her coat and ski pants as she began to soak in them. After a while she took off the rest of her heavy clothes and began to dance around. Her spirit felt like a child again. She had forgotten how much fun the world could be. The running with fear was too much. She was supposed to be happy and carefree. She found the place to be magical and beautiful. It was filled with happiness such as she hadn't felt for a long time. She felt a large smile pull at her lips, and she giggled as twirled around in the falling snow.

It soon chilled her to her core. It wasn't right. The temperature wouldn't drop suddenly like that. It had never happened before. It was all wrong. A shadow approached her from behind one of the smaller trees. She called out to it in greeting, but it gave no response. She ran towards it but it backed away.

It floated where it was hiding. The feet dangled from the ground. That was different. She had heard of such things but had never seen it. Her curiosity overwhelming her, she ran after it. The further she went the colder it became. Ice formed on her wet clothes. Soon she was freezing in the snow again like she should have been. She stopped and looked around. The woods had darkened, and she had become drowsy.

She found a tree and curled up against it. That's what she was told to do if she were lost. Its trunk held warmth but it wasn't enough. That was wrong. The trees always provided warmth against the cold. Why was everything changing? Everything was going wrong since that man came. She remembered his sense of fear and hopelessness. He had tried to protect them but failed. Against what, she couldn't grasp. She was still so young. She felt her eyes become heavy as the night carried on. The temperature continued to drop and her body shivered violently. She should have listened but she wanted to play. It was always safe before. She cried as her mind drifted into an unsettling sleep.

* * *

Evelyn's trembling woke her. The tears were hot on her cheeks before wiping them away. Her nightmare bothered her. She couldn't understand how she could come up with such horrible dreams. She wanted them gone. She couldn't take them anymore. All she wanted was a decent sleep, one of peace and happiness. She cherished the few she had. If only she could have more.

At least she was warm again. The heat was a constant and the source firm as she rubbed it through her sleeping bag. Maybe it was her grandfather. Maybe he had ventured out into the snow after Paige returned home alone. She nuzzled against the warmth hoping it were true. She sighed happily as she clung to the hope and the warmth filled her to her core. It was a welcome change compared to the unsettling cold.

It moved away from her and she protested. She mumbled for it to come back. She didn't want her grandfather to go. She was scared. She wanted him to tell her everything would be fine. She wanted his reassurance that the nightmares were not real. She would be safe with him. She stifled her cries as reality returned. Her grandfather couldn't find her out there. He had problems walking, and the cold bit at his old legs.

Everything was blurry when she felt brave enough to look. She rubbed her eyes to take the sleep away. She had to be focused to stay safe, though it was hard as her hands shook from the fear rooted deeply within. She slowly opened them again and noticed that the world was no longer white. It was wooden and was in good shape.

She was in her sleeping bag and wearing only her jeans and t-shirt. She found her winter gear and a green scarf hanging on a line close to her. A white cape over the top of her sleeping bag added to the warmth. On her other side was a fire, and sitting on the opposite side was Darrow. He was busy cooking over the fire and didn't notice her stirring.

She crawled out of her sleeping bag and sat on it. Another wave of panic washed over. She held her face in her hands as she tried to calm herself. She couldn't let him see her like that. He couldn't see any weakness or he could exploit it. He had some fish skewered and frying above the flames. Her mouth watered from the smell. She realized that she hadn't eaten since she had separated from Paige. Her stomach growled from the thought, and he looked up.

"So the snow sleeper is finally awake. I'm impressed."

She frowned. She was not expecting to have to deal with him that soon after waking up. The sarcasm in his comment caused more tears. She couldn't deal with that talk so soon after the nightmares. "I-I sleep in the snow, so what," she retorted. The break in her voice revealed too much, and she cursed herself for it. She was at her weakest when the night shook her. He shook his head and returned his attention back to the fish. He was silent for a while, and she wondered if he caught the fear. He obviously didn't talk much when his insults were thrown back at him, which was a positive for her.

"I thought you would've come in at some point. I guess you proved me wrong."

Her eyes narrowed at him. He acted like she had won a challenge but she never said anything. She bet that she could do it. "How did I do that?" She just wanted security with where she slept. That shady shack was not her top pick. "Oh, never mind. I was thinking out loud."

Something was off about him. He looked to be a bit more agitated. It was as if her defiance caused him complication. She liked that. Getting him off his game would hopefully offer clues as to why he was out there. He certainly wouldn't tell her if she asked him. "What happened to the nonchalant guy from yesterday?"

His head snapped back up. He was confused just as she was. He mouthed her words slowly. If he was going to be cruel to her, then she would deal it back in spades.

"What, my words too big for you forest man?" The growl was clear and the darkness in his eyes nearly scared her as much as her nightmares. Almost. "I mean come on. Yesterday you offer to help me but act like it's a big hassle or something. You even go on to insult me, which will get you no points with me. Make up your mind. Am I a burden to you or not?"

His attention returned to his cooking. He was avoiding answering her which was suspicious. It was a simple question. What were his motives? Why did he offer to help her if he was going to be like that? He sounded like he didn't care if she died but he kept coming back for her. Why was that? What was his goal in protecting her?

"You waiting for something 'cause I'm not answering. I like being alone and no snow girl will change that."

She frowned and crossed her arms. He was being difficult and obviously he wasn't going to tell her anything with a straight answer. "I need to know so I can figure out if I should just try to go alone. If you're going to act like that, then I'm putting no faith in you. I'll deal with the demons rather than be treated like this. I'm a person too!"

He returned his attention to his cooking as he snarled.

She blinked as she felt her fury grow. She shoved her feet into her boots before storming out the door. She couldn't stay in there. She had half a mind to beat him senseless but she wasn't a violent person by nature. She shivered as the cold licked her skin. She should've grabbed her coat but maybe the cold would calm her. The old wood touched her back as she leaned against it. She had to calm down. He was attempting to help her despite the attitude.

Her stomach growled again. She had forgotten that she was hungry. Anger tended to do that to her. She would have to go back in to cook her stew. She would have to swallow some of her pride and apologize to him, though make it clear that she was not accepting his attitude. That would be a mistake that he could use against her. She wouldn't allow it again. She had enough for a life time.

The flapping cloth caught her attention. He didn't look at her but handed one of the fish over. She accepted but looked it over. Was that his way of apologizing? The smell overwhelmed her as her mouth watered. It sure smelled good. "It's not poisoned. If I'm bringing you home, you need to be alive. You'd better come in, too, before you catch death. There would be no point if you died." There was the sarcasm she expected, though it was softer than before.

"Now you're nicer, why is that? I can't see my outburst scaring you, and I've met hermits; they still have manners."

His eyes avoided her gaze as he leaned on the door frame. He played with loose strands of his light brown hair mindlessly. Again she found him calculating his answers. She didn't like that.

"I would be nicer if you gave me honesty, Darrow." That was when she saw the first spark of kindness in his eyes as he looked to her. She recognized it, because she had given it before. He debated on whether he could trust her. "Come inside to eat. It tastes better warm."

She packed her things while they ate. She felt some of the tension wane. She was stressed enough with being lost and afraid of when the insects would come. It made her wish for small talk. That was one thing she couldn't stand when people approached her, but it was better than the silence. She could only hear the winter symphony for so long. It reminded her of when the power went out for a week during the coldest winter she knew. All her relatives gathered around the fireplace as the wind howled by.

"Thank you for feeding me." He paused while attaching his belt. It was odd. It told her how little he heard it. It was no wonder he was normally so rude. Perhaps he lacked the knowledge of courtesy and proper interaction if he was truly a loner.

"It's no problem," he whispered. "You look like you don't have much on you and winter can be harsh for hunting." She nodded as she understood perfectly. The stew would be saved until later.

Outside, the sun was shining brightly through the bare branches. It warmed what little exposed skin showed. The untouched snow sparkled in the morning light. A soft whistle could be heard as the pine trees swayed in the gentle breeze. She took a few steps as her eyes tried to soak in the view. It was magical that everything seemed so perfect. It could have been a picture on a holiday card.

He walked past her and motioned for her to follow. She looked back at the shack. In the light, it was much more inviting. It was only the outer shell that was crumbling. The inner structure was strong though sparse. She shook her head and followed him away from her first night lost in the woods. There would be more evenings of strange things to come, she was sure of it.

The day progressed while they travelled; the air no longer as bitter. It was quiet, and he didn't speak to her except for instructions. It was boring. At least with Paige, they could gossip about each other's lives. She got nothing out of him. Then again, she didn't want to if the attitude was still there. He attacked her less, but the roughness in his voice was still present.

He slowed down and crouched, motioning her to do the same. She obeyed but didn't sense any danger. The forest was quiet with the exception of the wind. That was normal for that time of year. The animals would hibernate and the birds had migrated. As far as she was aware, the white insects only travelled by night.

The slight movement past the bare bushes caught her attention. It caused her heart to race, which she pressed to calm it. His hand had a firm grip on his sword's handle. Whatever was out there, he deemed it to be threatening. Unease settled through her. He was usually uptight but not like that. It was normally about personal things if she asked questions. She held the hunting knife at her side, but it didn't leave much defense. She could do harm if they didn't get too violent with her. She hoped it was enough to run away from the danger.

He crawled forward quietly. The snow barely made a sound under his footsteps. Hers, on the other hand, sounded like an elephant walking on a carpet of nuts. He spun around and placed a finger to his lips. He was apprehensive at the disturbance, and her movement flashed panic in his eyes. A blush heated her cheeks as she kept still. It was astounding how quiet he was; it was no wonder she could never hear him as he followed them.

Through the fragile bushes was a small clearing. The sight of it made her stomach turn. Tossed about were what was left of chewed human limbs. Blood soaked the snow, leaving a crimson stain on the once pure blanket. It was fresh as it lay uncovered by the storm. She looked away as he pushed her to hide behind the trees. Blood had always been her weakness. It turned her stomach and caused other, worse symptoms. She was fine during movies, though anything else bothered her. Even the mention of blood curdled her stomach.

He motioned for her to follow, but she didn't move. She clung to the tree with her eyes closed. The smell of warm copper poisoned the air. She gagged when he tried to force her to move. Movement wasn't smart as she knew from experience. She covered her nose with her scarf to try to filter the stench. It had little effect which made her tear. Her phobia was taking over.

She sunk down to her knees as she kept her mind focused on the tree before her. The world was spinning, making the sickness worse. It didn't help that she hadn't eaten much since the day before. Nausea was a sign of her hunger. Combine them and there was no prevention of her reaction. She closed her eyes tighter as she wished for it to stop.

He grabbed her wrist and pulled hard. She whimpered pitifully as she staggered to stand. The dizziness progressed to a blurry reality. She cried when she tried to open her eyes. They burned from the sight of the sun. It came without warning, and she stumbled forward. Why did it have to happen then, of all times, to get a migraine?

He pulled her up harshly. It only caused her to fall forward, and the cold snow melted at the touch of her hot face. The darkness of it eased the confusion, and the cold numbed her. He pulled her up again and shoved her forward. She couldn't do it. There was no point walking with her eyes closed and her mind spinning. Every step she would fall. She shook her head. She felt him grab her coat to pull her along. She reached out and slapped him hard.

The sound of his grunt was satisfying. She wouldn't be pushed around so harshly. She refused to let it continue. She remained still until he pulled her up again. His nose touched hers which caused her heart to skip a beat. The skin was soft like a feather but his grip was rough. "Are you trying to kill us? You've seen what was back there, right?" Each word was breathed on her lips. It reminded her of more sensual, pleasant times with another man.

She opened her eyes to find the panic in his that burned her own. She steadied herself once she held his arms. Trying hard to keep sight of him, her vision blurred everything into splotches of colour. "I'm not well, Darrow. I need to sit and take the medication in my bag." His confusion was clear by the way his thin eyebrows bowed. The enlightenment appeared soon after.

He guided her forward and hid them in thicker underbrush.

She reached around and pulled her pack off. She dug through until she found a small pill bottle, a granola bar and a bottle of water that she had packed. The food had to be first as per instructions, which she gobbled gratefully. The pill slid down with the help of the rushing water. It felt so heavenly. She had forgotten what a luxury fresh water was.

She cursed the migraines. They stopped her from doing so much in her life. She had to stay home from school or work when they were bad. Events that she had prepared for were left abandoned. She even spent a birthday sleeping through the fog. Doctors had no answer for her as they were always random and never had clear triggers. She was thankful the last one was so long ago but also that she had come prepared.

"We have to get moving. It'll be dark soon, and I don't want to be out here with those things." The urgency was made clear. If only the world would stop moving, she could follow again. If he could understand her predicament, then maybe he would be gentler towards her. That hope quickly left when she was reminded of how he was. Kindness was not in his nature.

Again he lifted her from the ground. The world still moved about her as her legs refused to straighten. The snow chilled her knees. She couldn't do it. Everything was so unfocused it hurt her and made her limbs so weak. The medicine wouldn't take effect for a while longer. That was time they couldn't spare to lose. It was time she couldn't push further.

"If we don't move, we die. You remember what was back there, don't you? That will be us come morning." It was desperation. How late in the day was it? She couldn't see it being dusk. Then again she couldn't keep track of time out there anymore. It was always guesses until it was too late.

He had to understand. "I can't right now." Her voice was choked by her tears. Nothing had settled and the sound of her voice made her tremble. Why wasn't the medication working? "Everything spins, the light burns my eyes and my head... How I wish it would be lopped off."

She shifted, expecting a lashing from the silence. The most received was the cold wind against her skin.

"What would help to get us moving again?" She couldn't have heard him right. He was considering her current state. She had to take it. If she wanted to live, she had to take it. "I can't see and standing is an issue. So really, I'm useless right now at going anywhere."

His defiant snort stirred confidence. The weight of her pack was removed followed by an arm wrapping below her shoulders. The touch was foreign, and she desperately wanted to shy away from it. To feel that man so close to her was uninviting. She only stayed from the support she felt. He was strong and he was willing to protect her. Why would he protect her?

His personality would push her to walk on her own as he had been. At that moment, he was showing her a kindness that not many would. So many people scolded her or laughed at her. She only faked the symptoms for attention they would say. There's nothing wrong with her; this person on the other hand...

She had heard them all. If only they knew the confusion and pain behind her eyes.

They walked slowly. Time was lost. It felt like hours at the snail pace. The light behind her lids was dimming, a sign that dusk was falling. It was then the fog began to leave. She braved the light and opened her eyes. An orange veil descended on the barren trees and the snow lost its sparkle. It was normally a welcoming sign meaning that sleep was soon. It brought fear as the insects emerge and feed.

He set her down slowly and rushed to a tree. Creaks and snaps filled the air until he returned with light. He handed her the burning torch. The warmth was welcomed by her cheeks as they melted the cold. He pulled her up again and made them march on, faster than they had before. She well understood the reason why. The light was to keep the monsters at bay. The speed was to prevent them from being brave.

The darkness spread quickly through the forest; the mountains made sure of that. He tensed beneath her grasp. He was readying for the would-be predators that would spring without a moment's notice. He moved her hand from his shoulder and pulled her quickly by her wrist. He must have had confidence in her new found strength as he pulled her along. The sound of ringing steel made it obvious he wasn't as sure they would make it without incident.

As they marched forward, she looked around. It was a mistake she shouldn't have made. All around them were bright, glowing red eyes. So many that she couldn't count them all. Closer to the edges of the trees gleamed needle-like teeth encased in ghostly white exoskeletons. She whimpered and hurried faster. How could she have not seen them before? All those eyes staring greedily through the night. They were the embodiment of the nightmares. They could make worlds crumble from their ferocity.

That was when the clicking happened. That horrid sound. It made her cry out and run past him. He sped up along with her. They weaved through the trees, her feelings disoriented from the quick movement. That didn't stop them. They had found their meal and would catch it. They wouldn't give up until they ate.

She called out to him to tell him they were done. It was true. They always made sure of that. She never escaped them in the night. She always awoke to the sickness and fear of dying. The feel of claws disemboweling her forced louder cries to rip through her.

"I am not dying for this. These things can't have me. Screw the laws!" His strength was great as he pushed her forward. She tumbled and rolled when she tripped. The dull thud of the wooden floor caused tears. They had made it, barely. She wished she could have seen it rather than be forced into it but nevertheless, she was safe again.

The ferocity in his words was strange. What kind of laws was he talking about? Was he on the run from his own people? She had concluded long ago that he couldn't have been alone if there were others traversing the woods. It brought up the question again. What was he doing out there?

She threw the torch into an open pit as the sounds of clicking intensified outside. The roar of the flames bursting to life was welcomed. The warmth offered protection and the light peace. If Darrow was right, then the monsters would back off. They would be safe.

She remained still as the adrenaline slowly eased out of her system. Sounds of metal rang through the air. Screeches cut short, followed by more. The pounding of her heart echoed in her ears. It all made the ache in her head more apparent. She wanted it to stop. Medication could only do so much. She wanted quiet. She wanted sleep.

The night muted when Darrow walked in. Black ooze dripped from his sword like molasses. His green shirt stained where ever it caught. The insects didn't bleed like what she expected. She didn't know what it was. What were those things made of if they didn't bleed?

He cleaned his sword off with the door cloth before he stumbled. The grunt was muffled when he landed. He didn't move, but his breathing was deep and focused. What happened out there that made him so tired? She moved to check on him when he waved her off, signaling that he was fine. He turned with eyes burning with defiance. He obviously wasn't done yet.

Blood dripped from above his brow as colour drained from her face. She turned and dug out her medical kit. She needed to check the cut. If it was deep, then they would need more than what she carried. She hoped that it wouldn't come to that. If he was the only way home, he needed to stay alive as much as she did.

As she approached him, he hissed and glared deep into her eyes. The look was more animalistic when the pupils dilated. With a shaking hand, she swept aside the long strands. A long, thin cut ran from the hair line to his ear. "It's good that this isn't bad. I can fix this if you let me."

His eyes dropped before he leaned against a wall. "Why would you help me? I'm a stranger to you."

She sat back, mindlessly playing with the case clasps. The chuckle she felt lifted her spirits. She knew why. "It's how I am. I've always tried to help people, even when I was a kid. It's done me more harm than good, but I still try. Now sit still. This stuff stings a bit, but it will fend off infections."

She assumed his silence was consent. The alcohol was cold against her fingertips. His flinch was slight, but he remained calm. Those cool gray eyes watched her every movement. They were watery and held such a sadness it affected her. What was he thinking of to make such a feeling? Was compassion something so hard to come by for him?

Once the last Band-Aid was applied, he traced her work with his fingers. He nodded, which she assumed was his way of approval. His melancholy was not lost on her. Something was bothering him more than the scratch. She wished she could help him, but she needed to know what it was first. He would never tell. He was a quiet man and expressing his thoughts was rare.

He laid out his cloak while she put away her medical kit. He drifted off quickly. As she readied her sleeping bag, she noticed his light sleep. It wasn't deep, and each sound stirred him. He remained tense, his grip strong on his blade. When the sound of the zipper broke the silence, his eyes snapped open and darted to her. He settled quickly when all was peaceful.

"Get some rest, snow girl. You will need it."

Chapter 4

Obsidian Tower

The morning came too soon. Evelyn stirred before burying herself deeper in the warmth. It had been a while since she had such a comfortable feeling. Her sleep was deep and undisturbed. The darkness and lack of imagination was spectacular. That was the best way to sleep. Not feeling the time pass until consciousness the next day.

Crackling of a strong fire stirred her to take a peek. Darrow sat cooking and looking forlorn. The soup itself didn't have much smell, but it was enough to cause a growl. She hadn't eaten since the granola bar, which was longer than she had ever gone without food. He took a glance when she crawled out of bed. It was quick and she could have missed it. The solemn mood was off. She had pegged him as cocky and irritable. Sadness did not become him.

During the meal, he remained silent. Something was bothering him. If something was bothering, him it meant caution to her. The soup was fine, so it wasn't poison. He ate it too, so it wasn't that. Then again, if he wanted to kill her, he would have already. He had fended off those insects which was no small feat. That alone proved he was taught to fight and fight well.

The outside world was very bright. The sun felt hotter than it had since fall. As usual, the snow sparkled in the daylight. The further they walked the more apparent the heat. Small icicles had formed on the branches and dripped onto the snow. The snow was sticky. She would have made snowmen had it not been for her situation. Winter was deciding to end early or at least take pause.

By high noon, the calm turned tense. They moved slower, crouching behind bare bushes. The cold, damp air clung to them. It was the same hesitation from before. She prayed it wasn't more bodies and blood. She couldn't take more of it. It was too much the last time.

A small lake of ice spread out before them. It was longer than it was wide. The trees on the other side were noticeably greener than the ones she hid behind. She recognized it as Lake Obsidian. She had gone fishing with her grandfather there many times. It was a great spot and always produced fish.

He pointed to the other side of the lake. She followed the line and barely caught a glimpse of the shack waiting for them. It was closer than the others. That sent warning signs. Normally it would take the full day to reach the next one. A full day with no breaks. The one awaiting them was just over half. Was there something wrong in the lake to make it so close?

She was going to ask why when he raised his finger to his lips. Her stomach twisted with anxiety. Why did she have to be quiet? What was out there? There must have been another way to cross. If it was dangerous, then they would have to go around. It was longer but it would have been safer to cross at the river.

She turned to leave but he grabbed her wrist. He slowly pointed behind her. Looking over, she caught a glimpse of something dart behind a tree. His lips grazed her ear. It was so soft but the suddenness caused her to belt out a scream. He clapped a hand to her mouth and whispered quickly. "They are getting desperate and tracking us in daylight. They will not cross the lake and there are fewer on that side. Stay quiet and follow me."

He tested the ice. It supported his weight. He pulled her along with him as they made their way slowly. Why would they not cross? Would the water attack them? If it did, why would it be safe for them? Her heart beat in her throat, gagging her. She never was one for danger. Adventure, yes, but never danger. It was all she found since she met him. He was definitely bad luck.

Little more than midway, he stopped. The lake was quiet. It always was in the winter. Why would he stop when there was no danger? They should keep going. "Darrow?" she questioned. His cheeks, bright red from cold, turned ghostly white. What was he hearing with those ears of his? Did they allow him to hear better? What changed?

Suddenly the ice groaned. The snow remained unmoved, but the sound was loud. She gasped and looked around. He grabbed her wrist and ran at full speed. He obviously knew the danger approaching. Was the ice too thin where they were or was it something else? If the ice was breaking, then it would be better to go slowly. She knew that. So what was coming after them besides the insects?

He threw her forward. She stumbled forward and questioned him with her eyes. Why would he do that? What was behind them? She kept running, fear starting the adrenaline in her system again.

"Keep running and don't turn back, no matter what. Make it to the shore." His cold intensity offered no answers. She desperately wanted to know what was coming. She needed to know how to defend herself. She ran harder. He knew better than her. Something was coming, and he deemed her to be in the way.

A deafening crack resounded about the lake. The tremor that came knocked her off her feet. The snow was cold when she stopped rolling. Dazed and confused, she stared at the sky, its blue so misleading and cheerful. The shore was so close. His words echoed back. She had to move. She had to run. She had to get to that shore. Once there, she could survey the damage.

She slowly rose her feet. The knock to her head made her dizzy. Something black from the corner of her eye made her curious. Out of a snow scene, the colour black was not expected. It shouldn't have been there if he didn't know what machines were. Nothing natural was that black.

Except for creatures. When she focused on it, she wished she hadn't. A gigantic black worm cracked through the ice. The skin was as slick as black leather. Ice formed from droplets exposed to the air. The leech was beautiful with its sparkle, yet with that size it was so deadly. Under normal circumstances, she'd sprinkle salt on it. It would wriggle in agony and pop off her toes. Normally, it was no bigger than a finger. Seeing it there, she knew she was nowhere near home. It bowed the top of its head towards her, showing off the rows and rows of teeth.

"Run, stupid girl! Run!" His words brought time back in motion. His green shirt ruffled in the wind as he stood atop its head. A silver blade penetrated its flesh. That's right, she had to run. She had to get to shore. He better have known how to kill that thing. Not even the shore would stop it if they were camped so close. He better not die.

A few steps from the shore, the ice rocked. She fell to her knees and covered her head from the shards of ice. They stung her cheeks and ripped small tears in her coat. It dove back into the water, missing her by inches. With new motivation, she pushed herself harder.

Once there, she fell to her knees, breathing hard. She never thought for a moment she needed endurance training. Gym class was not her favorite. She was never fast. She swore this run was her best, and it took everything for her to make it. She decided it would be in her best interest to try running, even if it was a mile. If that ever happened again, she would stand a chance.

The lake was quiet again. The water sloshed onto the ice, freezing on contact. It was as if nothing had happened. The only thing missing was Darrow. Worry engulfed her. She couldn't find any green on the lake. Had he been eaten? Was he hurt? Was he drowning? If he was dead, how could she get home? It couldn't end like that. They had just started.

She was about to go look for him when the ice exploded before her. She screamed and ran for the shack. Deafening shrieks twisted in the air. It was new. It wasn't like the insects. There was no warning when it ate him.

She turned back to check, curiosity overcoming flight reaction. The leech waved frantically back and forth. Its screeches were unbearable to hear. It was in pain and its sounds were torture. How could it be hurting if it ate him? It was so big compared to him. Darrow would have been a light snack, a crumb. As it thrashed, it broke more ice. It was trying to get away from whatever was torturing it, but was unable to escape.

It stopped moving. It stood as a twisted obsidian tower surrounded by a moat. It would have been great inspiration for villains. So dark and menacing with such beauty. It stood at least sixty feet tall. Beneath the surface of the water must have been so much more. It was a deep lake, after all. It was amazing with its slick, shiny coating. No creature on earth was larger than what was before her. It terrified her to know that it existed in the back of her home. Were all creatures like that there? Were people at the bottom of the food chain there?

Out the side of it, an orange glow formed. It glowed like heated iron in the belly of a forge. The glow exploded, releasing a giant ball of flame. Bits of flaming flesh fell as a hole burned. No wonder it was crying. She would too if her innards were on fire. It fell forward and broke what little was left of the ice.

Something fell out of the hole and into the water. It failed feebly. She panicked, recognizing that he couldn't swim. She tore off her pack and ran to the water's edge. She slid to a stop when the creaking ice shifted. She dropped quickly to her stomach and crawled forward. When she spotted the brown hair, she stopped. He was eaten. He had sacrificed himself. How could he have done that? He made it clear that compassion was not his strong suit.

She pulled her mitts off. She wanted to keep them warm for later. She pulled herself to the ice's edge, balancing her weight. "Grab my hand," she yelled. He tried desperately to grab for her before his head started to sink beneath the water's surface. She cursed loudly until she grabbed his wrist. His skin was as cold as the water. A new panic washed through her. His temperature was dropping quickly. Death would follow if he didn't warm up.

Consciousness left him, leaving her with an image of his terror. Drowning was scary. She had almost done so before. She forced herself to get to safety then, and she would do the same for him. She slipped her elbows under his arms. She wiggled and fought and, with much effort, finally pulled him onto the ice. She didn't stop until they reached the shore.

Cuts and gashes covered his skin and clothes. The leech had done a number on him. Blood stained his clothing and caused her to gag. She had to keep working. There was no time to be sick. That man was dying. Through trembling hands, she checked his pulse which was soft. Everything was fine, but he didn't breathe. That was silent.

She had to act fast. She couldn't believe what she was about to do. The training would finally be used but she prefer not to. She lifted his chin, plugged his nose and pushed a breath into his lungs. She did this a few times. She checked for a pulse again as she was taught. It was gone. She was losing him.

She pulled out her pocket knife. She always carried it. It was handy if she needed to cut up a snack. In that case it was to cut open his shirt. She had to find the spot just under his ribs. Breaking them would be counterproductive. She tried to cut his shirt but it was too tough. All she managed was a small tear. She swore loudly and shoved it back in her pocket. Damn him and being prepared. She estimated where she should press and hoped for the best.

Round after round, she tried altering between forcing breaths and pressing on his chest. She was thankful that her workplace enforced CPR training. She would have never thought she would need it. After her eighth attempt, she could hear her instructor saying that it was done. It wasn't like she had a defibrillator with her. In the dead of winter and not being able to swim, he didn't have much of a chance.

She sat back as tears mixed with her sweat. She didn't want him to die. He was a person. He had so much more to live for. Sitting next to him, she blamed herself. If only she was stronger. If only she could have helped or gotten to him sooner. Perhaps then he'd have had a better chance. If she wasn't so damned useless, he could continue living. She would do anything if it meant saving him.

She noticed a soft, green glow grace her eyes. It started at his chest and spread outwards. Water bubbled from his mouth, spilling out. He coughed harshly. His body tensed and arched before thrashing. A horrifying howl echoed through-out the opening as his eyes snapped open and glazed over. The glow flashed brightly before dimming. Within moments it was over.

She let out a cry. Whatever that was, he breathed again. After a check, his pulse was back and strong. He was going to live. The outburst had somehow saved him. The relief was quick when the wind picked up. They were soaked. He was weak and in the cold. She pulled off her coat and dressed him. Once she pulled on her mitts, she struggled but stood with him on her back.

It took a painfully long time to make it to the protection of the shack. He was heavier than she was but not by much. That was something else she would have to work on. She was stronger than her female coworkers, but it obviously wasn't enough when she needed it most. The longer she was out there, the more apparent it was she wasn't suited for emergencies.

She ran back outside to fetch her pack. She needed to secure it to start a fire.

Her matches would work wonders on the dried wood piled in the pit. The bright red stood out in a sea of white. With a flick of her wrist, the fire roared to life, it's heat heavenly. With everything that raced through her, she didn't realize her arms had gone numb from cold. She changed into a dry sweater before moving on.

She lined her sleeping bag with a sheet she had brought for extra warmth. Getting it wet would be more than a mistake. It took forever to dry and it was the only thing to keep out the cold at night. It would also weigh more. That would slow her down. She wanted speed. The sooner that trip was over, the better.

Pulling off his clothes was harder than expected. He dressed in layers. It proved his intelligence. He wouldn't be cold, and this answered why he didn't have a coat. It meant it would take longer for her to undress him. The longer it took the more he bled. Blood loss was an issue that could not be easily fixed.

There was also a problem with a second, furry belt around his waist. She had noticed blood spots on the leg of his shorts which meant she needed to check there too. She hoped she wouldn't need to, but fate had different plans. She was curious as to why he would wear two belts. The only thing it held were the shorts but the shorts had no loops. She couldn't find a way to undo it and she couldn't pull the shorts off with it there. She would have to go through the legs. Hopefully they were loose enough she could fix the problem.

The first time she felt his skin, she paused. It was soft. She expected rough skin filled with scars. All that he had were multiple thin scars running from his shoulder to just past his navel. The longest ran the length while other shorter scars scattered around it, almost like something had shattered across his chest. The light from the fire illuminated them as a blue tint sparkled forth. She had never seen such a thing.

Cleaning and wrapping his wounds made her blush. He was a lean man. If it wasn't for the small muscle mass, he would have been but skin and bone. She had to admit he was handsome. If someone were only interested in looks, they could get no better. He must have had someone waiting for him back home. He looked about her age and, knowing most girls, they wouldn't leave him alone. If only his attitude was better, then she would be interested too. As usual, she was different from the others. As usual, she wanted more than just looks. She wanted a friend more than anything.

A friend was hard to come by. She was lucky with Paige. She was quiet and preferred her time in the country rather than the busy city life. It wasn't hard to notice that anyone her age wanted to party all night while balancing new careers in the day. She wasn't like that. She liked going home to the quiet of the farm to tend the needs of her grandparents. It was what she did. Her only yearning for adventure lay in the woods behind them.

She curled around her sleeping bag as best she could. She would rather be the one in it but it was a life or death situation for him. Heat would, hopefully, bring him around.

A yawn caused her to stretch and groan. The adrenaline was gone. She felt empty and exhausted. The only hope for recuperation was for the next day to be a quiet one.

Chapter 5

Your Name?

"You are one stubborn child aren't you?" The cold and cruel sneer sucked all the light in her soul. That voice, though never heard before, gave warning. A deadly warning.

Bones had been broken long ago, no longer pained. It was a dull reminder of what had happened. Open sores breathed in the infected air. Oh, did they ever burn like fire spreading from a spark. Movement was impossible. It was lost along all sense of joy. She remained defiant. Her father's words rang through. She had to be strong. They would win if she didn't. She had to do it for him. He lost everything just to give them a chance. She couldn't lose it.

"He won't answer. More beatings?" The excitement the violence gave them was wrong. That was not the teachings. They were peaceful. They healed the sick and helped the forest to grow. No one ever enjoyed killing. Why then? Why did that man control them like that? He wasn't supposed to. They worshiped life, all those people did was death. Why did The Mother forsake them? Did she not follow her like she wanted?

What did she do to make her so mad?

"No! You weaken the body too much and the soul will not linger. I can't use them if they are not trapped." The roar caused trembles. He wanted their souls, that was clear, but what for?

In a small voice she asked, "Souls are useful?" The cackle he let out was wrong. Why was the question funny? How did a stranger know about the adult teachings?

"That fool didn't teach you the true nature of your spirit? How does he expect you to defend The Mother if you don't fully understand magic?"

"That just made this much more entertaining. To think I was questioning the bargain I made with Devren. You have replenished my faith, boy." The laughter echoed throughout the room. While he gained faith, she was losing hers. No mother would ever abandon her children. Why was she letting him do this? She and her children had abandoned the people. Maybe he was right; maybe she should give up.

"You resist giving your soul to me but don't know why. Are you afraid that you will become a monster like the others? Afraid that your Mother would not accept you in death?" The clunking of boots on stone intensified the pain in her ears. She had been trapped and tortured for The Mother knew how long. Did her mother miss her? Did she think of her child as she looked at the night sky, praying for a miracle, like they did every night since the raid?

"Oh, how idiotic your father continues to be after death. All the mistakes that he's made. He should have taught you at least what your soul truly is. That knowledge might have saved you."

Frightening anger rose within. How dare he speak about her father that way! Her father was the best leader the village had seen in many centuries. It was recorded in all the history they kept. He was even awarded the life-giving sword. "Do not make fun of my father! He was a great man. You killed him." She was startled by the force of her voice. She didn't know she had so much left. The anger stirred something else, something that her father had warned her about. "You would be no match for him if it wasn't for your master!"

His snicker was sickening as the roots of her hair were pulled from her scalp. More pain. More suffering. She would not give in. Not like that. "Now is that you or Learthdelsea talking? Just to clarify, I have no master. There is only the Lord Devren, and that Mother of yours better be ready for us." At the sound of the threat, a wave a strength washed through her. Even with the little hope she had left, she still had faith in her and her children. She had to.

She started kicking and swinging. She had to get out. With the momentum it ripped more hair from her head. It was like needles but she no longer cared. This was her last chance. His laugh grew louder as he was too far from her reach. "Ah I see, even though I locked you away in that mountain you can still call out to him.

"Poor little Learthdelsea, no matter how hard you try, you can't win. The eldest of the bunch but so weak. Cenhelm would be a better challenge or even Raginmund. You were nothing. That bond you made, however, is nothing to sniff at." The boots circled her. She could hear the mumblings, but it was in a language she had never heard before. They stopped and swiveled. Cold, clammy hands grabbed her face. The stench of rot breathed over her. "Such a strong bond between a god and its people. Which would be better? Sever that bond or blend it better? Which one to choose? Either choice would be entertaining, for me anyways.

"I wouldn't be so worried about your father. His spirit is long gone." The strength failed, leaving her shivering and defeated. The rock felt colder than before. "The Mother couldn't stop Devren when entering her realm and no one else will be able to either. Soon, very soon, everything in this world will be mine." The creaking door slammed followed by the *thunk* of its lock. "Best of all, her guardian will be born in a decade or two. Plenty of time to whip up an army. When that happens, my boy, not even the guardians can stop us."

* * *

Evelyn startled awake and began to cry. The nightmare was terrible. It had never been so clear. She could remember every word, every thought, every feeling. They must have been something else entirely. No dream could ever be so real. It was if she was just there, in that room, being tortured to surrender. They had to mean something. A warning perhaps, or an explanation. All she knew is that the nightmares increased in clarity the more time she spent with Darrow.

She sat up slowly feeling the tenderness in her muscles. The adrenaline must have been gone. She had never before used so much strength or been so scared. It was a surprise she hadn't pulled anything. The cold sweat beaded down her face and her clothes stuck to her. That was always a sign the dream was powerful. She would give anything for a warm bath. Something to wash away her fears and the building grime.

The fire was down to hot embers. It glowed beautifully casting an orange shadow. No light penetrated the doorway, reminding her that it was still night. She grumbled as she moved to rekindle the fire. She needed to keep it going to keep them warm. She hoped that there would be a good bed of coals in the morning. Those were always the best to cook on.

As she watched the flames, she could feel them burn the fear away. They always offered her warmth and protection. The camping she had done with her grandfather showed her that. They would sit and tell stories till the stars were bright as candle flames. She pictured them together again, sitting on fallen logs in the summer. His teachings ever so precise. The birds twittered away while deer darted past. They would have to explore again once the snow was gone. It would be easier for him as age was catching up.

She changed her concentration to figuring out the nightmares. They became clearer the deeper she went. It was like the forest was calling out to her. Why would it do that? What was out there that would wake the spirits? She shook her head and sighed. Though the forest was alive, it was not usually thought of as a collective spirit. It sounded too surreal. Like magic. She loved her fantasy novels, there was no doubt there, but what was happening was a bit much. No one mentioned the horrors that a regular person from her age of technology would face. It was certain that man had conquered nature. Then why was all that happening?

Snoring erupted, causing her to jump. She had forgotten he was there. The quiet had deceived her. She crawled around as she heard deep coughing. The sound was sickly. The cold must have settled deep in his lungs. If it did, she couldn't help him. He would die there just like the leech.

She uncovered his face from the blankets. He was sleeping on his side and had dried since she had dozed off. His long ears twitched every now and then as he snored. She was curious about them as she had only seen costumes. The way they moved—it was like they were real. She lightly traced the top of one ear with her finger. It was smooth and soft like his skin, and it twitched away from her touch as if it tickled. He sighed as he rolled over.

The bag pulled apart as he stretched. His muscles showed their power as he tensed. He settled again but remained on his back. He calmed down considerably and his features were soft. Even the frown pulling his lips relaxed, allowing a slight smile. The edginess of his demeanor was gone. He had become a completely different person. Was he always so edgy when awake or was it only a cover?

She looked over his bandages and removed them. Some still bled but it was no longer a concern she had to deal with. Even though the sight of the crimson liquid bothered her, she learned to fight the feeling of sickness. She had to for his sake. The scars on his chest sparkled in the dim glow like snow. She had never seen such a thing before. They were magical, which didn't sit quite right with her. Magic was only a trick of the eye. It couldn't be real.

Curious, she traced the longest one with her fingertips. The scars were smooth and blended well with his skin. She couldn't tell by touch where he had once been cut. She felt a sting and pulled her hand back. Small cuts covered her fingers. She frowned and cleaned them. It was like a cut from paper as the bleeding stopped as soon as it started but stung more than it should. What was that?

Her touch alerted him and he gasped and shivered. A silent tear rolled gently down his cheek, followed by others. His sleep was as sound as her own. She wiped them away which caused more to fall. He trembled again before rolling over. The tears turned into soft cries. It was pitiful, like a child who was suffering. Suddenly he became violent and twitched as if he was bound. His cries turned into words that she had never heard of before. They were panicked and fearful.

Not wanting his nightmare to continue, she rubbed his back gently. Her grandfather would do it for her when she was a child. If the nightmares were bad enough, they would cuddle on the couch until she fell asleep again. Darrow's cries ceased but were replaced with warning growls. His eyes snapped open. They looked around wildly until they found her. The stare was so intense that she backed away from him. There was something wrong with the way his pupils dilated and his unwavering stare. They were primeval, that there was nothing intellectual within his soul.

He muttered something and his eyes softened. He was trying to tell her something but she couldn't understand. She looked at him apologetically. She wished she understood his mumblings, maybe she could help him. Calm his worries about the nightmares. He turned over and his eyes closed. She neared him slowly until she could hear him snore. His spell had passed. She tucked him in and decided she would ask him what happened in the morning.

The gnawing in her stomach woke her. She groaned before rolling over. She wanted more sleep. She could have slept for days and it wouldn't be enough. She opened her eyes slowly to see daylight peeking through the shack's fabric door. She grumbled as she sat up and stretched. The night was finally over. Continuing the journey should have been a priority as she wanted to get home. She had enough wilderness to last her at least until summer. Maybe then she could forget about the terror in the woods. First, she needed to eat.

The remaining stew smelled fit for consumption. That was one thing she could never tire of was stew. She cleaned the cast iron pot that was in the shack.

It was filled with dust among other things. She refused to eat from that. Every hut had one. It was good or else cooking would be hard if they could only find plants. The embers had nearly died so she added more logs before warming it up. Her stomach growled with anticipation from the smell that wafted in the air.

When it was finished, she put half back into the container and ate it with a smaller spoon that she had found. She couldn't wait for him to wake as she was starving. It had been too long that she had gone without food. She would need to remember to eat more frequently if she were to keep up her strength. Perhaps that was what she was missing yesterday. Her rescue attempt might have been better. She enjoyed her meal in the silence of the winter world that surrounded them. It was calming and offered a small chance of peace.

She had just finished the last mouthful when he began to stir. The bag moved and groaned. He poked his head out first and looked around sleepily. He missed her and curled back in with the pillow. She enjoyed watching him act like a regular guy who had just woken up from a good sleep. It made the vision of a tough guy dissolve. He was just like the rest and it made her smile. His hand searched around for his clothes. It retreated when it didn't find what it was looking for.

He looked up and about but still drowsy. He rubbed his eyes before settling back into the blankets. He nudged the pillow with his nose as he asked her a question in that language from the night before. She wished she knew what he was saying. She had a feeling she might have giggled as she could guess he was asking where his clothes went. His eyes opened a bit wider and focused on her. The gaze as calm as the liquid stone caused her heartbeat to quicken. She had to admit his eyes were beautiful even though they were an abnormal colour. Was it because of that that she like them so much?

She shook her head before going outside with the pot to collect snow for cleaning. She figured it should be washed before they left. It would have been the polite thing to do. As the snow melted, he grabbed more consciousness as he watched her. He was still tired but at least he was now alert.

"How did I get in here?" His voice was garbled by phlegm, and he cleared it while waiting for an answer. She shrugged her shoulders. "Take a guess but I can definitely tell you that you didn't walk here. You know, you're heavy."

His eyes widened. "You did this? You saved me?" The awe was uncalled for. She didn't appreciate it. In some ways it could be unbelievable that a strange girl save a man who was taller than her. It was rare for someone to help someone else. She wished he sounded grateful. "Guess it's hard to believe but it is what it is." He settled back in the bag. Something told her that she wasn't going to get an apology from him.

She shook her head as he dozed. He was supposed to be full of endurance. She had a feeling that whatever had happened between the leech and the glow had drained him. She walked over to him and pulled off the covers. He grumbled, but he seemed to be cold as he felt for the covers. She shook her head again. He was unbelievable.

He startled awake and stared wide-eyed at her. He looked down, and it was a like a brush of bright paint was smeared across his ears and cheeks. "Excuse me," he snapped as he pulled the covers back over. She frowned and growled at him. His attitude was getting to her. What happened to the kindness? "Considering you're in my sleeping bag and that I've seen everything but what's in those shorts, I don't think so." She understood the need for privacy, but at the moment he had none.

He sat up as his face burned red. "You what?!"

She felt her eyes tear as her anger grew. Coping with people yelling at her was not her strong suit. She didn't deserve to be yelled at. No one did. "Screw this! I'm sorry for saving you and disturbing whatever you were doing. Next time, you leave me alone and I'll let you die. How does that sound?" She stood and stomped over to the dried clothes and her pack before sitting. The ferocity was foreign. Never had she yelled so angrily before. Though it was completely against who she was, she wished she would have let him drown.

She felt the warmth of his hand on her shoulder. She shrugged it off. She couldn't bare his company any longer. He touched her again and she shrugged it off. Couldn't he take a hint to leave her alone?

"Sorry for yelling. I'm just..." he began. His voice was so tender and quiet it deflated her anger. He never sounded so sincere. "I'm not used to caring people. I usually find those who use others and are a curse to themselves. I thank you for saving me. I've never been good at swimming."

She placed her hand on his and felt its warmth. She believed him. His caring could be heard and made her wonder who he had helped before. "You're welcome, I guess."

She closed her eyes as he withdrew his hand. He walked before her and pulled off clothing. He jumped a bit and grumbled. She wondered why, of all reasons, he would change there. He had made it clear that he was offended by being seen nude. Out of courtesy, she kept her eyes closed. She would expect the same from him. Sometimes she wished her morals weren't so strong. The vision of him sleeping made her want to see more. It wasn't often she was lucky to see a well-figured man.

"You can open them now." She hesitated as she felt his breath on her lips. Did he know how much that tormented her? It was bittersweet memories the action restored. Some she would rather forget. She took a chance and opened them slowly. He was squatting right in front of her. He had dressed and was gazing into her eyes, almost reading her secrets. She was startled by how close he was. He either had no sense of boundaries or didn't care. He was amused as he let out a chuckle. It was light like his voice but held a power. "Are you afraid of me, snow girl?" She shook her head as she continued to look him over. She could see women trying to use him.

"What's with this snow girl thing?" Another blush made its way to his cheeks and ears. It was cute when he turned away to avert her questioning gaze. Something she wouldn't have expected from him.

"Well, you never gave me your name, so I had to give you something. You like sleeping in the snow so..."

It was her turn to blush. That was something she normally wouldn't forget. Knowing someone's name was important. She learned that lesson quickly. Then again, she thought she had told him. "Do you still want to know?"

He looked at her thoughtfully, his gray eyes filled with intelligence. There was the profound sadness within. It was deep and well-hidden, but it was there. Had anyone else noticed this pain? It was like he was longing for something but afraid. He looked down to his hands and remained silent. His hesitation was clear.

A growl came from his stomach. He looked up apologetically and frowned. She shook her head and gave him the warm dish of stew with the spoon. His eyes lit up as he took the first spoonful. He was delighted and continued to eat. The enjoyment of the flavor was apparent and he savored every bit of it. When it was all gone, he licked the spoon and the bowl.

He handed them back sheepishly. She raised an eyebrow. He would have been hungry, there was no doubt there. To lick the spoon and the dish was something else. "Is it honestly that good, or are you mocking me?"

He smiled and chuckled. "Honestly, it was the best meal I've ever had, and that's saying something. I've been around awhile." She returned his smile. He was opening up a bit. It must have been a miracle.

"You know that smile of yours is contagious," she complemented.

He looked at her confused as the smile faded. He thought about it before looking at her again. "I don't remember the last time I smiled. I don't think I ever have."

He watched his hands. She could tell he wasn't used to being civil with people. Being cold and uncaring worked for him in the past. With her it was different; she wouldn't allow being treated that way. He looked back at her with resolve. "Normally I don't ask this, but what's your name?" She shook her head with disbelief. His frown deepened.

"It's Eve," she answered. He moved his mouth as if tasting the word. "Eve," he finally said. "I've heard that word before. I remember someone saying new…" He moved his mouth again. The second time she realized that he was trying to sound out the word. English wasn't his native tongue. "New Year's Eve, the day before an event."

She nodded. It was a way around explaining her nickname.

She smiled at him. "Thank you, Darrow."

He was startled and looked bewildered. A bright blush glowed on his cheeks. "Y-y-your welcome," he stuttered. He cleared his throat and continued. "Well, we should get going. Night will come soon and we should be at the next shack by then." He smiled again as he gathered his supplies. "Though the insects are much fewer on this side of the lake, we'd be lucky to see one."

She nodded, feeling relief wash over her. She packed everything, dressed and let him know she was ready. She smiled as he let her out of the shack. She decided to ask him about what happened during the night.

His eyes pained and he looked away. "My past wasn't a happy one. I don't talk about it."

She nodded. She understood perfectly. There was something she had never spoken about before either.

"Though I'd like to know, what's the other language you speak?" She looked to him curiously as they walked. "I'm serious. I can tell that my language isn't your primary language. I don't trip over the word year."

He shook his head with disbelief. "In all the years I've been doing this, you're the first who's noticed."

She shrugged her shoulders and grinned. She had a feeling no one had noticed before. He would have been more cautious if it had happened before. "It's my job to see these things, makes my life easier."

He sighed and she swore she saw him grin. "It's Doolklian. Perhaps I'll teach you some one day. Depending on how easy you grasp new languages."

She smiled and nodded as they continued on their journey. That would be a promise she would make him keep.

Chapter 6

Protection of Innocence

Damp, terrified and cold, she felt the crudely cut rock pierce her flesh. She tried pushing herself up with her hands but no strength was left. She couldn't even move them into a position to push. She couldn't feel her legs, then again she couldn't feel much of her body. Her face was swollen to the point where she couldn't see. Even her stomach gnawed at her from what she knew was the days spent hungry.

She wished for the torture to end. Her spirit was fading. The retaliation from before couldn't last much longer, just like her body. She was weak. She was starved and forgotten in the prison of rock. The only release she could see was death. She wanted anything else but what she felt. Yet this small, weakening voice pressed her to go on. It told her that death was not the answer, that she couldn't let the light die.

Pounding came at a wooden door, her wooden door. Its rusty old hinges squealed defiantly as they were forced open. It was thrown and slammed against the wall, causing particles of dust and rock to fall and cover her. She could feel it invade what was left of her lungs as she breathed but couldn't move. They were coming again, coming to break her. It might have been the last time. Her body wouldn't take anymore.

She was dragged across the coarse floor by her hair. Strands, pried loose, fell like her dreams. Each stair was met with a dull thump from her body. It would be the same whenever someone remembered that scared little child in the dark. She would be dragged to another chamber, tortured and, if she hadn't changed her mind, she would be thrown back into her cell. She didn't know if the beatings occurred more frequently than usual. Time was a menace and a tease.

She was swung onto a metal table, its cold surface made her shiver, but the chill numbed the hurt. She was void of any clothing. Easier to break her. No safety she could cling to. She listened to the slumping footsteps leave the room. She couldn't understand why she was treated so horribly. What had she done? She didn't break any rules, she was a good girl. Her father always told her that. She was simply a child and nothing more. There was nothing special about her.

The door slammed open again. "The life of summer is still here!" That voice she had come to fear. It was cold and harsh. It never offered kindness. It played tricks with her mind to try to convert her to see his side. She would never comply. That little voice inside told her not to. "You leave me no choice. If you can still spread your life magic while trapped in that mountain, then I'll have to move you." He was desperate. He was never desperate. Calm and in control was how he worked.

"I would have thought you'd given up by now, but your spirit is strong so long as that god is with you. It probably begs you not to give in." He paced around her, mumbling in a language she had just begun to learn. Father said it was from people across the sea, people who reveled in war and death. Pages being turned drew her attention away from her past. Vials were combined and broken. Spells were whispered in the moist air. Each time made him more furious as he shouted.

"Give your soul to me, child!"

She could smell his rotten breath making her gag. It was always putrid, like he had died many years ago. She remained silent, her body beyond the point of sound. He would never get an answer. He would have to kill her. He screamed, and she flew across the room. She landed in a heap on the floor. Bones were broken. Her foot touched her face. She could no longer feel pain.

The room became quiet. He did not breathe, and her shaky breaths barely audible. His footsteps echoed as he begun to walk again. They ground across the floor. He picked her up gently as a father would a child. Comfort from him meant experimentation. More pain, more torture. Who would he make her see next suffering like her? She felt the cold steel of the table again. New to her were the ties of leather straps. A new fear crushed her spirit. They never tied her down before.

"I was hoping it wouldn't come to this but…"

She felt his cold hand press against her heart, cracking ribs that had already splintered. "This is my last option. I cannot prolong this any further." His hand burned where it touched. Though she thought she was done, she screamed with whatever energy she had left. It was as if he was extracting her heart. Why would he want that?

An explosion of heat washed over her. It pushed away the pain. She couldn't remember the last time the pain was gone. Warm winds blew the grease drenched hair from her face. Feathers brushed her skin. The sensation made her cry. It reminded her of her father, of his touches when she couldn't sleep.

"Yes! Yes! Resist the magic. Show me your memories. Let me tear them apart!" The sound of the man's excitement only furthered her fears. He couldn't take her father away. Take anything else, but let her keep him.

Just as suddenly as the warmth came, it left. Pain seared her skin and innards. Emotions were gone. She couldn't understand happiness or sadness. She heard laughing but didn't know what it meant. She couldn't remember who she was. Who was she? Where was she? Who laughed in the room? It was as if who she was had gone. "Now to be rid of this rebellion," she heard him mumble.

The door slammed opened again. The man was disturbed and seethed at whoever entered. "My lord, we've found it." He chuckled darkly. Was that what happiness was? He must have signaled to continue as the voice began again. "It's beyond that gate you wanted watched."

"Perfect, now to finish with you. Let see how your mother will react when you can't remember her."

* * *

Evelyn woke gasping for air. She tore open her sleeping bag. She felt confined and wanted to run. The burning of her skin still taunted her. She pulled off her sweater and t-shirt to feel the chill of the night cool her senses. She cried, frightened at what the nightmares had become. What creature would treat children like that? Why would she dream of such a thing? She sat on the wooden floor shivering in her tank top. She couldn't escape the terror that engulfed her.

Darrow's snoring caused her to scream. She cried harder and rocked where she sat. He jumped and the ring of his sword filled the night air. The trembling worsened from his movements. The forest made the nightmares worse. She wanted to be home. She wanted her grandfather and his safety.

A cool hand touched her forehead. "What happened?" he asked quietly. Looking up, she could see the worry in his eyes. Since she had saved him, he had treated her better. He held her hands in his. The softness of his stare calmed her but only a bit.

She shook her head. No one understood her nightmares; he would be no different. "Dreams are nothing to worry about." She had whispered it so softly she swore he shouldn't have heard her. He nodded as he caressed her cheek. Those eyes of his looked her over, allowing her a moment of calm before he returned to his rest.

She held her pillow, searching for a small sign of comfort. The nightmares were affecting her well after she woke. Even after his touch, her hands shook. She was scared to sleep. The torture that she went through was becoming more real. She could feel the pressure on her chest even after the dream had gone. It was hard for her to determine what was fact and what was dream.

She looked over to him to see him watching her. It was not usual to hear someone scream in their sleep like she had. She needed something to ease her fears. "Your home," she began. He sat more attentively. She knew he was interested in what had happened. "Does it have any places made of carved, stone blocks?"

He thought about it. He crossed his arms before answering. "Only in the pillar. I will never take you there. Everything else is made of wood or wool except for our tools. Why?"

She shook her head, losing energy to speak. She buried herself in the warmth before allowing sleep to take her.

She was awakened by him gently shaking her shoulder. She was groggy and exhausted. Even though the sleep was restful, she was drained. She opened her eyes slowly and found him kneeling beside her. He held an anxious frown. She groaned and rolled over. She needed more sleep, just a little more. The nightmare had taken much energy from her.

He shook her shoulder again. She complained that she wasn't feeling well and needed more rest. Her stomach turned as she slowly crawled from sleep. Usually it was rare, but the nightmares would take all she had. Leaving wouldn't be an option and neither would moving. She knew two things would have happened. One she would vomit. Second she would be slow and had a strong possibility of collapsing. She needed to stay to recover. She felt a shiver run through her and cuddled deeper in her sack before dozing off.

When she awoke on her own, the sound of metal being sharpened shrieked through the shack. She found a blurry, green figure across from her. She rubbed her eyes and could feel the crust. It was a sign that her sleep from before was not a peaceful one. Though she couldn't remember, it must have been upsetting to her. The crust was always a remnant of tears. Her grandparents would definitely send her to seek more professional help. That always resulted in medication that never helped.

She looked again to see him sharpening his sword with a small stone. She wiggled out of her sleeping bag and sat up. Her movement caught his attention and he stopped. As usual, he had a frown, and it wasn't long before he returned to his blade. She knew her sleeping in had halted their progress. She pulled on her t-shirt and sweatshirt. They would have to deal with it and walk faster to make it to the next stop.

Evelyn was starting to roll up her bag when he interrupted. "Don't bother, we're staying here tonight." His tone was cold and irritated.

It didn't sit well with her. She gave him a harsh look and sneered, though quickly softened when she understood where it came from. "Sorry..."

The grinding halted. He looked surprised when he looked up. "For what?"

She fidgeted with the bag's zipper, avoiding his gaze. "For sleeping in. I should have gotten up. I know how important movement is."

He sighed and sheathed his sword. "After that scream last night, I was surprised you woke up at all. It sounded like something was killing you." He moved closer and handed her a bowl of soup. She took it, searching the reason for his change. "Honestly, Eve, you're doing better than anyone else I've led through here. Most cower in fear; you've been facing it."

She shrugged her shoulders. She couldn't see it. She was terrified at what she had seen. There must have been braver folks than her. She decided to joke about it. "Maybe I've been prepared for it from cutting the heads off chickens and my nightmares."

His eyes widened but he shook his head and sighed.

As she ate the soup, a breaking of a branch outside caused her to jump. Darrow rushed to the shack's opening and held his blade ready to attack, his movements quick and precise. The flap opened and he pounced, tackling the intruder to the ground. He held the blade to the other's neck and roared in his tongue. It happened so quickly. She was right to assume he was good. He could have been a master assassin. The intruder thought the same as they didn't move.

He had caught a man who had the same long ears as him, though that was where the similarities ended. The trapped man had long, coal black hair tied by dark brown string. His eyes were that of dark chocolate and full of malice. He was dressed in brown with a white cape and he had a large build, much bigger than Darrow. To her, he was intimidating. He would have been more so if he didn't look helpless under Darrow's blade.

They exchanged heated words. It took a while before Darrow let him up. The newcomer looked around and noticed her eating the soup. His eyes lit up hungrily and he quickly looked to Darrow. His look darkened as she swore he sent deathly warnings. They both turned to her.

"I am Femil and I work in forest like Darrow." She noticed the difficulty in speaking right away, the accent heavy, nearly masking the words. It made her wonder how long her guide had been at it.

"Yes, though we don't all leave at once." Darrow's glare was frightening. She had never seen him express emotions openly before. Something was wrong. "However, normally we wait until the other returns from their patrol." It was odd how harsh he was being. It was different than anger. His words were sharp and tone dangerous. He was furious. It was almost like he wanted to kill the man.

Femil caught the hostility and backed towards the door. Evelyn finished her soup while the two talked, though it was more interrogation than talk. One word was spoken quite often. It was hinted that it was an important stressor. Each time it was said, Darrow looked over at her and he became more defensive. So much so he growled angrily until a full hiss came forth as he exposed his teeth.

Quickly he had his sword to Femil's neck again. He shouted at the second man with fury. His eyes burned with fire. Fire wanting to kill.

Evelyn couldn't handle more blood. She gathered her courage and decided to interfere. "What's a 'za-cree-lan'?" The feud paused as both men looked at her. The intensity in Darrow's eyes never wavered, while the other looked as if she had just saved him. She hoped Femil would remember that moment. She wasn't planning on dying.

"It's nothing you need to worry about." Darrow's reassurance didn't calm the atmosphere. The look in the other's eyes told her differently. Femil was still craving with unnatural hunger.

Suddenly Femil kicked Darrow in the stomach, knocking him nearly into the fire. He dashed out the door. Darrow jumped to his feet and followed, ordering her to stay there. She stared at the doorway. It happened way too fast. She couldn't let him fight without his sword. She pulled on her boots and coat, grabbed his discarded sword, and ran out after them. Their argument was about her. They looked at her way too often. What she couldn't comprehend was what about her had caused the fight.

The footprints darted through the trees. It was quiet. No animal dared to stumble upon the fight. Her gut told her that they had gone far. She quickened her pace. She didn't want people to die. She was never a fan of death though it was in the news to often. Femil may have looked to be dangerous but he wasn't harming anything. Not that she knew of anyway. She stopped and caught her breath. She listened intently for any sign that they were close. She had to find them.

While listening, she realized that perhaps Femil was going to kidnap her. Perhaps all Darrow was trying to do was protect her. Perhaps Femil wanted something more from her. She thought back to the hungry look from before. It was disturbing. That hungry look was not starvation. It was more. She had a bad feeling that he wanted her. What worried her was that she couldn't tell. He was cunning and judging from his actions, he was certainly good at battle.

She heard snapping branches near her. She hid behind a large tree and waited. She didn't want to encounter anything alone. Even with the sword, she was vulnerable. She didn't know how to use it. She waited for more movement. The more time passed, the more she wished she would have listened to Darrow and stayed put. She wasn't trained to fight. If Femil was coming back for her and had killed Darrow, then she couldn't beat him off. She grabbed the sword to help Darrow.

Two black shadows fell from the trees. She gasped and pressed herself against the trunk. She watched as the two fought. She was amazed at the talent she witnessed. Darrow was delivering blows with his fists while avoiding Femil's steel blade. He was good, better than any trained boxer. It was unfair as Femil had the upper hand. Her opinion soon changed when Darrow disarmed his opponent.

With Darrow having the blade, it was clear the sword came as second nature. His twists and turns were lightning fast, his strength just enough to cause heavy damage. When Femil tired, Darrow feigned to his left and then sliced

Femil's right arm to the bone. The stranger howled in pain and stumbled backwards. Survival burned in his eyes. He screamed at Darrow, but she saw the cold, uncaring eyes. He wouldn't live. He darted off to flee but was blocked by an ice wall erupting from the earth. He turned to face the reaper.

Femil mumbled something which caused Darrow to stop. His eyes softened but he shook his head. He was solemn and whispered something mournfully. Femil's expression blanked. Whatever Darrow said made no sense to the man. Gone was his pain but was replaced by utter confusion. He then growled and asked a question. Darrow's hard look returned, and with one swing he beheaded his opponent.

A dull wind brought the smell of warm iron to her nostrils. Her stomach churned and she turned away. She couldn't believe that Darrow had just slaughtered his own kind. There was no sympathy. No second thought. He didn't even give the man a second chance. He didn't let him explain. She wondered if he would do the same to her. Would he turn on her if she didn't do as he told her?

She was about to turn and run when he appeared. She held his sword tight. She would fight her way out if she had to. She pointed it at him with distrust. He looked at it solemnly. He held the blade between his thumb and forefinger.

"If you want to kill someone…" He moved the blade to point at his throat and pressed the tip into his skin. "This is the quickest way to do it." His eyes were cold yet begging. He was dead inside as the stare held hers.

She stood shaking, not understanding what he was doing. She released it and let it fall into the snow. She couldn't kill someone. She refused to do it. It was and always had been against her to kill things. When she helped her grandparents on their farm with the chickens, she would cry afterwards. She hated to admit it, but it took many tries for her to be able to kill one. They were all beautiful creatures with lives. She couldn't end them.

He picked up his sword and led her back to the shack quietly. He refused to look at her. She felt herself still shaking and couldn't care less. She felt that hunting animals was one thing. A person planned on eating it or selling it. When one was a farmer, raising the animals was like raising a family. What she witnessed was horrifying. She couldn't understand the reason for it. Why would one kill another for nothing?

He helped her sit on her sleeping bag before sitting next to her. He put away his sword and stared at his lap. He was waiting for something. She figured it was any sort of reaction from her. At that moment she didn't know how.

The sunlight had faded from around the door frame when she felt pulled out of her shock. He was cooking again but his eyes distant.

She closed her hands into tight fists and glared at him. "Why," she asked angrily. Her voice surprised him as he snapped up. "Why did you kill him?"

He looked back at the pot and shook his head.

"Do you think I'm too stupid not to know?" She was furious. Life was precious and he stole it away. She had stood and was leaning over him. He looked up slowly, and she saw the pain behind his eyes. He shook his head again and returned to his cooking. His actions continued to infuriate her. She roughly turned him to face her. "Why won't you answer me?!"

He stood. He looked angry with her behaviour, but there was something else. He walked towards her and she retreated. She felt the wall behind her and stopped. He raised his arms and she flinched. He was going to hit her.

Instead he grabbed her shoulders gently. His stare was hard, but she noticed the softness that had appeared in his stone gray eyes. "Because unlike the others I've led through here, you are innocent. You bare no grudge and see the good in people. You value life. There's a light in you that I don't want to see be taken away.

"That is why I had to quiet him. He's a scout. If the lord finds out about you..." He paused and looked down. She felt a slight tremble in his hands but it was controlled quickly. He sighed and let her go. He sat and returned to his pot. "Someone so pure should never be touched by that evil."

She stood where she was, not comprehending what he was telling her. Her, pure? Was he joking? "You think I'm pure?" She shook her head in disbelief. She thought many things about herself. The words pure and innocent never came to mind. She thought newborn children were innocent until they understood the concept of good and bad. Being an adult, she definitely didn't think of herself as pure.

He handed her a bowl of soup. "I have been around many years, Eve. I've seen and led many people through these trees. Not one has made my mind as clear as yours. You have a gift, one that needs to be protected." She continued to look at him, confused. He looked her age, which was just shy of twenty. How old was he and how many people did he escort? He shook his head and looked at her kindly. "Don't worry about it; just know that you are safe. I won't let anything hurt you."

She didn't turn away as she slowly ate her supper. She wanted to understand why she was different. She was as normal as anyone else. She had gone to school; she had a job and a home. The only out of the ordinary thing was that she lived with and took care of her grandparents. She sighed and handed him the bowl once it was empty. She wouldn't get a straight answer from him. That's how he was.

As she crawled into bed, she noticed him crawl over to her. She realized that more recently he was becoming more open, more caring. She would even dare to say softer with her. She wondered if he did that with everyone. She watched him stand and step outside as the moonlight entered. He was lost, and she had no idea how to help him.

Chapter 7

Shifting Stones

Snow crunched beneath her feet. What lay before her were untouched mounds of freshly fallen snow. Its softness had built up on the trunks of trees and left blankets on their branches. Twinkling ice particles made it look like stars during sunlight. It was deep, which made her inner child tremble with excitement.

The air was a bit chilly but was more of an autumn breeze than the winter wind. The sweat built up in her clothes, making them sticky and damp. She decided to take off her coat and, soon after, her sweater. She found it still warm and removed her mittens, scarf and toque. She smiled and twirled around, lifting a whirlwind of white. Out of all the fear and terror her life had become, she deserved a bit of play time.

She ran over and fell into the snow. She waved her arms and legs around. When she was satisfied, she stood. Her chest puffed up at the sight of the perfect snow angel. Giggling, she jumped around. It had been too long since she had made one. She nearly forgot how much fun it could be.

She ran this way and that way. She would stop and make something out of the snow and then take off again. She grew tired from her play. She stopped and looked at her creations. A few more snow angels guarded the land. A snow family stood lovingly with the snowman, woman and child standing together under a tree. She had made many snowballs and had piled them in different sections. She had even made an igloo.

She sat from exhaustion. She had been very productive and had the snow creations to prove it. She wished she could show it to her mother. It was then she noticed that the air had cooled considerably since she started. Night had descended, but the moon offered light. Because of all the work, her clothes were damp and the wind pushed through them. She shivered and rubbed her arms as she walked to where she had dumped her clothes. Everything was gone. She looked harder and saw footprints bigger than hers walking away from where they had been. It must have been her mother. She followed them.

She walked and walked. The further she went, the colder it became. She shivered as the wind picked up a storm. The snow pushed against her, slowing her progress. It became too cold for her to walk, and she huddled next to a large tree. She could see the prints walking further ahead. She tried to force herself to keep going, but her body was too cold.

She waited for what felt like eternity. The beautiful golden hues turned into a hellish scene of blue and death. She began to cry. She should have listened and stayed with the group. She wished for her mother's safety. If she were to live through the night, she could hear her mother scolding her for taking off on her own. She closed her eyes.

Out of the howling wind she heard a small branch being snapped underfoot. Her eyes snapped open at the sound. A shadow appeared from behind a tree. It was tall and its cloak billowed in the wind. In one hand she saw the missing clothing. In the other was a blade made of clear blue ice.

Click. Click. Click. She shuddered knowing what the noise was. It was the sound of death. It had taken a beloved from her. The shadow tossed her clothing while it walked towards her. It reminded her of a ghost as the cloak hovered over the snow, never touching it.

Click. Click. Click. It stopped and looked around. She felt fear seep into her heart. The shadow wouldn't save her. It would harm her just like the stories. She had to run but was too frozen to move.

Click. Click. Click. It looked around and then stared in one direction. She wondered if it was also afraid of the insects. They were fearsome creatures that killed without hesitation. They had no soul or emotion to care about their victims and killed mercilessly. Her hypothesis was false as it returned to its walk to her.

Click. Click. Click. Once it was near it raised the iced blade. The gleam of its sharp edges caused her to cry. It was going to kill her. Beyond the trees she saw the shadows of the insects with the red glow in their eyes. Death was imminent; if the shadow didn't kill her, the insects would.

Click. Click... "We t-t-trusted you," cried a woman through chattering teeth. Before she looked to see who it was, the blade slashed downward. It hit her right shoulder and shattered as it continued to slice down her chest. It's pain burning, freezing her blood.

SCHEECH!

* * *

Evelyn gasped as her eyes snapped open. She could feel bile erupt from her stomach and climb up her throat. She tore out of the sleeping bag and only made it a few feet before vomiting in the snow. Her body trembled violently as it forced more digested food from her system. The power of the nightmare clouded her thoughts and caused a third dry heave before she was able to breathe again.

The immense pain from the ice blade penetrated her shoulder and chest. She held in hard cries but couldn't contain the softer ones. She pulled her sweater off her shoulder to see that nothing had damaged her physically. Yet it continued to burn as if she was injured from the dream.

She remained on her knees waiting for the spell to pass. She continued to tremble, but the pain subsided to a dull pulsing. Her pants became wet from remaining in the snow for so long. She only had her sweater and thick jogging pants. She slowly looked over her shoulder to find her winter gear still beside her sleeping bag. Darrow was still sleeping on his cape.

She took a deep breath. She had to get back to bed. He had told her that the morning would bring the last part of the journey. She would finally see his home and be one step closer to hers. She placed her hands on her knees and pushed herself up to stand. It was slow but halfway she trembled again and lost her strength.

She sat back and rocked herself. The motion usually lessened the pain in her stomach and lessened her fears. Her grandfather taught her that. Once she had calmed, the voice of the woman returned to her as well as the fear. It was if the nightmare had triggered something deep inside. A memory she never had. "We trusted you," she whispered after the third failed attempt.

"Hmm… What was that, Eve?" She heard him yawn and stretch. She looked over slowly and saw him watching her. His head tilted as he tried to get a better look. Her stomach cringed, and she turned around quickly before heaving again.

The snow crunched behind her as her trembles worsened. A warm hand was at her back as she felt his presence beside her.

"What happened," he asked worriedly.

She shook her head slowly and drew in a shaky breath. She felt a cloth wrapped around her and she saw it to be his white cape. When she felt her stomach settle, she answered him. "Nothing, I'll be fine."

She heard him snort. "No one I've brought through here has ever been sick, and you were fine last night. So honestly what happened?"

She looked up and saw the care in his features. The calm eyes, the slack frown. She had noticed it a day or two before, but now it was filled with worry. "Just not feeling well, that's all." He rolled his eyes and shook his head. He knew she was lying.

He grabbed her under her knees and back. After a bit of difficulty, he lifted her into the air. She gasped and buried her face in his shoulder. She didn't like being picked up. She remembered being dropped one too many times by her aunts and uncles and didn't want to get hurt again.

He sat down on her sleeping bag but kept her in his lap. She let out a slow breath, feeling safer on the ground. She couldn't fall from there. He removed his hand from under her knees. He removed the thick leather glove from his free hand with his teeth, showing longer canines than hers. His fingers fumbled but found the edge of her shirt. She growled and pulled back her fist when he caught it. "You think I'd pull that when you're ill? If that was my goal, it would have happened already. If your stomach is truly upset, I'm going to fix it so you can sleep."

She growled a warning but let her arm relax. She glared at him but he kept his calm, soft expression. He placed his hand under her shirt and on her skin. His skin was rough but his touch was gentle, so much so that it tickled her. She smiled and snickered but tried to hold in her giggles. She felt warmth emanate from his hand. He moved slowly, and she could feel him press parts of her stomach.

When he was done, he removed his hand and tucked her shirt in. "Whatever it was has passed." She rested her head against his chest. His heartbeat quickened at her touch. She closed her eyes and listened to the rhythm. The sound quieted her nerves. She felt peaceful and she could tell sleep was embracing her.

The touch of a finger brushing her cheek startled her. Her eyes snapped open and she watched his hand brush away a few strands of hair from her face. She looked up to see a strong blush across his cheeks and up his ears. His eyes glistened in the ember glow of the fire. It was then she noticed the openness in his eyes. He was no longer tense and something within her whispered it was a rare sight.

The woman's voice echoed in her ears. She sighed and cuddled closer to his warmth. "Do you think I trust you?" She watched his features harden and his peace fade.

"Why would you…" His voice trailed off. She waited for an answer as he began to rock them slowly. She continued to watch him as his expression turned darker. He was furious and she could feel his fingers grip her shirt.

She pulled gently on his sleeve. His face softened once again, though it held sadness.

"It seems like it is in your nature to trust people fully."

She thought for a moment then nodded. It was true. She gave many people the benefit of the doubt, even when she shouldn't. She noticed pity surface in the depths of his gaze.

"Which I think is quite unfortunate as you're not warned of those who will hurt you."

She frowned at his words. She had some sort of gut reaction to those who would hurt her. She stayed away from those reactions. There were few times her instincts failed at warning her, but they were usually on point. She sat up and stared into his eyes. "What do you mean unfortunately? Trust is what friendships are based on."

He shook his head. "There are some things in my life that are better off unexplained. I learned early not to trust people."

She watched him, confused. He gazed at her as a blush crept across his cheeks and ears. He lightly brushed the loose strands of hair from her face. He treated her so gently and kindly, yet his words were harsh. She wondered how his upbringing created such a complicated man. She felt herself blush the more she looked into his eyes. He may not have shown emotion, but she had discovered that his eyes spoke volumes.

He placed her in her sleeping bag and tucked her in. She watched as he stood and walked away. The absence of his presence pulled at her chest.

"Do you trust me," she asked quietly.

His ear twitched and he turned back to her. She felt her heart clench at the sight of his watery eyes. "I wish to. I'd give anything to trust someone."

He returned to her and kneeled. He kissed her forehead, and she felt his cracked lips linger longer than any other had. He withdrew slowly, and she heard him draw a quick breath. "Just remember that I'll be here to protect you." She felt herself tremble slightly but could feel the sincerity in his words.

He left and curled back into his spot. She could still feel her heart pounding from his touch. She felt herself smile. It had been a long time since she felt that way about anyone. At least that was how it felt. She knew that only one other made her heart pound and that they had moved shortly after she realized her feelings.

She played around with the end of her pillow case. She found herself acting like a young teen who was smitten. She snorted then nuzzled her pillow. She figured the forest was getting to her. She felt being alone with someone for so long may cause the feelings. Even though she knew it was probably nothing, she couldn't help but wonder how it felt to be in his loving embrace.

She shook her head. If anything, he was probably anxiously awaiting a loved one at home. A man as gentle as him would have someone. She then thought about how he first acted. She sighed and looked over to him. He was snoring softly and was off to sleep. She smiled and settled into her bed. She'd find out her answer soon enough.

The morning was greeted with a bright light. She grumbled and rolled over to avoid it. She wanted more sleep. She felt her mind cry for the same. She settled again only to have the light blind her. She groaned and covered her head with her pillow. Just another hour was all she needed. Just a few more minutes.

She felt a chill come from her side. She felt it inviting. She had grown hot overnight. It grew the longer she remained still. Suddenly, the coolness turned cold, and she felt fingers lightly touch her sides causing her to giggle. They continued on playing her nerves like the ivories of a piano. She flipped over and howled in laughter. She couldn't stand being tickled but couldn't defend herself either.

She begged for it to stop but it persisted. She grabbed one hand but always seemed to miss the other. He was too quick. She kicked trying to escape but never made contact. "You going to get out of bed now?" She nodded and looked at him with tears in her eyes. His smile drew his lips up revealing teeth. A true smile and joy as his eyes matched his expression.

She breathed heavily after the attack. "You're mean," she complained. He shrugged and patted her shoulder as she stuck out her tongue.

She sighed. "I'm still tired from last night."

He nodded and smirked. "I know but you can sleep once we reach my village. It'll be safer at my house." She remained silent as she looked at him. His eyes were different; they held a light within them. He had come alive from the one night of sleep. The eyes from before were dead and somehow new life was breathed within them.

At that moment, she felt mischievous. She raised her hands slightly and he didn't notice. Her smile changed and she saw the flash of alert in his eyes. "What happens if I don't," she exclaimed just as she began to tickle his sides. His arms shook as he started chuckling. Once the roars of laughter started, he lost his control and fell.

His laugh was deep and he buried his face in her shoulder. She loved the sound but stopped to allow him to breathe. He continued to chuckle well after. His arms had wrapped around her and she could feel the strength they held. She sighed and wrapped hers around him and held him in a tight embrace. She always returned hugs and they were one of her favorite things. She felt her heart pound in her chest and could feel her face glow. It had been too long since the last one.

He pulled away slowly. "Eve, do you remember what I said last night." She nodded and tilted her head. She noticed his arms flex and tighten. "I meant every word I said. I will protect you; I'll always protect you."

Her curiosity grew and she felt a bit of frustration bubble forth. "Why though? I thought you didn't like people like me."

He sat up and frowned. "I never said I didn't like you."

She felt herself frown along with him. "If not, then why were you so cold towards me?"

He fell silent and looked away. It was long before he stood and walked to his cape. "You'd better dress. We need to make it there by nightfall."

She went to apologize but turned to her pack instead. She couldn't understand his sudden change. Her confusion soon turned to anger. She wanted to know why he was harsh before.

She tied her sleeping gear to her bag harshly and dressed. She walked briskly past him without making eye contact. She was cheerful for once, and it had vanished. He would always remain shrouded in mystery. The gloom and secrets never lifted. She felt hurt because he wouldn't trust her. She didn't pose any threat besides falling into traps.

She heard him speeding up and walked faster. She didn't want to be near him. She wanted to be alone. She growled and quickened her pace again. The faster she went, the faster he got. Soon they were running. She breathed heavily as she pushed herself farther. Her need for solitude drove her while her body yearned to rest.

Suddenly, she slipped and fell. She felt her head hit something hard. She screamed from shock and pain. She cried as she covered her face and drew up her knees. Her head felt as if it would split in two. She remained in her ball as she heard his hurried footsteps approach.

She tried rolling over to sit, but her backpack hampered her progress. When she'd strain to turn, it would cause the pounding to intensify. She found it to be like her migraines. The more she struggled the worse it became.

She felt his hands pull her from the snow and turn her over. He looked her over. Worry set in when he looked at her forehead. She growled at him and shoved his hand away when he brought it near. She tried to move away but he kept her in his lap. "Eve, please," he begged. "You're bleeding and your struggling is making it worse."

She froze. She didn't feel blood. She quickly removed her mitten and felt around her face. She felt warm liquid and a cut in her hair line. She brought her hand down and paled from the sight of crimson. It smeared down her fingers as her stomach churned. "D-Darrow," she whimpered. She closed her eyes, afraid of having dry heaves again.

He shushed her as she felt a rough material wipe at her face. She opened her eyes slowly and saw his cape stain with her blood. He let it go and placed his hand on the cut. She felt comforting warmth from his touch. After some time, the pain in her head subsided and he took his hand away. He sighed and looked at her. His worry dwindled and he looked caringly at her.

"Is that better?" She nodded slowly and settled against his arm. He chuckled as a small smile crept across his lips. She blushed and felt her breath catch in her lungs. Such a strange man she had found. "I'm glad some colour has returned to you." She looked away quickly, feeling embarrassed.

"I still don't understand why you were mean to me."

He sighed deeply but remained silent. He kept her in his arms. He shook his head and his look softened. "I acted that way because..." He looked away, and she could see the conflict burning in him. He tensed and growled before letting out a long breath. She waited for him, a bit annoyed that he couldn't say anything but remained silent. "I have a job to do, Eve. One that I can't get attached to people or else I will get hurt."

"I'm not going to hurt you." She couldn't dream of hurting someone. His cold hand met her cheek which caused her to shiver.

He smiled sadly but it quickly disappeared. "I know but…" He sighed and walked away from her. He leaned against a tree, his back towards her. She followed him but stopped when she heard a shaking breath. "You're so different from everyone else. You shouldn't…"

She watched as he shuddered and clenched his fists. She knew then that something was tormenting the man. There was an agonizing battle going on within that was causing him to break. She worried for his safety as well as her own. From watching movies and listening to her grandfather, a warrior who loses themselves to their emotions is useless in battle.

She decided to change the subject. "We should get going. You said we had to make it there before dark." He took a deep breath and let it out slowly. He nodded and started off again. She followed behind him, knowing that the first half of the journey had ended. She shoved off the feeling that something horrible was going to happen, something that would change the course of history.

Chapter 8

Welcome to the City of Light

The night stars twinkled more brightly than she had ever seen them before. Evelyn gazed up at them and watched them dance against the black sky. They were little crystals sprinkled across the sea. She felt oddly peaceful as her eyes wandered. If it wasn't for every sound making her jump, she would have fallen asleep against Darrow's cape.

He instructed her to stay still and silent while hiding in the thicket. He needed to fetch something from his home in order to keep her hidden while bringing her pack with him. If she were to keep her ears hidden, she would be just like him. Perhaps his people were violent. Perhaps they killed people for fun. She shivered at her thoughts as they were not happy ones.

She felt herself nodding off when she heard the sound of footsteps crunching towards her. She remained still and listened. They had dug a bit of a hole in the snow so she would be hidden from view. Was it another scout? They were trained to see things that were abnormal. It wasn't until the footprints were gone when she let out a slow, quiet breath.

She waited longer. All was quiet before she was yanked from her hole. She was pulled to her feet then shoved back down. She groaned as she fell on some of the dead bushes. Their brittle branches snapped and cut her face. She looked up to see a person with long ears whom she didn't recognize. She stayed still as they drew their blade on her. She stared at them in horror. He was going to kill her.

They spoke in Darrow's language. She wished she understood. They sounded threatening and demanded answers. When she didn't answer, they pressed the tip of their sword into her neck. She whimpered but didn't know what to say. They may not understand her. She couldn't see all of them learning it.

Their agitation ceased but was replaced by a tone she recognized before. They sounded hungry. They quickly returned their blade and brought her up to their level. It was another male.

His eyes were intense as he licked his lips. "Sacrilan," he whispered hungrily. She began to struggle as she remembered the last time she heard that word. It did not end well.

As he placed his hand on the hem of her coat, he stiffened. A threatening voice growled menacingly behind him. It was, thankfully, one she recognized. The stranger growled something in return before falling limp against the blade. Darrow carried the body back to where her hole was and dumped him in.

After burying the dead man, Darrow returned to her. "This was what I meant by my home is dangerous to you." He spat at the grave. "If it was his choice, he would have brought you back to his place and had his way with you."

She shivered at the thought. The more time she spent around his people, the more she had the feeling that they were cannibals. Either that or lawless murderers. Made her wonder about him. Was she in danger?

He was dressed in white from the strange hat that covered his face to the coverings on his boots. If he were to have lain down in the snow, he would have looked like lumps. He had a large, white blanket in his arms and he handed it to her. "We will need to be spectres descending into my village. I will need to carry you the rest of the way." She nodded but wondered if he could do it. He was barely taller than her. Judging by what she saw from healing him, she was also larger than him. He smirked at her and patted her shoulder. "Though I may not be used to carrying as much weight, I can still do this. Have faith."

She put the blanket on to discover it was an oversized cloak. The more she inspected it, the stranger it was. It had pockets to put her hands and feet in. She placed them in the pockets assuming it was supposed to be that way. He adjusted a few straps then knelt down with his back to her. "You will pretend to be like your pack. Do not move or speak or we will both die." She nodded and climbed on.

He groaned at first but lifted her in the air. She whimpered but settled quickly. She hadn't been lifted since she was a child. He let out a soft chuckle as he walked slowly. "Come now, Eve, it's not that high."

She snorted. "Sorry if I'm not used to being picked up like a sack of potatoes," she spat. He glanced back at her with a confused looked but smiled soon after, followed with another chuckle. She smiled, happy with knowing he could understand her joke.

Through the trees was a clearing; within, it had a large depression with a pillar of rock towering in the middle. Atop the pillar was a large statue with wings made of stone. She wondered who the statue was a depiction of as it was hard to make out the rest. Surrounding the pillar were gigantic trees. She figured they must have been fifty feet tall or more and crowned near the center. The entire sight reminded her of an angel food cake bowl with dead broccoli in it. During the day, she could imagine being blinded by the snow that covered it all.

"This is my village," he whispered to her nearly inaudibly. "We call it the City of Light, but the elders say there was another name. It's only a legend now." He sighed as he stood at the rim. "My mother told me that this place is beautiful during the other seasons, but the snow never melts. The younger generations think she's lost her mind. The other elders think so too. Even I'm starting to doubt her stories, but they give me hope." With that he descended into the village.

They slipped and slid until they reached the bottom. She clutched onto his shoulders tightly. She was terrified that they would fall. She knew that one misstep would be the end of the both of them. Not even the soft snow would cushion them. It seemed that he read her mind and he shushed her. He paused for a moment and looked at her. His smile assured her and she loosened her grip.

As they walked by the closest tree, a man appeared. She could feel Darrow tense and stop his progress. He let go of her leg and removed his mask before lifting her again. He was proud from the way he strutted. From the glow of the starlight, she could tell that the newcomer was much taller and leaner than Darrow. His coarse black hair dangled messily and the very dark eyes hid his pupils. The feeling she got from the new villager was danger, a strong sense of danger.

He spoke to Darrow. The longer the conversation carried, the more tense he became. The stranger motioned to touch her, which caused Darrow to growl menacingly and retract a few steps. The other man held his hands up and motioned Darrow to calm down. Darrow continued to growl as he circled around.

He sighed and shook his head. The other waved and walked off back towards one of the large trees.

Darrow stomped off. His growling intensified. While he walked, he turned back and spat in the direction of where the man used to be. Obviously, Darrow did not like him. She couldn't blame him. His actions and movements during their meeting made her think that he was one of those womanizing stereotypes that acted better than everyone else. She couldn't stand men like that.

Darrow neared one of the trees and circled it. When she saw rungs carved into the tree, he began his accent. She began slipping and adjusted herself. The more he climbed, the less she wanted to look down and the more she knew she didn't want to fall. He pulled them up for what she felt was an eternity. Her arms and legs would give way at any moment.

He finally crawled onto a platform. It was small. Large enough for two, perhaps three, people to stand on. A door was carved into the tree with a golden handle. He shifted her a bit, and she felt his hand on her buttocks. She growled but he ignored her. He reached out and grabbed the handle. It glowed with a warm light and she heard a soft click. He sighed and pushed it open.

Inside was dark. He walked a bit and set her down on what felt like a comfortable lounge chair. He walked back to the door and closed it. Then it was pitch dark. It made her gasp. She closed her eyes and curled into the chair. She heard the floor creak as he walked. A candle was lit and the room came into view. It held a small kitchen with a wood stove, a small table with three chairs and the lounge chair she was in with a side table all made from wood. It was quite cozy and reminded her of home.

He approached her and removed the cape. He smiled softly as he moved a few strands of hair from her forehead. "You can speak now," he whispered.

She smiled back at him sleepily. The excitement and horror from descending into the village had taken its toll. "Why are you whispering?"

He shrugged his shoulders and chuckled.

He leaned forward slowly as the light gave a slight shimmer to his eyes. She felt her heart quicken. He truly was a handsome man. She could see why many would follow him through the forest as she had, though for different reasons. She felt her breath catch when his nose scraped against hers. "Eve, I really do care for you. I—"

A knock came at the door. It startled him as his head whipped around to look at it. It came again and an urgent voice barked orders. He was hesitant to answer but did in what sounded like a startled voice. There was panic in his eyes as he picked her up, swung her on his shoulders, and took her down a hallway.

He turned into a room and set her in a closet. He buried her under any clothes and blankets he tried to find in there. "Please don't say anything ok," he told her urgently. "I can't have them find you."

Again the voice came to the door and sounded furious. He looked back at her with pleading eyes. She smiled, hoping to calm some of his nerves. "I promise I'll be as quiet as a backpack." He relaxed somewhat before he ran back out, shouting at the visitors.

She listened to the tones of the voices of the people who were in the entrance. She could tell there were Darrow and two others. Their conversation started as one of business. The calmness of the one reminded her of a typical mafia boss she'd see in movies. She shuddered at the thought that he was some hired thug. Not with that kindness that had grown.

The voices soon escalated. There was shouting by what she assumed was the boss and then the pleading of another. The boss, though at first he sounded calm and reserved, hid a darker side, one that was filled with malice and an enjoyment of abusing authority. It became silent but was soon broken by his small voice. She heard some footsteps leave but couldn't tell who it was.

Silence filled the house again. She heard walking down the hall, and the footsteps stopped before the room where she was hidden. "I will warn you, Darrow. If I discover that you are hiding a sacrifice from me, your punishment will be worse than my grandson's." The warning was in her language. Her eyes widened and she wondered if he had done that to make sure she understood. Perhaps he thought she would give herself up to defend him. There was the perfect use of grammar and no hint of an accent. "Give a full report once you have slept. I'll be expecting full details as to why this one died. Considering your reputation, it's hard to believe that you failed."

The footsteps left the room and she let out a breath. Her feeling was right. He was a dangerous man. "Remember, boy, no soul escapes this village. No one!"

The door slammed shut and sent shivers through her. She thought that the leech was terrifying. It was nothing compared to that voice. She knew that if she were to ever meet the man that it would be unhealthy.

Silence once again filled the house. The heat was getting to her. Not only was she still in her full winter gear, she had the cloak and a closet full of clothes on top. The room temperature was also a factor. She was used to the cold after spending so much time in it. She moved as quietly as she could. As soon as she felt a comfortable spot, she felt herself begin to drift into sleep. It had been a long day. She pulled a cloth over her head and closed her eyes. Once she had, sleep took over.

Chapter 9

Ghosts

The room was cold. The surface beneath her was like ice. The sound of dripping liquid could be heard from nearby. It was a sound she had become accustomed to as her days were spent strapped to the cold metal table. She couldn't understand it. Why she had been taken? She only wanted to look for her friend.

The sound of a creaking door echoed in the room. Shuffling feet entered slowly. They were different, as if they had aged greatly within the past day. That offered some satisfaction. The smooth fingers touched her skin. She felt repulsed by him. She wanted to fight. She wanted to run. She had tried for days to escape, but her bonds were too strong.

"In all my years here, I have only met one other like you." It was a cold yet old voice.

She remained silent and still. She couldn't care less if she was rare. As far as she could tell, there weren't many people to begin with. There were only a few who visited her, and she used "visited" loosely.

"Yes, quite unique, quite the good distraction from the real thing."

She felt herself growl but couldn't understand why. It stirred something within her. His words meant nothing to her yet caused her anger. Perhaps it was the man itself who enraged her soul.

She felt his fingers trace along her collar bone and under her chin. "He would have been amazed by your soul. So very large compared to anyone else's. Cre-anni has certainly out done herself with you." He paused while he traced back down her neck and down her arm. It was sensual. If she weren't tied, he would have been flat on his back. "It's still not good enough to trick my master. No,

Devren knows better. This is not her true guardian. The one who holds the key to the ultimate weapon still roams these woods."

He snickered as he placed both his hands on her face. "Do you bare a grudge against her now? How she left you in my care to follow some stranger into the darkness?"

Her lips peeled apart and she sneered at him. She wished she could see the cause of her torment. That damned cloth kept her eyes shut. She wanted to tear at his face and end him as he had done her.

"No, as a true friend, you remain loyal to her. You would follow her to the bitter end. You won't even give away her location."

She wanted to cry. She knew that death was her only escape. The cruel man would never let her go. He had told her so many times. He wanted her soul, though she didn't understand what he meant. To her, a soul was nothing but her personality. It was her upbringing. It was how she presented herself to the world. Nothing could take that away from her.

"It is only a matter of time before I find her again," he cackled darkly. He hit her chest hard. She felt her ribs crack where her heart was and she let out a long cry of agony. Hot flames spread from the impact and intensified as they spread. She wanted to die. She begged for it as he roared with insane laughter. "Yes only a matter of time before I end her. I will do what I should have done to that child twenty years ago. If only I knew what she was then, we wouldn't have this problem. Once I do have her, that cockroach can't save her. Then his memories and the key will be gone forever."

* * *

Evelyn awoke in a daze. The room spun wildly as she stared wide-eyed at the wooden ceiling. The longer she looked, the more sickness swirled in her stomach. She tried closing her eyes. It only made it worse. It had transformed into endless twirling which caused her stomach to eject.

She rolled until she found the edge of the bed. She breathed heavily as she tried to keep her last meal down. She cried from the pain and from her frustration. She wanted her sickness to end. She wanted her nightmares to leave. They had overstayed their welcome, and she wanted to force them out. As the cool night air filled her lungs, she could feel herself tremble from the cold. She had built up a sweat from her sleep and the dirty clothes stuck to her.

After a while her breathing calmed as well as her stomach. She settled but near the edge. The exhaustion from the nightmares had taken its toll. As she thought back, she realized that the last one was different. She never had it before. She wasn't a child. She was an adult. She wasn't addressed as a boy either. The voice, however, was the same. It was the same tormenting voice that wanted the world for his own.

She took deep breaths as she settled back into her sleep. She welcomed its embrace. She had yearned for its comfort. She sighed tiredly as she closed her eyes. More sleep was needed. Just a few more minutes. As she dozed, she felt a presence shift beside her. It made her gasp and she twisted around. What she saw made her scream.

Darrow jumped from the bed and to his feet. He took a fighter's stance but was slower than usual. He wobbled as he looked around wildly. He did a few passes before stopping and looking at her. He breathed heavily and sat back on the bed. "What happened?"

She shook her head angrily and pointed at him. "What are you doing sleeping with me," she seethed.

His face fell as he cuddled under the sheets. He yawned as he closed his eyes. Soon she heard deep breathing and she knew he had fallen back to sleep. She shook his arm violently. It was one question he was not getting away with. She needed to know. His eyes opened again slowly. The longer he looked at her, the more she realized how exhausted he had become. His eyes had grown dark circles and focus was gone. He reminded her of herself after the nightmares.

He groaned and rolled to face her. "I'm keeping my promise." His pace was slow and words formed awkwardly. She shook her head and shook him again. He grumbled but stayed in his position. "I can't leave anything unsupervised here, especially you. I did the only thing I could think of to keep you safe."

She frowned as she wasn't satisfied with his answer. "I thought you said I'd be safe here."

He reached out and grabbed her hand, squeezing it gently. "You were until last night."

He grumbled as he sat on the edge of the bed. In the very thin slivers of light, she saw he wore only shorts. She could see the muscles work and contract as he rubbed the back of his neck. She gasped quietly as he stretched. Under his clothes, he looked like a mildly built man. Even when she had rescued him, the power of his muscles didn't show. As she watched him stretch and flex his arms and back, she saw the true power that hid behind the blade's blows.

He stood and walked to the closet after stumbling a few steps. He mumbled something to himself as he leaned against the door frame. The more he mumbled, the angrier he became. Soon he sighed and returned to the bed with a dress in his hand. He handed it to her, but she simply stared at him. She didn't wear dresses or skirts. Her personal dress code was strictly pants or shorts. The only time she wore a dress was for graduation because of her grandmother's wishes. "It's only until I get yours clean, unless you wish to remain in two weeks' worth of dirt."

"Two weeks," she breathed. She couldn't believe what she heard. It didn't feel like two weeks. It felt much longer. Maybe a month or more. She sighed as she took the dress. It would have to do. She frowned as she looked it over. It was green and plain as his shirt. It also only went to her knees and had very short sleeves. She figured it would be something suited for the summer, not winter.

As she looked at herself, she noticed she only had on her undershirt and sweatpants. She snorted as she began to laugh. "Couldn't resist could you?"

He watched her curiously as confusion clouded his gray eyes. He frowned at first but soon blushed brightly as he turned away. He cleared his throat and opened his mouth but didn't speak.

He shook his head and sighed. "I suppose you would wish to bathe," he asked quietly.

She smirked knowing that her family's history of humour was getting the better of her. "Not with you but alone, yes, a bath does sound good." She watched as he stiffened but didn't turn to face her. She wondered if she had gone a little too far.

He finally shook his head again and snorted. "You certainly have a sharper mind than you show."

She snorted and crossed her arms. She didn't know how to take his comment.

He looked back at her and smirked. "It's meant as a compliment. Not many render me speechless." He then motioned for her to follow.

They walked down two hallways and climbed two sets of ladders. He completely bypassed the second floor and hurried her along. She wondered why but remained silent as she climbed the ladder. On the third floor was a single door. He opened it and steam filled the room. He led her inside, and she was amazed by the bath. Half the floor was sunken in and filled to the brim with hot water. In the ceiling was a metal fixture that she assumed was to let the water in.

He explained where everything was and provided a large towel. It was soft to the touch and reminded her of her favorite blanket. He gave her a few bottles and explained how they were used. She smiled when he provided bubble bath for her and then proceeded to mix it with the water. She couldn't help but giggle when she saw the bubbles begin to foam. She knew she was in for a rare treat.

"While you bathe, I'm going to try and fix what happened last night," he informed her. She looked at him curiously and knew that his explanation wouldn't be good. "You must have heard at least a portion of the fight." She nodded and explained what she had heard the man say. He nodded back and held her shoulders. "That's what I'm going to try and fix. If I can convince them that you died in those woods and that's why it took me so long, then I can finally sleep. Until then, however..."

He pulled out a small bottle with a cork stopper and placed it in her hands. "You've seen how I light fires, correct?" She nodded. She couldn't explain why, but they suddenly caught ablaze. "It's a small bit of magic. What I'm about to do is something that is... well, frowned upon here." She frowned and looked seriously at him. Magic was nothing but illusion to entertain children. The fire trick could have been done easily. What he was telling her was that it's real.

He smiled softly and gently placed his hand on her cheek. Again it was soft and caring. "I see your doubt, but you will see." He placed his fingers over his eyes, and she watched as his muscles tensed. "A light will be put in that bottle. Once you see all of it in there, replace the topper. You will then have to escort me out of this room and slam the door behind me." At this point she was bewildered and couldn't comprehend what he was explaining. Did he think she was so gullible to follow through with it?

His hands glowed with a dark light which caused her to retreat a few steps. "Do not open the door back up until you are finished with your bath. By then, I would have left and you can do as you wish. Don't go outside or this will be for nothing." He sighed tiredly, followed by a hurtful groan. Something was wrong. "When I return, make sure I'm alone and then uncork the bottle. The light will return to me but before then I will think you dead. Understand?" She whispered a small 'yes' to him which caused him to smile. She really didn't but had to trust him. She had no other way of getting home.

Suddenly a bright green light erupted from his eyes. The light turned to mist and swirled slowly around them as his arms lowered. She watched as the mist sparkled, and she found it to be horrifying yet beautiful. A portion of the mist hit the bottle which caused a reaction. It glowed brighter before gathering quickly in the bottle. She corked it as instructed when all the mist entered. That was definitely magic.

He slumped to the floor and coughed heavily. She panicked as she was afraid that he had hurt himself. She hoped he hadn't. She also didn't understand what she had witnessed. He stood up slowly, breathing heavily. She helped him straighten but gasped when she saw his eyes. They were glazed over and had a lack of focus. His constant mumbling didn't help her worry, either. What had he done?

She took a deep breath. She had to follow his instructions. That's all she had to go with. She led him to the door. He was hesitant at first but followed. He stumbled like a drunk. She made sure he was away from the ladder. She could see him coming out of his state and falling through the hole. If that were to happen, she knew there would be no way home.

She walked back into the bathroom and started closing the door. She went to close it quietly but remember the last of his instructions. She opened it wide and slammed it as hard as she could. On the other side, she could hear him gasp followed by more coherent mumbling. Soon his voice vanished and she assumed he had gone down the ladder.

She found the entire situation strange as she undressed. She looked at the bottle as it glowed brightly. What was it? She had never seen mist suddenly erupt out of someone, let alone glow an eerie but beautiful green. She had never seen hands glow as dark as night. The more she thought about it, the more she felt she had been taken in by her novels. Maybe she was in a coma from being lost in that blizzard. That was more story-like than anything.

She slipped into the water. The heat penetrated her icy skin. She groaned as she couldn't remember ever being so cold. She felt a large smile spread across her face. She knew then she was going to enjoy that bath as it would wash away any pain. It was going to be bliss.

She lathered her hair and body and sat on one of the seats under the water. She found it disturbing how quiet the room was. She had grown accustomed to the howling wind or being constantly alert to the breaking of branches. To hear nothing at all made her feel on edge. It had become unnatural.

"To think I find this unnatural now and how I longed for it so much at home." She washed the soap from her hair and laid back to float on the surface. It was large enough to be a small swimming pool. Darrow was lucky to have such a large bath. As she watched the ceiling, she wondered why the adventure happened to her. She didn't ask for it. All she wanted was a vacation from the busy city. All she wanted was a few days spent in her favorite place. It always called to her. It pulled at her as if it wanted her to return to it, as if she was supposed to be with the forest.

The forest reminded her of her grandfather's stories, how there was a land within the forest that was timed back before humans. It was covered in a lush forest that held every creature imaginable. Its people lived in trees. These people helped one another and protected those who traveled within its depths. These people were one with forest and knew of its shifting conditions.

She remembered his stories of the village of the angel food cake bowl. Its trees were greener and livelier. The people loved deeper and their commitments meant something. The warriors would protect those in need while still keeping the forest in balance. She remembered how he explained their magic, that it depended on a person's soul and their stamina. The more unnatural the magic, the more stamina it took and the more a person lost themselves to it.

"Why did you tell me these stories," she questioned to the room. "Why did you feed me these tales? Did you know that I would be lost within them someday? Did you expect me to find a hidden meaning?" She hit the water angrily and caused the bubbles to break away from her. She stood back up and began to cry. "Grandpa, why did you do that? What makes me so damned special?"

She crawled out of the water and sat holding her knees. What made her so special that Darrow would protect her? Why was she so different from everyone else that had been through that forest? He said so. As far as she could tell, she was ordinary. She had regular grades in school. Her friends were normal; she learned to drive just like everyone else. She wasn't even the most popular person in school or at work.

The more she thought about it, the more it frustrated her. Out of the millions of regular people on the planet, why was she handpicked to be different? She roared out to the room and felt little of her anger leave. She wasn't innocent, a past love made sure of that. She wasn't pure for the same reason. She may have been sharp, but there were many others like that better suited to the task.

She picked up the closest thing to her in her anger. She began to throw it when she felt a sharp pain in her palm. She brought it into view. It was the bottle with his strange light. The bottle had cracked and she had cut her hand. She frowned, wondering how she was going to bandage the cut. She didn't know where her pack was and there was nothing in the room that held first aid.

The sound of glass cracking caught her attention. She looked down to the bottle and her eyes widened. The initial fracture split longer and branched out. She held it delicately thinking it was her but it continued on. She set it down and backed away. Things shouldn't break on their own, and she knew that. She then remembered the mist.

It shattered and the mist swirled around the room. It wasn't calm as it was before. It was frantic as it shot to the ceiling and spread and tried the floor and walls. She couldn't register what was happening. What was that thing?

She squealed as it barely missed her in its bizarre quest. Her sound made it stop. It collected itself and floated before her. She remained still as she was afraid of what it might do. She wished for Darrow to return. He would know what to do. He always seemed to know the answer.

The mist made its way towards her and began to circle her. She reached out slowly and it went through her fingers. It was warm, and she could feel a comfort from it, like his touch. "What are you," she asked it quietly. It must have had a mind of its own as it made its way up to face her. She felt as if it wanted her to guess but she had nothing. It returned to her outstretched hand and formed a dull orb which floated in place.

She shook her head and decided she had enough. She dried whatever was left wet and dressed. She brought her clothes and orb with her. She knew that the mist was important but had no clue why. It enjoyed being near as it never left her hand.

She returned to the second floor. As she passed by the first door the orb flew and hit it. The door opened with a slight creaking noise. As she followed the mist through, she created a cloud of dust. With the amount that swirled up and around her ankles, she wondered how long it had been since the room had seen life.

The room was small, and the large window's curtains were open. The window itself had become glazed with dirt, and it was impossible to see out of. The light that pushed through gave the room a ghostly feel. She saw a bed large enough for a child. The sheets were still crisp and without a single wrinkle, but it held a second covering of dust. Shelves lined the walls. They held dried flowers, dusty polished stones and wooden toys. An abandoned rocking horse sat in the corner, begging to be played with again.

As she looked around, she felt an overwhelming sadness. It was unbearable to think that the rest of the house was used except that room. The mist settled at the head of the bed. Unlike her, it didn't disturb the dust. She watched as a part of it elongated to point at the bedside table. It was small and made of wood like the rest. It held two objects. One was an emerald leaf fastened to a golden chain.

The second was a picture frame. She picked it up. It was caked in dust and the glass no longer transparent. She took the edge of her dress and wiped it clean. She wanted to know what it held. It was a black and white photo. There was a beautiful woman with long hair and kind eyes who wore the leaf pendant on the side table. Next to her was a man who looked to be Darrow's twin. The only exception was the man had broader shoulders and his long hair tied back.

In their arms was a little boy. His grin spread wide as he held on to both his parents. All of them looked to be happy. It was if nothing could separate them from each other. A tear fell from her eye and landed on the picture. Then another fell, followed by another. Something inside knew the happiness didn't last. She knew that this family was torn apart. Somehow she knew the boy never smiled again.

She put the picture down as she felt herself begin to tremble. The tears continued as she looked around the room. She knew it was the little boy's room. As she looked at the once-loved toys, she knew that after that day he never played with them again. Ever since that day, the room was never touched.

"Why, daddy," she cried quietly. "Why did you leave us?" She fell to her knees, unable to contain her tears. She held herself as the overwhelming emotions took over. She had never seen any of these things before, yet they brought memories that she'd never had. She was a child again, scared and confused.

She felt the warmth of the mist. Its comfort quieted her tears. Something whispered in her ear and acted like a feeble breeze. "Spee…" she began. She tried sounding out the word, hoping its distraction would calm her. "Spiraney?" she questioned. The mist moved and rested in her hand. She had never heard of such a word. She knew that she would have to ask Darrow when he returned. It must have been important.

Feeling calmer, she left the room and closed the door. The experience was otherworldly. She felt surrounded by ghosts. Each visit was by another who needed her help. As she walked down the hall all she could think about was her nightmares. She had only thought of them as that. As she learned about magic and whatever was in her hand, she saw them as, perhaps, something more. Something pointing to disaster.

As her feet touched the first floor she heard an agonizing cry. It startled her and she froze on the ladder. She could hear three others in the house besides her. One was crying while the other two chatted amongst themselves. She kept quiet as she walked to the end and peered around the corner.

Two men were standing with arms crossed. Their backs were to her and facing the chair. They pointed to it and drew her attention to the furniture. Her breath caught and looked away when she saw who sat. From the brief glimpse, she could tell Darrow had been beaten. She felt her fury rise and her fists clench. She couldn't comprehend why people would beat him.

The men chatted for a bit longer before she heard stirring. At first, it was groaning but it soon turned into harsh coughing. The men laughed and commented. She looked back again to see them make him sit up and look at them. They seethed at him and their laughter started again.

He looked up and she saw the fight left in him. He growled menacingly which caused the men to jump and back away. He stood from the chair and breathed heavily as he took his fighting pose. He shook and stumbled but remained upright. He snapped at both of them which made them retreat further. One had gone so far that he fell over the chair. She could only imagine what he was telling them.

The air felt dense and a green light emanated from his body. The sight frightened the others as they ran for the door. As the door shut, he fell to the floor. He didn't move as his breaths were laboured. She felt that whatever had happened was all due to her. His pain was her doing.

She rushed over and slowly rolled him onto his back. She could feel the fight was gone. He didn't even resist the movement. He started to mumble which reminded her of before. She brushed the hair carefully away, avoiding the bruised eyes. "Darrow, what happened," she asked quietly. His eyes snapped open and stared. He stumbled away quickly and pointed at her while crying out.

He fell into the lounge chair while tears flowed freely. She walked slowly closer and he pressed himself deeper into the chair. She couldn't understand why he was afraid. His hand caught fire and he threw it at her. She felt the heat slip passed her cheek as she gasped. Why was he attacking her? He told her to stay there.

He fell out of the chair and crawled to behind it. He would peer out weakly and cry out to her again. The pain she could see tortured him. She wondered why and walked closer. Again his hand lit but vanished quickly. His consciousness was fading fast. She needed to know why he was attacking her. She couldn't help unless she knew.

"Darrow, speak to me in my language. Why are you so scared?" He shook his head slowly as he slipped to the floor. Again she gently rolled him onto his back. She lifted his head slightly and tried to coax him awake again. His eyes opened a sliver and more tears fell. His fingers grasped tightly to hers. She asked him again but he shook his head.

"Ghosts haunt me..." he croaked weakly. "Femil killed you. I watched him and did nothing. I watched while he stole the only person I ever trusted."

Chapter 10

Last Visit

The days felt as if they crawled by. She had removed his clothes once again. The cuts were deeper than the run in with the leech. They were made by knives and deep enough that it would take time to heal. Then there were the bruises. Their shades of black and purple worried her. How much torture did he go through? She wrapped up the cuts that bled with torn pieces of fabric. It was the least she could do to heal him without her bag. She had to carry him into his bedroom and tuck him into bed. He had remained unconscious the entire time. Even after a day or more, it was rare when he would awake.

She discovered she had more free time than she needed. The mist wasn't much for conversation. It hovered around her, interested in everything she did. She had washed all their clothes in the third floor tub and hung them to dry on the first floor. She cleaned his closet and found her pack. From this discovery, she properly cleaned his wounds. She wiped down the table and counters. After the third day, she had even washed the floor.

She refused to let her mind idle. The feelings would overwhelm her if she were to stop. She wished she had never entered that room, the room of lost innocence. Ever since then, if she had any lack of distraction, it would cause her to cry. The feeling of loss was great. Even still, she couldn't explain why. That was what bothered her the most.

She sat beside him on the bed, rubbing her hands. She hoped that he would soon wake. He said to open the bottle once he returned, but he never explained what to do after. How could she fix what had happened? She didn't die. That was the only thing she was absolutely sure of. If she had, she definitely wouldn't want to stay in the village. There was nothing there for her.

He stirred and groaned but returned to his still state. She sighed. Her need to return home intensified with each day. Surely by then she would have been considered dead. She had been gone for far too long. If she ever returned, there would be a mess. She would need proof of who she was and an explanation for what happened. No one would believe her story, except perhaps her grandfather. The thought of him made her shudder. She knew that her grandfather would punish her greatly for breaking his rules.

"Why are you still here?" His voice startled her and made her jump. It was slow and mournful.

She stared at him a few moments before she realized the question. "Well, you still have to show me the way home," she explained.

He sighed while flexing his fingers. "You're a spirit, follow the tug home. I can't... I can't help you now."

She shook her head. "I'm not dead." He had to believe her.

His eyes opened and focused on her. He grumbled and shook his head. "Do not lie to yourself. He ran you..." He closed his eyes tightly, followed by his body. The sound of sobs clenched her heart.

She shook her head. "You told me to open the bottle with the light in it when you came back. It broke while I bathed, and the light floats around the house. I don't know what to do with it." He opened his eyes and looked at her again. Questions burned while tears squelched the flames. She hoped that he started to believe her insanity.

He asked to see the light and she brought it to him. It had been swirling around the room as if it was running a course. As he examined it, he became more confused. He looked up to her and back to the dull orb. "A piece of my soul... my memories... how did you get this?" The trust they built was draining away. He tried sitting as he growled deeply at her.

"Hey, I don't do this magic stuff. This is your doing," she snorted while pointing to the orb.

He sighed while sinking into his pillow. He shook his head and closed his eyes. She had a strong feeling that he wasn't going to answer on how to fix their issue. She didn't like being told she was dead. She knew she wasn't as she wouldn't bleed when she hit her head. Even still, he denied it. At least he wasn't going to kill her.

She decided to change the subject, one that she desperately wanted an answer for. "What's a spiraney?" she asked. He quickly looked at her and his eyes widened. She wondered if it was a bad topic.

"Where did you hear that?" His features angered further as his lips peeled back to show his teeth. She explained everything that happened in the room. He was angry for her entering there. He softened quickly with the mention of the misery. He reached out to her and held her hand. "Oh, Eve... seems like more ghosts haunt you than me."

He shifted his weight and sat up slowly. He grumbled something as he tried flexing his arms. She watched him worriedly as he stretched his toes, legs and neck. He was slow which she understood. The beating must have been harsh. At least the bruises were healing. She helped him stand, which took a large amount of coaxing. He still thought she was nothing but air.

Once he dressed, he sat back on the bed. He had aged a great deal as he held his head in his hands. He continued to mumble to himself which began to annoy her. She wanted to know what was going through his mind. She wanted to help him.

The mist floated between them before gathering into an orb. "You should really take this back. I don't think it's a good thing to leave it lying around." She felt like a mother telling a child to pick up his toys.

He frowned and let it float in his hand. "They've taken so many memories already. I'm almost an empty shell now," he whispered. His words disturbed her. She had heard a few people talk as he had, but they didn't have the magic factor. How much had he lost?

Then an idea came to her. She put on her best smile. It had to be convincing. "Then make new ones. I can help, but you have to take that one back. I don't want to be a ghost anymore."

He looked at her slowly. His eyes cried out to her. It reminded her of when she held his sword to him. He begged for it all to end.

"Come now, it won't be that bad."

She thought for a moment or so. It had to be something uplifting. "How about once you take me home, I show you how I live? We can go shopping, I'll take you for a car ride and I can take you out to dinner and a movie." She stopped when she mentioned her last suggestion. She felt her face flush as she realized she had just asked him on a date. It wasn't intentional. She only wanted the man to have something to look forward to.

"I've heard of those things from others but they normally mention something called a 'boyfriend' too. What is that?"

She felt her cheeks burn and she looked away from him. It was a question she really didn't want to answer.

He chuckled softly and placed his hand on her shoulder. "Perhaps another time then," he offered. She shook her head and looked back at him.

"It's just a bit embarrassing and sad for me." Thinking on her past relationship, it was more hurtful than anything. Darrow folded his arms. She sighed. She wasn't getting out of that one. "For a girl, it's a guy who she does romantic things with and kisses. It's a stage before marriage to get to know each other... Oh never mind. I can't explain it," she grumbled.

He thought about it as he stared at the wall. The silence that stretched between them became uncomfortable for her. He nodded before looking at her. "It's like two people before they combine their souls."

At first she was bewildered by his statement. She believed a soul was what made a person who they are, that it was their life experiences. The more she listened to him, the more she felt it might be an actual thing. He smiled kindly and continued. "Marriage, in my culture, is when two people give their souls to each other and conceive a child. Once they do, they can never be with another. The separation is worse than any torture."

It was her turn to think it over. She was used to the idea of wedding rings and a party. He was explaining something greater, something like in her grandfather's tales.

As she thought, a bright light startled her. Out of instinct, she looked over but shielded her eyes quickly. It was intense as it burned her pupils. When it faded, she looked to see Darrow slumped on the bed. He whimpered as he curled up near his pillow. She went to approach him but he waved her away. He took a deep breath and let it out slowly. "I was right," he mumbled quietly. "Ghosts do follow you, more than you know."

She was about to ask when a knock came at the door. She gasped and was about to hide when he stuck out his arm. He stood slowly and left the room, limping. She listened as he answered the door. As was his usual interaction, the newcomer began to yell at him, but the difference was he remained silent. The door closed and he returned. She began to ask, but he just shook his head and assured her that nothing was wrong.

"Before I take you home, could I show you a few things?" His attention was caught by the floor which was unusual. He was one who talked by looking at the intended target. She didn't answer and remained on the bed. She noticed a slight nervousness as he shifted his weight. She shook her head and explained why she had to go home as quickly as possible. He stopped moving and looked up sadly. "At least is it alright if we visited my mother? I can't leave you alone in here anymore and..."

He shook his head and walked away. He was acting strange. She went after him and found him sitting on the lounge chair. His head was in his hands and he was mumbling. His trembles were wrong. The visitor had brought bad news. She took a dining room chair and sat across from him. He didn't move until she placed a hand on his knee. He stiffened but slowly looked up. He shook his head and settled back in the chair.

"I'll take you back in the morning. I need more sleep before I leave again." He yawned and watched her through closing eyes.

She shook her head. "No, we'll go visit your mom first. Parents are very important." She smiled while resting her arms on her knees. He smiled back tiredly before standing. He instructed her to stay where she was and that he would return soon.

He returned with a large pile of clothing with some false ears and gave it to her. "It's my mother's old clothes. They will fit to you. At least I hope so. I think this will be the first time an outsider wore our clothing."

She felt the green material. It reminded her of her hair after bathing. It was silky and soft but it was strong and thick. She looked up wondering what he meant.

He smirked while putting on his boots. "It's made from my mother's hair just as my clothing is made from my own. When we learn how to control magic, we learn how to make and expand out clothing. In a matter of speaking, I've been wearing the same clothes since I was a child."

Her eyes widened but she didn't say anything. She knew that magic was very prominent in his culture. It was apparent with the removal of his soul and that strange glow when the men were teasing him. She even thought back to when he had killed Femil. The ice wall appearing from nowhere to block his path was also beyond belief. It all pointed to one thing: Magic was real.

Eve followed him through his village. People looked at them either darkly or fearfully. They all avoided Darrow and gave him space as if he had a deadly disease. She wasn't even seen walking behind him as they all kept a close eye on the leader. She couldn't understand why they were fearful. He was one of the nicest people she had met on her journey. Any other person had been very violent or cruel.

Besides the people, she was in awe with how they travelled. Many walked on the ground, but above were bridges connecting the closer trees. The large earth pillar was integrated into the web of wooden bridges. It looked to be the business center as many went through its doors. The hustle and bustle was like the large mall, but something was missing. There was no laughter or joy woven between the trees.

Even in the hospital center the mood remained the same. Very depressing, very dry, uncomfortably inhuman. He guided her through the halls but remained silent. She learned that they had a different alphabet. Symbols were carved into wooden plaques that hung on a few doors. She wondered what they meant. She assumed they were different doctor's offices or permanent residence wards.

He led her through a doorway and closed the door behind him. In the room was an elderly woman laying on a bed. She looked much older than Eve's grandparents. Her long silver hair was loose and scattered across her pillow. Her skin was very worn and loose for her frame. Eve felt sad at the state of the poor woman. Something within her knew that she was a lively soul, one that defied monsters.

Darrow approached the woman's bed as she slept. His normally hard exterior softened as he held her hand. His face held great worry. He rubbed her hand and persisted she woke until her eyes opened. It was hard to tell if they were related until she opened her eyes. The stone gray shimmered in the window's daylight. She smiled, which was hard for her to do. Eve wondered how much longer the woman had left. She had seen many elders in the weakened state during checkups with her grandparents.

They exchanged many words. She listened to him as he rattled off a story. She could only assume it was his adventure with her. The longer it continued, the more animated he became. It was a strange sight to see the man excited and filled with life. Seeing him happy made her smile as she stood silently in the corner. He needed some brightness in his life.

When he finished, his mother patted his hand and then looked over to Eve. Eve felt nervous and avoided her gaze. She could hear him say something then switch languages quickly.

"Sorry Eve, I got caught up."

She looked up to see a bit of red in his cheeks and ears. He stood and led her to the bed. "This is my mother Rosena. Mother this is Eve, the umm... the lady I've been guiding."

Rosena smiled at Eve tenderly as she held her hand. "Nice to meet you," she greeted softly. Her voice was light and reminded Eve of bird song.

Feeling the nervousness and being cautious of who she spoke with, she remained silent.

"Eve, it's alright. Unlike the others, my mother won't hurt you."

Rosena nodded and looked at her sheepishly. "Yes, unlike the younger folk, I remember the old ways. I do not hunt for souls and never would."

The mention of hunting souls made Eve's stomach turn. She noticed Darrow avoid his mother's harsh stare. It was strange. He didn't do anything wrong.

Rosena sighed tiredly. She asked him something in their tongue. He nodded and left them alone after instructing Eve to stay. Rosena settled back into her bed and looked at the younger woman. "So tell me, how is young Christopher these days?"

Eve stared at her and tried to speak but couldn't think of anything. How could she know him? It must have been good memories as the smile was comforting.

Rosena giggled and patted her hand. "Surprised that I know your grandfather, child? Yes, we go back a long time. He and my husband were great friends..."

Her expression darkened and she looked to the door. "That was until the evil came."

Eve's heart clenched as the mention of the evil reminded her of her nightmares. Something inside her knew what she was talking about. "Is it a shadow, this evil?"

Rosena looked over and her eyes widened. "Yes, it was until it took form. The form of a holy man who now guides this village."

Eve frowned feeling she knew more about the never ending snow than she cared for. "If I tell you a story, at least a few parts that I know, can you tell me if it's true or just craziness?" She felt that Rosena was the only person she could get answers from. Someone who was there in the beginning. She would know the cause of her nightmares. She just knew she would.

Rosena agreed and Eve began her tale. She started with the father and insects. Followed by the cold and ice blade and finished with the scenes from within a dungeon. Rosena remained silent throughout the tale, never once interrupting. She found it strange that Darrow was gone so long. When she had finished, he still hadn't returned. Where had he gone?

"Seems like ghosts haunt you more than my son." Rosena was emotional throughout the story, and Eve wondered why. To her, they were nothing but nightmares or at the most a warning. Seeing her reaction to it made her think there was something more than that. Her words were also the same as Darrow's. What ghosts were they talking about? "Have you told my son these dreams?"

Eve shook her head. She told him about her breakdown in the room but her dreams remained secret.

"I will tell you the meaning of your dreams if, and only if, you promise to never tell him of them."

Eve could feel the old woman look into her very soul as she awaited an answer. She wanted to know why she couldn't tell him anything. What made them dangerous to him? Rosena could have told her not to tell anyone but was singling him. She hoped that she would tell her why, if she agreed. "I promise I won't say anything," she swore.

Rosena's features relaxed and she closed her eyes. "Those are not dreams but memories you carry. Memories that my son had lost decades ago." Her eyes watered. The memories were not pleasant. "After his father was murdered in the village, we fled to the forest. He had gotten lost from the rest of us, and I knew I'd never see him again. I searched for days. When I found him, the man who was leading us through the forest cut him from shoulder to navel with his blade of ice. I'd never heard a child scream so terribly before.

"The entire camp was captured and taken back to the village along with my son. I prayed every night for him to return whole. When they finally returned him weeks later, he was not the same. His smile had faded. He never cried, never laughed. All he was then was an empty shell filled with violence and anger. My happy little boy gone," she cried. Eve sat next to her and held her, trying to soothe her.

As she did, she thought about it. She somehow had Darrow's missing memories. It was like that ball of green mist. How they got there, she had no idea. She couldn't remember a time when she had encountered magic before the trip. She sighed somewhat, regretting asking. She had more questions than when she started.

"I do thank you, Eve."

Eve was a bit startled from her words. She had made Rosena cry with her question and nightmares. She smiled at her and she could see the happiness in her eyes.

"He was filled with life when he came in today. He was so exhilarated when he was telling me his recent adventure through the forest. I haven't seen him that excited for more than thirty years. I had my little boy again."

She felt her lips part as the man didn't look older than twenty. If she had to guess on the new information, he had to be in his forties or more. She heard a chuckle.

"It would be a bit shocking knowing he's probably twice your age if not more. Unlike your race, we do not age as fast. Just as birds differ, so do we. It would amaze your grandfather as I am twice his age. Seventy is just getting into middle age to us while your people consider it old."

Eve shook her head and groaned. There was more to magic than she thought.

Rosena moved gingerly in bed and settled down again. She grabbed Eve's hand and held it caringly. "It seems that my soul cannot hold the curse off much longer. As I have explained your dreams, can you please do me one favor?" She was too weak which caused Eve alarm. She nodded slowly as she knew the decline was there. Even when she first entered, she knew that Rosena didn't have much time left.

"If Darrow takes you to see the midnight dancers, flee as quickly as you can without his notice or anyone else's. Let this place be nothing but a memory and follow your heart home. I will not allow Christopher's child to fall. If he takes you to his special place deep in the woods, protect his soul and allow him happiness, however short it may be. Can you do this for an old mother," she pleaded.

Eve nodded but asked, "You can't hold up much longer to whatever is ailing you. Is this why you're asking me?"

Rosena nodded as more tears rolled down her wrinkled face. "Again do not let him know. He will learn in time. He must focus on the choice he has ahead."

She looked out the window. She followed her gaze and watched the setting sun. He had definitely been gone for a long time. "I wished to have seen the green of spring before I departed, but it looks like it wasn't meant to be." She looked to her and saw her weakening smile. "Please guide my son to the light spiraney. I know without you he will be forever lost in darkness."

There was that word again. It bewildered her, and as she was going to ask, a knock came to the door. She twisted around to see who it was when Darrow entered.

He was carrying a platter covered by a wooden lid. He set it down on the bedside table and smiled kindly at his mother. "Sorry it took so long. I had to cook it myself since they were being as kind as usual in the kitchen," he mumbled apologetically. His mother shook her head and patted his hand.

He stood awkwardly as he looked at the two of them. She mentioned something to him in their language and he nodded. He asked Eve to move and sat next to his mother. Again they talked in a language Eve didn't understand. She pulled him close and held him tightly as he returned her tight embrace. Tears ran down, filling wrinkles as they went. Eve felt awkward watching them and turned around. Whatever they were doing was a private matter.

A few moments later he turned her around with a tired smile. She looked to his mother. She had the platter on her lap and had begun to enjoy her meal. She had a feeling that it may have been her last. She moved from around him and approached the bed. "It was nice meeting you Miss Rosena. I'll keep my promise and tell grandpa what happened."

Rosena smiled kindly and patted Eve's hand. "It was nice meeting you as well. Please keep him safe."

Eve waved her bye and exited the room. She waited for Darrow patiently. Some nurses passed her giving threatening glances. She wrinkled her nose at them and remained where she was. She couldn't stand those who were rude to others. She was doing nothing. She decided she wouldn't complain about the nurses at the hospital if she had to go, at least they tried to be nice.

He exited and pulled the door shut. He took a deep, quivering breath before walking away. She wondered what the conversation was about. His mood had turned quickly. He kept his head down and avoided everyone's glare. Some even spat at him as they passed. He was definitely not welcome in that place.

He walked slowly as the sun settled behind the mountains. Its light gave the trees a ghostly orange glow as a light mist covered the village. She found the scene was beautiful with its hues of orange. She smiled thinking that it was as if it was on fire. A beautiful contrast to the cold of winter.

Once back home, he turned to her. "What did you and my mother talk about? Why did you say you'll keep your promise and you will keep him safe?" His frown and focused eyes showed he meant business.

She smiled at him. She knew she had to lie to keep her promise. If it meant keeping what was left of his sanity, she would do nearly anything. "We were talking about my grandfather. Seems like they know each other from long ago. I promised that I'd tell him why she hasn't visited in so long and that I'd take care of him."

He was content with her answer as he nodded before walking away. She looked back to the door and felt her heart clench. She knew that the visit was the only time she would ever see his mother. It was the last time that he would see her alive. That realization cracked whatever seal that was placed on her emotions and she began to cry. He had gone through enough. More heartbreak would kill him.

Chapter 11

To Feel is to be Human

The next morning Evelyn sat at Darrow's table and ate soup quietly. The taste of soup bothered her. She would be avoiding it for a long time. That's all they ate which she found a bit odd. They must have something else. She couldn't wait until she was back at home. She planned on having eggs with bacon, pizza and anything else that didn't involve vegetables and liquid. The thought of the alteration in meals made her stomach growl louder.

She looked up from her food to see he was lost in his own thoughts. He had been quiet since she had woken. Not that it was unusual but the distant gaze wasn't right. She reached over and touched his hand which remained still on the table. He jerked and pulled it away before looking up. He was exhausted even from the night of sleep. He shook his head and looked back at his bowl, mumbling to himself. She frowned and returned to hers.

She packed her bag and folded her gear next to the chair. When she was finished, he was still staring at his bowl. It was wrong. From when she first met him, he always did things with a purpose. Looking at him, she couldn't help but think that he was lost.

"Something wrong with your soup, you've been there all morning," she asked. He shook his head, mumbling again. She asked again what was bothering him. He pushed away from the table, walked to his room and slammed the door.

She stared at the wood dumbfounded. She hadn't done anything wrong. She ate the food that was given, even though it was bland. She packed her things to make sure she was ready to leave. Organization was always key before leaving on trips. When she looked to her things, a small realization came to her. She had been getting hints that he liked her more than just a friend. He was overly protective and thought more highly of her than she did of herself. He'd touch her face with the utmost delicacy while moving strands that strayed. As she thought about it, the more she understood.

He didn't want her to leave. He didn't want to be alone anymore. If what he said was true when she was a 'ghost' haunting him, he trusted her. It was something that he desperately wanted. He had said so before getting to the village. What he wanted more than anything was to trust someone again and that he had. He more than likely didn't want to lose that person.

She walked quietly to the door and pressed her ear against the warm wood. No sounds were heard in the room. She found it strange and knocked. No answer was returned. She frowned. She didn't like the idea of no noise. She had learned that a lack of noise meant something bad.

She opened the door quickly. When she looked in, the room it was empty. There was no lump on the bed. No one hiding beside it. No one hiding behind the door or anywhere else in the room. She began to panic. The man entered the room. There was no question about that. However, with magic he could have easily slipped passed her.

She was about to leave when she remembered the closet. She couldn't believe he would hide in there. Only children would hide in the closet. She couldn't see the point. She wasn't going to hurt him and there was no one else in the house. She would leave whether he liked it or not. She needed to get home. She needed to repair whatever life remained for her.

She walked over and opened it, finding him asleep on the floor. It wasn't a restful sleep as he kept fighting and jerking. She was about to touch his shoulder when he jolted awake and stared wide-eyed at her. He was confused at first, before he sighed and rested back on the floor.

"Darrow, you promised you'd take me home today."

He looked away and shook his head. His eyes squeezed shut and watered.

"I need to go home. My grandparents will worry."

He shook his head again before squeezing out of the closet. He was acting strange for his standard, and her worry increased. He stood behind her for a moment before running out of the room.

She took off after him. He climbed the rungs quickly, and she heard him run while she started her climb. He was fast. It surprised her how fast he could be. She didn't expect such speed. She climbed quickly to the second floor. It didn't take her long to see that the first door was open. In the time she stayed there, the door was never open.

She found him staring at the double bed, mumbling franticly, his fingers twitching erratically as if trying to sign. He turned and placed his hands on the glass stand just inside the door. Just as in the child's room, the glass was thickly coated in dust and grime from the years of neglect. He wiped it slowly as if in a trance.

"Memories fill this room," he whispered, his voice hoarse as if he had been crying. "They tell me of this sword. How it protects people from evil yet…" He breathed deeply as he began to tremble. Tears fell from their stone prison and splattered, cleaning specks off the glass. Soon the tears turned to sobs and cries.

He turned to her and his eyes screamed anguish and despair. "Why couldn't it save my parents? Why did my father have to die? Why is my mother on her death bed? If it's supposed to protect people, why can't it protect the people who keep it?" He balled his hands to fists and looked to the ground, shaking angrily. His questions were valid. If the sword did such a thing, why did its holder perish?

He moved suddenly and grabbed her shoulders. He squeezed hard which made her eyes water. His fingers dug into her skin. "I keep losing everything I love and for what, Eve? What did I do that was so wrong to lose my parents and my memories? Why?" His hands slipped and pulled her into a tight embrace. She rubbed his back as he cried into the crook of her neck.

She could see then he was nothing but a child who didn't understand. He was never explained the cruelty of the world but was forced to commit its crimes. Whichever evil was controlling the village, he was forced to follow. He was one of the few who fought against the evil in his heart. Due to his resistance, even with the lack of memories, he was targeted. From what she saw, he was not a liked man. He had never known peace.

"That is the nature of people, Darrow," she whispered. She pet his head, feeling the soft hair against her skin, hoping to calm the tears. She knew because it was her job. She had people lie to her every day and never thought twice about it. They did it because they wanted something from her. As people will do anything to get what they crave, they will hurt others in the process. "As it has always been and always will be, those in power or those who are desperate will lose what we all hold most dear."

He pulled away and held back more tears. "What's that?" he asked quietly, wiping his eyes with his sleeve. She placed her hand on his cheek and rubbed it softly with her thumb. She could see the years of restless sleep rise to the surface of his tired eyes. Dark circles had formed and he had aged in the days she was there with him. "Their humanity," she whispered.

His eyes lit up as he blinked at her. She wondered if her words brought realization to him. As he did with new words, he tasted it though it was longer than the last ones. "Humanity," he asked, confused.

She nodded, knowing that it was new. "The feelings that make us human or civil. Feeling sorry for someone losing a loved one. Feeling genuinely happy for newlyweds or new parents. Feeling for other people.

"Not like I can talk though. Seems like every day more people convert to the non-caring ways. Makes me sick," she spat. She growled as she thought about it. It intensified when she thought of a particular cousin who would do anything to gain their grandfather's favor. He wanted the farm to sell it off to the highest bidder. She snorted as she knew it never worked. Her grandfather saw through his kind. He knew the kind of person someone was by listening to them talk.

He nodded but looked back to the sword. He wiped the top of the glass clean with his sleeve. She could see a small smile pull at his lips. "To feel is to be human," he mumbled. He continued to wipe the glass as he switched to mumbling in his own tongue. She sighed but had discovered it was how he processed things. She wouldn't bother him as her grandfather would do the same.

He looked back to her, and she could see determination burning in his eyes. "I want to know more about this humanity. I want to know more about what my mother talked about. I want answers about who I am and why I lost my memories."

She nodded not really knowing what else to do. A new life was sparking in the darkness.

He took her hand in his dusty one. He softened as he looked at her. "I want you to come with me," he told her softly. "I want to show you my special place. We will find answers there. I know that's where it is! All we have to do is look. Please, Eve."

She paused and shook her head. "I need to go home, Darrow. You promised me once we got here that you would take me home. I've put it off because you were sick, but now I really need to go," she explained harshly.

His face fell and he looked to the floor. "But..." He shook his head and let go of her hand. He sat on the bed, sending up clouds of dust. He held his head in his hands.

She sighed, wondering when he had started to get to her. "Fine, but on one condition will I go." He perked up and looked at her expectantly. "As soon as we see this place, I go straight home. Is that fair?"

He nodded vigorously before standing.

"Wait here a minute," he ordered. She nodded as he ran to the ladder and jumped in the hole. She heard him land with a soft thump and speed off again. It wasn't long before she heard him speed back up and then was back in the room. He was elated as he held a small key in his hand. "The lord will be looking for this soon. I heard his guards talking about it. 'The Sword of Learthdelsea' is what they called it. A weapon that can decide the fate of many people. I remember the elders claiming it can take away lives to instill them in others."

He paused and looked in the clean spot. He suddenly was distant but shook his head and his focus returned. "There was a poem my mother would sing to me. Learthdelsea's Grace, she'd tell me," he explained. "Being so young, I didn't know what it meant. It was only a lullaby. Thinking about it now, I swear she was talking about this sword." As he opened the glass container, he recited it to her.

"Turn back fate
Speed up time
Let my whims be your design
Let earth be my canvas
You are my brush
Together we will create ash and rust
Yet let your kind soul
However frail it may be
Turn this ancient stone heart free
Let birds fill the air
Fish fill the waters
All at my command through the voice of the forest
This home, this earth
Forever be free
Let Learthdelsea's grace flow peacefully"

He turned to her and presented the sword. She gasped in awe at the beauty of it. The guard and hilt were gold with thin, silver vines curling around them, as if they were alive. An emerald leaf sat in the guard, glimmering brightly from the window's light. The blade was crafted with blue-tinged steel. Engraved from the guard upward was a moose like creature staring at the moon. Its sheath was equally as beautiful with its wooden-like material and silver vines crisscrossing down to the tip.

"I will get supplies for the trip there and then the trip to your home today," he explained. He was distant to her as she continued to look over the sword. It didn't look like a weapon. It was more like artwork. Masterful artwork. He couldn't be planning to use it on someone. His chuckle brought her back to reality. "Tomorrow we leave."

Chapter 12

Spiraney

The sun was bright and warm as they walked past the sleeping trees. Droplets of water fell from the broken canopy above. It felt like cold rain whenever they would walk beneath them. The trees had formed icicles from their frozen branches. The snow crunched loudly beneath their steps. It was soft but it stuck to their boots, perfect for play in the snow.

She smiled as she felt the warmth of the sun soak through to her skin. She hadn't realized how cold his world was until that morning. They had been travelling for a few days and each day brought warmer weather. She wondered if it was the first sign of spring. If spring never came and if it was always cold, was a day as hot as that a sign of the evil leaving? She hoped Rosena still held on to enjoy it.

They were close to the mountains. They loomed ahead of the forest but were inviting. Its slopes were gentle and sharp edges couldn't be seen. She recognized them from the mountains far behind her grandparents. She knew it was a long drive between the two but walking was longer.

He led her to a large outcropping before carefully guiding her around it. They climbed quite a ways before he stopped by a large boulder. She breathed deeply and leaned against the cliff wall. He smiled at her. It was brighter than ever. Genuine happiness was shining forth. It was something that was never there before. She could tell his energy had returned as he didn't breathe hard. He encouraged her forward as the entrance was close. She nodded but continued slowly. She had to keep an even pace if she wanted to keep up with him.

They walked until they found a small gap in the rocks. She could tell from its position that one couldn't tell there was a small opening. She never knew it was there from her adventures in the park. He pulled out a stick in the pack he had brought and placed his hand over it. A small flame erupted and covered the balled end. She stared at him in awe. She had only seen flame conjuring in movies.

He chuckled and pointed to the back of the opening with the torch. A small, simple door built into the rock face awaited them. As they approached she noticed writing carved into the stone above. It was written with letters she had never seen before. She squinted to try to make out what it meant but couldn't guess.

He touched her shoulder and brought the light closer. "To all who enter, beware. Only those chosen by her hand will find my sacred place. All others will be forever lost in the chaos of their hearts," he deciphered.

She shivered at the thought of being lost in a mountain. "You sure you want to go in there," she asked.

He nodded and opened the door. It squealed and groaned against the movement. How long had it been awaiting to be used again? "I come here every time I'm done in the woods. My special place away from the noise of my village."

They entered and he closed the door behind them. She could hear the howling wind through the tunnel. The darkness closed in around them as their footsteps echoed in the small space. She could hear the dripping of the stalactites onto the stalagmites. In all, it disturbed her. The few times she had seen a horror movie, it usually had such tunnels. She was not pleased with the thought that the mountain could cave in on them at any moment either.

As they walked, he kept hold of her hand, which she was more than pleased about. There were multiple split offs, but he knew exactly where they were going. It was impressive that he knew the direction. She felt lost by the second turn. She was paranoid that they were lost. If they were to be separated, she knew that she'd never leave.

He stopped when the small tunnel opened up. The cavern was so large that the torch barely penetrated the space. The light could spill on the wall behind her, but there was nothing it could touch on the path ahead. Her curiosity pulled her forward. She took a few steps when he stopped her. He shook his head and smiled before pulling her back. "Hold tight," he whispered. She nodded as her fear increased. She wrapped her arms around his waist and held tightly.

He tossed the torch in front of them. It rolled on the strangely flat stone ground. It was polished and perfect, cut from the same slab. The torch continued on until it fell. She watched as it grew dimmer and dimmer until there was nothing. She squeezed tighter as she searched for light. She should have known better. The distance they had travelled meant they were deep in the mountain. As she hadn't heard the torch hit bottom, it meant walking off the platform would cause death.

She buried her face in his chest and closed her eyes tightly. She wasn't fond of the dark. She didn't like the idea that they couldn't see where they were going. He chuckled, which she could feel come deep within him. He turned her around to face the cavern, which she fought the entire way. As a child she never explored the dark. She always needed a light. He held her against him and asked for her to open her eyes. She refused. He asked her again.

When she did, she gasped. The cavern was bright, as the glow of endless symbols and patterns covered the walls. They pulsated with blues, violets and greens. He guided her forward slowly as she took in the sight. She could never imagine there being such a place near home. It was too magical, too surreal. She could see there being a village in the trees, that wasn't so farfetched. The magical cave with glowing walls was something else.

He stopped them at the edge of the ledge. Three bridges made of gray, white and multicolored light symbols stretched across the endless pit. As she looked down, the glow continued down to the bottom with more colours but never stopped. She looked back at him.

He smiled at her and sighed. "This place is called Prophecy Mountain. Written on the walls is the history of the world. It tells us the past, present and future, if you know the language," he explained quietly. "It continues to be written by an unknown hand. Legend has it the first spiraney was the first to decipher its meaning.

"Now choose a bridge," he instructed. She looked at him bewildered. She had never been there before, unlike him. She didn't know the way. She shook her head. He continued to smile at her. "If you are as special as I think you are, you will choose the right one." She shook her head and stared horrified at the empty space.

She felt his rough lips tenderly brush her ear. "Trust your spirit," he breathed. His voice and touch made her shiver, his breath as gentle as a summer's breeze. She wanted to feel it again as her breath had stopped. She trusted him that far, a few more steps couldn't hurt. She looked at the space and closed her eyes. She had to trust him.

There was a small pull at her chest. It beckoned her forward. As each foot touched the surface, she felt a presence. She recognized it. Though she never thought of it before, she trusted it. It lead her through life. All the way up to the trip in the forest. Then it was lost in the blizzard. She followed it, feeling safe in its embrace, but kept her eyes closed.

When she couldn't feel his presence anymore, she opened her eyes. She screamed as she could see through the floor. She was standing on the white bridge. Its markings blinded her as she stood still. She didn't want to move. She should not have been standing on open space. There was nothing to hold her. It defied all sense of logic.

She looked around tearfully until she found him standing on the multicolored bridge. He walked across as if he had done it many times. He probably had. She shook her head. "Where are you going," she cried out. She was terrified. She was not used to magic. Flames was one thing, a magician could do that. The coloured mist was a necessity, but science could have answered that. That bridge, in an age void of technology, could not be explained. She needed something to make sense of it all.

He climbed up to another tunnel opening which was one of four on his out-cropping. Each entrance had a symbol of a creature she had never seen. He sat at the entrance and looked back at her. He held his smile, but the look didn't calm her like before. He was a Wildman with an addiction to adrenaline. That must have been it. She couldn't follow that.

"Trust yourself Eve and I'll see you soon. I believe in you. You're the only person in the village's recorded history that can walk the clear path." With that, he pushed himself into the tunnel and was gone.

She trembled as she swore loudly at him. When she took a closer look at the bridges, she noticed a difference. The gray one was completely formed with the symbols, almost too full as more circled around it. The multicolored one less crowded but still formed. She couldn't see through them as she watched the symbols swim around. Hers, on the other hand, only contained three. Two to stand on and a third for the next step. She wondered why hers was so differ-ent. She wanted to run back and test the others but the thought was quickly dismissed.

She walked forward and ignored the endless abyss beneath her. If she ob-sessed over it, she would never leave that place. Once she was across, she would never have to walk that way again. At least that was what she hoped for. She couldn't handle going across again. Each step she took was guided by a new white symbol. When her foot touched the outcropping on the other side, the bridges disappeared.

She felt her heart hammering against her ribs as she fell to her knees. Her entire body shook. Never had she been so scared, and that trip certainly had plenty of fear. She did not enjoy the idea of nearly falling to her death. He said to trust her spirit. She found if her spirit guided her to do reckless things then she would never listen to it again.

She took deep breaths and centered herself. When calmed, she looked up to the wall before her. An opening, just as large as her, was the only way to proceed. It looked dark. It was unwelcoming. She quivered as she stood. She wished she wouldn't have agreed to go with him. She would have been fine had he not left her alone. He was used to the unknown and magic. She wasn't. What she was seeing was insane.

As she inched closer, a ghostly figured appeared. It was a woman, a beautiful woman. Her pure white dress flowed out around her as her long sleeves blew in a nonexistent wind. The silver, diamond and pearl jewels gleamed and acted much like the symbols on the walls. Her hair that blew about was also white and long to her ankles. Her skin was as pale as moonlight and her eyes held no colour. She looked fragile from the tips of her fingers to the end of her long, slender ears.

She beckoned Evelyn forward and started down the tunnel. Evelyn followed but only to the entrance. As the ghost walked, her glow lit the darkness. Evelyn breathed deeply and took a few steps in. The entrance quickly closed behind her which made her scream. Rock was not a live thing. She knew that but she witnessed it cover the entrance.

She looked to the woman, who beckoned her forward with those tiny fingers. Evelyn shook her head. "Who are you?" she asked. The ghost smiled and sprinted off. Evelyn took off after her, calling for her to stop. The woman never turned around, never motioned that she heard. All she did was run.

During her chase, Evelyn tripped over a loose stone and fell. She stayed where she was and breathed deeply. She was tired from running and was starting to crave food. She must have been crazy. She had chased a ghost not only once but twice. Then again, the first one was Darrow.

She sat up and watched the faint glow turn to black. Once again, she was trapped in the darkness. She sighed heavily and crawled until she found the wall. At least it was what she thought was a wall. The new portions of the tunnels were smoothed out. It was polished like the flooring in the cave. If she could see, she could tell if they were manmade or not. In the darkness, she could only assume they were.

"Spiraney," called out a soft voice, the accent very much like Darrow's. She looked around but only nothingness was seen. She stood up and followed the wall further. The voice repeated itself as she followed its source.

"What's a spiraney?" she asked to it. If it was using the term, she would hope that it would know what it was. She needed to know. Why was the term used over and over again by ghosts? No answer was returned. She called out again but still nothing.

Suddenly, something rushed through her. It was bitterly cold yet it felt as if she were on fire. She screamed as it tore through. She begged it to stop as she fell to the ground. She thought she could hear it circle around as it swiped at her. Each swipe made new wounds, wounds that bled and burned. She felt like she was in a tornado the way it tossed her hair and scarf. It was unending. It was relentless.

It pulled at her chest. She could feel the same burning sensation as in her nightmares. They were trying to take her heart. She cried for her grandfather. He needed to come and wake her. She couldn't stay sleeping any longer. She had to escape but she knew she couldn't. Unlike her dreams, that was reality. She couldn't escape that easily.

"The true spiraney, give me your soul!" The voice forced her eyes open. She recognized it. It was the same voice from the nightmares. It was the same voice that visited Darrow's house. That man was the one who took away Darrow's life. He was the evil that plagued the land.

She growled menacingly. She wasn't about to give up hers. "Get your own soul! This one's mine," she spat.

She swung her fist at the darkness. It exploded into fragments of shimmering dust. She breathed heavily but begun to run. She wasn't going to stay with that evil. She needed to find Darrow and get them out of there. He wasn't safe there. If he knew that she was there, then Darrow would be killed. A dim light filled her portion of the small tunnel. She didn't know where it came from, but she was thankful it was there.

When she felt a safe distance away, she stopped. Her heart beat wildly in her chest. The tunnel returned to its normal self. The soft voice began calling out "spiraney" again. Soon after, the woman appeared before her. Evelyn stopped as she turned. The ghost beckoned her forward and began to leave. Evelyn shook her head and crossed her arms. She wasn't going to follow.

"Enough games, tell me what a spiraney is and maybe I'll follow you again," Evelyn growled. The woman smiled knowingly before approaching her. She placed her hand on Evelyn's chest. A warming sensation engulfed her but, unlike the last, it was pleasant.

The ghost extracted a clear orb. A shimmering mist of gold and silver danced around it. The mist reminded her of Darrow's soul piece. "This," she whispered with her soft voice, "is why you are the spiraney, just as I am. You possess more power in your soul than the evil does in its true entity. You who have no magic can use the most powerful of all.

"That is why he hunts you," the ghost informed her. "You have always been a threat, so has Darrow. That is why he extracted the boy's soul and implanted it in you. He removed his rebellion while trapping your powers at the cost of his father and your parents' lives. Do you understand me, Evelyn?"

Evelyn nodded slowly. She didn't understand but knew Darrow would. Having a physical soul was his thing, not hers. She sighed. Why was she pulled into the mess of the world? She never chose it.

The woman stepped away. "You were created to cleanse his soul. Someone caring but firm, much like I was with my husband. He must prepare for battle as the eve of war is upon us." She bowed as she slowly vanished. Evelyn ran forward to see where the woman went, but she was not to be found. It didn't make sense. Couldn't they have chosen someone from the village to cleanse him? Evelyn couldn't understand the warning of war. She didn't see people preparing for battle. The village was a bit rough but there were no soldiers about.

Evelyn sprinted down the tunnel until she saw a new light source. It was green like the summer leaves. She quickened her pace hoping that it was sunlight. She slowed down and stopped when she reached the source. The wall was made of crystal, and she could see through to another large cavern. Around the walls were pictures depicting something. The middle of the room had a large stalactite and stalagmite set. In between them, hovering between the spikes, was a gigantic green and gold orb of light.

Near that orb she saw Darrow. He was meditating. He never did that. She descended the stairs beside her. She would need to ask him and give him a piece of her mind. He was never allowed to leave her like that again. She ran out and turned around. From the inside of the cavern, the crystal looked like rock. It was a two-sided mirror.

"Eve," he croaked quietly. She spun back around. He remained seated but leaned on the base of the stalagmite, his trance broken. As she approached, she saw tear stains on his scarf and the red in his eyes. He was also tired as he fought to keep them open. She sat next to him. and he closed his eyes, leaning against her. "I found some answers," he said. She nodded as she had found more than she wanted. The answers raised new questions.

He breathed deeply as he rested his head on her shoulder. "I'm sorry I brought you into this."

She shook her head and rubbed his shoulder. "From the sounds of things, I was involved the day I was born. Didn't really have a choice," she snorted.

He looked at her then shook his head. He snickered. "Same here, and to think I'm supposed to promote life. My mother must be disappointed in me." She asked him what he meant but he dismissed it immediately.

He handed her dried meat. She ate it thankfully as her stomach gnawed at her innards. She hadn't eaten since the morning, and she could only imagine what time it was then. As she ate, she could hear him snoring softly. She watched as he slept peacefully. It was the first time he didn't fight or twitch. She had a feeling his ride through the mountain was just as emotional as hers. Once she was finished, she curled up with her pack and napped along with him.

She awoke to him curled around her as he breathed near her ear. She tensed at first but soon relaxed in his embrace. She loved having him there. His warmth and protection reminded her of her grandfather's, but his was wild. His threats were deadly. He may have been cold at first but he had changed from their travels. Her cheeks warmed as she thought of him. She had changed him; though she had a feeling it had more to do with his soul completing itself rather than her presence. He was a complete man again and not just an empty shell.

She wiggled out of his embrace. She didn't want to wake him. She walked around the cavern taking in the paintings. It was written by the first spiraney. She hoped to find the history of the world. As she looked around, the word 'history' did not come close to mind. From her understanding of the village and the woods, they were an advanced people but did not build tall structures or buildings of any kind. Yet they were there in muddy colours. As she looked at them, she read it more like a prophecy rather than forgotten history.

It started with darkness born into the world. At its peak, the creator locked it away in an Eden, turning it into a desert. The darkness laid in wait for many millennia before growing strong enough to break the bond. It stayed hidden, building an army, while it sent a piece of itself to the past through a gate. There it created a cycle. It would suppress the people, a hero would arise and destroy it in a desert only to revive and start again.

It was very depressing. The darkness would always return. It was an endless battle. If she were to prepare for battle, it was for an endless war. Yet there was no war in her time. There was knowledge and technology. There was crime, yes, but no wars. They called it an era of peace.

"Amazing, isn't it?"

She gasped and spun around to see him. His eyes were more focused and the fatigue was gone. She nodded but frowned. "It's sad though. It never ends."

He shook his head. His fingers traced the tree markings, following them to a moose creature. "I think it will but it won't be our choice," he sighed.

He guided her to another part of the cavern. He pointed to a rectangle carved into the wall. Within it held more writing like the ones on the entrance's doorframe. "Its corruption will travel to a time forgotten and change the destiny of Garlandon. Only those chosen by my hand will save us, and the cycle will begin and repeat until time's end. This is Creanni's prophecy and the destiny of the Gates of Life." He then pointed further down. "Only when the ultimate child is born and the evil brought to its knees will I give them a choice. That choice will bring an end to the darkness but at a cost. What my children choose is up to them.

"See, Eve? There will be an end. Most likely, we won't be able to see it, but it will end."

She nodded and continued to look at the cave paintings. She wanted to know what her part was in it all. She was to help Darrow, but was that truly all she was there for? Couldn't they have sent someone else from his time?

"It's the reason why I come here. It gives me hope that all this suffering will end. I get away from the selfishness of my village and depression here. Here I feel like the person I was meant to be if I had all my memories," he explained quietly. He shook his head and sighed. "I know it might sound weird but... It's the way it is."

She looked at him and smiled. "Nothing weird about it at all. I used to go into my grandfather's backyard when no one was looking. Still do when I feel the world is out of place."

He smiled back at her.

She had returned her attention to the walls when he grabbed her hand. It was warm and made her realize how cold hers had become. She would have to fetch her mitts later. She looked to him to see what was wrong when she noticed his eyes. They were soft and, for once, peaceful. It was the same caring look that he had given her many times.

"Maybe you're just weird too," he chuckled quietly.

He pulled her gently towards him and put his arms around her waist. She didn't resist as she felt mesmerized by his haunting eyes. She couldn't tell if it was just them or the chuckle she heard, but she knew her mind wasn't with her. It had gone long ago. As the gap closed between them, she placed her arms around his neck. His eyes regained their shimmer as his hard stone eyes softened into liquid.

She felt his nose scrape against hers causing a jolt to reality. "What are we doing," she asked quietly. He had told her not to trust him, that he was a threat, but it was different than before. His trance was broken by her words as his eyes widened.

He pulled away and shook his head violently. "I don't know. I don't know anything about what I'm doing anymore," he growled pitifully.

He backed away until he leaned against the wall, his back to her. He trembled before falling to his knees. His sobs echoed throughout the mountain as he pounded the wall with his fists. His spirit was broken and he was certainly confused. As she approached him, she could feel the only threatening thing about that man was his blade. He had proven his fighting skills. She knew that it wasn't much of a threat as it sat with their packs.

She squeezed between him and the wall before wrapping her arms around him. He tried to push her away, mumbling furiously, but she held strong. He gave up quickly and buried his nose in the crook of her neck. She rubbed his back to calm the tears. She tried soothing him and began to rock him as best she could. It was hard to do with someone slightly taller than her. Soon he quieted and nuzzled her neck.

He sat up and gazed at her. His eyes were irritated from the tears and the salted water expanded the stain on his scarf. "When we get back, I need to tell you everything. What I do for a job, why the village is a mess, everything. I can't keep it from you, not when I feel like this..." He took a deep breath as he covered his face. "I'm a mess. I'm not used to feelings. These feelings I get from you whenever I feel you near are the worst. I can't tell if I'm supposed to be happy or scared or sad or angry. Everything is so instinctive! It's wrong for a warrior to feel like this. I just—"

"It's wonderful isn't it," she interrupted. He looked baffled before a small smile pulled at his lips. She smiled back and sighed peacefully. Her heart was a different matter. It beat wildly in her chest at his words. He wasn't used to feeling. He just explained the complications of love and it was because of her. At least that was what she hoped for. When had she begun to care for that wild man from the woods?

"This feeling is something that you would only hear in stories. Something so magical that it can melt the thickest ice. Something that can break the chains around your heart even if—"

His lips interrupted her. His cracked, dry lips caressed hers ever so gently. He pulled her closer as if he hungered for more. She had no argument as her own body yearned for it. How long has she yearned for his kiss and his caring embrace?

A low moan escaped him before he pulled away. He was breathless as he leaned against her forehead. She felt a little helpless as she whimpered from the loss of his touch. She opened her eyes to see a tear roll down his cheek but a smile graced his tender lips. He licked them as his smile grew. "I'm definitely alright with feeling," he whispered against her lips before stealing another kiss.

She nodded and giggled. She could feel her chest inflate. She knew then she was in trouble. She cuddled against his him and closed her eyes. His heart skipped a beat. She had unwillingly fallen for him. Worse yet, she knew that they wouldn't stay together long. Once she was back home they would split ways and never see each other again. She shook her head and allowed herself to be buried in his hold. He wouldn't let this feeling go. It sounded like one he actually enjoyed. She wouldn't give it up easily.

After a while, he helped her stand and looked to the orb. Its light was brighter than it was before. He extended his hands towards it and called out in his own language. It responded by glowing brighter and letting out a pulse of energy. The blast pushed them back, but he held strong. He called out again, which resulted in the ground shaking and the light dwindling.

The orb had broken free and zoomed around the room. It soared and collided with him, engulfing him in the light. As it did, a small green mist was slowly drawn out of her. The mist spun around her before joining the green orb. It filled the room with warmth and springtime. Grass crawled out of cracks and tulips bloomed. She found it spectacular as the gold and green danced around his shadow.

It slowed down and the orb shrunk in size. Darrow glowed with the gold and green light until the orb had gone. He flexed his fingers and stretched before looking back at her. He smiled greater than before and his chuckling began. "You truly did have ghosts but they are gone now, spiraney. I have them back. I promise that my dark memories won't haunt you anymore." She looked at him bewildered at what just happened. He shook his head and patted her shoulder. "A way to put it is, Learthdelsea's guardian has finally awakened and I am a complete person again. At least I hope."

He held her hand as he led her from the cavern. He was a whole man again. She knew she felt lighter and more cheery. The dark cloud that hovered over her had gone. The fear of sleep parted with it. The reasoning could have been many more things. One thing was for certain. She cared deeply for that man and she loved the person he was.

As they left the tunnel and marched into the light, she could hear the woman call out to her. "You are the beginning and eventually, spiraney, you will also be the end."

Chapter 13

Village Sickness

Their journey back to the village felt like a short one. Darrow talked nearly the entire way, except to take a break to sleep. He wanted to share everything that he had learned through the journey in the mountain. She was more than happy to listen. The change was welcoming; it meant he was whole again. It was extremely odd though as the man didn't talk that much normally.

He explained how the magic worked. How basic elements took less energy and a lesser soul compared to the dark, unnatural magic. How the greater or larger one's soul is, the more powerful the magic would be. A person's soul made the difference between a tiny flame and a raging fireball. She found it all interesting but, when she tried nothing, would come. She would sigh and feel pitiful, yet she remembered the first spiraney's words. She could not use magic for whatever reason. Yet she was the most powerful being to come.

He explained how his civilization was before the evil corrupted it, how his people were in tune with the forest. They would hunt but only to feed them-selves and prevent overpopulation. They would cure the creatures and plants of any illness with their magic. They would grow crops but only in the clearings they found to not harm the trees. Also due to their connection, the artwork, clothing and jewelry represented everything that nature did.

As they neared the village, she could feel a sense of dread. She explained the feelings to him; he frowned and nodded but said nothing. She was afraid of what was causing her such emotion. She knew from experience that when she felt that way, bad things happened. It was starting to look brighter and everything was coming together. To break his spirit now would be awful.

They entered the first few rings of trees. The quiet was disturbing. He touched the first rung to his house when a man ran by. The stranger turned and shouted something while rushing to the center pillar. Evelyn looked to Darrow for an explanation. His face paled considerably and his expression darkened. He lifted her hood and covered most of her face. She was confused by his actions. Her instincts had warned her of the bad approaching. His deepening frown confirmed it.

"You said you trusted me, right?" he asked. She nodded and noticed the urgency in his eyes. Something was wrong. He breathed out slowly but the light mood didn't return. "Promise me whatever happens from this point forward that you will trust my judgement. No matter how strange or cruel it is."

She hesitated and she stepped towards the tree. She didn't like where it was going. "What's going on?"

He shook his head and sighed. "I'll explain everything when we get back. If I'm missing from this, they will look for me. Just please, Eve."

She looked around him and noticed more people gathering towards the center. Her sense of unease didn't falter. She looked back at him. The urgency never left. "You promised you would protect me no matter what, right?"

He nodded vigorously. "Yes, I put my mother's life on the line for you," he mumbled. His words surprised her and her frown deepened.

She couldn't quite place why her safety involved his mother's life. She didn't want him to sacrifice his mother if it meant she could go home. That was wrong. Everyone needed their mother. "I want something to defend myself just in case we get separated."

He nodded and pulled a knife from in his pack. It was long and sharp. It would do. She took it and they followed the crowd.

They ran to the central pillar. It was decorated with gold, silver and greens. It was like during the holiday time back at home. A large outcropping way above the populace was the main attraction. From what she could see, there were two people tied to wooden poles with their heads covered with sacks. Beside each of those were bulking black shadows. If it wasn't for the sun, one could never tell they were heavily armoured knights.

He kept them near the back of the crowd. She couldn't blame him. The villagers were rowdy and particularly violent. They were trying to force their way forward and pushed their way through. Some even beat others to get out of the way. They were never close enough for whatever was to happen. Evelyn held tightly to Darrow's hand. He was the only safety she had. No knife could defend her there. It helped that one glance from Darrow sent most flinching off while spitting back.

A door opened with an echoing squeal. The village fell eerily silent. Not even the wind moved. An elderly man slowly limped from the beautifully decorated door. His peppered hair was long and tied back like his beard. The long, white robe he wore was greatly adorned with golden accessories while the black scarf that wrapped his neck dragged along the ground. Watching him walk towards the crowd, Evelyn felt like she had seen him before. The way Darrow growled assured her that he knew him.

He raised his arms and the crowd cheered. The only one who didn't was Darrow. The man shushed them and again the crowd was silent. When he talked, she knew then who he was. His voice was unmistakable. It may have been raspy and old but the cold, harsh tone could not be cloned. He was at Darrow's house warning them that she could never escape. He was the one who haunted her dreams. He was the cause of all the chaos in their lives.

He slowly circled the captive on the left while he continued his speech. The crowd booed and hissed, throwing balls of snow, but were quickly hushed with a wave of his hand. He enjoyed the sound of his voice and he had complete control over the villagers. When he revealed the person on the pole, everyone gasped. Even she recognized him from the first decent into the village. It was the man who Darrow very much disliked and had spat at.

She could hear him scream something into the crowd but was muffled from the gag in his mouth. He struggled to try to break free. She could only imagine what was going on. He quickly gave up when everyone spat at him. Growling came from everyone's lips. She thought of it like being among a pack of rabid, angry wolves. She understood if the man was a criminal; but, even still, most criminals had family or someone who cared from them. Not a soul cared for the one under execution.

The old man withdrew a black blade from one of the knights. Evelyn felt herself shiver and huddled closer to Darrow. He held the blade high over his head and shouted to the crowd. They all cheered as the black steel cut through the captive's leg but it wasn't loud enough to drown out his screams of agony. The blood spattered as the limb lay in the melting snow. Crimson falls appeared soon after.

Her stomach retched as the wind picked up the scent of warm copper. She turned and hid her face in Darrow's shirt as the old man swung again. She covered her ears and tried to block the screams as much as she could. Even with her hands pressed hard against her head, she could still feel his cries echo over the crowd. It sickened her that the people were overjoyed by the man's suffering. The entire village consisted of psychopaths.

Suddenly the crowd fell silent. The only sound was the wounded man's cries and the persistent ramblings of the torturer. His words stopped and were soon followed by an abrupt end of sound. Evelyn felt herself tremble and buried herself deeper in Darrow's chest. No one deserved that torture. Nothing deserved to suffer as he did. It was wrong. Those people were wrong. The stories were wrong. Everything happening was wrong.

Soon a new sound washed over the crowd. It started as a low hum. It then grew. Even with her ears still covered, she could hear the name. "Baltazar," she whispered quietly. She looked up and froze. Darrow was as pale as the snow and was as still as a statue. His eyes held tears but they were void of emotion. She pulled on his shirt and he snapped a look to her.

His eyes widened before he sighed. He leaned forward until she felt his lips against her ear. "He's the elderly man up there. He's the one who warned us that no one escapes him. He is the one who has caused so much trouble in our lives," he explained. His voice was so low she barely caught it. He looked away before returning his attention to her. "Remember when you asked me what a sacrilan was?" She nodded quickly. The word caused a death by his hand to protect her. Sadness built in his eyes, a pity a he gazed at her. Perhaps she didn't want to know. "You're about to find out what it is."

She turned around to see what he meant. Atop the outcrop was now a flaming pillar on the left while the old man had migrated to the right. The sight caused more unease, but it was the smell of burning flesh that caused her to bury her nose in her scarf. It was no wonder there were no burial mounds or sites. They burned the bodies. They removed all traces that the person had ever existed.

She remained hidden as Baltazar continued on with his show. This seemed to happen often as Darrow knew that he would be counted on to be there. It raised the question on what he did. Everyone was scared of him yet was enraged when they saw him. He was an essential piece in the workings of the village, but they would beat him till near death if he did anything less than perfect. He acted like a hunter but fought like master warrior and talked as smooth as a salesman. It was a jumble of skills that didn't match one career. What did that man do with his life?

The crowd cheered and she shivered. She wanted to go home. She couldn't stand those who gathered around her. She couldn't believe their bloodlust. It was disgusting how a civilization would promote such barbarism.

A tear had escaped from his wide eyes. She noticed the shock before his expression hardened. Unlike before, he didn't look down when she pulled on his shirt. She looked over to see what he was staring at. When she did, she felt her knees buckle.

Even from the back of the crowd, the copper hair stained with blood was blinding to her, a beacon in the madness. She knew exactly who it was. She had followed her through the forest. She warned her not to run away. She was the smarter one that time around. Evelyn cursed herself. Because of her stupidity, she got caught. Because of her pursuit of the shadow, Paige was going to die.

Darrow held her tightly as she started to make her way to the front. She cried as she struggled against him. He muffled her noise by burying her face in his chest. She needed to rescue her friend. She needed to save her from the fate that she knew that was coming. She could hear him mutter but she couldn't care less. The people of his village were going to end her friend.

She wiggled free but he was quick. He placed his hand over her mouth and held her tightly. She could hear him struggle, but in the end he was stronger than she was. She stopped, knowing that nothing she did could stop it. She watched as Baltazar's hand glowed black. He pressed it against Paige's chest and she began to scream. It felt worse to Evelyn than the previous man. If her dreams were anything, Eve knew exactly what was happening. She had seen the torture Paige would go through.

Baltazar raised the soul above the crowd. The swirling blue and silver light dispersed over the area and past them before flying off into the forest. Paige's head slumped against her chest and the cheering began again. Evelyn fell to her knees and cried. The woman who she considered a sister had her soul ripped from her. She had dreamt about it for years. It was a fate she did not wish on anyone.

"You're nothing but a pawn." The voice was strong and resilient but a whisper to everyone. The voice silenced the village. Everyone looked around. No one could find the source. "This talk of prophecy and you defeating the hero is beyond dumb. She will see to it that you are destroyed. She's good at that."

Baltazar yelled and ripped Paige's body from the pole. The people moved as it fell to the crowd below. A shot of blue light fired in the air and took the body with it. It hung there, which made everyone scatter. As usual, they avoided the man and parted around them. Evelyn watched as it burned in a white flame. She swore she could feel Paige's gaze burning through her.

"Eve, get to your house. You must get out of here before he finds you." Her warning was clear. She understood the danger well.

She called out to her friend but didn't get a response. Screams of fury came from the man above. She growled as glowing black magic surrounded him. She wished nothing but death for the man before them. She hoped his death was filled with torture and pain. He would feel everything he had ever done to those who suffered.

"Run, Evelyn!"

She was helped up and guided away with the remaining crowd. The heat of something was behind them before a pulse of light knocked her off her feet. She shook her head and got up quickly before running. She had to blend with the crowd. Darrow was not far behind which put her at some ease. Her friend was gone. Nothing left but glimmering blue and silver dust.

As they reached his home, Evelyn felt a darkness approach her. She stopped and twisted to look. A dark shadow cloaked the trees as it spread from the pillar outward. Darrow forced her to climb quickly. He shoved her in the door. Before he slammed it shut, a black shadow of a hand reached up. From beyond it, the sounds of the raging evil could be heard. "I will get her, Darrow! Mark my words, she will be mine and then soon my master will know true life once again."

Chapter 14

"It's My Job"

She sat alone on the big arm chair. She was void of feelings as she stared at the darkness above. Scenes of what happened replayed themselves through her mind. What could she have done to help her friend? She had to find something that would have indicated that she was there. The more she searched, the less she found. The knowledge that nothing could be done infuriated her. There had to be something, anything, to prevent it. There had to have been a way to save Paige.

The darkness pounded outside. Darrow had left to check on his mother but assured Evelyn that the shadow could not enter. It was not invited. His home was picky that way. She could only assume that the tree was guarded by magic. She watched as he cut his hand and smeared his blood on the door. Even after he left, blood dripped down leaving a thick crimson trail.

She couldn't tell when the sight didn't bother her any longer. She was usually made ill from the sight of blood, but this time it didn't faze her. She would have never guessed that she would have gone through all that she had. She had seen the death of people. She had rescued a man from drowning and then freezing. She had held a sword to someone's neck. She had crossed over a magical bridge and witnessed a rebirth. The worst part of it all was that she had fallen for a man who had a secret. It was one that she knew could take everything she held dear. Even after it all, the journey was still not over.

She heard the demanding voice of Baltazar through the pounding. It started with convincing her to leave. She ignored it completely and remained in her emptiness. It was better than the emotions that would run wild. He changed to bargaining, promising that he would allow Darrow to live. She snorted and shifted in her chair. At that moment, Baltazar had shifted to demanding and threatening for her to leave or he would kill Darrow. She couldn't care less. Nothing mattered, not even her life. She wished for death but she would never give up to him.

She dreamt of being at home. She could envision her room with her large bed, dresser and desk. She had beautiful curtains that covered the large window. She would spend many rainy days listening to the pitter-patter of the raindrops while doing homework. The wonderful comforter that covered her bed held the warmth of her room. She and Paige had spent multiple hours giggling and gossiping about boys as teenagers.

So many days the two of them would play in the fields. They would hide in the tall grass and try to catch each other. They would climb the trees and see who would reach the top first. One time, Paige had fallen and broken her leg. The trip to the hospital was not a pleasant one. She thought of the first time they camped in the forest, how even then they were being watched.

The door slamming shut brought her back to reality. Heavy breathing brought some sense back to her and she quickly hid behind the chair. The footsteps of the newcomer dragged along the floor. Each footstep was forced and no energy was behind it. She looked around and watched the shadow of a man slowly made his way to the hallway. His posture was slumped over. Before she heard the door close, she thought she heard him say 'moma.'

Feeling no threat, she decided to investigate. She enjoyed the thought of a distraction. It was better than going over what was and what could have been. She checked the entrance and watched as the bloody hand glowed and faded. She hoped it was a good sign that Darrow was home. She didn't know how to replace it.

She silently crept down the hall to the bedroom door. She pressed her ear against it and strained to hear the quiet sobs. She tried the knob and found it open. She peeked inside and sighed when she found Darrow lying on his bed and stripped of clothes. The odd, furry belt curled up beside him. She was glad it was him but found it strange that he said nothing as he entered. As usual he was mumbling to himself, though it was angrier than usual.

She walked into the room cautiously. It wasn't until she sat on the bed that his mumbling stopped. He lay on his side, his face buried in a pillow. He breathed heavily but didn't move. It wasn't long after when his muscles loosened and his breathing changed. It wasn't like him to ignore the presence of a person. He was much more cautious than that.

She crawled onto the other side of the bed and loosened the pillow from his grip. His face was red and eyes swollen. A new tear formed and dripped from his nose. He hadn't finished when he had fallen asleep. She took a corner of the pillow and dried his cheeks. At first, he jerked then twisted until he was a tight ball on the bed. He growled and shifted before becoming still again.

A golden chain was clenched tightly in his hand. She wondered where it had come from as he had never had one. She tried pulling it free but quickly realized it was entangled in his fingers. She tried to relax his hand but he only held on tighter. She wondered what it was as the golden chain glimmered in the candlelight.

His other hand reached out and pushed her down on the bed. The wild eyes from the night of the leech were back, and they glared at her. He snarled menacingly, his lips pulled back revealing longer canine teeth than her own. She had never noticed them before and at the moment she feared them. He had become more animal like, and she could tell from a dog she had owned that he was not happy. The furry belt whipped wildly, snapping at the bed.

He kept her pinned for quite a while, but his snarling had ceased. He acted like he didn't know what to do with her as he kept looking over her. She remained still, afraid that any movement would set him off. She wondered what had happened to change him again. It must have been like a defense mechanism while he slept to keep him safe. He changed only while he slept.

He let her go and cuddled in the blankets. He kept watch on her but the anger had gone. She moved slowly but the movement didn't bother him. She wondered why he acted as such. He was an intelligent person. He was civilized as he had demonstrated before. At that moment, it was all gone.

He sat back up and looked at her curiously. She didn't know what to do as he moved around her. The tail of his belt brushed her face with its soft fur with each pass. When he was satisfied, he sat in front of her. He watched her, looking expectant. When she didn't move, he inched closer. It wasn't until he touched her nose that she saw him blush. He gasped and shied away quickly.

She shook her head. His behaviour was definitely off. He approached her again slowly. He rubbed his shoulder against her as a cat would before settling on the bed again. She felt herself rub his shoulder and back absentmindedly. His tail curled and stretched lazily with each stroke. She smiled as it reminded her of her past dog. It wasn't long before she heard a deep purr. She jumped, not expecting the sound. She looked over to see the blissful smile on his lips.

She shook her head and continued to rub his back. She wondered if the change would be permanent. He would definitely be an odd pet, and she doubted that her grandfather would allow her to keep him. He flexed his fingers, which let the golden chain fall. He yawned and stretched as he nuzzled the pillow. Soon after he relaxed and fell asleep.

She stood and picked up the chain. A pendent hung off of it. It was a small emerald leaf encased in gold. It was beautiful as the light played in the jewel. She frowned as she had a feeling to whom it belonged. She placed it carefully on his bedside table. Her feeling of it being the only visit she'd have with his mother must have been correct. It could be the only reason he had been nonresponsive upon entering.

She tucked him in before changing. She crawled into bed next to him after blowing out the candle. She enjoyed his company. It was better than being alone. She settled into her pillow and looked at the ceiling. She wondered how long her time with him would be. She felt her heart tighten. She hoped he wouldn't leave her; she had grown to love the man. She would ask him in the morning. She had to.

When she awoke she discovered she was alone in the room. She sighed and stretched. Normally he would stay and watch her sleep. She had caught him doing it many times. Usually it was with sleepy eyes before he would drift off again. She sat up and noticed the necklace was missing. It wasn't long after when the memories from the gathering returned to her. She frowned and stared at the floor.

"Oh, you're awake," she heard him say quietly from behind her. She looked to see him dressed in only his undershirt and pants, the newly discovered tail swaying behind him. She nodded and saw the sadness in his features. He avoided her eyes. "I hope I..." he began. He shook his head and walked back out. Her frown deepened. His mind was back but his behavior was still odd. She stood and followed him.

She found him packing at the table. He would stop, stare at the wall, mumble something angrily and continue packing. She shook her head and tapped his shoulder. He stopped but didn't turn to look at her. She watched his fists clench and a tremor go through him before he returned to packing.

She tapped him again but he only shook his head. "Darrow, I know you're busy but I have a question." He stopped but refused to look at her. She frowned, hurt by his actions. She sat down beside him and he turned away. This made her angry. "What the hell did I do to deserve the cold shoulder," she spat. He shook his head and ignored her.

Her wrath only increased. She turned his chair to face her. He looked down at his hands that were in his lap. She grabbed his face and forced him to look at her. "Why won't you look at me," she yelled.

"Because I ruined your life," he roared.

She sat back on her chair. She wasn't expecting that. His eyes watered and he looked away from her again. "No, I ruined—"

"No, you didn't. This is all me. It always has been." He took a deep breath and leaned on the table, his head in his hands. "It's my job to bring people here. What you saw yesterday was what happens after I'm done. Only a select few from this village do it. We are the soul hunters, the kul runders." He pounded his fists on the table as she stared at him.

He shook his head and looked at her. "We are trained how to deceive and kill people at a young age. It is ingrained in us to make everyone do what we want at whatever the cost. That's why everyone here hates me. It is the most respectable job, but it is also the most hated because you never know if what we say is truth." His eyes hardened as she saw the anger grow.

"You want to know what a sacrilan is? The direct translation is sacrifice." Her eyes widened. She was called that many times by others from his village. "I chose you to be the next sacrifice. You were the one that was supposed to be up there, not your friend. I chose not to once you saved me from that leech, and since then everything has been wrong!" He stood and hit the wall, fury shaking every limb. "There was something different about you. Most would have left me to die, but you didn't. I didn't even know what a spiraney was supposed to look like until we went through that cave."

He took a deep breath and leaned against the door frame. "I'm supposed to be the guardian of life just like my father, but here I've been destroying it!" He dropped to the floor, tears streaming down his face. "I promised my mother after my graduation that if I found anyone pure that I would protect them. I didn't know what she meant but soon after my first job she got ill. Baltazar promised that so long as I brought him sacrifices that he would keep her alive.

"For years, I never wavered; I always brought him people. They were all cruel or would throw themselves at me. You were the first that I hid from him. You've been the only kind-hearted soul. Since I didn't bring him a soul, he killed my mother, once your friend was sacrificed so was she. She was my payment because I didn't give you up..." He breathed heavily as he was holding back more emotions.

Evelyn stared at him, trying to process what happened. She was the one to be killed, not Paige. He decided not to sacrifice her and in doing so, they found and killed her friend instead. These people lived from sacrifice to sacrifice, for what? All the stories of missing people were not due to carelessness but to these monsters. Everyone who had gotten lost in the forest would have been fine if it wasn't for the society living deep within it.

What she couldn't comprehend was out of all the people, as usual, why was she different. She was simply a spiraney, a pure soul that was created to cleanse his soul. She had done her task from what she could tell. He was a whole man and could think clearly again. Couldn't she just have been killed and let her friend be free? She shook her head. By the time they learned all this, he said he cared about her. He would never give her up.

Then his statement about why the village was cold towards him came to mind. He was trained to be deceptive. He lied on a regular basis. Could he have lied about his feelings as well? Perhaps, in reality, he hates her and is keeping her just as another sacrifice. For all she knew, he could have killed his mother. He was trained for it.

There was also wildness with him. It was willing to kill her but hesitated. It was curious about her as if she was something different. It was shy when it got near but then acted warm towards her. It was comfortable enough to sleep next to her soundly and enjoyed her affection.

"Who are you?" she asked. He looked up at her with confusion but didn't answer. She felt a lump form between her breasts. It pulsated with warmth she could vaguely remember. It made her mind spin but her anger pushed past it. "Answer me! Who are you?" Her voice was distant but still strong. His eyes widened and he blinked a few times before sitting on his knees. He looked away and shook his head while mumbling in his language.

She growled and picked him up by his collar. He looked horrified and held onto her wrists. "I said answer me, boy." The lump pulsated through her arms, which she hoped was what was giving her strength. She normally couldn't pick up someone who was her height. His eyes watered and he closed them. He shook his head and she assumed he answered her in his language.

She dropped him and she felt the pulsing leave her. "Fine, don't answer," she spat. She stomped down the hallway when she heard him speak.

"I did answer though," she heard him cry.

She looked back at him bewildered. "What, in your language? I know only four words, be realistic."

He shook his head but didn't turn to look at her. "Then why were you speaking it?"

She growled and slammed the door of the bedroom. She didn't speak his language. She only knew two words properly and they were titles used on her. She couldn't complete sentences. She clearly spoke in her language.

She sat on the bed and glared at the window. It was bright outside, though she felt a hurricane blasted throughout the tree. As she breathed deeply, she thought back to his tone. It reminded her of her younger cousins when they were in trouble. The youngest would cry when he was scared. She quickly dismissed it. He was an adult. He was also one who wasn't used to emotions. She sighed. It hadn't been long since he had acquired them.

She grumbled and stood again. Damned emotions and guilt; her grandfather raised her better. She shouldn't have been so harsh on him. He was only a pawn in the chaos just like her. He lost his mother because of his decision just as she had lost Paige. At that point they were stuck in the mess together. If he was going to see her out, she needed to help him through those pesky emotions.

She found him sitting just where she left him. He looked defeated as he shook his head between his mumblings. She shook her head. It was one of the man's quirks. He picked it up quickly since becoming emotional. She tapped his shoulder which made him gasp and cower from her. "I'm not going to kill you." He frowned and looked away.

"You're right though," he whispered. His words confused her. He smiled and looked at her with his own will. "I don't know who I am anymore. I don't want to be a kul runder. I was never meant to be one."

She sat on the floor with him. He had settled as he wiped his eyes with his hand. "Then who do you want to be?" He looked as if he was going to answer until he blushed madly.

He shook his head and returned to packing. It was a weird change.

"Seriously, who do you want to be," she asked again.

His blush returned as he tied up his bag. He tried to say something but stopped. She tapped his shoulder. He rubbed the back of his head. "You're not going to leave me alone until I answer, aren't you."

She smiled and nodded. It was a bad habit of hers. She only did it to help those close to her.

He chuckled and smiled back. "I want to be a man who loves his family and can protect them from anything. I want to be like my father, he tried to do that and I feel like he's still trying."

She stared at him and frowned. It was another answer she didn't expect. He frowned soon after and turned away. "I'm not discouraging it. You just keep telling me things that don't sound like you. It's surprising that's all," she explained. She had hurt him from her reaction.

He snickered, "Finally my turn to confuse you."

She was about to retaliate when she thought of all the times she left him speechless. She shook her head as he patted her on the shoulder.

"Help me finish packing. Tonight we leave this village and I get you back home."

Chapter 15

Wild Swarm

He helped her down the ladder, his presence never leaving from below her. She was thankful for the bright full moon and cloudless night. It allowed her vision where normally there shouldn't have been. She was also glad that the shadow had gone. The voice offered no comfort and never ceased to control her. Once Darrow had returned, Baltazar had given up.

She had the white cloak which covered most of her original winter gear. It was quiet as they walked through the village. It was night and most would be sleeping, but she figured some people would be out. They had to have someone patrolling for miscreants. The more she looked, the more she noticed that there were no guards. It was strange considering the violence level of his people.

Suddenly, a man ran out in front of them. He ran up to them and was begging Darrow about something. The stranger shook him and sank to his knees. He was crying. He pointed towards the direction they were heading in. Darrow whispered to the man. He nodded and handed Darrow a few pieces of gold before running off.

"What was that all about," Evelyn asked once the man was gone. Darrow's focus sharpened, his body tensed, it wasn't good. "Trouble," he stated while putting them in his pocket.

They made their way carefully around the trees. Each step had purpose and was quiet like the wind that blew through. Near the outer rim, Eve saw the danger. It was just like the massacre she had first witnessed. The bodies were torn apart. From what she could tell, it was of a little child and a mother. Her stomach churned and bubbled. The blood stained the snow. She was disgusted by the sight but also saddened.

Atop the bodies was a large insect as white as the snow. It tore off the woman's flesh with its thick needle teeth while its long mandibles held her head still. Its small eyes glowed red while its head was long and curved to its back and the antenna flickered around creating a clicking sound. Its six legs were powerful and all had three, long, sharp claws covered with blood. It stood and it screeched to the moon, revealing transparent wings hidden underneath an outer shell. She covered her ears. This was a beast from her nightmares. What made it worse was that it was taller than her and it was real.

"Zakulnea," Darrow seethed. He withdrew his sword quietly and charged at it. It didn't react quickly enough and he knocked it off the woman. It spun and charged back. He gracefully dodged and blocked a barrage of swings. Evelyn was surprised at how quickly they both moved. It was a blur of green and red. It ended just as quickly as the insect screeched a battle cry. It allowed Darrow time to slice it upward, splitting it in two.

He motioned her to follow and began running up the incline. Leaving hidden was no longer an option. They needed to move fast. She met him at the top and found him fighting off a group of them. Close to her was a small family. The woman clutched the man who was gravely injured while some children cowered behind them. They waved Evelyn over. They spoke to her in Darrow's tongue. She looked at them apologetically since she didn't know what they were saying.

As the last insect fell, Darrow ran over to them. With glowing white hands, he tried healing the man and gave instructions. The woman motioned to Evelyn. Darrow smiled and had quick words with the woman. She nodded and looked to Evelyn.

"You make him strong?" the woman questioned. She nodded thinking of how her husband had changed. She smiled while squeezing Evelyn's shoulder. Her eyes were bright with crystal blue as they watered. "You good for him, keep safe. No lose, yes?"

Evelyn watched as they made their way back home. She needed more of an explanation. Darrow told her who the woman was or else she wouldn't have attempted communication. That was a dangerous move. He had them start to run.

"She's known me since we were kids and always knew I was more than what I believed I was. For a long time, she pursued me and tried to show me how to feel; but I shoved her away, knowing that there was nothing there. She was thanking you for freeing what was lost." Evelyn nodded and tried to keep up with his pace. She understood the urgency. Being caught by one of the monsters meant death.

They slowed their pace when he started to breathe hard. They took a brief break and ate some meat that he had brought. He shook his head and growled.

"He must really want you to allow those things in," he mumbled.

She nodded and chuckled. "I'm a rare commodity, you know. Not everyone has a soul like mine."

He shook his head again and rolled his eyes.

They travelled for a few days, and Darrow was tense during each minute that passed. She woke many times at night and noticed the animal in him blossom. It watched the woods intently but always lingered a few moments when his gaze passed her. She couldn't blame him for being apprehensive, as the insects would attack them from time to time. He had to be focused and always alert. He was the only one with a weapon and speed to defend against the creatures. Evelyn was useless.

It had grown warmer since they left. Evelyn had removed her sweater from her coat during the day. The snow had started to become slush. Icicles dripped everywhere. Even Darrow mentioned the heat and removed his scarf, allowing it to flutter aimlessly in the warmer air. He was confused with the change and didn't like how slippery it was. He stated he didn't have as much grip in the wet stuff. If it was always winter, then slush and fresh ice would be bad for navigation.

During midday, they found themselves at a gorge. Evelyn's spirits brightened. She had been there before. It was a leisure day's walk from home. She smiled and told him of the good news. He nodded shortly and glared at it. The only difference was the rope bridge that was strung across. It wasn't there the last time. She frowned and wondered when it was built. Also, the campsites that littered the open land were missing, another oddity.

He had them walk cautiously out of the trees. With his sword drawn, he surveyed the area. She couldn't understand why. The gorge was safe. The only thing dangerous about it was the sudden drop at the cliff's edge. If a person were to survive the fall, the fast river would certainly kill them. Once caught in the current, one was swept into the underground river that nurtured the land.

Darrow peered over the ledge. He looked back to her and motioned to keep quiet. He tested the strength of the bridge before fully trusting it. When it creaked, he cringed. He looked around again with focus in his features. He shook his head and motioned for her to follow.

The crossing was agonizingly slow. She was not one for the open gorge. It was beautiful but at a safe distance. The thought of crossing it on something held by old rope was not appealing at all. A breeze had also started, which rocked the structure slowly. She only held on tighter. She was not interested in falling to her death that day.

The sound of dull buzzing echoed from beneath them. He froze mid-step and snapped a look down. The longer he stared, the more his eyes widened. As the sound grew louder, he looked back at her. He was trying to think of the best option. He took in a quick breath before whispering, "Run."

His word seemed to have summoned whatever he feared. Large creatures shot up from below, causing the bridge flail violently. She screamed as the buzzing drowned it out. She felt him grab her arms and guide her forward. She shook her head and, when she opened her eyes, she regretted it. Flying from below them and gathering above were what looked like enormous yellow jackets.

Her eyes widened at the sight of them. She was as tall as one segment of their legs, if not shorter. Their wings drowned out any sort of sound and hurt her ears. Their slender shapes would dive at them only to pull up at the last moment to hopefully catch them with their stinger. She was horrified by their size. She had been stung by a small one once. It had hurt and swelled, but she knew that the ones they aggravated would certainly kill them if caught.

Near the end of the bridge, Darrow threw her forward. She tumbled into the snow. She knew it might have been necessary, but she would have hoped for a warning. She felt him pull her up only to shove her forward again. Once again, she tumbled as she lost her footing. The slush offered no friction to stop. She couldn't understand his strategy. It would be better to have her running for the trees rather to have her stand and fall.

Evelyn looked back when he stopped. The wasps were after them as she remembered they ate meat. In a frozen wasteland of a forest, only foolish animals would traverse the gorge. The way they swung in and tried to grab at them certainly made her think that way.

Darrow blocked their stings, but she could tell he was tiring fast. He was becoming sluggish in his movements, and the stingers were starting to tear at his clothes. She crawled slowly to the trees as she knew they were better coverage, though she kept an eye on her protector. He backed away slowly when he could but was blocked usually by the swarm.

She heard him scream. When she found him, she held onto the tree for support as her knees buckled. One of the stingers had caught him in the shoulder. What made it worse was that it was caught there due to how it was barbed. He cut it free but fell while breathing heavily. As he lay, the wasps didn't stop as they attempted to cause more damage.

She wanted to help him but didn't know how. She had no weapon strong or long enough to fend them off. She didn't have the training to use a weapon if she had one. She didn't have enough knowledge to know how to distract them without endangering herself. She knew that he would have a great issue if she were to do that. All she could do was watch and wish for his pain to end.

She cried out begging them to stop. He didn't deserve it. Everything that had happened to the man was caused by the evil in the world. Her head began to pound as the world began to spin. She sat on her knees and cried harder. There was no time for her spells. She needed to help him. She couldn't sit there while the world moved on its own accord.

The spell worsened as a burst of pain engulfed her. It had never grown to such an extent. In her chest, she could feel a large bubble of discomfort. She wanted it all to end. She wanted the pain gone. She wanted the bubble gone. She wanted his suffering gone. Everything.

As she felt the world begin to depart, she felt a small voice in the back of her mind. It was instinctual. It felt like a part of her history. It was part of who she could have been. The small voice demanded her to push. It instructed to push the pain. Make it burst forward. Make it leave and explode in the distance.

She tried. She pushed in her mind as what she felt was right. She started to growl. She felt her hands push on the tree as her nails dug into the bark. The pain intensified. Her tears turned into screams as she began to feel weak. The voice inside became clearer and pushed her harder. Knowing nothing else but the instinctual push, she continued. It was as if something was keeping the pain inside, but she knew deep down it could leave. It needed to leave.

She was frustrated. She wanted the pain to end. Her inner voice gave the promise it would so long as she kept pushing. She had to break free on her own. She had to undo what had been done to her ancestors. She had to break from the choice. "Leave me," she screamed as hard as she could.

A deafening boom covered the forest and the pain left with it. Evelyn leaned against the tree, exhausted from whatever had happened. As she breathed hard, she realized a sound had gone missing. The buzzing of the wasps had passed. She tiredly opened her eyes and frowned. They had all disappeared. All that remained was Darrow lying in the snow.

She stood slowly. She saw the bridge was nothing but two charred posts. It was the regular sight she was used to. She walked trance-like near him while never looking away from the gorge. It was beyond strange. They should have killed him. It was in their nature. They wouldn't have just vanished without reason.

As her trance slowly left her, she noticed ashes falling from the sky. She held her hand out and collected some. They were definitely ashes that fell but were far too many for just the bridge. The wind also didn't blow in the right direction to blow it to her. As she looked up to the sky, she felt small drops of water splash her. The longer she stared, the more fell. It had started to rain.

She couldn't understand it. It was winter. It shouldn't rain. It was too cold for it to rain. Yet, there she was getting drenched in it. She had to get out of it but her feet wouldn't move. Her head had begun to spin again. It was different from her spells, she was exhausted. When she finally could take a step forward, her body released her consciousness.

Her mind faded in an out many times before she fully woke. She was warm and dry, but she could still hear the forest and the crackling of a fire. She wanted to know where it came from. She hadn't made one, and Darrow was certainly not in any shape to move. Her eyes fluttered opened to see the light of the flames. It was bright and full of life. It made her smile.

Wheezing disturbed her. She quickly looked over to find Darrow hunched over. He sat near her but his greasy hair covered his face. She worried about him. He shook every time he took a breath in. It was not normal for him. He was strong. He was healthy.

She crawled out of her sleeping bag; she assumed he had put her there. No longer sleepy, she could tell a few changes. Poking through his thin, light brown hair were small antlers resembling that of a fawn's. She had never seen them before. Twitching next to her bed was a long ape's tail the same colour of his hair. She traced it back to his bottom as it awkwardly stuck out of his pants. He definitely had a tail, but he hid it. Why would he leave it hanging out?

She carefully reached out and touched his shoulder. She snapped her hand back when he looked over and snarled. Through his hair, she could see that his eyes had changed. The wild was back in him as his pupils had slits and dilated much like a cat's. He barred his fangs at her while he hissed angrily. The tail twitched madly as the hissing changed to growls.

She retreated back to her bag and sat. He was no longer himself. She wiped her eyes as a few tears fell. Her heart clenched. She felt sorry for him. He never had control of his own soul. He rarely had the chance to be him. She shook her head and took in a deep breath while closing her eyes. She would just have to deal with the animal first.

When she opened them again he was staring at her merely an inch away. The anger was gone and he was curious again. He licked her cheek gently and she felt him take away a tear. He saddened before he began to cough. It was violent and shook his body. It stopped as soon as it came but he was tired from it. He was a curious creature by nature but wise.

When he turned away she gasped. His back was bright red with long, infected cuts running down it. She found the initial sting. It was mostly healed but looked to be infected from being exposed for so long. She began to panic and quickly dug out her first aid kit.

Her movement startled him as he turned to her quickly and growled. She shook her head and took out the bandages and alcohol. "You need care. Those things are very bad, Darrow," she explained. He shook his head but winced at the movement. It opened a few wounds and his blood began to spill. She sighed and pointed to his back. "See, that's why you need this and a new shirt."

He breathed deeply before awkwardly laying on her sleeping bag. She wondered if he remembered her from before. He was content then. She also wondered if he understood her. She patted his head and he looked tiredly at her. She asked him a few questions and she assumed he gave her answers. She found it hard to tell as he answered in his tongue. When she began to clean his back, he cringed but didn't turn to harm her.

She was as gentle as she could be. Once his chest and shoulder were bound, she helped him into another shirt from his pack. He was still wheezing and in pain, but she felt better from having the cuts disinfected. He curled up in the bag with her and quickly fell asleep. She listened to his snores as she rubbed his arm. She knew she had to remain awake to protect him. He needed the rest.

She gazed up above and realized they were hidden underneath a large pine tree's branches. She had made such a structure with her grandfather. She had even spent a few nights that way with him. Some of her favorite memories were those cold nights. In all ways, he was her father just as her grandmother was her mother. They raised her and loved her as their own child.

She laid there until the embers died, and even then she watched the sun rise from the pin-sized holes in the branches. He coughed more and had started to whine. She felt his forehead and cheeks to find a fever. She packed up everything and convinced him they had to leave. He needed more medical treatment than she had in her bag.

She helped him out of the branches and watched as he walked much like an ape with his knuckles. They had only taken a few steps when she gasped. Ahead of them was a sight all too familiar. It was a wooden, forest green doorway. The frame was made of normal wood, but it stood on its own and grew roots like a tree. The two green doors held diamond windows with pure golden sunlight shining through. The top sprouted healthy vines covered with brightly coloured flowers and hung down over the door.

She had seen it many times. It was a short walk from her home. She had made a promise to her grandfather that she would never tell anyone of it. He was protective of the strange phenomenon. She would visit it from time to time. It was welcoming and allowed her clarity when needed. She promised she would never tell a soul about it.

She began to walk around it as there was nothing but forest on the other side, as expected. It was nothing but a door in the middle of a forest. It was an odd place but it belonged there. Darrow pulled her to the door and opened it. A hot breeze embraced her which sent alarms off in her mind. It wasn't right. He smiled and tried to guide her in. She shook her head and turned around.

Then stopped. Hundreds of glowing red eyes peered out from the branches followed by white shining claws. She backed away to the door when the clicking began. She felt all hope drain from her. They were cornered and had no way for escape.

"Eve," she heard him strain to say. She looked back as he started pulling her through.

There was nothing there. Only those monsters were on the other side. It was a regular door. Couldn't even he recognize that even if his mind had gone wild?

The brightness from the door blinded her and she couldn't see within it. When she was clear of the door, it shut behind her and heard it lock with a loud clunk.

Chapter 16

Twisted Fate

When she was younger, Evelyn always wondered what would happen if she were to open the door and go through it. When she had her bad days, she wished for it to take her away to a safe place. When she felt like she wanted rest, she wondered if it would take her to the tropics. When she was happy, she wondered if it would take her on an adventure. When she needed answers, she wondered if it was the door to an all knowing sage.

As they walked through the light, she swore she saw a glimpse of blowing red sand. She shook her head, knowing nothing like that existed. It must have been her imagination. Within seconds of entering the light, it faded, leaving nothing but the vision of trees before her. Her heart hammered hard in her chest as there was danger on that side. She grabbed Darrow's shirt and turned to run back, but the door had already slammed shut behind them.

She twisted back around to face their death. She frowned and was confused when the white insects were no longer present. Instead, a worn snow path big enough for a horse drawn cart was before them. She recognized it as she had walked it many times. It was the path she was on with Paige on their camping adventure. They were on that path when she first met Darrow. She was back at the beginning.

She stared at the clear path. The storm had passed and any trace of people walking there had been buried. She swore when she looked before, it was just the forest with only trees behind the door. No path present. It was surreal. She couldn't believe she was home. She had spent so many days away, she found it unbelievable. She wondered how her family would feel when she would meet them. She had been gone long enough that they may have lost hope. She must have been lost for at least a month, if not longer.

Darrow's harsh coughing disrupted her thoughts. He shook violently until he vomited in the snow. His light wheezes deepened. She cleaned off his face with her mitt and washed the vomit off in the snow. She saw the pain in his eyes as they started to water and his body trembled greatly. She needed to get him to the house. He needed warmth and a doctor.

She coaxed him to follow her after tying her scarf to one of his antlers. She wanted to make sure he was there but needed to keep an eye on the forest. There could have been more monsters waiting to kill them. If they ran into any, he was in no shape to fight. Their best chance would be to flee, and advance warning was a must.

She smiled when the path opened up to reveal her home. The snow-covered barn and rustic two-story house caused her to cry in joy. How she had missed the picturesque scene. She missed playing in the barn. She missed watching her cousins play in the snow. She missed the hardy home cooked meals, the smell of a fireplace and the sound of laughter. She knew all of it would grace her soon.

She started to hurry when her arm pulled back. The sounds of him being sick reminded her that she had to take it slow. Again she cleaned him up, but this time he refused to move. He painfully made his way to her lap and whined as he rested on it. She petted his head in silence. He couldn't push himself any further. He was done.

She couldn't carry him with the packs. She would struggle with just his weight. If she were to leave the packs there, they could disappear. It wasn't a choice. She would have to leave them. He wouldn't survive much longer if she were to prolong his exposure. She dropped the pack off the path. She moved him to her back with very little help from him. His strength was gone.

As she tried to lift him, the sound of a readying gun made her gasp. She quickly looked behind her and cried as she saw who it was. It was an elderly man wearing a green hunter's cap and green, one-piece work suit. His hiking stick was left abandoned in the snow causing his limp leg to bend to carry the weight. In his hands was his hunting gun; and his deep blue eyes were focused, ready to threaten whoever walked on his property.

Her grandfather's features softened as his wrinkled face smiled at her. She jumped up while dropping her load. She pulled him into a tight hug while crying. She was truly home. The sight of her grandfather was proof that she was finally there.

"Hey kid, I've been looking for you. I started to worry since you're late from your trip," he said as he patted her back. She shook her head while she continued to cry. It made no sense. It should have been much longer than that.

An agonizing cry startled them. She looked over and watched as Darrow's tail curled and uncurled quickly while he rubbed his head violently in the snow. She petted his back to calm him and apologized. He continued to cry but stopped moving. His stone gray eyes opened slightly and he begged for whatever it was to stop.

She looked up at her grandfather and he nodded as he picked up their packs and stick. "You obviously will need to answer some questions once we get it back to the house."

She frowned and felt angry by his words. "He is not an *it*," she grumbled as she got Darrow on her back.

"Couldn't tell with the hair and those screams," her grandfather mumbled as they began to walk.

She sighed and shook her head. "Since when do girl animals have antlers?" He started to laugh as they made their way to the house. She had made her point.

Once she got past her grandmother's kisses, Evelyn placed Darrow on her bed. His consciousness had left and she feared his breathing would be next. Her grandfather followed her shortly after with a small wooden box in his hands. It was old and the design reminded her of things she had seen in Darrow's house. She couldn't remember ever seeing the box.

She quickly got out of her winter gear and helped get Darrow's shirt off and roll him onto his stomach. She watched as her grandfather nodded. He opened the box and pulled out a small needle with clear liquid inside. She frowned and placed herself between them. She was protective of the dying man and needed to know what was happening before she gave consent. She promised she'd keep him safe.

Her grandfather smiled at her. "It's ok, Evelyn. I'm assuming those are wasp stings from his time. This is the anti-venom," he explained.

Her frown deepened. "What do you mean 'his time'?" She had called it that since they were behind in technology, but the forest still had unexplored places within it. Darrow's people could have lived in one of the places that were left untouched by technology.

Her grandfather shook his head. "His people are from at least thousands of years ago. Pretty impressive for an old timer, eh, Evelyn?"

She shook her head. If Darrow was from the past, then she must have been in the past. Having changed him, she must have changed future events but everything was the same. She shook her head again. There was no way for them to be in the past. It was impossible. Time travel was impossible.

He instructed her to hold Darrow's arm still as he injected the antidote. Darrow twitched and whined but the slight consciousness left quickly.

"You might find it improbable but it's the truth. Two of my best friends came from there and it's all because of that gate in the forest. It links all of us." They changed his bandages and finished undressing him. Her grandfather left and returned with old voice monitors before they left the room.

"With your reaction to all this, there's no doubt in my mind you went through that gate. Explains your confusion with time," he mumbled. They sat at the table and ate lunch. He explained the gate after she explained what had happened. To Darrow's people, it was called the Gate of Life. It was the creation of the world's creator to link the past and present, the reason was unknown. His two friends had passed through it frequently before the one died and the other never returned.

"I have a feeling that's how your adventure started. He had guided you through the gate without your knowledge." Her grandfather looked out the window and she followed him. The snow had started to fall again. She sighed tiredly. Knowing what really happened, how she was lured into the past, drained whatever strength she had left. He patted her shoulder. "Don't worry too much about it. You're home safe now and life can return to the way it was once we sort out what happened to Paige."

Evelyn shook her head as she took her dishes from the table. She knew better. "Grandpa, my life will never be the same."

She showered and changed into fresh clothes. She searched for her pack but was dismissed by her grandmother. She smiled as she knew the woman had already taken care of it. She curled into a chair and watched a movie with her grandparents. It was odd how everything hadn't changed. It was as if the man healing in her bed never existed. As she watched the old film, she fell asleep.

She stirred and woke again. She rubbed her eyes and then stretched her arms. She could feel that she had been tense for too long. She wondered how he could do it. How Darrow had managed to live his life that way.

She looked to the clock and realized it was the early hours of the morning. She shook her head. She had slept a long time. She couldn't remember finishing the movie. She couldn't remember her grandparents going to bed. She snickered. She was definitely tired.

She went into her room and checked on Darrow. The wheezing had ceased and his features were peaceful. The wild was still there. The antlers, fangs and tail had not disappeared. She gently stroked his cheek which caused him to stir. He stretched and whined before licking her fingers. It made her smile. Even the wild enjoyed her presence.

She pulled the blankets up to cover him. He rolled over and nuzzled the pillow before settling again. She giggled quietly. If only he knew how cute he was as he slept. She could only think if he couldn't return to his normal state that he could still stay. She would keep him safe and happy as long as she could.

She took an extra blanket from her bed and returned to her chair. The brief alertness had returned the feeling of exhaustion. She stretched and wondered how long it would take for her to reach normality again. She knew she couldn't go back to the way it was. Her best friend had been taken from her. It was her fault, though Darrow insisted it was his. She sighed and buried herself in the chair. She would have to find balance in the morning.

When she woke again, she could hear voices nearby. She stirred, refusing to return to the waking world. When the discussion became louder, she opened her eyes. In the dining room were her grandparents and a few policemen. She frowned and wondered when they got there. She didn't hear the phone and, once again, she didn't hear her grandparents stir. She stood tiredly and joined them.

"Ah, she's finally awake," commented her grandfather. He rushed her to sit and her grandmother gave her breakfast. Evelyn frowned and looked at it confused. It was odd that it was done as clock work. They were never that efficient.

One of the officers sat next to her. She recognized him. They had gone to school together. He placed a tape recorder between them. She sighed. She was not ready for that. She shook her head and looked back at them. "Seriously, I just woke up. Don't you think this has all been traumatizing enough," she complained. She pushed away her bowl and went to the bathroom.

There was a knock at the door. She hissed. She didn't want to be disturbed.

"We just need what you saw, Evelyn. We won't bother you again," encouraged the officer she knew. She snorted. She knew otherwise. The gossip from the other missing people reached her ear frequently. The officers would be back. She shook her head and went back to the table. The more she cooperated, the less they would bother her.

They started the recorder and she started her tale. "Everything was going as planned for the trip. We had made all the checkpoints and eaten our food. It wasn't until the third day that things went bad," she began. She felt herself shiver. She knew she was going to have to lie. No one would believe the truth unless they already knew about magic.

She took a deep breath and continued. "An unexpected blizzard hit us midday. It was then we got separated because I pressured her into continuing." That was her first lie. They got separated because she chased Darrow to clear him off her grandfather's farm. "During that I fell and hit my head on something hard, it could've been a tree." This time a half-truth. She had hit her head but it was much after the blizzard. "When I woke up again, I was alone. I tried looking for Paige but, for all I know, she could be buried under all that snow. Then I came home when I found the trail again." Another lie, she knew exactly what happened to Paige and the memory would haunt her forever.

They nodded but continued recording. "You didn't see anything unusual?" the one asked.

She shook her head. "Only thing strange was finding one of my grandpa's tarps stuck to a tree, but he had lost that a while ago. Made me think it was a monster." If people would have believed her, she'd tell them she travelled through time and found a village ruled by magic. In doing so, she freed a man's soul and the animal within him was sleeping on her bed. She knew that wouldn't convince anyone. It would be written off as a hallucination from the cold.

They asked Evelyn a few other questions and a description of what Paige was wearing. She provided all the answers that she could. By the end of the session, at least an hour had passed. Hunger gnawed at her and she had begun to tire once more. The stress of the past had drained her fully. The officers thanked them and left. She knew they'd bring some dogs to sniff Paige out; once they didn't find any leads, she'd be pronounced dead after a week. No one ever returned past that. They never were seen again.

Evelyn ate her breakfast in peace. Afterwards, her grandmother insisted on a hot bubble bath. She didn't feel like it but agreed. It would relax her muscles and calm her mind. She needed to empty her mind of all thoughts. She wanted it clear for the questions she would sure answer soon. It wasn't long after she sunk into the bubbles that she slept.

She was woken up by her grandmother gently. She groaned but slowly opened her eyes. Her muscles had finally loosened and she sighed. The happiness that she had once known seeped back into her soul. She stirred as she wanted to return to whatever bliss her dreams had created. Her grandmother was insistent, however, as she was panicked. The urgency woke Evelyn fully and she quickly got out of the bath.

With the towel wrapped around her, she hurried from the bathroom behind her grandmother. Some trinkets off the shelves had fallen and shattered on the wood floor. She could hear loud, menacing snarls coming from within the room. When she found the source, she frowned. Darrow had wakened from his unconsciousness, but the wild was clearly still present as he crouched into attacking position. The hair on his tail was on end as were the smaller hairs on his head. He barred his fangs at her grandfather who was standing still from across the room.

What would have set him off? He was safe in her room. Nothing could harm him there. Her grandparents posed no threat. The scariest thing about the old man was his marksmanship and his gun was nowhere near them. The most threatening thing about her grandmother was the chores she assigned for punishments. Neither were on the verge of letting loose their weapons, therefore they were no threat.

Evelyn slowly made her way between the two while keeping her eyes on him. He shifted while she crouched. His snarling settled into a low growl. His eyes blinked making her focus on them. His pupils were dilated much like that of a cat's, while his stone gray irises hid the whites of his eyes. His wild transformation had gone even further as pale green vines appeared at his temples and grew across his cheeks. If she had to guess, the civilized man was no longer in his body.

She sat on her knees and remained still. It wasn't long before Darrow approached cautiously. He sniffed her outstretched hand and looked it over thoroughly. He made his inspection up her arm and began to circle her. She heard him hiss when someone moved from behind her. They were worried about her safety, but she advised them not to move. Every time the wild would appear, Darrow was very cautious. He did not trust anyone.

Some time had passed and he finally sat in front of her. She held out her hand and he rubbed his cheek against it. When he stopped, a few tremors pass through him. She patted the floor, testing to see if he would lie down for her to inspect the wounds. He obliged and stretched out on his stomach while his tail curled tightly.

She cautioned her grandparents to move slowly. As they did, Darrow watched them warily. When they went on to their business, he relaxed and closed his eyes. She hoped it was a sign that he trusted them to an extent. She explained she would return quickly and went to change.

When she returned, she touched the stings gently. When she approached the site of the stings, he yelped and growled at her fiercely. She frowned and returned his cautioning glare. "I need to fix these and I need to touch them to do that. Do you understand?" she asked harshly. He sat up very slowly and stared into her eyes as he balanced his weight on his knuckles. She felt like she was fighting for dominance and that, if she were to look away, she would lose.

She smirked feeling his challenge. It was the first time that an interaction with the wild showed intelligence. "You understand when I talk to you, don't you?" That was when a devilish grin spread upon his lips. Seeing the grin made her want to test her theory. Without moving her head she requested, "Nod your head for yes." It didn't take him long before he nodded.

It was then her grandfathered entered. He sat on his chair which earned a growl from her experiment. Darrow obviously didn't approve of new people within a certain parameter. He stared at her grandfather and leaned forward.

"I'll take your test a little father." Her grandfather looked into the wild creature's eyes. Evelyn knew that stare. It was one that he used if he wanted answers.

"Do you know this Darrow fellow?" her grandfather asked the wild creature.

The question was beyond unnecessary. Of course Darrow knew who he was; it was him. Evelyn was about to dismiss it when her grandfather held up his index finger. Slowly, Darrow nodded but had begun to growl in the process. It was odd.

Her grandfather's next question confused her. "But you're not him, right? You're someone else entirely."

She stood and made her way next to her grandfather. She was about to ask him what he was doing when the devilish grin returned and Darrow nodded.

Her grandfather sighed and shook his head. "I was afraid of that." She frowned. She knew him longer than her grandfather but he knew more about him than her. Her grandfather patted her shoulder and sat back in his chair. "The man you explained on your adventure doesn't suit who we have here. This Darrow sounds emotionless around people he doesn't know, where this one has made it perfectly clear that he doesn't trust new faces. Makes me only come to the conclusion that he has developed what his people call a 'kulpsylin' or split personality, to put it simply, though it's more complicated than that. Not something that they usually promote."

She looked between the two, more lost than before. She thought it was just the forest getting to the poor man, but he was suggesting something different. She had met someone with split personality because of her work but their appearance didn't change like Darrow's. She shook her head as her grandfather continued.

"Do you have a name?"

The creature's bravado melted away by a profound sadness. He turned and headed back into the bedroom.

Her grandfather shook his head and looked at her. "That will have to be corrected. I'm sure you can come up with a good one," he told her.

She looked at him bewildered. "Why me, you're the one with kids. You have experience." She didn't like the idea of calling him anything but Darrow. It was the name that she had associated to his person.

He laughed and shook his head. "I think it would mean more to him if it came from you. Something tells me you're the first person he's ever interacted with."

She shook her head and glared at him. "How do you know so much about his people?"

He stood from his chair and patted her on the back. "The summary of it, Evelyn, is I was entrusted to know about them by those friends I told you about." He led her to his room and pulled out an old book that was bound by cracked leather. "This farm was given to me by an old friend when he passed on." Within the pages was a letter written with fancy lettering.

"Dear Christopher,

I do hope this letter finds you. If it has, then you already know my fate and my soul has returned to the earth to help continue the eternal cycle.

I have entrusted this land to you and only you as it states in my will. I do this because I trust you to protect my family as I have yours. As you know, within the everlasting green is a very important gate which commands this forest. It is the only connection I have to them. I know you will protect them as you have protected me throughout the years. I have faith in you and always will.

My son will visit soon to retrieve a few of my things. He is much like you. He has that ambitious spark and cunning that had driven me mad countless times. Just as you have he, kept asking me to return home. The boy has never fully understood the true importance of your era. Even with that difference, I know the two of you will be the best of friends, like-minded spirits always do.

May Creanni bless your family and Learthdelsea's spirit lead you to a long life, my old friend.

Edgar Tisen"

Evelyn handed back the letter and frowned. It was the first time she had seen it and the book. His work-worn fingers traced the strange, gentle looking creature on the cover. "Without knowing it, he had been grooming me to become his people's first line of defense. I've stayed despite the countless offers I've had to move elsewhere." He sadly put the book and note away again. "Seeing that boy the way he is made me feel that I had failed at it. I know they would never allow one of them to split this far.

"I also feel that way because I had let a power hungry man into their world."

She stared at him. She couldn't believe what she was hearing. He couldn't have been the start of the cycle, he just couldn't have. He was an average farmer with a normal wife and had regular children. Something that grand could never be started by him. "Evelyn, before your aunt was born, I let a sinister man named Leigh Baltazar get into that gate. Ever since that day, the first day I witnessed magic, everything has changed."

Chapter 17

Start Training

A few weeks had passed since she had walked through the gate. She returned to work and all its regular, repetitive glory. It gave her peace in what had become her twisted life. As she had predicted, the police dogs had searched the forest and as she knew no body was discovered. Paige was later pronounced dead and assumed to have been eaten by animals just as the others had. The police once again asked her what had happened on their trip, and again she told them the same story. They had returned a few more times to make sure there was no news, but Evelyn had not seen them since.

The alter ego of Darrow she had named Alder after a few days of hard thinking. It was fitting as he was very much a part of the forest. He was wise and mostly quiet but his curiosity about the new world concerned her. Her grandfather always promoted curiosity in all his grandchildren; with Alder, he tried to divert it. His reasoning was that he liked to take things apart, as they unfortunately found out when the old television was unplugged from the wall and the parts scattered across the floor.

Alder had a hard time trusting new people. In the beginning when Eve was home, he would stick close to her and growl at anyone who got near. She was told when she was gone he would hide in her room under her bed and refused to join her grandparents. When he felt more at peace with the new people, he would spend time in the same room but didn't interact with them.

He was awfully strange, she couldn't deny that, but she had a feeling he was trying to replace the man that was lost. He would try to communicate with them; but when they couldn't understand right away, he would scream and hide in her room. She would find him later talking angrily with himself and would burst into tears if she interfered.

That particular night was different. He would pace from the living room to the bedroom, sit and stare at her and begin again. She watched him worriedly as he had never behaved like that.

Her grandfather must have felt the same as he commented, "Think he's sick?" Alder looked over at him and shook his head.

He looked out the window and snarled. His hairs stood on end as he roared fiercely. She looked to the window and screamed. Watching them was a strange man who had a thirst for them. He opened the window and crawled in, holding them at gun point. "Call off the monster or I'll shoot the old hag there." His voice was gruff but there was no mistake of a promised threat. Alder did as he was told without a word from her. An evil grin spread across the intruder's lips. "It thinks for itself, I'm surprised. I was told it didn't have smarts."

"Enough insults, what do you want?" barked her grandfather. Even under threat of his wife, he held his authoritative tone.

The two men stared long at each other before gunman chuckled. "You don't know? You hide the world's most powerful weapon and you don't know? Now you're just insulting me." All three of them shook their heads. She had never heard of it before. It was a farm not an armory. Alder grew quiet. "Seems the monster knows, be a good boy and tell me."

In a matter of seconds, the man was disarmed and sprawled out on the floor. Adler stood his full height and pointed the weapon at the stranger. He retreated to the wall but the panic of the sudden attack shook him. A low chuckle echoed in the room. It was mutated, making her shiver, but it was one she recognized. It shouldn't be that way, not filled with darkness.

The man pleaded with Alder to let him go but he shook his head. "Engardonians are pathetic. You wave your weapons aimlessly and threaten those who cannot defend themselves, but once the tables have turned, you run like worthless pigs," he spat. His voice settled a worry she had but the tone rose another. How many had heard it before their deaths? Did he really think of them that way? "Now tell me why you desire that power or else your death will be a slow, painful one." The stranger shook his head and cried. Alder grabbed him with his free hand and slammed him against the wall. He said nothing.

Alder shot the man's leg. She shook as she cowered behind her grandfather. The screams were horrid and rang in her ears. He couldn't kill people like that. It wasn't like him. He protected people.

"Please, I know nothing! We were promised a million to bring it back. An extra five if we got you alive," the intruder cried out. Alder pushed the muzzle against his arm and began to pull the trigger slowly. "It was bounty set by the inventor of robots, didn't say why, just that he needed it to complete something."

Alder growled as he straightened, the hair still on end. "I don't know what these 'row-butts' are but no one threatens my family."

He grabbed the man's collar and started dragging him to the door.

"You'll let me go, right? You said if I talked that I wouldn't die, right?" the man pleaded. Evelyn watched as Alder looked down at him.

His eyes were cold and void of feeling. He held no pity for the life he held in his hand. "I said your death wouldn't be painful; I never said you would live." The man begged and struggled to get free but his flailing was pointless. His leg was tied by Alder's muscular tail, so tight it would break. He hissed as the sickening thump of the stairs filled her ears. "You should have thought of this before becoming a mercenary."

When the door slammed, she held onto him. The man's screams were heard through the clouded night air. It was surreal. She then knew why he was feared in his village. He was ruthless. He could be a caring man but his actions were cruel. Alder returned and her grandfather asked what he did with the other man. His answer was indirect but he promised that they would never be bothered again.

Her grandfather wiggled from her grasp; the answer was sufficient for him. He grabbed one of Alder's antlers. "Listen here, boy, and listen good. You may have saved my granddaughter from whatever business you have; but if my family continues to be in danger because of you, I will drag you back to that gate dead or alive. Do you understand?" he warned. Only once had Evelyn heard him so furious, who it was directed at was never heard from again. The look in Alder's eyes was indifference. He couldn't care less. She knew that her grandfather's wrath was something she couldn't save him from, but she couldn't believe that he wasn't taking consideration of his words.

The antler softened and turned into Darrow's light brown hair. It flowed through her grandfather's fingers and brushed Darrow's face. He straightened again to his full height and took on an intimidating stance. He looked at the enraged man.

"You know nothing of me or my people. I might look young but I'm probably much older than you. Do not lecture me," Darrow growled back.

Evelyn watched as her grandfather burned with rage. He then did something she did not expect and from the reaction, neither did he.

Her grandfather grabbed both Darrow's ears, twisted, and pulled hard. His knees buckled and he cried out as the other man's grip remained, squeezing hard. Tears streamed from his eyes as he begged him to stop. Her grandfather kept holding on. "As I said, listen, boy, because I know who you are and I know your age. I probably know more about you than you do. Now do you understand?" Darrow nodded before he released his ears.

Darrow sat on the floor, rocking, with hands to his head. The pain lingered as new tears swelled in the corners. "Why… why does it hurt so much," he asked through his cries. Evelyn wondered the same. Her grandfather only crumpled his ears. She had done it to herself as curiosity and it was only an irritating sting. She wondered why it hurt him more than being eaten, beaten or stabbed.

Her grandfather settled in his chair. "You have nerve endings back there that we 'Engardonians' don't. From what I've heard from your father, it hurts worse than a knee to my nether regions."

His crying slowed. He looked up, and she could see his emotions had returned to him. He smiled softly at her grandfather.

"Yes, I knew your father. He was my best friend until that gate locked up from the incident."

Evelyn's grandmother looked over to him with eyes wide. "You mean he's that adorable little baby they brought with them that one time?"

He chuckled while nodding. Evelyn saw the excitement in her grandmother's eyes as she left the room.

When she returned, she held a small photo album in her hands. She opened it to a page and handed it to Darrow. Evelyn was curious about it. Like the book, she had never seen that album. Where did they keep it all? It made her wonder if they were actually keeping an all powerful weapon in that house. She would have to go look.

"It was the only time we were allowed to take pictures of them. I think your father knew what was coming. I can see it even in those pictures. The pain in his eyes, poor thing," her grandmother told Darrow. He was entranced by the photographs. He flipped through them slowly and, when he finished, he began again.

They had gone about their normal night routine when his nose emerged from the album. He looked at them with new tears. "These are my parents?" he questioned quietly. They nodded as they turned off the television. "Mother looks so young... what happened?"

Her grandfather patted the chair next to him. Evelyn knew the twinkle in his eyes. He was going to teach the boy; and, by the look in his eyes, Darrow was ready to learn. "I can teach you nearly as well as your father but you need to listen. Can you do that?" He snorted and his eyes darkened. He laughed as his famous smile lit his old features. "You're as stubborn as my granddaughter. That's perfect!

"We will start the training in the morning, though. Unfortunately, I can't pull off all-nighters anymore," he yawned.

Darrow watched him walk to his room and sighed. Her grandmother followed only after she patted his head. He looked over to her, and Evelyn could tell he was also ready for bed.

"You better get some sleep too. I can tell he's going to be putting you to work in the morning," Evelyn warned. She watched his sleepy smile spread. After readying the couch, she crawled into her own bed, knowing full well what her grandfather was about to do.

The next morning was peaceful. Evelyn awoke, changed and left her room. She found it odd that the couch was empty but knew her grandfather was an early riser. They would have left before her. She did her regular before-work routine and sat down to eat breakfast. She enjoyed having her own time again. It was also strange. Alder was always at her side during the morning. She missed him sitting next to her, watching eagerly for a berry to fall.

As she walked to her car, she noticed the two men standing at the wood pile. She smirked knowing that Darrow was made to chop wood. She walked over and greeted them. Her grandfather returned her greeting, but she got a grumble from the other man.

He stopped and looked over to her while taking deep breaths. "Can you tell him that I know how to do this? He won't listen to me and we've been here since dawn. Unless it's tolerance to old men, I don't understand what he wants me to learn," he complained.

Evelyn snickered. She knew what was going to happen. He made her do the same thing.

"Can I tell him, grandpa," she asked. He nodded and sat on log. He followed suit and took a deep breath. She could tell he was working hard as the beads of sweat rolled down his face. "He's teaching you how to be a farmhand so you can blend in better and increase your stamina. I've gone through grandpa's 'training.' You'll be a farmhand in no time, trust me." She watched as his face fell and he glared angrily at the wood. "I thank you for doing this too, because this is normally my job. They can't really do it anymore; and, believe me, cutting this stuff is much harder at night." A small blush coloured his cheeks as she headed for her car.

When she returned home that evening she found him sleeping soundly on the couch. She couldn't help but giggle. Darrow slept like he did after life-threatening events, but that time it wasn't because he was nearly killed.

Her grandfather patted her shoulder. "I was right in saying he's stubborn but has no stamina without his magic. This is the third nap today." She looked to him confused. He smiled warmly and hugged her shoulders. "Based on what I've seen from his father, their energy comes from the earth's life force. I want to get him away from that. It would make him a better and stronger man. "Once he learns to use his own strength and builds that stamina, I can see him withstanding much more."

Evelyn felt more confused than before. He must have sensed it as he continued with an example.

"Let say he's like that TV. You give it electricity and it works, take it away and it doesn't. It's the same with him. Take away the earth and any living thing, his electricity, and he wouldn't be able to swing his sword for more than a few strikes." He smirked and patted the sleeping man. Darrow grumbled and rolled over, trying to hide his face. "He may show muscle definition but that's all it is. It's a show, reason why he's so thin."

She nodded and watched while he slept. She never thought about it before. She knew she wasn't light, but he was still able to lift her despite his size. It reminded her of an ant, and she wondered if that was how they were able to carry things ten times their size. It made her wonder if anything else could use magic. Perhaps that only people like her, what he called Engardonians, couldn't. She wondered if in the past they could and something stopped it. She couldn't see such power be dropped by people so willingly.

It then returned her attention to what happened the night before. The mercenary had mentioned an ultimate weapon and the inventor of robots. She first had to get past the fact that mercenaries still existed. She believed they were only part of stories. Knowing they existed caused her to shiver. They were dangerous and that man had threatened to kill them for the weapon, something that they knew nothing about but was determined that they did.

However, as was pointed out, Darrow did. Even Alder knew what this weapon was and he was supposed to be a younger soul than his. She could see his sword being the wanted item. It could take life from things and instill it in others. She wondered if there were others like it. She imagined there would have to be. In all the stories, there was always talk of magical weapons, many of them. The thought of only one was strange to her.

Then there was the mention of the robot inventor. There were many out there trying to create the computerized life form, but one man stuck out in her mind. Damian Airiman wasn't much older than she, but had already started a company looking into robots and had successfully made a prototype. He was cruel and paid for everything he desired. If he wanted someone's research, he would pay them. If they didn't accept, there were rumors that he would have them killed and take the research. They disappeared if they didn't accept the offer.

The more she thought about the man, the more fear crept into her heart. His perfect cut black hair and cold brown eyes continued to haunt her from the day he visited her office. He wanted the whereabouts of a client and she refused to give him answers. He became quiet and made her skin crawl until another worker interrupted. He followed her instead and let her be.

"What are you thinking about?" Darrow asked, pulling her from her thoughts. His voice startled her and she gasped.

She shook her head as he watched her sleepily. "It's nothing. Just a bad memory of someone," she lied. She watched as he raised his eyebrow. He wasn't fooled but wasn't going to press the issue. She was glad that he had learned better.

When it was time for bed, he followed her. She crossed her arms and explained that they couldn't share a bed anymore. Her grandparents wouldn't allow it. Before, it was for special circumstances. He sat on her bed and watched her. He was silent but his actions told her that he wasn't leaving. She sighed heavily and left him there to change in the bathroom.

When she returned, he remained sitting on her bed, watching the door. Again she told him he couldn't stay in her room but he didn't move.

"Are you sure it's alright for me to stay?" he finally asked. She nodded and couldn't think of a reason why he couldn't. "You've got nowhere else, and I'd doubt that lunatic would let you go back after letting me escape. Besides, I think grandpa likes you. He hasn't offered to train anyone in years and people do come and ask."

Darrow nodded but looked out the window. It was her turn to wonder what he was thinking about. She asked but he slowly shook his head. She sat down beside him and patted his back. "A good looking man like you is going to fit in. You just have to find a way to hide your ears... and that tail." She watched as it twitched lazily on her bed. Her grandfather said it was irregular for them not to have one and that his friends did.

Evelyn watched as a strong blush burned his cheeks and ears.

"You think I'm a good looking man?" he questioned quietly.

Her eyes widened. She didn't quite realized what she had said until he repeated it. She turned away as she felt her cheeks burn. "Well..." She cleared her throat, feeling her embarrassment crush her. She couldn't believe what she had said. "Nearly every girl wants a hero to rescue her. Looking like an elf is usually a bonus."

She felt his hand turn her face towards him. Quickly after, his softened lips pressed gently on her forehead. She felt her heart quicken. It had been a long time since she felt his tender kiss. The last she remembered was in the Prophecy Mountain and even then it was surreal. As he pulled away, she could feel her heart wanting him to stay. She watched his sleepy yet content smile pull away from her.

"Have a good sleep, Eve. I promise you'll see this work horse in the morning."

Chapter 18

Two-Year Explosion

A few years had passed since Evelyn came out of the gate and her world had drastically changed. She couldn't complain. She remembered how she always wanted change so desperately, how she was bored of her regular routine of work and sleep. Lately, she had been finding herself wanting her old life back. She remembered how there wasn't as much drama then as there was in her present.

All of it revolved around Darrow. She could hear them gossip at work about how this foreign man showed up at her farm. He had become a large part of the farming community in the few years he'd been there. They always asked where he was from, but Evelyn didn't really have an answer. The only thing she could think of was that he was from one of the more remote islands off the coast. She couldn't tell the truth. She could hear others sneer that he was a slave that was bought from one of the poorer islands. She could only snort at those people. As if her family had that much money or morals to promote such behavior.

Though she couldn't blame them for gossiping about him, the man did appear from nowhere. Once he mastered the work on her grandparent's farm, he helped the others out. Soon they paid him for it. Once he earned their trust, he started using his magic and herb knowledge to heal their animals. The farmers were always astonished by how easily he could cure them. His excuse was the herbs he would feed the sick animals, but she saw the bits of magic that he threw in secretively.

His fame with the neighbor farmers spread. The city folk drove out to see him if their pets were sick. It gave him enemies from some of the local veterinarians, but he gained far more allies. It had gotten to the point where they wanted to take him to court for misconduct of animal practice. No evidence was found. It had the opposite effect as they discovered his medicine was far healthier than those who pitted against him.

His presence gave him a better sense of his peaceful self. It took quite a few months before his tension had nearly ceased. He was comfortable around her grandparents. He regarded her grandfather like his own father, almost to replace the one he lost. Even Alder was more open and receptive to new people as she watched him bound through the fields.

It was another thing about him that had changed. Darrow allowed his wild side through more often. The more often Alder was out, the more he matured. At first he was like a toddler, curious with everything and playing with anything he could get his hands on. With more practice and experience, it was hard to distinguish between the two personalities. Darrow and Alder were very much like twins, having their own likes and dislikes. One thing they did share in common was their gentleness towards her.

His fondness raised more rumors from her workplace. Her co-workers spun tales of how he was there to woo her, how he wanted to take her back to his island and marry her. She could only sigh and ignore them, as denying it only added more fuel to their gossip. When she denied it, they talked about how she had to stay with her grandparents, and how once they'd pass, Evelyn would run off with her strange suitor. It was completely unbelievable. The most that they had done remotely romantic was her taking him out to see the city. He wanted to know how she lived and it was the best thing for him to learn.

She couldn't deny that she enjoyed his company. The times they spent alone, whether walking in the forest or at the busy Redgate mall, she cherished. He would sometimes tell her that she had calmed his angry soul, but she felt the opposite was also true. He showed her how to trust someone again. She was afraid to be used as the past few boyfriends had. She knew she could trust him as she had in the forest.

She felt like he pampered her. The moonlit walks and quiet discussions were enticing. He had tried to cook her dinner a few times. A failure from his lack of cooking skills, but she appreciated the effort. With his new contacts, he had arranged for her to try horseback riding and getting her a dog from one of the litters he helped deliver. From the way he treated her, she could see why they would come up with those rumors.

That evening, they were invited to a party by an old friend of hers. The invitation was for a formal dance. She could only smile as she knew the man well. Celthric Ledgerwood was the inventor of a popular strategy game called 'Deathclysm.' It would suit that the dance's theme was a masquerade ball. She wouldn't admit it to her coworkers, but she was thrilled to be invited as, for once, she had a guest.

As she waited with Darrow at the front door, she could feel her heart pound in her chest. His hair was cut short. He refused for her to buy him a new dress shirt. He had insisted on making it in his people's traditional ways and had used most of the hair he had grown out to make it. She wouldn't admit it, but the forest green colour really did suit the man. The black suit he had gotten with dress shoes made him look formal, which was an unusual sight.

He hid the slenderness of his ears with magic and he had tucked his tail within his dress shirt. He would still stick out, but it wasn't because of his heritage. The years he had been working without his magic made him bulk out. He was no longer the slender man who had more strength than what his body showed. The tone he had gained made her think of some of the movie stars she'd seen on television. She wisely hypothesized that he would be getting much attention from the female crowd.

She hadn't told Darrow, but she found him quite attractive. She had mentioned that he was for society's view, which was proven by the way his female customers swooned, but not her thoughts. Secretively, even from the first time she met him, she thought he was quite handsome. Watching him become the man she stood next to made her heart beat harder. She couldn't even look at him without feeling her face flush.

Darrow donned his plain brown mask as she passed their invitation to the door attendant. He smiled at her as she led him into the mansion. His eyes widened as they walked from the hallway into the ballroom. From its mahogany wood floors to the white marble and gold pillars to the spectacular three-story ceiling, she couldn't blame him for being overwhelmed. She had seen it many times before, but the crystal chandeliers still amazed her with their ambiance and beauty.

They walked slowly along the outside of the main crowd. She wanted to let everything soak in, since he lacked his usual focus. She watched as Alder's curiosity seeped out as Darrow touched the marble and gold. He asked her questions about the materials used. He then moved on to why her family didn't live in a house like that. She could only giggle and answer truthfully that her family was not as successful as her friend's.

They were led to a table by one of the waiters. Many sat with them. She recognized Celthric's wife, and she nodded curtly to her. His wife thought of Evelyn as a threat as she was friends with her husband, and she had made it clear many times. It was the reason why Evelyn didn't visit him anymore. She couldn't see the woman's reasoning. She had made clear she thought of Celthric as a brother since they had been best friends since childhood.

Soon Celthric joined them. His eyes lit up when he found Evelyn. "Evelyn, I'm so glad you could join us. It's been way too long since we've seen each other," he said cheerily.

Evelyn smiled as she missed his company. They spent countless days running through his house playing and scheming. "Yes it has. I bet I couldn't beat you at your game anymore. I haven't practiced," she laughed. She could remember the many nights they'd play as he was creating it, how she would roll the lucky number and mortally wound his character.

Celthric looked over and noticed Darrow. His smile grew and he walked over. "This must be the famous healer we've been hearing so much about. It's nice to meet you," he greeted while extending his hand.

Darrow stood and looked Celthric over. He hesitated, which was odd, but shook the offered hand. The brief instant they touched, he growled and bared his fangs. The smile on Celthric's face faded. He whispered something quickly before returning to his seat.

As Darrow sat next to her, she asked what bothered him. He shook his head and mumbled something about the water. She snorted and called him out on his lie. He had nothing to drink since they arrived. He shook his head again and told her to drop it. She glared at him, but his warning stare forced her to look away. Something about Celthric had set him off. She wished she knew what it was.

The dinner was pleasant with the slow-cooked roast, rich gravy, potatoes and various legumes. She had some wine with her dinner, which she also enjoyed. It was rare for her to like alcohol, but she knew Celthric would have chosen the best for his table. The talk was cheerful but there was tension between the two men since their handshake.

It wasn't long before couples started to dance with the music once their dinner was finished. Evelyn smiled at the scene. It was one of happiness. Once the partiers consumed more alcohol, there was doubt there would be scandal the next day. At least they could say they were having a good time. She was detached from the table she sat at. Besides her and Darrow, everyone else was a top manager of his company and was discussing business. It was always boring. It was why she never went alone.

When Darrow stood, it startled her from unfocused observation. He walked into one of the hallways and was soon followed by her friend. She frowned. Celthric was going to start trouble. With trouble came embarrassment, if it went too far. She rarely saw him mad and it was usually at the bullies from school. She excused herself and followed them.

The hallway was dark, but she could hear their heated conversations from one of the rooms. She quickly walked along trying to find them. A few times, she thought she had found them but opened the door to only find an empty room. She frowned after the failed third attempt. By then, she had become lost in the many hallways.

She sighed and sat down on one of the wooden benches. Normally, she was good at following voices, and they hadn't left that much before her. She had seen Celthric's tailcoat as they turned a corner. She shouldn't have lost them. She also should have seen them as she turned the corner shortly after them, but she didn't. When she realized that fact, her frown deepened.

The longer she sat, the clearer she could feel an uncomfortable pulse in the back of her head. She rubbed it and knew what it was going to become. She took the pins out of her hair and massaged her scalp. It had been a few years since she had her migraines. Ever since Darrow had received his memories, to be exact. Why were they returning if he had them all?

"I know what you are," she could hear someone whisper from the shadows. She groaned as she tried to open her eyes. Just as before, it was painful to keep them open and she couldn't see anyone. She took a deep breath and rubbed her eyes. "I know what you can do," she heard the voice again. She shook her head and asked them to leave her alone. She didn't want to be bothered. She didn't have any pain medication with her and knew that the headache wouldn't leave.

A hand grabbed her shoulder and she gasped. She tried opening her eyes again and saw a shadow of a figure through her watery vision. She shook her head and pushed him away. She was in no condition to fight and hoped they would take the hint. Instead, they grabbed the other shoulder and pushed her back onto the bench when she tried to stand. "You're not going anywhere like that," they teased.

"You'll be perfect," they whispered in her ear. The deepness of it was a man. She shuddered from his tone even still. The voice reminded her of an abusive love of hers. "You will draw him out and then we will have the weapon." She felt her breath catch in her lungs. They were still after whatever Darrow kept secret. They hadn't been after them since that night but they still pursued.

"I-I won't help you," she sneered defiantly.

He chuckled, his hot breath heating her neck. "What makes you think you have a choice?"

He grabbed her arm and made her stand. She stumbled and whimpered when her hands found the floor. Her head made it hard for her to hear what he was commanding her to do. He pulled her to her feet by her hair which made her scream. He slapped a hand to her mouth as the painful throbbing continued. She couldn't stop the tears. The pain was too much.

He guided her as she stumbled down the hallways. She wanted to find a bed. She wanted to pass out and hope that when she awoke that the pain would be gone. The kidnapper meant her hopes were in vain. They wanted her to lure Darrow to them. She hoped he would be smarter than that. She hoped the old, calculated man would know better.

She felt the cold winter night air pinch her bare shoulders. She recoiled and tried to push back to the heat. He pushed her forward, causing her to trip on some loose gravel beneath her. She cried out and shivered as the pounding intensified. He ordered her to stand, but she remained still. Some rocks had cut her face, shoulder and hands, stinging as warm blood beaded loose. She cried louder when he picked her up again. He made her take a few more steps before shoving her into what she assumed was a trunk.

"Now be a good girl and enjoy your new home," he snickered as he slammed it shut. The noise made her whimper as she held onto her head. She couldn't believe she was being kidnapped. She thought Celthric's home was the safest place to be and yet she had been shoved in a trunk. She cried silently as she heard the vehicle start. First, she followed a stranger through a blizzard, and her luck evolved into kidnapping.

She jolted as they started to move. They were driving slowly by the sound of the engine. It was loud even at that speed. As they went down the long driveway, she could feel her migraine worsen. She remembered the wasp attack. It was the same as before.

As the pain increased, she felt the similar push instinct. It encouraged her to push past the pain. It promised an escape if she would listen. She tensed all her muscles until she heard the man's voice.

"So it seems our client wants the Ledgerwood guy as well. Says this girl will lure both," he explained with glee.

The other one laughed. "Why those two would chase this trash is beyond me. Honestly, if I had my pick, I'd go for the guy's wife," she heard another man speak.

A stretch of awkward silence fell between them before they started again. "Do you know why he wants these people," the one asked.

The silence happened again before the other answered. Why were they hesitant to talk about it? "Seems this foreigner knows of an ultimate power that can change the course of history, and the client wants it. Ledgerwood, well I'd guess it's the company this client wants, but there's this rumor that his family has deep roots to that place. There's this one that says he can use magic, like what you see in movies, a sorcerer."

Her eyes snapped opened. Her friend knew nothing like that. He showed no sign of magic. She should know as she had seen more than her fair share in the last few years. She shifted over on her other side and ignored them. She needed a way out of there quickly. She had no worries that Darrow could track her. It also worried her. He couldn't get kidnapped and used. He needed to be free, just like the forest and its creatures.

She growled. The lump in her chest returned and her breathing stopped. She continued to push but felt it was easier than before. She pushed harder until she screamed. The lump expanded and grew along with the pain. Again, she exclaimed for the lump to leave. Within seconds, the lump exploded in a wave of heat.

She was launched from the trunk as the migraine subsided. The wind whistled by her ears as she flew. Her flight didn't last long as her body met with snow which turned deeper and covered long grass followed by leaves and branches. She lay still. Her screams ripped her throat. Her body burned at every nerve.

There was another explosion. The world spun. It must have been the vehicle she was wretched from. It ended like the wasps. Nothing but ash and pain. When the world faded, she swore she heard a furious howl in the distance.

Chapter 19

Partner

The world spun as Evelyn could hear a steady beeping. She wanted to open her eyes and find the noise. It was irritating and rhythmic. As she tried them, like everything else, they were too heavy for her to lift. It frustrated her. Her memory was worse. She couldn't remember much. She couldn't remember where she was or how she got there. The last thing she could remember was the ball, her running after Darrow and a car.

Her consciousness faded and cleared many times before she could focus. There was the beeping near her head. She wanted to silence it, but she had heard it before. The origin remained unclear. She could hear voices. They were muffled and somber but they were there. Why was their mood so gloomy? Since there was a party, people should have been happy.

Something pricked her. Her vocal cords let out a harsh groan. It burned like sandpaper. Shortly after, her entire body was washed in pain. She cried out to make them stop. She didn't understand why there was so much pain. She didn't drink to beyond her limit. She never did and never would. She was certain nothing bad had happened, but something in the back of her mind told her differently. As soon as the pain came, it went and her consciousness with it.

She awoke again. Her mind felt clearer than it had been before. She could feel the stiffness in her joints and the throbbing in her body. She wondered where it had come from when her mind sent her a vision of an explosion. It was one she had caused by pushing that lump out. It reminded her of the kidnapping, and with the kidnapping came the information of her friends.

She opened her eyes slowly. It was difficult as they were heavy. Her persistence was greater. She wanted to see where she was. As she opened them, she could tell her vision was a bit hazy. She blinked a few times before the vision of a white room was before her. She recognized it from the visits she had with her grandparents. She had somehow managed to get into a hospital.

As she looked around, she found a nurse adjusting her IVs. She groaned inwardly, knowing that needles were inserted somewhere. She wanted to get the nurse's attention but all she could manage was a grunt. It worked as she looked over. The nurse's eyes lit up when she noticed her opened ones. The woman instructed her not to move and quickly finished her task before running out of the room.

It wasn't long before a doctor followed the nurse. He asked Evelyn if she could hear him. She tried responding but could only manage another grunt. He explained a system for answers, and she blinked once for yes just as he instructed. After some questions, he left the room with the nurse in tow.

Soon after them, Darrow sulked into the room. He looked exhausted as he rubbed the dark rings beneath his eyes. Tears stained his dirtied face. He hadn't been home since the party. He was still dressed in his dress shirt and pants which needed a wash. They were covered in dust and torn. He curled up in the only chair with his head facing away from her. It was hard to look at him; she couldn't move her head well.

She was about to try and get his attention when Celthric walked in.

Darrow perked up but didn't move from his seat. "I don't want to hear anymore," he whined angrily. His voice was harsh and scratchy but held a warning.

"I'm not here to try to convince you to leave. I wanted to check on her before I visit the office," Celthric snapped back. She sighed. They were both so stubborn.

She was about to interrupt them when they started talking again.

"I feel just as at fault as you. I usually have someone keep an eye on her. It was the reason why I challenged you. I know who you are, and I wanted to make sure that she's kept safe. I don't call her my little sister for nothing." It was true. Celthric was protective of her even when they were kids.

She heard Darrow snort and stir in his chair. "They're after me and the information I know. How does that involve you?"

She knew exactly why and wanted to tell them.

As she was about to try and get their attention again, Celthric continued. "There are many things you don't know about this era. Some I want to tell you but I can't for special reasons. I can tell you that you are not the only magic user." He rubbed his face and leaned on the bed, back to her. "The old decision is breaking because of that discovery made in Mordon. Whatever that thing is, it's making more users than the chosen families, which is a problem. Normal people cannot use it properly, like history has proven all too well."

"I don't care about your history. It's you Engardonians that made my life a living hell! Your decisions stripped me of my father, my mother, my home, my memories and now... I was finally happy, without anger, and this..." The room grew silent.

Celthric shook his head and walked to the door. "All I'm saying is be careful, Darrow. You not being in the past may disrupt the future, and she may not be here without you there," he lectured before leaving.

She heard his pitiful cries soon after he left. She hated seeing him cry. She wanted to comfort him but couldn't move from the bed.

Darrow started to mumble to himself angrily and pull at his hair. She grunted but he didn't hear her. Not knowing another, louder sound she could try, she stuck her tongue between her lips and blew.

The noise startled him and he looked up and around the room. He settled down and held his head in his hands. Again, she tried to speak but ended up with a squeak which caused her to cough. She whimpered from the burning in her ribs. She had a feeling a few of those were broken or bruise.

Her movement caused him to stand and look at her. When he met her eyes, more tears flowed. He moved quickly and she felt his dry lips against hers, desperate for affection. Her heart beat quickened, which showed on the monitor. She had missed his kiss. She tried avoiding them, fearful he would leave to return to the village. She couldn't deny it was hard to do.

He lingered there before pulling away. She felt him mouth 'oh mother' before he stood again. "I'm so sorry, Eve. I should have been there with you. I shouldn't have gone off. I..." He pulled back, tears splashing on her cheek. She sighed knowing he was tired. He had a hard time keeping his composure the longer he stayed awake.

It was a few days before the staff let her out of bed. Her tumble through the bushes dislocated her shoulder. She had broken a few ribs and bruised some others. Her leg had also broken from the impact. Doctors were surprised she survived the explosion as the other two had died, their bodies couldn't be found. All that was left were their charred wallets and clothes in the woods. When she was able to talk, the police interviewed her again. She explained everything she could remember, omitting the talk of the ultimate weapon and her being the reason of the hole in the road, but keeping that they were hired to get at Celthric.

A few weeks afterwards, Evelyn was able to return home under the condition that she wouldn't do anything strenuous. She wanted to beat the doctor who explained the rules in front of Darrow. He had taken his words to heart and wouldn't let her do anything on her own. He babied her. With some things, she was grateful that he helped, but with others, she wished he wouldn't. It was hard for her to accept assistance for things she knew how to do. She discovered that she was quite the independent person.

He had also become overprotective of her. Any visitors he would inspect and he'd order them to empty their pockets and bags. He refused to sleep in his bed and settled for sleeping on the couch. He insisted on keeping a baby monitor there in case someone was to break in and he couldn't hear it. By the end of the few months, she swore she wanted to kill him. She understood where his worry came from, but his reaction was extreme.

If what she overheard was any indication, he cared about her. The possibility of losing her had shocked him. He didn't want to lose someone else that was important to him. She asked if he took care of the mercenaries but said nothing on the subject. The dark expression spoke wonders, however, and that if he caught one that they'd wish they hadn't been.

His behavior changed. When he wasn't hovering over her, she found him rubbing something small in his hands. His hands glowed silver and green. She had asked a few times what it was. His answer was always nothing but his cheeks and ears would glow a dark red. Whatever it was, it was either about her or was too embarrassing for him.

When she had the casts removed and her physical therapy completed, she convinced Darrow to go for a walk. It was too long since she was able to walk in the forest. She missed the trees and sounds. The seasons had passed without her. He refused to let her as the doctor told them that she shouldn't push herself. She was elated when she was cleared. It meant greater independence and peace.

Darrow held her hand tenderly as he guided her through the branches. He was still protective but allowed freedom. One thing he refused was for her to carry a backpack. He wasn't convinced she was fully healed. His excuse was to make sure that she could complete the walk on her own. It was the condition before he agreed to take her anywhere.

She sighed as the warm summer breeze played with her hair. She enjoyed the sunlight on her skin as her light summer dress swayed. She didn't plan on a long walk. She just wanted to be outside. The days of being stuck in a chair frustrated her when she wanted to run. She had never thought of herself as an active person. Taking it all away was torture.

He led her to a clearing and laid out a large blanket on the ground. He helped her sit before removing his shirt, complaining it was too hot. He lay down beside her and stretched. A smile graced his lips and his tail twitch lazily. She cuddled close to him and rested her head on his shoulder. She could hear his heart quicken its pace. He squeezed her shoulders gently with his arm as he yawned.

"Eve, have you ever thought about having children," he asked quietly.

Her eyes snapped open. He normally didn't ask questions like that. She didn't expect him to ask it either. "Yes," she answered slowly, "why?"

He didn't answer but his train of thought did not falter. "How many?"

She shrugged her shoulders. "I never really thought about it that far. It would depend on the father I guess."

He grew quiet but it wasn't long before he continued. "Have you found a father," he asked, voice barely above a whisper. His questioning was odd. He would know if she had been seeing someone. Everyone else thought she was with him. Not like there were any hints that they liked her.

"No one has approached me, but you would know that." She sat up and looked at him. He sat up and turned away. She frowned but felt a shy smile when she noticed his ears turn red.

She decided to ask. "What's with all the questions?"

He shook his head and she noticed his shoulders tense. "Ha-have you ever thought about marrying someone," he asked nervously. Her frown returned. His questions were leading somewhere. It was a place where she didn't know if she wanted to answer. She noticed his ears turn a deeper shade of red from her silence. "N-n-never mind, Eve, forget I asked."

She shook her head. He was acting strange even for him. When she saw a slight tremble after he took a deep breath, she crawled around to investigate. He had been known to have anxiety issues since he regained his memories. She worried that it was one of those times. As she sat he took another deep breath. The nervousness had passed. He was playing with a golden chain in his hands like the one his mother wore.

He looked up to her with determination in his eyes. "Would you be my partner, Eve," he asked.

She looked at him confused. "Partner for what?" If he was going on an adventure, she knew she was not strong enough to go. She needed to heal more for that. He held her hands and she could feel a warm metal leaf against her skin.

"I-I mean marriage, Eve."

She stared at him dumbfounded. She had difficulty believing his words. He couldn't mean that. He was the one that told her a few times that they couldn't be together because of their differences. He would have to return to his own time one day.

Yet there he was, asking her anyways.

"You said we couldn't," she pointed out.

His face fell but he was persistent. "I know I did but... what happened to you last year made me think differently. Watching you lay there like my mother made me realize that all this..." He paused and sighed heavily. He still had issues expressing himself. He shook his head. "All this happiness was because of you. Everything that I've done here is because you helped me. This would not have happened if you weren't there with me. I want to keep living like this. I can be the man I want to be with you here." He smiled and pressed the metallic leaf in the palm of her hand. "I would rather risk giving you my soul and lose you to never love another knowing that, for that brief moment, you had my soul in your hands. I'd rather that than knowing I'd spend a lifetime never finding a partner that means to me as much as you."

She couldn't believe what she was hearing. The entire thing made no sense. He wouldn't want to marry her. He just wouldn't. She was too plain for such an extraordinary man.

They sat in silence. As it passed, his smile disappeared. He turned away from her and curled his tail around him. She looked to the leaf in her hand. It was made of dark green polished stone with golden rippled edges and veins. She thought it beautiful and felt his personality within it. She felt herself smile and knew the answer.

He had tried to always be there for her and had shown it when she couldn't care for herself. He was already a part of her family as he had lived with them for a few years. His touch was ever so gentle, and he tried his best to protect her. He had even given up his life and his mother's safety for her.

The more she thought about it, the more she was sure it was right. She had grown to love him. Not just anyone could accept his quirks. The way he mumbled to himself in his language to process things. How he'd purr when he heard the sound of rain on the windows or when she'd rub his back. His love for hunting and his gentleness to heal the animals then let them go. The fact was that he had two personalities in which the other was an animal first but still intellectual. There was always only one answer.

She tied the pendant around her neck. As soon as she did, she felt his warmth explore her from the inside. It was if his embrace was holding onto every vein, every nerve. She teared from the feeling. She adored his cuddles and felt like it was that feeling that was staying. She smiled and crawled to face him, still feeling the tingle of the magic.

He looked up slowly from his hands. When he saw the pendant, his eyes widened. "You weren't…" he began as his eyes lingered. "Eve?" he asked a bit confused.

She giggled before kissing him gently. "Yes, and we can hold the wedding next winter. I need time to organize everything," she whispered to him. She watched as he went from confusion to enlightenment to tears.

Suddenly the ground shook violently. She could hear the disturbance in the birds as he quickly held her under him. The trees groaned as some other snapped and fell. She watched as deer galloped past in terror. In her soul, she was frightened. Earthquakes never happened, ever, not in any history she'd heard.

They slowed and stopped. She held onto him tightly as lifted her from the ground. He looked around apprehensively as he continued to hold her. When he was satisfied, he packed up the blanket quickly. He shook his head, mumbling furiously. He put the pack on her and lifted her onto his back. She started to protest, but he snapped at her. She had no choice. As soon as her foot was off the ground, he ran for the house.

It didn't take long to get back. He opened the door and found her grandparents unharmed, but her grandmother was shaken from the quake. He let her down and breathed heavily. As he did, she noticed her grandfather sat calmly but had a dark look in his eyes. Darrow noticed as well as he commented on the other man's mood. Her grandfather shook his head and went to his room.

Her grandfather missed supper, which was unusual for the man. It was clear that food was his favorite thing. For him to miss it was extremely abnormal.

As the others ate, Evelyn told her grandmother about the proposal. She saw the brightened look in the old woman's eyes before she got up, hugged her and congratulated them both. When she let go, she began discussing everything that they would need to do.

It was well into the evening before her grandfather emerged from his room. He looked frustrated and walked around with the old leather book in his hands. They all looked up at him from their started wedding plans. He didn't acknowledge their presence as his hands continued to trace over the strange deer on the cover. He shook his head and left for the basement.

They were heading for bed when he climbed the stairs. In his arms were more books. It worried her that he had nothing to eat since lunch. He sat at his chair, put the books on the end table, opened one up and started going over it. When they didn't leave, he ordered them to go to bed. She frowned but knew better than challenge him.

Darrow didn't. "Are you alright, Mr. Ashmore," he asked. Evelyn shook her head and knew the storm that approached.

"I said go to bed! No questions," the old man barked. He was brisk, which made her worry more.

She decided to tempt fate. "Grandpa, you've been acting weird since the earth shaking. Did anything bad happen?"

He snorted and glared at her. "Yes, you got married in his tradition. Did he even explain to you how that works?"

She looked over and frowned. He only proposed.

Darrow looked away sheepishly. "She didn't give me time to explain. She put the necklace on before I could," he mumbled.

Evelyn held the pendant and looked back at the two of them.

He shook his head. "Sounds like my granddaughter." He paused before he continued. "I knew exactly what he'd been doing while rubbing his hands and that glow. In essence, Evelyn, you are holding a part of his soul in your hands. He'd been imbuing it with his power. It's like his promise ring, but in his culture it means you're married to him."

She looked between the two of them and understood his anger. Had she'd known the pendant was part of his culture's wedding ceremony, she wouldn't have put it on yet. She didn't give him a chance to explain.

Darrow was embarrassed as he continued to look at the floor. "You forgot a part," he whispered.

Her grandfather nodded and his features lost a bit of his anger. "Yes, the binding isn't complete until you have an offspring." He looked at Darrow darkly. Evelyn sighed, remembering how he treated the few boys she brought home. He wasn't treating this man any different.

He looked up and she could see rebellion in his eyes. "I have nothing but the utmost respect for you and Eve. If that's what she wishes, then I will not stop because of your warning," he stated. His courage faltered somewhat as he frowned. "She's the first that I've ever wanted to be with and I don't want some other female. Trust me when I say the feeling's mutual." She knew he meant; Alder felt the same.

Her grandfather nodded and stood from his chair. He grabbed Darrow's hand and shook it. "You better not hurt her or I will hunt you until I die, and even then your spirit won't be safe from me," he warned. He nodded, and she watched as Alder's mischievous smile pull at his lips. "I mean the both of you." Darrow's lips pulled past his teeth before he snorted. She knew that it was a signal that the challenge was accepted by the inner animal.

He sighed heavily and slumped back into his chair. He ran his hands over his face and into his thin, wispy white hair while mumbling. He normally didn't mumble or stress over anything. He shook his head and looked to the two of them. "I have a feeling that you don't believe that's the only reason why, isn't that right, Darrow."

Darrow crossed his arms and nodded. "I could tell it was the shaking. I didn't like it either. My question is why? The girls were upset but you have sensed this before haven't you?"

Her grandfather nodded as he stood from his chair again. He only became restless when something bothered him. He turned off the lights and opened the window curtains. The stars were brighter than usual and were beautiful. Evelyn joined him at the window and saw that he wasn't as impressed. "You're right, I have. The magic that is buried in this world made everyone forget the magic of that day. Everyone but me..."

Chapter 20

The Beginning

The sun was hot as it beat down on his darkly tanned skin. The summer sun was determined to dry out the crops that year. It was nothing unusual. Every five to ten years there would be a dry spell only to promise double crops the following year. As he was told by many farmers including his own parents, it was just the way of Garlandon. The cycle never failed.

He sat on a stump just outside the field and wiped the sweat from his face. It was his first year owning a farm. Sure, he had been a farmhand for most of his life, but he felt owning one was harder. There was more to worry about than just if the job got done. He had to make sure ends met, as well as his wife's happiness. He smiled as he knew that his wife would never be an issue. The woman was naturally happy and her smile glowed like the sun.

"Christopher, lunch," he heard her call.

His stomach growled as he could only imagine the savory flavors of her cooking. "Coming, Jocelyn," he called back. He stretched as he stood. He couldn't believe how the time flew. He swore it was still early morning when he last checked. He decided to leave the plants be while he ate. He had faith that they wouldn't wilt by the time he returned. It was as if Edgar's farm had magic buried in its dirt. It was always the only one unaffected by the shifting sun.

As he walked into the house, he could smell the stew cooking on the stove. His stomach rumbled louder as it demanded to have the aroma. He climbed the few steps and sat at the table. On his plate was his usual sandwiches and large glass of milk. He smiled up at her as he felt his heart flutter. They had known each other since they were children and, like him, she knew the last owner of the farm.

"We are expecting company in a few days," she informed him. He stopped mid-bite and waited for her to continue. She sat as she laughed. She shook her head and patted his arm. "Yes, before you ask, it is them. Three of them will be coming this time."

He smiled and felt his spirit soar. It had been a while since he had seen his new friends. He missed them. Last they were there, they mentioned they would bring their son with them. He was curious as to which one the boy would look more like.

He finished eating his lunch and was about to head back out when a knock came to the door. He frowned knowing that he wasn't expecting someone that day. As not many people visited, he cautiously checked. He looked through the window and saw a scraggly man with greasy black hair. The man's eyes sent shivers through him and knew who he was. He came to the house nearly every day. Christopher saw the evil in his eyes and never allowed him more than a few steps into the house. Ever since he lost the battle at the court hearing, he had been returning.

"Don't make me call the police again, Mr. Baltazar. You have your answer and it will never change," Christopher warned angrily. At first he claimed the land was his inheritance as his family was the rightful owners. It never held in court as the records showed it was always in the Tisen name. His current bargaining tool was all the money he would ever need.

"I want this land, Ashmore," Baltazar bickered through the door. "It has the best soil in all of Garlandon. Can you not share the wealth with other farmers?"

Christopher signaled to Jocelyn to call the authorities. He was in no mood to hear him that day. "This farm was given to me and my wife. Unless you've changed gender, you do not fit the description." He remembered in school, even though he was one of the older children there, everyone teased Baltazar about how much he resembled a girl. He was feminine with his smooth skin, long hair and lack of muscle definition. He didn't find it as amusing and ignored the more popular people. It was not part of his morals to insult others. This man became an exception.

He watched as the comment infuriated the visitor. He had a feeling the bullying still haunted him.

Baltazar slammed his fists on the door. "Give me what is mine! The lord demands it," he screamed. It startled Christopher and he backed away from the door. It was the first time the man was violent. Christopher reached for the old pistol that was concealed nearby. Edgar was prepared for lunatics like him.

He warned Baltazar again to leave, but he continued to pound on the door. "I'm tired of waiting! I will move you by force if I have to. This place is mine. All of Garlandon is mine! You will not keep me from my lord's promises." He continued to rant.

Christopher refused to allow Jocelyn to worry as he noticed her fleeing to the bedroom. He opened the door quickly and pressed the cold metal of the gun to Baltazar's forehead. He froze as his arms hung in the air where the door used to be. "This is my last warning. I will not let you threaten my wife. You come here again and I will kill you. Just remember, I own that forest and there are plenty of places to hide a twig like you in it."

He watched as Baltazar quickly ran to an expensive car and drove off. He shook his head and hid the gun again. How that man grew such a fortune was beyond him. Baltazar was from an impoverished family and had to be one of the smallest children of that district. He had never graduated from elementary school and didn't have a job. When Christopher had inherited the farm, he suddenly had all that money and no one questioned it, as if some higher being helped him.

It wasn't long after he sat at the table, once again, with the policemen. The only difference was the report. He didn't enjoy threatening people. He was also graciously given a restraining order from the man but it never helped. He bothered them anyways, acting like he was above the law.

Christopher grumbled as he lay in bed that night. The man was such a bother. If it meant just giving up the farmland, he would do so in a heartbeat to be rid of his torment. However, the farm meant more than that. Not only was it a place where he spent a good portion of his childhood, it meant a great deal to his late friend. In Edgar's letter, he asked Christopher to guard his family, explaining that, in the forest, was a gate that connected him to them.

He never questioned how odd it was. He swore he would never enter it. As a child, Edgar would tell the children stories of gigantic insects that could swallow them whole. It frightened them enough that they never went too far into the woods. As Christopher grew older, logic took hold. He walked around it many times. It was the same on both sides. Logic dictated that it would simply be the same if he walked through it. He remembered trying to open it once, as his curiosity got the better of him but couldn't. It was locked and refused to open even though there was no keyhole to be found.

It was like everything on the land he inherited. Everything was made of wood. Out of curiosity, he invited an expert in antiques to look at the farm. The man spent a good day looking at everything and was more astounded by each piece he looked at. By the end of the day, he concluded that everything was hundreds of years old but was as lively as the day it was cut from the tree. It never rotted and kept its lively quality.

The few days that passed were not eventful. He was impatient to see his friends, and the days dragged on. The sun was hotter than it had ever been, and he felt his skin burn. The trees had become his friends as he had to take constant breaks to allow the baking flesh to cool. He could tell the cows and other animals felt the same as they joined him in the shade.

It was on one of those breaks when he heard the whinny of a horse. He perked up and looked at the large path that was carved into the woods. Two tall, wooden posts marked the entrance. They had stood guard for decades. He knew the sound of the horses. He knew when they came from that path that his friends had arrived.

He watched as two beautiful deer emerged from between the posts. Riding the buck was a lean, muscular man. His deep green eyes surveyed the area as he sat proudly on his steed. His long, blond hair was tied back with a green string which matched his short sleeved tunic. His rough pants were brown and were tucked into his leather boots, his fingerless gloves were made of the same material. Around his neck hung a pendant of a brown feather, held on by a golden chain. His ears were long and pointed, much like that of an elf from stories.

The doe carried a beautiful woman. She was slender and her long ears were pierced with golden hoops. Her brown hair was long and was left to play in the wind. She too wore a green tunic, though it was long and fell past her knees. Her boots and gloves were made of leather much like his. Her stone gray eyes watched caringly at the head of light brown hair in her lap. It was dressed just like the man as it clung to her waist and wasn't much longer than his arm. Emerging from the pants was a small, monkey-like tail which twitched lazily.

The man found what he was searching for. He watched as a large smile spread to reveal long canine teeth. He descended his horse and jogged over. Christopher braced himself before he was pulled to his feet by the visitor.

"Christopher! It's so good to see you again," exclaimed the man excitedly as always.

He could hear the man's thick accent as some of the words were forced. "Yes, Arron, almost too long," he greeted breathlessly.

He heard the woman's chime-like chuckle as she guided the deer over to them. She said something in her language and Arron promptly released him. He took a deep breath as he patted him on the back.

"Sorry about that friend. I forget that you're not like us." He nodded and stood up straight. He was an enthusiastic man and extremely energetic. His partner was quiet and reserved.

"Good afternoon to you, Rosena," he greeted. She smiled and nodded. She was never one for many words.

They let loose the deer as they always did and followed him to the house. Inside, Jocelyn was busy cooking what he assumed was supper. He could smell the fresh pork that he had traded a few baskets of vegetables and milk for. The night's supper would be more than fantastic. When she noticed them, he saw her smile brighten as she walked over to greet them.

They sat around the table and, not soon after, Christopher heard the question that he wanted to know about.

"What's his name?" Jocelyn asked pointing at the young child in Rosena's lap. She chuckled and spoke to him quietly. The light brown hair shook, and he remained cuddled in his mother's arms.

Arron laughed and petted his head. "Unfortunately, my son isn't used to travel. It's his first time away from the village, really." He looked over to his hosts and smiled. "His name is Darrow. He's usually full of energy, but I think I wore him out before we got here." He began to laugh as Rosena shook her head.

"You keep forgetting he's just a boy," she said quietly. He shook his head, but he could tell the boy's mood did not falter. "The boy is turning ten next year! When I was his age, I was able to run circles around my father, Creanni protect his soul."

Rosena sighed and looked at their hosts apologetically before looking back at her husband. "Yes, but you also jumped off the tallest tree as a child trying to prove that you could do anything and nearly died. I do not see him being so reckless." Arron wanted to retaliate but looked away. She had won.

Just then, Darrow's little head looked around sleepily. His grey eyes, only half-open, tried to survey the room to find the noise. His searching stopped at them and he rubbed his eyes. He looked up to his mother and pointed at the two strangers. She smiled and whispered. His eyes widened as he looked back. He was a bit frightful as he jumped onto his father's arm, climbed onto his head and tried to hide in his hair. He was pulling some strands; Arron flinched from the movement.

"He can be a bit apprehensive with new people," Arron explained as he tried to untangle him. Darrow growled and buried himself deeper. Arron sighed as he spoke to his son. The boy shook his head and continued to hide. "Give him a bit. He'll come out."

Christopher nodded and smiled. He had seen many children hide behind their parents when around new people. Seeing one small enough to nearly hide on his father's head was new.

"At least you know he won't try to do anything to hurt himself," piped in Jocelyn.

They looked at each other sheepishly. "Not quite true, friends," he said. He chuckled nervously as rubbed his back. He could hear purring follow as the child nuzzled the top of Arron's head.

"The boy has a unique talent which caused us to step on him a few times." Rosena sighed and shook her head. "He has an uncanny ability to hide anywhere by using the things around him."

Darrow smiled as he untangled himself from his father's hair. He was quite proud of his ability.

"In the house, he'll blend into the carpet. Out in the grass or in the trees, you'll never find him. Quite the escape artist."

They stayed the night and packed to leave the next morning. It was a short trip. It was all they could spare as they were needed back home. It upset Christopher as he enjoyed the man's company and he didn't have the pleasure often. He would learn a little more about them each visit but it was never enough. Learning about Arron's people was one of the few things that truly interested him.

As Arron prepared his saddle, he turned to Christopher. "I have a present for you," he said with odd seriousness. He passed him a book bound with leather. Etched in its front was a curious creature. It looked like stag with moose antlers. Its hooves were replaced with strangely shaped paws where new sprouts grew. The sight of it caused a strange peace and security within him. It was as if he knew the creature was there to protect him.

Arron looked up to his friend and saw the smirk. He placed his finger beside animal, seemingly careful not to touch the depiction. "I know your people have forgotten everything of the old ways," he told Christopher softly. He continued to smile. "This is to explain my people, as I see the curiosity stir in your soul when I talk of home." He opened the book and the title page held a coloured depiction of the creature in all its earthly tones. "Read this and you will know all about my people. You will know of our function and, most importantly, you will learn about one of the forgotten children."

The more Arron spoke, the more it confused Christopher. He chuckled before Darrow leapt from his mother's lap onto his head. He spoke excitedly to him before looking up. He could see that the boy was filled with life and happiness, which made him smile. It suited him well. Darrow held out his little hand to Christopher as he leaned on his head. He reached and touched it with his opened palm. Where Darrow touched tingled.

He held it there before the child said something, smiled brightly and jumped back onto his mother's lap. Arron reached over and ruffled his hair. Darrow giggled and hid himself in her arms. He looked back over.

"He trusts you, which is surprising. The boy doesn't trust any soul back home." Arron smiled, and Christopher noticed a hint of sadness. "Children seem to know more about the world than we do. I wonder when we lose our connection with our Mother."

He jumped onto the stag and settled on its back. He looked to the sky and Christopher's gaze followed him. Dark clouds were forming. It was not a good sign for travel. His crops, on the other hand, would love a good rain. They looked back at each other. "May Learthdelsea's grace protect you, Christopher. A storm is coming. One I fear will do more harm than good."

Arron's prediction had come true. There was a storm, one that drowned the crops and killed every field. The animals cowered in the barn, trying to find an escape from the heavy rain fall. Christopher could feel them jump every time thunder roared. He had to admit it frightened him as well. He had talked to a few farmers and never in history had there been such a storm.

It ravaged on and off for days. It would break only to start again with more anger. It was like the heavens themselves were furious over the land dwellers. As the storm raged outside, he would sit away from the windows and comfort Jocelyn. She trembled in his arms as she also claimed that the storm was unholy. Nothing natural would last that long.

A few months passed and with it brought the earth shakes. The land flooded and shook; the water from the outside splashed against the house. He worried for the animals. They couldn't escape easily and had less protection than he did. He cautiously looked outside during one of the breaks. He had to focus as he swore he saw a nearly transparent orb protecting the barn. He shook his head. Nothing like that could exist.

As they listened to the radio, hoping for some sign of relief, he tried reading the book given to him. It explained otherworldly things. It explained the ways of magic and how to use it, which he frowned at. Magic didn't exist. It depicted monsters and creatures that he had never seen before, and most likely no one else had either. Giant insects and leeches didn't exist. It told of four god-children, one of conflict, one of knowledge, one of life and one of death. How they were to guide their guardians on their culture's way of life. How they were actual beings that mingled with the people. Those gods didn't exist either.

It told of The Mother Creanni and how she had created those children to watch over the world as she slept. He believed in Creanni; the world believed in Creanni. It told of the Gate of Life. How it was a link between the present and the past. How The Mother told an ancient family that the land needed protecting in the future. She told her first child, Learthdelsea, to pick a guardian and send them to the future to protect its land, how that family could blend in with the 'round-ears' using magic. The Gate was true; it was there in the forest. The rest made the book unbelievable.

Edgar must have been one of the chosen. It made him think. Why would he give the land to Christopher if it was supposed to be in his family? His god was supposed to choose an heir. Was something going to happen to them? Something so destructive that he had to pass on the role to a... round-ear?

The earth shook again, followed by thunder. What was left of the china fell to the ground. He had to find Arron. He could use magic. He could do something to stop the chaos. If what the book said was true, then he must have been a guardian. If he understood the scripture right, only the guardian could pass through the Gate. He told her to stay put and keep safe. Arron was the only chance they had.

He ran as quickly as he could to the basement. He put on his farming clothes, followed by chest waders and his hunting coat, hat and gloves. He looked around. If he was going to cross that door, he would need protection. If that book was right, then he would be at the bottom of their food chain. An easy prey. He found his shotgun locked in its case. He knew it would be his best option, his only option really. He packed it up in his hunting case and ran back up the stairs.

He looked around for a good exit that didn't put his wife in danger. He couldn't use the door. What they'd been trying to keep out would probably burst in. As he looked around, he felt something pull at his arm. He looked over and saw the terror in Jocelyn's eyes. He smiled softly at her.

"I know you're going to find, Arron," she whispered as her eyes watered. She handed him a small bag. He had a feeling she packed him some food. He was usually always hungry while hunting.

He kissed her softly and held her tightly. "I promise I'll come back. Dead or alive, I'll come back for you."

He didn't want to leave her. If it wasn't for the unknown, he'd bring her with him. She was a strong girl and a better shot than he was, but she didn't have the stamina like him. He could push himself if needed. She, as they had found out, couldn't push hard or else she'd need a doctor. He went to the door and handed her the hidden pistol. "If anyone threatening comes in here, I want you to kill them. With what's happening out there, I don't care about the law. I want you safe." She nodded and placed it on the table.

He found a window he could fit through and removed the screen. The sound of the outside was worse with it open. He closed it and turned to her. "I love you, Jocelyn, and I will come back. Just like when we were kids, I promise to come back for the princess." He saw her bright smile as she returned his feelings. He chuckled at he kissed her forehead, remembering playing knights as children. He always protected and rescued her and when he would leave, he always promised he would come back. He kept his word every time. He pulled away, opened the window and jumped through.

As soon as he landed, he could feel the wind push him every which way. It was strong and it howled loudly. He could tell getting to the Gate could prove to be a challenge as he slowly trudged along. The water splashed at his knees while the wind picked it up and drenched his face. He growled angrily. He had to be insane to be out there, but he had to protect her.

As he neared the tree line, his thoughts changed. He noticed a strange dark light emanate from it. It was wrong. He could feel in his gut that it was un-natural. As he watched the trees, he could see their bark being burned off as the leaves shrivelled and turned to ash. It couldn't have done that as the rain pounded on the canopy above. The black light meant death.

As he neared the gate, he could feel his body react to the exposure. He could feel it burn his face and squeeze his insides. He turned away and wiped his face with his gloved hand. The feeling was still there. He wanted to turn back. He wanted the protection of his home. He turned towards the glow. If he were to return, the light would spread and hurt Jocelyn.

He neared enough that he could finally see the gate. Its white light washed over him and soothed any pain the dark inflicted. A shadow of a man stood before it with arms outstretched. The black light came from him as he directed it to the gate. The more he watched, the better he understood. The unnatural weather was caused by those two. The shadow was attacking the gate while it defended itself. From his readings, this battle was what caused the weather.

"Open to me! I command you to open the past. Lord Devren demands it!"

Christopher recognized the shouts. It explained why Baltazar didn't pester him anymore. He had snuck onto the land and had gone after what he wanted. It then made sense why Leigh Baltazar wanted his land. It was never for farming. It was for the Gate of Life.

"Since that damned farmer wouldn't give up his lands, I have to take them by force," he cursed at the door. The door groaned in return. They must have been fighting for a long time. "The trees may listen to him, but he has no real power. You must know this." He turned away as a greater flux of white light disturbed the forest. "It's the truth and it angers you. He can only stand by while I destroy everything he loves. Isn't that right, Christopher?" Baltazar looked over to where he was hidden. He couldn't believe he knew he was there. He never said a word and was quieter than the wind. He even blended into the trees.

He cackled as he turned back to the door. "This is what your ancestors gave up. They chose to lock away the power because of a war that nearly destroyed the planet." His laughter increased as the black light grew to overpower the gate. "All this locked away by the choice of some insignificant guardian!"

He quickly reached for his weapon, readied it and shot Baltazar's shoulder. Both lights vanished along with the earth shakes and the storm when the bullet made contact. The black clouds parted and welcoming sunlight burst through. The man stood swaying and mumbled to himself. He didn't scream. He didn't cry. He stood and stared blankly at the ground.

"The protector shot me," he heard Baltazar call out. His head snapped up. "You see what he did, Creanni? Your child defiled my flesh."

Christopher walked from the woods and readied another round.

Baltazar looked from the gate to him. His face elated. "You are like me, both against Mother's wishes. Come with me and I'll share my power."

Christopher frowned and aimed for his head. The happiness left and replaced with a dark look. "I'll make one thing clear, lunatic. I am not like you and never will be like you. I am Christopher Ashmore and I protect my friends and I love my wife. I warned you I would kill you if you came here again," he growled menacingly.

Baltazar backed away slowly. "Now, now, Ashmore, there's no need to be hasty. Remember, I can give you anything you want."

He snorted and began to pull the trigger. "I have all I want with the exception of you. You want to make a deal? You want to make my life better? Then disappear! Leave my family and this gate alone. Can you do that? Can you make that wish come true," he spat.

Baltazar smiled, which confused him. What did he say that was so funny? "Open that gate and I'll give you that wish," he offered.

He circled and stood with the gate behind him. "That's not my wish and it will never happen."

Baltazar chuckled and stepped towards him. Christopher retreated until his back touched the door. He didn't like the look he was getting. He aimed and shot for the man's head but it went through him. He looked at him in horror. It was at point blank range, there was no way he could have missed.

"Poor farmer can't even hit a lunatic at, what, one…" he took a step. "Two," he took another step. "Three paces? Poor baby farmer." The lunatic laughed as he stood mere inches away. All sense of bravery drained from him. He felt like a child again, one who was facing the monster under his bed. This time the monster was real.

"Let's show you how to really kill someone." He smirked as he placed his hands on Christopher's chest. He wiggled against the door and tried hitting the wounded shoulder hard, but his attacker never flinched. He felt his skin burn where the hands were placed. The pain intensified the longer they stayed. He cried out as he tried escaping. He couldn't and soon felt his feet lifted from the ground. "Now give me that strong soul of yours. I'll make good use of it."

Christopher felt something pull at his heart. It hurt far worse than anything he had felt before. He tried kicking as he saw the black light again. He had to get away. If that was what magic was used for, then it was good riddance. It was nothing but another weapon to kill things, something else to tear families apart.

As he felt his consciousness slipping away, he felt the door open slowly behind him. He begged for it to stay closed. It couldn't allow the evil into that place. Arron said it was peaceful. Everyone helped each other. It was beautiful and free.

"Please," he cried, "don't let him in. Let me die, just don't let him in." It opened more and he fell to the ground, into the darkness.

Chapter 21

Where It Started

His mind stirred. He was exhausted as if he had been running for hours. He felt hot and drenched in sweat. He rolled over and was disturbed that his pillow was missing. When he tried to bury his face in the mattress, he felt sand instead. He opened his eyes quickly. He was staring at the dirt. He sat up and felt the world spin. He held his head in his hands and tried to grab at what happened.

Slowly he remembered the storm and how the earth shook. It led him down the watered forest path to the gate. Attacking the gate was Baltazar. He shot the man and injured him. He then used magic on him and was saved by the gate.

He looked up and saw that he was lying next to the forest door. Its normally bright, lively leaves were shrivelled and tinged with brown. He stood up slowly. The forest was bright and the path missing. It was more than strange. As he looked around, he found his gun had also vanished. He turned and walked to where he thought his home was, but when he knew he should have reached it, he got nothing but trees. His farm, and his wife, was gone.

He turned back. He couldn't have been in past. It was illogical. He remembered the lights and the horrid pain. He shook his head. At that point, he had to know it could be possible. He had been subjected to enough magic to know better.

He tried opening the door. It was locked. He looked for a way to unlock it but quickly gave up. He knew better. He pushed and pulled and it wouldn't budge. He cursed at the magical structure. It wasn't supposed to let him in. He would have gladly died if it meant keeping that insanity in the future. Having access to the past, he could change everything that he knew.

He turned around and explored the forest. He hoped that he was heading in the right direction. He had only one option. He had to find Arron. He was his only way home. He rubbed his face with worry and felt the stubble that grew. How long he was out for? He hoped it wasn't for too long. Judging from the sun, he had to guess it was morning.

He walked until dusk. The setting sun caused an unsettling feeling. He had nothing to defend himself against whatever beasts prowled the night. He looked around and saw a pine with its branches sweeping the ground. It would have to do. From the other pines surrounding, it he found the widest branches to further hide himself from the creatures. As he curled close to the roots, he wondered if Jocelyn incessantly worried about him back at the farm.

The next morning, he was greeted by the sounds of snarling outside the branches. It was loud. As he looked around franticly, he found something large just outside the branches. He remained still. Whatever it was did not sound friendly, and he had no wishes to meet death early anymore. He watched as it slowly moved away from his hideaway. As it did, it removed some branches from their places. It unveiled large amounts of fur but it was far too big to be a bear. The book came to mind, and for all he knew, it could have been one.

He was no longer safe being exposed as he was. When he was sure he heard the creature had moved on, he slowly crawled from behind the branches. He looked around carefully and let out a sigh of relief. He could see his journey ending quickly if caution wasn't taken. When it was clear, he left and continued his journey.

He soon met with a gorge he was familiar with. It was a deep scar in Doolk-fae's landscape. As he cautiously looked over the edge, he saw the familiar rapids that ran the span of the continent, mostly under the trees. Near him was a newer rope bridge. There was no crossing the gorge without it and could potentially save walking distance. He took a deep breath. He would have to chance it.

His journey was slow but thankfully uneventful. He did not enjoy being left open to attacks. It was a tactic that he used when hunting deer. He would lure them into the open and strike. He was happier being in the trees. As he walked, however, he could sense that perhaps something was watching him. He stood next to one of the large trees. Perhaps he was being hunted. He shook his head. He was beginning frighten himself. He needed a clear mind. It would be better that way.

Most of his day was as it was before. There was nothing but the sound of birds and his walking. As the sun began to set, he searched for another wayward pine. He found one but, as he approached, he stopped. The birds quieted and the forest along with it. He looked around franticly. He couldn't see any danger but the silence was unnerving.

Something hit him from behind. It had enough force to knock him over. He quickly flipped to his back, just in time to kick, hard, the attacker. He saw the shadow of a man tumble into the forest. It was his cue to run.

He sprinted through the trees and hurtled over fallen logs. He was thankful that his school had done track meets. It had certainly prepared him for his sudden flight. As he ran, he heard howling. It sent shivers through him. It had to belong to a wolf. He cursed his luck and powered forward. He hoped that they would give up on him and that his sudden dash would confuse them. It was either that or find Arron's village.

He had just jumped a log when something tackled his side. It knocked both of them over and the wind out of him. He swung his elbow and connected something. It cried out in pain. He quickly got up and ran again. His pace was slower than before as he felt his side pulsate with pain. Whatever it was hit him hard but he couldn't stop. Mother only knew what they would do to him.

Night had fallen and he kept running. The shadows hadn't stopped their pursuit and he was tiring fast. Running away was one thing. Keeping the pace all night was another. He tried jumping over another log, but his foot caught it. He tumbled over but quickly rolled under it. He hoped it would distract the chasers. As he lay hidden under the log he knew he couldn't go any further. His chest wouldn't allow it.

He heard them land but, like him, they stopped. He heard them talk amongst each other. He recognized the language. It was the same as his friend's. He looked up and could make out five human figures in the moonlight. Much like his friend, they were slender with long ears and a tail. Unlike him they had large antlers on their head. Christopher cursed at his luck. There was a chance they were from his village and there was a chance they were not.

They stopped when the one held up his hand. The leader sniffed the air and his lips parted to reveal the long canine teeth. The way they glistened in the moonlight chilled him. He remembered the movie that he brought Jocelyn to, a horror film about a werewolf. The way the men acted reminded him much like a pack.

The stranger neared the log and reached underneath. Christopher backed away as quickly as he could. He couldn't get caught. If he did, it would have been the first promise he would have broken to her. It would be his last. When the man didn't find anything, he looked under it. His bright blue eyes glowed freakishly in the dark as they dilated to see. He smiled and reached for his quarry. Christopher pulled his fist back and struck the man in the jaw.

He howled in pain as he escaped from the other side. He was about to run again when another man jumped him and pinned him to the ground. He whimpered from the impact. He had a bad feeling that some ribs were damaged. Another man grabbed his ears and pulled them up.

Then quickly dropped him as he gasped. Christopher looked up dizzyingly as the one he assumed grabbed him babbled quickly while pointing at him. He was lifted in the air and slammed hard against a tree. He felt himself cough from the force. He was not used to such abuse. He looked into the man's blue eyes. It was his last chance.

"Arron," he gasped at him. "Do you know Arron?" The hardened expression turned confused. The mana soon raged and slammed him against the tree, taking his consciousness.

He was confused but almost grateful when he awoke again. At least he wasn't dead. There may have been a chance to return back to his wife. As he stirred, he listened to the sound of dripping water. It was slow and it had formed a puddle below. As his mind focused, he found himself cold, unbearably cold. He shivered, irritating his broken ribs.

He opened his eyes to find his clothes were gone. He could feel the cold stone on his exposed skin. They left him with only his briefs. He sighed as he saw the shackles on his wrists and ankles. The chain led to the floor. They probably thought he was going to escape. He chuckled as he thought about his run. He gave them a good fight.

He groaned as he tried to sit. He was stiff. He could only guess it was from the dampness in the air. His lungs burned when he breathed. His only guess was that he was in a dungeon of some kind, one that his wife would explain to him from her books. He smiled as he thought of her. How she told him she longed for an adventure, just one she'd tell him. He could imagine her jealously when he would return home.

He heard the door open and looked over. It was one of the men that hunted him. The man forced him to stand and walk to the door. He frowned as he didn't resist. His fight was depleted and, without knowing where he was and being chained, there was no use trying.

He coughed deeply as his captor walked him down the halls. He couldn't have been in Arron's village. Arron said everything was made from wood like the house. All Christopher saw was stone. His hopes slowly dwindled as they faced a door. He was on his own in the strange world.

He was shoved roughly through and found himself in a cage. He sighed. It wasn't like he was going to run. He couldn't the way his feet were chained. He felt the heat of the room lick his skin. He welcomed it hungrily as it slowly calmed his shivering.

He looked around as he heard the dull roar of a crowd. There were a dozen or more of his friend's kind there; most were older and graying while the five from the forest sat on inviting chairs. They fell silent as another man walked in. He felt his hope return. At the head of what he assumed was the council sat Arron.

He looked bored and refused to look at the cage. He looked at a scroll and around at the people. They watched him hesitantly. One spoke up and he nodded. He looked over to the hunters and listened to their story. His posture clearly stated he was not pleased to be in that room. He looked over the scroll again and he spoke with his serious but board tone.

Everyone looked to Christopher. He coughed when his lungs demanded it. He could feel an illness start to bloom within them. The stares he was getting made him self-conscious. He wasn't going to say anything. He didn't speak his language and had no idea if he was being addressed. Again, he said something but more irritated. The audience shifted away from him when he didn't answer.

Arron pounded his fists hard on the wood, cracking it. He glared furiously at the cage but quickly changed when he finally saw the man in it. "Christopher?" he asked strangely.

Christopher nodded slowly before his coughing returned. He heard a soft thump and the squeaking of metal hinges. The shackles fell from his ankles and from around his wrists. He felt his friend's warm hands on his shoulders and he shivered at the touch.

"What in Mother's name are you doing here?"

He could only smile at his friend. "You wouldn't believe me if I told you," he chuckled, which triggered more deep coughing.

He heard Arron order the others. His friend helped him into a thick robe, and he sighed happily in its warmth. He addressed the other people who began to talk heatedly with each other. Obviously, he was quite the abnormality. Arron handed him warm liquid and he drank from it hungrily. He felt it heat up his innards and clear out his lungs. He asked what it was and was greeted with a smile. "Think of it as special medicine that can cure any illness, though your ribs will be another matter."

He nodded and returned the bowl. He took a deep breath. He most certainly had some explaining to do and the quicker it was done the better. "After you left we had a storm rage on for a good month, which was followed by earthquakes. Not knowing what else to do, I left Jocelyn there to search for you. I read the book; and, if magic was real, then you would be the one to stop the chaos." He frowned as he shivered again. Thoughts of her fear plagued his mind and he wanted nothing else than to protect her.

Arron urged him to continue. "Everything was flooded and when I reached the gate..." he paused. The horror of what he saw and what Baltazar had done engulfed him. "I'm sorry, Arron, I... I broke my promise." He trembled. The memories of the evil man terrified him. He was a brave man but that man caused fear.

Arron rubbed his arm and tried to calm him. "This is obviously something that you'd rather forget. Plug your ears. I'm going to place my hands on your head and you will feel a slight discomfort but don't move. Understand?" he ordered. He nodded and covered his ears.

He felt a discomfort in his mind. Whatever Arron was doing made him feel like he was going through his memories. He watched through closed eyes the events that happened at the gate. He whimpered as the pain pricked at his chest as he watched Baltazar grab his chest again. He relived his flight through the forest and then when he finally woke up in the stone room. The room was silent.

In a matter of minutes, it was finished. He removed his hands. He muttered something darkly to people in the room. They agreed and he watched as they left. Arron helped him to his feet. "You will heal at my house and then I'll take you home." He smiled kindly as he led him from the room. "I know of a young boy who will be thrilled to see you. He's been asking for you since we got home a few weeks back."

As they walked through the forest, he felt in awe. Giant trees towered above them like skyscrapers. He watched while people ran between them on bridges and enter doors cut into the trees. It was decorated beautifully with flowers, and everything was carpeted in green and brown hues. The large canopy covered the entire central village and kept them cool from the summer sun. It was as if he was in the middle of a story book.

Arron looked over to his friend as he began to chuckle. "It seems this is a bit otherworldly to you. I can tell by your face," he laughed. He smiled as he looked around. "I suppose one would be; it is quite the magical place. One tends to forget when they live here for so long."

Christopher rubbed his face but could help but continue to stare. The thought of it all was almost over powering.

As they walked to the outer rings of trees, he noticed how many people approached Arron. They bowed politely to him before speaking. Many asked him questions. He answered every one of them. When they asked, they looked to him. He frowned as he could only assume they were talking about him. He was the only one without long ears. He remembered the words of the book. He was the 'round-ear;' he was different.

Arron stopped at a tree and turned to him. "You're probably wondering what everyone's been talking about." Christopher nodded but didn't want to explain that he felt like an attraction. Arron smiled and patted his shoulder. "They're curious about you. Your people haven't come to this land yet. They trust my judgement to let you walk around without restraints. Normally, we don't take kind to strangers, as we're protecting something that was left to us by The Mother. They have to trust me anyways. If not, what kind of chief would I be?"

Christopher stared at the man. His best friend was the leader of a very large village. This man who looked bored sitting atop the council table discussing his fate. This man who visited him every month. He understood why he couldn't stay for very long. "Then why do you come visit me at all if you're always so busy?"

Arron patted his back and helped him up the ladder built into the tree. "Keeping that farm safe is one of my duties.

"That's what my father was doing before he passed, I'm his successor. Normally, once the elder chief dies, the current one lives there while his child takes over," he explained. He sighed as they climbed onto the platform. "Darrow is too young to understand the implication and my father knew that. I've been different compared to my ancestors. I had my first born, my only child, very late in my years. He should be older than you by now if I followed tradition properly."

Christopher shook his head. He couldn't believe it. Arron couldn't possibly be older than he was. They looked to be the same age.

Arron laughed as he opened the door. "Don't be so surprised. My people age much slower than you due to our connections with magic. Besides, because of my rebellious nature, your family has the chance to live on the best land in Doolkfae."

When he entered, he smiled. The sight was familiar to him as everything was made of wood. The entrance was part of the kitchen and dining room. The small family table sat on one side while the kitchen with its cupboards and wood stove was at the opposite. It was very cozy as he was led down the hall and into a door. Within was the living room with a large armchair and long sofa. As he looked, he wanted nothing else but to stretch out on the sofa and take a long nap.

Arron sat on the armchair as he invited Christopher to sit next to him. He nodded and groaned as he felt the soft cushion's embrace. His consciousness wouldn't stay for long as his eyes quickly fluttered closed. He heard Arron chuckle again. His reaction to everything amused his friend. He couldn't blame him. He felt like a child with each new sight.

He heard a gasp and looked over slowly. Rosena stood in the doorway and looked at her husband. She asked something and pointed at him. He assumed she asked what he was doing in their home. How, most likely, he had broken a rule by being there. Arron's expression darkened and he answered her. Christopher saw the pity she held and rested his head on the back of the couch. How his body craved for rest, a long uninterrupted sleep.

She sat next to him and patted his hand. He looked over and smiled at her tenderness. "I'm glad you made it here in one piece," she told him. He nodded and stifled a yawn.

Arron moved and she sat on the other side of him. "Yes, we both are. I'm surprised you made it considering how overrun the forest is with creatures who would eat you," he said.

He snorted and looked at the two. "Trust me when I say I know. I've never been that frightened."

They continued to watch him. He frowned. There was obviously something they weren't telling him. "Why did he want to come here anyways? How did he know about the gate," she asked. He watched his friend sigh before shaking his head. She sat oddly still which made his frown deepen.

"Christopher, do you believe in fate," he asked suddenly.

He thought about it as he never really had to before. He shrugged his shoulders as he figured he didn't have an answer. It was his turn to frown. "Since the beginning of creation Mother had prophesised that the evil buried in an Eden would travel from the future and bring chaos to the past. This would provoke a cycle of endless strife to critical points in Garlandon's timeline.

"Unfortunately for all of us, I believe the cycle has begun," Arron explained quietly. Rosena shuddered beside him. He looked away, feeling a heavy weight on his chest.

"And I started it," he whispered as held his face in his hands.

"Oh goodness no, Christopher, don't blame yourself. No one could predict it would be now," she tried to comfort.

He shook his head and stared at the wall. "I should have aimed for his head with the first shot."

Arron heard him growl before lifting him to his feet. "Listen, you did the best you could do without magic. I bet my life none of your people could pull off what you just did. Most would cower and let the earth die." He let him down slowly and let out a shaken breath. "My father chose well."

They heard a squeak from the door and turned to look. Nothing was there. Christopher watched as she stood and walked over. She quickly snatched something and turned around. Young Darrow playfully growled and teethed at her hand, tail swinging wildly. She sighed as she brought him to the couch. "He was supposed to be sleeping," she grumbled. She freed her hand and he jumped for it only to fall to the floor. He whimpered and slowly got up. He shook much like a wet dog and tried grabbing her hand again.

He quickly stopped when he saw Christopher. His smile spread and he quickly climbed onto his lap. He reached out with one hand and quickly said something. Christopher chuckled and ruffled the young boy's hair while obliging to his extended hand. As the last visit, he felt warmth emanate from it. It spread into his lungs and the irritating sting vanished. He looked curiously at the child as he felt his ribs. The pain had gone.

He heard Arron laugh. "I told you he would be excited to see you." He patted the boy's head. "It's a shame he won't remember all this." He looked over curiously. It would be strange that he wouldn't, not if he were to see him every so often. He shook his head. "Children's memories are strange things. I've seen far too many in my life forget these early years as they grow older. It wouldn't surprise me if he doesn't remember any of this in a few years."

He was about to ask when a knock came to the door. Arron left and he could hear some hurried words at the entrance. He saw Arron rush past the living room and heard thumping above them. Soon after, his friend rushed into the room, and he could see the worry in his features. "They found that other man, but he has already convinced the younger generations that he is a prophet from a distant village."

He looked out the window and he followed Arron's gaze. The clouds had darkened. He looked in horror as white snowflakes gently floated down. It was the middle of summer and it certainly wasn't cold enough for it. He noticed the anger on his friend's face.

Arron growled and walked to the window. "How long has he been here? The earth cycle is nowhere near winter." He quickly looked over to Christopher with eyes burning with questions.

"I don't know, Arron. I don't know how long I slept in the dungeon or at the gate. It could have been a week or longer; and with that gate, he could have come much earlier than me."

He quickly walked to the hall. "Rosena, help prepare him for travel. I need to get the armour," he ordered as he left again. She tried taking Darrow from his lap but the boy nestled under his arm. She looked at him fearfully and he nodded.

He moved the child from his hiding spot and looked into his terrified grey eyes. "I need to go now but I'm sure we'll see each other again. Alright, little one?" he told him calmly.

Darrow nodded sadly and pulled out a small golden chain. A tiny leaf dangled from it and he put it around his thumb before running off.

Christopher looked at it curiously and then at Rosena. Her beautiful eyes held tears as she shook her head and looked away. She mumbled something and looked back. "It's his charm. It holds magic from both of us to keep him safe," she explained quietly. She stood and looked out the window before looking at him again. "I wouldn't be surprised if he ends up saving people one day. He's always trying to protect people."

Outside was cold. The temperature had dropped since he entered the house. As Arron stood waiting for him, the snow had built up to his ankles. He watched as his figure returned with a stag. Normally, there were two and he asked why the difference. His face still held the anger as he explained that he didn't plan on returning home right away.

Christopher climbed up behind him and they quickly made their way to the center of the village. He recognized it. It was the only thing that wasn't made of wood. A rock pillar grew from the earth and sprouted taller than any of the trees. At the base he could see many people dressed in the same brown armour as Arron. The chief addressed them and they nodded and answered. He turned and forced the stag into a gallop out of the village.

They ran up the gently sloping walls of a depression in the land. As Christopher turned back, he thought it was much like an angel food cake bowl with dying broccoli. He was saddened as he felt it would be the only time he would see such a place. He turned around and held on tightly as Arron urged the steed faster.

After a few days travel, they returned to the gate. By then, the snow blanketed everything in sight. The temperature made their breaths produce clouds. He shivered slightly in his hunting gear. It was worse than what he was used to. Spending nights outside was one thing when he had a sleeping bag. The chill that spread through the forest was something different entirely.

Arron let out a shaky breath as he stood before the door. He looked at Christopher with profound sadness. He frowned and placed a hand on his shoulder. He had never seen the man so distraught.

Christopher smiled weakly. "I can't help but feel this will be the last time we see each other, friend," he confessed.

Arron shook his head. "I'll see you in a month, as always." He smirked but it quickly disappeared. "I need you to do a favor for me."

He nodded. He would do almost anything for him. He had already shot a man and would have killed him if he had the chance. Arron took a large pack from the deer. Christopher had wondered what was in it as it was odd to carry with them. He passed it to him along with a small note with a strange depiction on it. "I need you to hide this in the hidden room in the basement," he whispered. "That paper has enough magic to get you there. Place it on the wall, you'll know which one."

He nodded as he knew exactly which one he spoke of. The one with a strange stuck out brick. Arron had shown it to him before.

His curiosity overpowered him. "What's in this sack?"

Arron patted his shoulder. "You've always been so curious, Christopher. I can see why father loved you so." He pulled him into a tight hug. Through his actions, he could feel the upending doom. Something was not right. "What you carry is what the future guardians need to succeed. You carry our past and wisdom and hopefully a child's future."

Christopher pulled away and tears gathered in his eyes. He opened the door and he felt a warm breeze embrace him. He looked at it and then his friend. He refused to accept it may be the last time he'd see the enthusiastic man. It couldn't be. He couldn't lose his best friend as he was.

He reached out much like his son had with him. Arron responded the same way and placed his hand on his. As before, he felt the warmth emanate from it. "I hope you live a wonderful life, my friend, one filled with many children and much laughter." He felt his eyes water and blink. "I hope what I unleashed doesn't end up killing you. I wish I could help. This is all my fault."

Arron smiled his usual smile. It was brighter than the sun itself. "You've done more than enough and I thank you for it. Do not think for a second longer that you started this. You didn't know of what was to come. None of us did."

He nodded as he watched him climb back on the stag. He raised his hand and waved. "May Learthdelsea's grace protect you, Christopher, and all your descendants," he said proudly before turning and running off.

Christopher watched him go sadly before he turned to the gate. He felt his heart fill with sadness and a realization he wished he would have seen sooner. "May Learthdelsea protect you too, brother."

* * *

Years had passed and as Arron predicted, once again, he never heard from him since. The pain of knowing that he had probably lost one of the most important people in his life hung over him. It took time and much convincing from Jocelyn that he couldn't have predicted what happened that day. As the years passed, even she had forgotten about the storm as well as the rest of the world. It was if it had never happened.

Christopher had many children and even they started families of their own. With each new arrival, he felt he had a purpose once again. He had to protect his own family as the farm had steadily declined with his age. It saddened him to see it become what it was, but his body could no longer handle the work.

Watching his grandchildren play in what once was a daily chore brought new life to the old barn.

It was when his youngest died that new life was breathed into him. His son and his wife had died tragically in a car accident. What happened still remained a mystery to anyone who looked into the matter. As they died horrifying deaths, their only child, his granddaughter, had survived unscathed. A miracle some claimed. As he took on the role of father once again, they didn't know just what sort of miracle she was.

It wasn't long after they adopted their little Evelyn that she had gone missing. The girl was curious by nature and loved to explore. He hated to admit it, but she was much like him when he was younger. It unfortunately led her wandering off on her own. Being but just a toddler still, she had the stamina to go far. They searched everywhere for the young child but she was gone.

A few days after her disappearance, she was found giggling on the living room rug, dressed in her pink winter clothing. When they asked her where she went, she would reply 'out.' They looked at her confused. It made sense that she was outside because of her clothes but not how she returned. When they asked how she got home she would reply with 'awow' and giggle more. When they undressed her, Christopher smiled. He saw a small golden leaf on a chain around her neck. He felt, deep down, that he knew who returned her.

Chapter 22

Only Night

A few months had passed since her grandfather told them of what had happened with Arron. It had put Darrow in a daze. He couldn't remember meeting Christopher. He couldn't remember the times he had spent in the future. His memories of his father were hazy. His first, clear memories were of the snow and running from the darkness with his mother. Even with his soul intact, parts were still missing.

What bothered him most was he couldn't remember meeting her before the trip with Paige. During his training to be a soul hunter, the trainers had said they would lose their memories of the first hunt. Such memories would be removed, for they only know the feeling of stalking their prey. He could remember the feeling; but, unlike the others, his explanation was different. He didn't feel the excitement or bloodlust. He only remembered the intense need to protect the innocent. Being that she was so young, she couldn't remember anything either.

He had discovered the secret room in the basement and spent days pouring over the ancient scrolls and books that filled the shelves. She could see the interest in his eyes but when she asked about them, he would only shrug. When he had finished, he sealed the wall shut. He shook his head and sighed tiredly. His reasoning was the information was everything he already knew. It was his culture's traditions and history that was locked in that room along with old armor and a strange staff.

Since the first quake, the forest had settled, but more would come again without warning. They were not as violent as the first. Only they remembered the quakes as the rest of the world would forgot. No one made mention of them once they'd pass. She remembered the way her grandfather explained it. It was the old magic in the world erasing their memories.

Summer had passed, as well as fall. The snow fresh on the ground blanketed the continent beautifully. She would sit at the window and watch the piles sparkle like his scars. She would smile as she thought of her wedding day. She chose the winter because that was when they had met. The snow was what brought them together. It should be there when they made their vows.

Her family had gathered that evening for a holiday feast. They wanted to celebrate the end of the year with everyone. It was a tradition that they religiously followed. She smiled at the merriment as they accepted Darrow as part of the family. As usual, when there was people around, he hid his ears and tail. No one had ever noticed how different he was all the years he had spent with them.

After the preparations, the supper completed and clean-up finished, Evelyn felt herself yearning for the outside. She could see the snow fall lightly out the window and wanted to be with it. She was confined with the amount of people gathered on the inside. She decided that she would leave for a bit and return within the hour. She couldn't see her short disappearance to be a bother to anyone. She did it all the time. She quietly slipped on her complete snowsuit and left the house.

Outside, the crisp air nipped at her skin. It was wonderful as the heat from the stove was unbearable. The glow of the house lit the rest of the farm. It carefully caressed the contours of every building and snow heap, from the barn to the workshop. The light danced off the flakes making them little lights that floated from the sky.

She made a path in the deep snow left untouched from her younger cousins. She had to admit even after what had happened within those trees, she still loved the snow. She listened peacefully as the sounds of her feet crunched quietly as she passed. She loved her family dearly but did not enjoy the bustle that came with the holidays. She could feel the anxiety slip from her heart the longer she remained outside.

She sat in a large snow pile, hidden from sight. She remembered the many nights she spent outside while it snowed. How everything was that more magical. How she would giggle and laugh as she would have snowball fights with her grandfather. How some nights they would sleep in their igloos and still be warm the next morning. How, as a child, everything was less complicated. Back then, there were no worries besides her grandmother making her eat her peas.

Her mind drifted away from her consciousness. She could see their wedding day. She envisioned Darrow's smile and the rare peaceful shine in his eyes. How he'd somehow sneak in his snow girl comment and they both would chuckle. Only they knew its true meaning. It was a fitting name. She was connected with the white fluffy stuff. Everything happened to her when it fell. Some would joke that winter was the only time something would happen.

She opened her eyes when she heard someone approach. She found Darrow walking towards her in his old green tunic, brown pants and leather boots and gloves. He sighed happily as he sat next to her. "Since its only you, I felt like being nostalgic," he joked.

She giggled and moved closer. He was more content in the winter as he stretched out over the hill. "You've picked up the language well since being here. You're accent is almost gone."

He chuckled and scanned the forest. "That's what happens when you live somewhere for a few years. I've picked up the Engardonian habits well."

He sat up and continued to monitor the trees. "We're wearing the same things we did when we first met." He looked over to her and she noticed the loving calm in his gray eyes. "Still think I'm a stalker?" he asked lightly. She laughed and shook her head. She couldn't believe that he still remembered her name calling those few years ago.

"When I couldn't find you in there and saw your winter clothes were gone, I was afraid that you went back in those woods. I told your grandfather and came out here," he told her quietly.

She shook her head. "If I went in there tonight, I believe both you and my grandfather would have a cow, especially after what happened when I met you." She could hear him hold in his laugh.

"We can never tell with you. You're as wild as that forest and incredibly unpredictable. Can't be too safe letting you wander off anymore."

She sighed and shook her head. "Look who's talking. First you wanted to kill me by making me a sacrifice, and then you protect me, followed by a kiss. Later you tell me you can't be with me because it causes conflict with the timeline and then you go and propose. Please explain why I'm unpredictable."

He simply smiled but remained silent. There was melancholy as he watched the snow. She frowned and asked what bothered him. He shook his head and looked up. From the gloom that spread, he couldn't shrug it away. She wanted to know.

She persisted further until he looked at her. He held her hand and rubbed it gently. Her heart clenched as she saw the few tears dribble down. He looked away but retained his grasp. "What if I told you I had to leave? That The Gate of Life has been summoning me to guard it and I have no guarantee of returning. I've been putting it off but it's been demanding and I can't any longer," he whispered. She squeezed his hand. He couldn't leave. Their life had just started. His had just started. He had finally found peace. He couldn't leave.

"Would you consider me selfish if I wanted to finish the combining ritual before I have to go?"

She looked at him bewildered before realizing his words. She smiled. He was still a man within everything that was different. She wrapped herself in his arms and didn't answer. There was no doubt in her mind that she would become pregnant. He was the guardian of the life god from what he explained. It was expected. If he couldn't return, she would have to raise the child alone.

She looked up to him and watched him slowly nodding off. He had been running and helping everyone since they arrived. He slept better in colder weather. She removed her glove and gently cupped his cheek. He startled awake but frowned. She stood and smiled mischievously. She made her decision. "Well how would you woo me if we had time," she asked. He looked up quizzically. She giggled and stepped away. "I mean if you don't come back, we better make this worthwhile."

She watched as his face lighten and he smiled. Soon after, he frowned again as he mouthed a word. "What's this 'woo,' or do you mean courting," he asked. She nodded and said he was correct on his guess. She watched his ears and cheeks burn red as he turned away. He rubbed the back of his neck and looked at her. "You do know that I've never done this before, right?" She shrugged her shoulders and grinned. She knew exactly that he had never been interested in the girls from his village and that he was already interested in her when he started living with them.

He stood and walked past her. He swirled his hand in the air as a blue glow appeared and caught the descending snowflakes. He moved both hands and caused the snow to dance into a familiar scene. She remembered it from before. She watched as vague patterns of people danced around them. He returned to her and held her waist. "If I had a lifetime, I would take you dancing like this," he whispered as he guided her through the crowd. She felt the wind pick up and heard it play soft, whistling music in the branches.

He held her close as she rested her head on his shoulder. "I would take you to every strange dance your friend Celthric would have and show them how truly a beautiful gift you are." He spun her and she stopped suddenly as she gasped. The snow had shifted to what looked like a beach off one of the coasts. She watched as people played in the water and the birds flew in the sky. He hugged her from behind. "I'd take you to one of those beaches I've heard of and you can teach me not to fear open water."

He spun her again for she'd face him. He continued to dance with her and show her the different things he wanted to do. How he longed to walk into Prophecy Mountain again. He'd take her on a proper date and show her a few places that his friend had showed him. He would bring the old farm back and get animals and care for her. He wanted to travel to see the rest of the continent. If he could, he'd do everything possible. He'd spend a lifetime with her.

He let go of her hand and built up the snow between them. It started with a feminine figure which blossomed into a gown. It sparkled in the blue glow as the veil covered the face with beautiful ice flowers. He reached out and began to make a snowball out of the dress. As he waved his hands around it, she watched him make a small ice flower.

He approached her and tucked it behind her ear. She felt the chill but didn't remove it. He held her waist and brought his lips near her other ear. "I'd give only the best for my snow angel," he breathed. She felt herself shiver from his voice as her heart hammered hard in her chest.

She buried her face in his shoulder. He nibbled the top of her ear, making her giggle and causing him to chuckle. He hummed a soft tune and the sound of his voice melted her. She couldn't remember if she'd ever heard him sing before. She wondered if all of his people courted the way he was, if they all had wonderful voices like his. If not, then it was something uniquely his own and she was falling deeply.

She squeaked when he lifted her knees and began to carry her into the forest. She could hear the creaking of the branches. He would look down and smile peacefully, but she could see a new fire burning. There was conflict between the two souls. They fought to be present. She held him tightly and nuzzled his arm. She hoped they wouldn't fight.

When she looked back, she watched wooden walls be built around them. The wood creaked and groaned. A bed was made from wood and some soft material with a small fire in the corner. He placed her on it and gently kissed her forehead. She growled and quickly grabbed his shoulders and pulled him into a deeper kiss. He followed with no hesitation.

She had never felt such passion from the man. Darrow kissed her tenderly yet heatedly as he hungrily removed her winter clothing. She felt his cool fingers touch her bare back as they slipped inside the bottom of her shirt. She giggled as he found a ticklish spot and buried her nose in his shoulder. He nudged her away gently before entrapping her lips again.

He growled and moved away quickly as he snapped at the air. He supported himself on the bed while keeping some distance between them. He breathed heavily as he trembled. He shook his head as he looked at her exasperated. "S-sorry," he apologized before he growled again followed by a whimper. He breathed deeply as he shook again. "We've never fought like this, never both wanting to be present at once." He rested his forehead on the pillow.

He breathed heavily as he trembled. She asked if he wanted to stop but he shook his head. The fabric of his clothing began to fall apart and shed. She watched as the antlers shaped and grew while pale green vines grew from his temples. He looked over and she saw his eyes dilate more like Alder's. She frowned a little as she didn't want to lose him. He smiled and kissed her softly as the violence lessened. "It seems we'll have a visitor as he's agreed to share at least. Would that bother you?"

She smirked and rubbed his back, earning a loud purr from him. He arched his back as he rubbed his cheek against hers. She turned her head and kissed him lightly. "As far as I'm concerned, there's only ever been one," she whispered tenderly. He smiled and rubbed her cheek again. "A coin is only one coin but has two sides. I think the same with you two."

He pulled away slowly and looked at her. She noticed the passion of the other as the purring intensified. He licked her cheek and pulled her closer.

When she awoke, she was unusually happy. She could feel her smile spread as she rolled over and cuddled with the warm body she slept next to. She watched as he snored. He was just as content as she was as he subconsciously nuzzled the top of her head. Her movement caused him to stir but he quickly settled, the snores didn't falter.

She watched him as she slowly woke. He dreamt peacefully as his small smile never faded. She traced the vines still present on his cheeks. She wondered if Alder still persisted to have dominance as normally the green would have vanished along with his consciousness. She looked up to the antlers and knew for certain that he was determined to spend the last few moments with her.

She looked over to the wall as she felt the sadness blossom. He would have to leave to go to war. There was no certainty that he would return. She thought back to her history lessons. The continent never saw war. Everyone lived peacefully. As she delved into her knowledge, she realized there was a gap in time. There was never any mention on his people. No artifacts found and nothing to say they amalgamated into the society she lived in. His people vanished.

It was the same with magic. He said that her kind used it. That every living being is capable of using the world's gift. It raised the question as to why no one could. Her migraines were caused from some form of magic. She came to that conclusion after the last incident. Her guess was it was due to her being a spiraney. She was different from normal people. A soul who supposedly has the greatest magic of all but, as she discovered in the mountain, she had none.

He stirred and opened his eyes. He stretched and held her tightly when he noticed her near. He whispered good morning to her and she returned his greeting. He kissed her softly and she knew that was the end of the happiness. He frowned and looked at the walls before sighing.

He stood and stretched more. He held out his hands and she watched as the hair that had fallen the night before clung to his form. It shifted and changed before becoming his regular clothing. He pulled on his boots and gloves before turning to her. She shook her head. He couldn't leave yet. She wouldn't let him leave yet.

He sat beside her. "Unless you want to be out there in the nude, I'd suggest putting your clothes back on," he tried coaxing her. She sat up and wrapped her arms around herself. She didn't want to leave. She knew as soon as the wooden structure was gone, the brief period of happiness would follow. Those few years that he'd been there felt like they would be for nothing.

"Eve," he whispered quietly. She could hear the hesitation in his voice. She didn't like it when he sounded that way. "Eve, please don't look like that." He touched her arm and she held it tightly with her hand. She shook her head and looked away. He couldn't go.

"We both know that my life hasn't always been about what I wanted."

She nodded as she felt tears gather in her eyes. He had few choices to make in his lifetime. He made one by choosing her life over his mother's. He made his second by staying with her. He made his third when he decided to marry her.

Throughout all those choices he was still being told what to do by whatever entity controlled the earth.

He held her tightly in his arms, pulling her into his lap. She felt the wanting to stay as he held her close. She knew better. "I promise you, Eve, that whatever I chose, it will always be to protect you. It may not make sense. Half the things I do don't to you some days. I have a feeling that you may want to burn my corpse by some of the choices I've made and will make. Through all that, be assured that it's for you. That you don't have to go through that hellish journey you made with me those few years ago. This is really the only promise I can make. I'll try my best to come back. It wouldn't be fair if I didn't see you one last time to try and explain what happened. I can't promise I will, but come hell or high water, I will try."

She looked back and smiled. The man who she believed could do anything would surely come back in one form or another. She wouldn't be surprised if she would see a small piece of his soul float back to her. She held him tightly and kissed his cheek. "You better not forget that promise," she warned. He chuckled and kissed her forehead.

She dressed and, as she zipped up her coat, the walls sunk back into the earth. The sun had just touched the night sky as a glow was seen over the horizon. Her family would be sleeping. She knew they would have questions about where she went. She wouldn't be surprised if her grandfather knew. He was a sharp man. She could only hope that he assured everyone that she was fine.

Darrow walked her back to the house. They were quiet and their steps were slow. He didn't want to leave and she didn't want him to. He held her hand firmly as his eyes were lost. They didn't scan for danger. They didn't look at the dark scenery. All they did was stare lifelessly at the path.

He helped her undress from outside and walked her quietly to her room while avoiding those who camped out on the floor. As she sat on the bed, she quickly looked over to him. She had an idea. "I'll walk you to the gate. We should have gone there first," she stated.

He shook his head. His eyes hardened as he watched her. "Knowing you, which I do, you'd follow me in and get in trouble. I refuse to let you follow me this time. I don't know what's there, and I cannot protect you properly if I'm scanning for danger."

She stood up quickly and started for the door. He grabbed her waist and spun her to face the bed. She growled and struggled to free herself from his arms. He held tight and refused to let go. She swore at him as she swung her arm back. If she had an ability to make things explode, she could help him. She had to be useful. She didn't want to sit back and be protected. In her mind, he needed to be protected.

He grabbed her arm and shoved her harshly on the bed. She let out a quick yelp as she hit her head on the headboard. She turned and was about to get up when his hand held her down. She grabbed it and tried tearing it away. She felt his other hand on her forehead and looked up. His eyes held the loss of when they first met. He leaned forward and whispered in her ear. She couldn't understand what he said; but soon after, her consciousness faded quickly and she fell back to sleep.

Chapter 23

The Calling

Darrow watched as his magic lulled her to sleep. It was the first time he used magic on her besides healing. He frowned and hoped it wasn't too powerful. She was an Engardonian after all. One who was from the future and had no magic. Even with a spiraney's soul, the strongest mage of all, she had no control over it. He knew those two explosions she caused were magic but he listened to her story. It was forced by her migraines.

He sat on the bed and held her hand. Seeing her so calm reminded him of when she was kidnapped. With Alder's help, he tracked her down quickly but found no signs of the abductors, nothing but their wallets and bits of clothing. He sent another warning to the group of assassins anyways. It was one they would not soon forget. He was always praised for being discreet and intelligent by Baltazar. His warnings were of dead comrades as the first intruder had discovered. The second warning was the exposure of nearly every gathering place to the law enforcers. They needed to regroup and, for an order their size, it would take time.

He kissed her forehead softly. He always did before leaving her room. His soul trembled with anxiety as the feeling of sadness rose. He held onto the railing and paused. Even through the years of practice, some of the overwhelming emotions caused him great stress. He sat shakily on the steps. He breathed deeply and quietly as he focused on the room.

He learned her family was great in numbers as they filled the bedrooms upstairs and most of the living room floor. He wished he could have experienced the feeling of family like she had. Though it was crowded, they shared the room. They were happy. They cherished every moment they spent together. He only had his mother and even she, at times, was difficult to read. Some days, he could remember hiding, wondering if she contemplated killing him. When she grew ill, he learned better. It was his training that distorted his thoughts.

When the spell passed, he quickly made it to his room. It was simple with a small bed, dresser and trunk. He opened the trunk and searched through his old pack. He pulled out the few things he had brought from home with him and placed them carefully on the dresser. He opened the small wooden box and listened to the soft melody before returning to his digging. From the music, he could still hear his mother's lullaby. She would sing it to him every night to chase away his nightmares.

As he pulled out the letters he had written, he stopped and listened to the music. He sat on the floor as his mind drifted. He began to hum and soon he sang quietly. "Pretty baby look at me..." he began. He stopped as he felt the tears return. He missed his mother. He wished he could have done something to save her and Eve. He had spent many sleepless nights analyzing what could have been done. All his conclusions were the same. Rosena was doomed the day the darkness engulfed the land.

He closed the trunk and stood. He watched the box as it slowed. He couldn't leave it unwound. He cranked it again and closed the lid. Whichever child got hold of it could hear its beautiful sound. It would not mean the same to them as it did to him. The box kept not only the sound of his first memories but his parents leaf pendants. They might have been empty then, but he knew they once held their souls.

He climbed into the closet and moved a few boards from the ceiling. He reached into the hole and pulled out the ancient sword. He dusted it off and tied it to his side. It was as beautiful as ever. He hoped it was strong enough to bring him home. He promised to return and that's what he would do.

He slowly crept down the stairs and back into Evelyn's room. She was still peaceful as she had buried herself into her blankets. He watched her sleep. It was common for him. He smiled as he knew she loved being wrapped up in her blankets. He caught her giggling before falling asleep as she made her nest. It would be one of many things he would miss.

He placed one letter on her desk. He had written it when the forest first started summoning him. It called to him, beckoning him to the gate. It told her of the hiding spot of where he hid most of the money he made while staying with them. He hoped it would last long enough for them to live out their days.

He knew financial matters were not something he was good at. In the village, he would only have to perform his job and he would get his weekly rations. It was not as complicated as the system that he learned from them.

It also held all his feelings for her. All his wants and desires. His dream of being a good father to his children. His promise was written in words, though his handwriting would be hard to make out. He had problems forming their letters for writing words. He remembered smiling while writing it. He couldn't be good at everything.

He left and noticed the sun starting to enter the house. The light would wake them up soon. He would have to leave by then. He couldn't explain what was happening. None of them knew who he truly was besides her grandparents.

He placed the last letter on the kitchen table. He addressed it to her grandfather. He hoped he would understand more about the situation. Christopher Ashmore was a decent man and understood the strange complexities he'd throw at him. He was fortunate to meet him and have him as a teacher. He was lucky to have him as a father for even a short time.

He turned and headed for the door when a hand caught his chest. He looked wide-eyed at the man. Her grandfather was the last person he wanted to see before leaving. Judging by the fuming expression, he was in for a long lecture, one he no longer had time for.

"Please explain why you would impregnate her and then leave," he seethed darkly.

He let out a long breath. He knew he would be asked. "She consented and she knew the consequences. If you want more of an explanation, you'll have to follow me before it starts up again. I don't want to aggravate The Mother more than I have," Darrow explained. Mr. Ashmore nodded and quickly changed before following him outside.

The temperature dropped drastically since he had entered the house with Evelyn. He shivered as he walked with him past the barn. They followed the trail, and he could feel his heart pulling him back. He looked over to him and saw the sadden look on his features. Perhaps she wasn't the only one not wanting him to go.

"You're not the first I've seen leave like this," Ashmore said. Darrow nodded and understood. It was clear from his story that his father had left the same way. "It still raises the question as why you would leave a child here. There are women there who would bear your children."

He smirked as he felt the entity within him stir. "None are like her, and I wish my child to live a happy, peaceful life. A life that all Doolkfaerians are naturally born for, a life without violence, greed or selfishness. One that is nowhere near like my own," he answered. Ashmore nodded and fell silent.

He could feel the entity push forward. He wanted a turn with him. He chuckled as she had named him properly. He was as strong and stubborn as a tree. What he never told her was he wasn't an alter ego. He never denied he was kulspylin, but he knew it wasn't true. In truth, Alder came to him the first time he entered the mountain. The animal wasn't an animal but an ancient soul. The soul protected him but only through instinct. He hadn't grown a conscious until recently; even then he didn't know his name.

"You remember how to fight?" Mr. Ashmore asked suddenly.

Darrow nodded. Once he finished his daily rounds, he would continue to train in the forest. He would spend a few days tracking and hunting animals. He felt him smirk on his lips as he remembered a few people he stalked and chased for trespassing. "That's one thing I didn't let fade. Knowing my level of combat skills is not something you want to lose," he said confidently. Mr. Ashmore nodded curtly and continued.

They reached The Gate of Life. Its vines had shrivelled and browned as the green peeled off the doors. It looked sick which caused unease within Darrow. It was always healthy. It was the only thing warm in the unforgiving land he hunted. Something caused it sickness.

Darrow heard Mr. Ashmore sigh before placing his hand on it. "I heard the call the same day as the first quake," he said quietly. "The monster I let in is wanting back here with his new army no doubt." He looked to Darrow. "I've grown too frail as you've pointed out over the years. I can't go off adventuring like I used to. You need to protect all of us.

"Please save us from that darkness I let in all those years ago. Don't let them hurt my granddaughter again," Ashmore pleaded.

Darrow knew what he meant. He didn't want what happened to her parents happen to her. He nodded but stopped when he felt the fear in his chest. He was used to battle; he was used to living in fear. He had a feeling the war was different.

He felt the old man's arms embrace him. He slowly lowered his head and rested it on his shoulder. He wondered if that was how a father would comfort his son. "Mr. Ashmore..." he began.

He shook his head and hushed him. "You've done a lot for this old man, Darrow. I've lost a son and I thought I lost a part of me that day. Evelyn can only fill in so much of that emptiness, but she's still a girl. In these past few years, you've filled the rest. You've given me a son back and it's more than anything I could ever ask of you."

He pulled away and looked at the teary-eyed man. Ashmore considered him his son. The person who originally was going to kill his granddaughter and caused so much suffering in her life. He couldn't comprehend it. He watched the old man smile. It was one that always warmed his heart as he knew he was doing something right. "Mr. Ashmore I... you've..." he wanted to tell him. He wanted to say exactly what he had told her.

Ashmore placed his finger to his lips and hushed him once more. "I've known for a long time that you've been looking to me as a father. I've seen that glimmer in your eyes the times we've gone fishing and hunting.

"I could never replace Arron. He could show you so much more but I've had the pleasure of seeing you mature. I saw you as a child and as a grown boy and watched you learn to be a man." He extended his hand and Darrow took it. He felt the tears crystallize and sting his eyes. "If I've taught you how to be a good boy and you never return to your old ways, then it's enough for me. I think I've fulfilled my duty to your people."

He nodded but stopped. He shook his head and felt his face sour. "You can't die yet. I'm not going to defend this place if you're not here for her," he snorted.

He laughed and he felt his spirits rise. "Don't plan on that for a long time yet."

The sudden squealing of hinges startled him. He looked to the gate and watched it open. It wasn't like before. Inside was black as night instead of its usual bright glow. A bone chilling mist billowed from within. It was less inviting. He didn't want to voluntarily enter the darkness.

Darrow looked back. Mr. Ashmore held a smile. "I never wanted to send you in there." Darrow nodded. He didn't want to leave but it was necessary. He could feel the hesitation from Alder. He didn't like what was happening either. He watched as Mr. Ashmore held up his hand. He felt his heart swell and placed his against it. A strange, familiar warmth was felt at the touch with the word 'trustworthy' bursting from his mind. He knew he had felt it before but couldn't pinpoint where.

"Funny how old feelings bring up memories," Mr. Ashmore whispered.

Darrow looked curiously to him. Then he remembered his story. He did do that before with him. "I said something to you then, didn't I?" He nodded but remained calm. He smiled and knew what he had to tell him. "Trustworthy. It's the only thing that came to my mind when we touched."

He watched as a glow came to the man. "That I am, son, and always will be."

Darrow sighed and turned to the door. He couldn't hold off any longer. The sun had dawned and he had a feeling the house would begin to stir. He wouldn't be surprised if they wondered where their father had gone. He started walking towards it when he was stopped. He looked back, smiled and raised his hand again.

"May Learthdelsea's grace protect you, son," Mr. Ashmore wished him.

He chuckled. "May Learthdelsea's grace protect you as well, new father."

Chapter 24

Darkness

The doors had closed behind him which felt like so long ago. It left everything in darkness. He couldn't see his hand as he lifted his arm up. The smell of the woods was gone. There was no smell of the city or any buildings. It was if it was taken away. It was the same with the sound. With his heightened hearing, he would hear the smallest quiver in the wind or scurrying of mice. There was nothing. All of his senses were disabled.

He pressed forward carefully. He couldn't stop. Something besides Alder's spirit told him to continue, that stopping would kill him. He couldn't chance death. He promised he would return to her. He reached for the small glass orb that hung from his neck. Inside was an orange blossom. It was such a pure flower and it represented the spiraney soul nicely. He played with the smaller glass orb that had a few tiny, pink flowers inside. He smiled as he chose those to represent Eve. She may have not been able to infuse her soul within them, but it was right to have them around his neck.

He had walked for hours. The further he went the more energy it took to take a step. He breathed heavily as if he had been running for days. His fear rose. It had been a long time since he rested, but that was nothing compared to the days he travelled with no sleep. He wondered if being inside for too long was affecting him. Normally, his passage was quick. It was through one end and in seconds he was out the other. His current journey dragged on.

He fell to one knee as his eyelids drooped. He could feel himself push forward but his body wouldn't take it. He pushed up but fell in a heap. His breathing was harsh as nothingness continued to be his surroundings. Why should he continue? There was nothing but the endless space. He knew he was lost within it. Even if he turned around he couldn't guarantee he was going to find the door. He had finally met his end. As he suspected, he would die alone.

Press on... he heard feebly. He looked up and found a dim light. "Who are you," he asked. He realized he had lost his voice. The voice was familiar but he had never heard it before. He forced himself to stand and concentrate on the light. *I am... another...* It had begun to answer before it faded.

He took a step forward. He needed to know why he knew that presence. There were few things he trusted in the world. Every one of those things was outside the gate. None were with him. He felt his lips part and show his fangs as he pressed on. It was a twisted smile that he knew Alder showed when he was laughing while mocking something. He wondered what it could be when he realized Alder was mocking him. He should have realized that he didn't leave everything behind. He had the old sword and an old friend.

He stopped when his foot caught an edge. It was clean cut. He could safely assume it was like the Cavern of Knowledge. One more step and he could have been falling for eternity. His heart pounded in his chest. He was never fond of close calls. He knew he had to turn back. He took one step and felt that the floor behind him had also gone. His boot felt the sharp edge. He felt the ground to his sides. They too were gone. He was somehow standing on the only block. It led to the question of how he got there. He had just fallen on a much larger square.

As he stood, beginning to panic about being cornered, the block vibrated. The intensity knocked him off his balance and he fell. The supposed air pushed his clothes and hair before him but the sound of rushing air was absent. He was falling but there nothing was normal about it.

He twisted and tried to reach for a ledge, anything to stop his fall. Hitting the ground would kill him. No amount of magic could save him. He pictured the few people he witnessed fall from the tops of the trees. How their bodies would splatter if they were high enough. He could only imagine the radius of his corpse when he landed.

As he fell, he thought of his friends. He thought of his newly found brother who was part of the police force. The officer's smile and enthusiasm never ceased to amaze him. He thought of Celthric. The man may have been harsh with him, but it was for a good cause. Eve was always a good cause. He smiled as he thought of her. That strange woman who slept in the snow despite being cold. The same woman who saved his soul. The same one who he grew to love and from her he learned to trust others.

Then there was her grandfather Christopher. The man had a unique ability, there was no doubt. He retained the information of Darrow's people better than most of the elders in the village. People naturally followed him and trusted the man. He was a leader and a teacher. He was more than worthy of the title trustworthy and father.

The decent continued far longer than he liked. He opened his eyes and gasped as he had to close them again. It was bright. As his eyes grew accustomed to the light, he knew exactly where he was, or at least he thought. Covering the space around him were the multicolored symbols from Prophecy Mountain. He knew them well. Did he walk that far? It wouldn't have surprised him, but surely he would have walked into a tree or something.

He began to hear again. The sound of rushing wind was still absent but he could hear a voice. It was singing and very pleasant. It was a woman's song as her voice was as light as a small bell. It was comforting. If he were to spend eternity listening to her, it would not be torture.

He felt Alder rush forward and roar at the air. The song continued but it enraged the entity. He clawed at the space, having no control over what he wanted. He was desperate to get to the voice but couldn't move from the rushing air. He could feel the burning frustration from Alder.

It was overcome by unbearable sadness. It confused him. Why he was sad at the song? It was comforting. Why would a beautiful melody cause him so much pain? What happened to him? Who was the entity who had been protecting him all those years?

He felt his body transform. His hair stiffened into the antlers. His fangs elongated and he could feel them burn with the deadly poison they carried. He felt the vines grow from his temples and invade his cheeks. Unlike any other transformation, it burned his entire body. He cried out for it to end. He couldn't stand the pain.

A force struck his side. He swung to hit back but caught nothing. It hit him again and again. Each time more specks of something accumulated. As more and more formed, he recognized what they were. It was red sand, the fabled property of Emptharen. It was what supposedly lies between the gate entrances. It was another story if someone would ever see it or not.

Knowing what it was, he had an idea of how to disperse it. He spun around and could feel the air dance around his arms. The bruises pulsed painfully as the sand kept its distance. His mind had difficulty grasping the concept. The specks of dirt had intelligence.

In the brief moment of confusion, it attacked again. It struck his face, sending him spinning through space. He squealed more from shock than pain. The sound set it off as it came back and forced its way into his nose and mouth. It began filling his lungs.

It burned as he tried to keep it out. He cried. There was nothing he could do to stop it. His breathing shallowed as he prayed for it to end. He hoped that if his death was by the sand that he would be able to see his parents again. That somehow Eve would be given notice that he was gone. He closed his eyes and embraced his fate.

"Breathe," he heard someone order from the distance. "Darrow, breathe, you have to breathe!" The male voice was commanding but he should know better. He was being buried in the sand. Though the voice was familiar to him, it was from a distant memory, one he could faintly remember from more peaceful times. "Breathe dammit!"

He felt a shock run through his system. It was unbelievable how painful it was. He coughed but could still feel the dirt cutting him apart on the inside. He could hear the man cursing. He could hear another voice say it was too late. That he was going to die. He agreed with the second one.

That voice then went on to say it was over before it begun. He wondered what it was. He had gone into to the gate to protect something. His main goal was to protect her. Strange thing was he didn't know what was causing the danger. It wasn't like him to charge off into something he didn't know.

He felt the shock again. He coughed and took a deep breath. It didn't burn. Where had the sand gone? He was dying wasn't he? His limbs pulsed dully as he flexed them. It was painful. He felt tired. He wanted to sleep more.

He felt cool water wet his face. He gasped and opened his eyes as he sat up. He felt his head spin as he caught glimpses of a tent. He could hear pounding in his ears as he slowly lay back down. His strength faded.

He sat up again quickly when he felt someone's lap. It wasn't normal for him to be there. He spun quickly to see who when his vision darkened. He felt faint. He only had his spells when his emotions were running wild. It wasn't the case.

"Settle," the man hushed. He couldn't understand why his voice felt secure. He groaned as he rested his head on the ground. Whatever had happened sapped any strength he had.

"You're safe for now but not much longer." Darrow looked up slowly. He stared at the man in awe. He felt like he was looking in a mirror. The only difference between him and the man was his green eyes and his long hair tied back with green string. He shook his head and closed his eyes. He couldn't be seeing that man. He had to be dreaming. The man before him was supposed to be dead.

He sighed and made Darrow face him. "You need to grasp the new reality quickly if you want to win this battle," Arron informed.

He shook his head but could feel him agree. He couldn't accept it. The dead remain dead. Their spirits power the earth and its yearly cycle. "My father is dead! This is not reality; I watched him die. You are not here," he roared.

He shook his head. "This is Emptharen, son. As I learned, the dead are not dead here. We live on between the strands of time, forever waiting till the end.

"Mother Creanni has a purpose for us all and she can no longer afford to let the cycle continue. The seasons have stopped because of Baltazar taking every soul you bring him for his army. In doing so, she had to stop the cycle to have some defenders here for when he decided to go after time itself," he explained.

Darrow sat back, lost by his words. There were other dead souls within the gate but that didn't explain him. He was very much alive when he entered, unless the sand killed him.

Arron smiled and continued. "Have you played chess with Christopher, and don't act like you don't know him. I saw the small bit of his wonder in you."

Darrow nodded before he smirked. He had won a few matches against the man but normally he was the one who lost. He wasn't used to commanding an army.

"To explain easier, you are the king piece and I will go with you as the queen. Everyone else you see here are the other pieces. I am here solely to protect you and make sure you don't die. Everyone else is to fight the opposing pieces with Baltazar as their king. The goal is to kill him as you both are the only living souls in this place, though I use the term living very loosely for him.

"Oh and don't worry about his 'queen.'" He could see the smirk on Arron's face. It made him worry. "I'm proud of what you've done by protecting his granddaughter. By doing so, you removed his queen from play. From our sources, you were supposed to be his head Zakulnea. He was grooming you for it, but you ended up betraying him. Bravo!"

Darrow shook his head. He knew the leader had bigger plans for him. He always thought it would be to lead the kul runders. He could never imagine him planning to take his soul and make him what everyone feared. He wondered if other hunters were out there as a few had disappeared.

Arron sighed as the life left with the breath. "So much has been lost because of this evil and I know it will not end here even if we win," he mumbled. He looked to him and looked away. "I've felt her passing, you know, her pendant no longer glows with her radiance. Our people have lost so much since my death. We have lost our culture, our children, our village and our future because of this madness. Those of the future have lost many loved ones as they trespassed on the Lochden farm. Christopher has lost his son and nearly lost his granddaughter.

"And you," he paused. Tears collect in the tear ducts. The profound sadness he portrayed made Darrow's heart swell with pain. "You've lost more than anyone. I've felt you grow since I was trapped here. I felt the devastation of my death. I've felt the torture you've gone through, and then him separating your soul nearly killed me twice over. I've felt the wandering boy who was trapped in a hunter's body while being protected by an entity that is older than us all. I've felt all those unwanted choices be forced upon you and all I could do was wait here and feel it all. This useless soul that could do nothing to protect his son but watch!

"I watched for decades as the darkness continued to suffocate your soul. Then there was a beautiful, daring little light. It gave you hope and clarity. You were able to see truthfully again and turn back before he fully consumed you. That little light guided you through the darkness that had spread over Lost Lorne Forest to those few precious years of happiness. I don't think she will ever know how truly a wonderful gift she is to this bleak world."

Darrow sat in silence as he listened to the man. Hearing all that had happened for most of his life made him realize how dark it truly was. He smiled as he clutched his pendant. Through all that time, he thought he was saving her life. The reality was she had been saving his. That strange, stupid girl saved his soul and had put it together again.

He knew there was only one way to repay that. He looked up at him and felt some of Alder's mischief crawl across his lips. He stood up straight and saluted. "So where do I start, sir," he asked enthusiastically. He saw the smile return to his father's face. It caused joy within him to see his smile, one that he had forgotten.

Arron stood and patted his back. "Now this is why I'm so proud of you," he laughed hardily.

He led him to the tent door. He could hear his heart beat in his ears. Whatever awaited him on the other side would be the last struggle. He would either come out of it alive or the evil would spread and consume everything. He carried everyone's future on his shoulders, which he didn't like. The animal's pride burst forth as he was also proud of his decision. Arron stopped him at the entrance and his smirk grew. "Welcome to the Emptharen War and the fate of Garlandon."

Chapter 25

The First to Die

Darrow had to shield his eyes from the blowing sand. As it settled, he gasped. The vast red desert stretched for eternity before him. It rained with the red flecks. Dotted among the dunes were large, crimson rocks. It certainly was a magical place as the sand glowed a ghostly yellow, keeping them warm. It allowed him to make out the thousands of people stretching out before him on the sand dunes.

He turned around to see the tent flap was gone. All that remained were those who stepped out. The laws of Emptharen made poor sense. He hoped that he wouldn't have to stay long. His concerned was marked by Arron. "It is the ways of this place. If something is needed it will appear as if a gift. Even though most of us feel forgotten by The Mother we still get reminders that she knows we're here," he explained. Darrow nodded as he was guided to the back of the army.

He saw the many souls that stood, waiting for battle. There were mothers, fathers, sisters and brothers. There were elderly, adults and children. He recognized many of them from the first village purge. He didn't understand at first, but he knew what had happened. Their souls were sent to their deaths in hopes to fuel the Zakulnea. He noticed there were also many Engardonians standing among them. Some he recognized as choosing them for the next sacrifice.

He was asked to sit on a large rock formation and he followed instructions.

"It will begin soon," Arron stated quietly. "All these people will fight the oncoming army in hopes to save their loved ones who remain outside." The melancholy returned and he looked to the folded hands in his lap. He returned his focus. "The armies will clash here. Our mission is to find the gate and protect it. Once we find it, we wait for Baltazar and kill him unless someone else got to him first. I have my doubts but I can always hope."

Darrow nodded and returned his attention to the field ahead. The sight stirred Alder's anger. It grew and grew until it started a headache. He couldn't understand the creature's fury. He didn't get angry at many things. He was more enthusiastic and mischievous but never angry. As he tried to question him he pushed forward. The fury blinded him as he held his head. He was fighting to burst forward as he tried to maintain his sanity.

Through the wild pounding of his heart, he heard the familiar distant screech. They were coming. The sound set him off as he retreated back into his mind. The impulse shook him as he felt someone help him to his feet. He looked over at the concerned man and looked away. "Christopher called me a kulpsylin, though it's only half true." He looked up shakily and drew in a breath. "Shortly after Baltazar split my soul, something else found me. We've been together ever since, but he sometimes forces his way through when he deems it necessary. I've never felt him so angry." He looked over to Arron as he guided him. He wanted answers and he may have had them. "Why does this place make him that way?"

Arron stopped and looked over. "If we have time for a break, I'll try my best to explain what I think he is. Right now we need to focus on that."

He pointed back to the army. It had already begun. The army of Zakulnea dove for the first row. The spirits used fire magic which drove the enemy back, but the land marchers took them out quickly. Then all hell broke loose. He had only seen such devastation once and that was when he had lost his father. The blood spurted everywhere while corpses burned and shredded.

He turned away and felt Evelyn's sickness for blood. He had seen more than his fair share. He was the cause of so many deaths. He had slashed, decapitated and mutilated many people and monsters. His job was to knowingly lead people to their deaths. Death and blood were a normal sight.

The sight of battle, however, bothered him. He was always alone whether it was at home, hunting or walking through the forest. Watching the thousands of people gathered, killing each other, was not right to him. They were all kinsmen at one point in their lives. They shared Garlandon in one existence or another. The clash of two like groups was wrong. The war should have never happened. There should have been peace and happiness.

Their sneaking through turned into a run as a few of insects had infiltrated the ranks. He could hear their ever deafening screeches and beating wings. One sounded too close. He spun around and withdrew the old sword. The magical blade sang hauntingly louder than the clash before them. He could never remember a time where it sounded so sad. The depressing note bore into him.

The sound made every monster stop. They turned to him as his allies continued the fight, taking more down. He felt his instincts, and his body vibrated with the feeling. Alder knew the power of the blade. He allowed the suppression of his soul. He knew that allowing his body to cripple would be costly. He could sense his arms flexing, followed by his legs. They unleashed their coil and he felt resistance of something.

Within moments he was forced back into consciousness. He panted as his head spun. A great deal of the insects were gone as black ash fell from the sky. A power pulsed into his arm. He looked over and saw the blade glow with immense light. It burned his eyes, but within seconds, it seeped into the sword. He looked over and saw Arron shake his head. Obviously he had never seen it work either. It was something else of legend much like the land he ran in.

The wind had picked up since their flight. It pushed against their backs but would then turn to hinder them as it blinded them with sand.

"I see you, Darrow. You know running has never suited you. I much preferred my strong statue. This thing you've turned into is quite appalling," Baltazar called out. The voice carried around the space as it echoed, almost as if through time.

Darrow growled as he continued to run. Allowing words to affect his judgement was fatal. It was that way in any combat.

His father didn't know that lesson. Arron grabbed Darrow's wrist and stopped them both. "It's always suited you though, hasn't it," Arron challenged back. "You ran from Christopher and then from me. As we hunted you, you cowered in the shadows like the pathetic insect you are. I know you're terrified of our lineage. Once you break life, it's not liable to come back.

"The only problem was you allowed my son to live," Arron shouted. "You now resent that as you were sure he would never escape the darkness you implanted in his soul. You never anticipated that he would find the spiraney of legend and be purified by their light. That oversight of yours has cost you your greatest warrior and he's now your most feared ally." The ground shook as an explosion went off near them.

The man was insane as the wind caught and caused a twister. They ran again as Baltazar laughed. Darrow's suspicions of insanity increased as he felt his heart hammer in his chest. He did not find the humor in the situation. If they were to have been caught in the blast, they would have been dead. If they would've been pulled into the twister they would have been dead. Why the man decided to insult the most powerful magic user known was beyond him.

They ran at full speed as Baltazar targeted them with fury. Darrow couldn't blame him. He would have tried to kill his father too if he was the receiver of his insults. He could faintly remember when the elderly insulted him when he had first taken over the village. Within a few hours each person was gone without a trace. The other villagers had all assumed he removed them from existence for treachery. There were a few who were executed before the village within the moment the words left their lips. No one dared question him.

As the sounds of battle died, the frequency of the explosions vanished. They hid behind a rock and breathed deeply. Darrow whimpered as his arms and legs pounded. He was accustomed to lifting things and short bursts of speed. The prolonged running was not something he ever had to do. He'd escape but would quickly dash out of sight and hide in the snow. He'd lay in wait for the pursuers to wander off and then leave.

He noticed a glow near them. It was different than what the sand offered. It was a white light. He smiled. They had found what they were looking for. He looked over and saw the Gate of Life. Its vines were shrivelled but held green patches as the green moss on the door had browned and had fallen off in places. It was normally magnificent. At that moment it was pitiful. The wonderful creation that he had used to lure the unsuspecting Engardonians was dying.

He patted his shoulder and smiled. He was out of breath and his skin shimmered with sweat. Even through the exhaustion, the determination was still present. He could see why he was such good friends with Christopher. They were both stubborn when it came to survival.

"Now that we have a quick break, I will answer your question from earlier," he stated. He frowned but quickly remembered he asked about his anger. "Since Emptharen is timeless, I sense all there ever was and will be. It is normally a jumbled mess and it takes a great amount of meditation and focus to gather feelings for just one existence. It is easier when you are connected with the one you want to visit." He smiled and wrapped his arm around his son's shoulders.

Darrow found it odd but allowed the man the small bit of pleasure. He most likely wouldn't have it for long.

"I focused on you so I could still have some sense of family. It then changed when he came." His mood darkened and his voice saddened. "I felt the history of the new entity. His life unending and ancient as he clings to a promise he made to the life he cherished most. He has walked this earth for far too long and had nearly lost his purpose until he met you." Alder stirred and his sadness leaked out causing tears to flow.

"I cannot say much as even his life is twisted in time strands too long to follow. He has somehow even weaved himself through history until he met you. I do know he has been to Emptharen before, though not through the gate. It was after that incident that the gates appeared and linked, though no one knows their true purpose." Arron stopped and looked up. Darrow followed his gaze. His eyes widened as he saw a flaming torch falling from the sky. The singing from before could be heard gently above the howling wind. It was for a brief moment but he saw the symbols of Prophecy Mountain before vanished with the music. It landed with a dull thud in the sand.

He stood, checked for danger, and jogged to torch. He brought it back. He was in disbelief as he recognized it. It was the first time he had used thicker cloth with straw and a ring of metal to not burn his hand. It was the one he let fall over the edge when he had entered the cavern with Evelyn. Knowing the small bit of his history, he came to a conclusion. It was correct as the rage bubbled forth again along with unending sadness.

He looked at Arron as he felt the transformation began to take place. "I know how he came here. He fell like that torch from within the mountain. He fell into the space between time and became trapped for eternity," he breathed between his fading control. He felt his hands on his shoulders. He looked up tiredly before his knees buckled. He didn't want to hand over control. He wanted to stay as long as he could with the man he knew wouldn't be around afterwards. Could the animal not understand that?

"Yes, the poor soul that wandered these sands eternally. At least he was supposed to until you took him," chuckled the cold, old voice he wished would vanish from history. "I know you're out there, Darrow. I feel the anger and the desire to remain with your father. I know you're near that despicable light. Be a good boy and come away from its glow."

Darrow snorted. As if he would ever listen to the leader again. He lied and killed every decent person from the village. Only those who praised darkness remained.

"If you surrender, I'll allow you to live and keep what your heart desires, that woman you hid from me," he bargained. Darrow growled. He had a feeling that Baltazar had lied but his comment confirmed it. "She is quite the female because of her soul. Nothing much to look at; she didn't have the wonderful red locks of her friend. Now she was a beauty, quite the good distraction Mother played."

Darrow roared loudly as his own anger was amplified by Alder's fury. He held onto the rock as his body shook with hatred.

"Listen to that beautiful anger. How I crave to hear you howl as you once did. Perhaps when this useless war is finished, I'll keep your soul alive. I will keep you only to make you scream as you watch me take the spiraney as my own, her choice or not."

Darrow darted forward, no longer able to contain their rage, only to be caught by a strong hand shoving him against the rock.

He pounded on the rock and hissed loudly at his father. Arron kept him still though he could see the effort. He twisted to free himself but was kept pinned. He screeched out but had his mouth covered. He felt the impulse to bite. He tried but was unable to as Arron was faster. He glared at him as he explained it was a trap.

Baltazar snickered from nearby. "I thought your people were of honor. Here I am insulting and threatening to take your wife and all you do is howl. She must be nothing to you but a power source."

The words shattered whatever civilized barrier he had. He shoved the man harshly away and leaped onto the rock. His feet barely touched the stone when he was hit squarely in the chest and flung into the air. He hit the ground hard and cried out from the impact and magic. He could feel the dark energy course through every cell in his being. His body trembled as it felt as if the magic tried dismantling his nerves.

The slight touch against his cheek brought him to focus on that point. He could hear his father's voice slowly telling him to breathe. He assured that the dark energy would dissipate soon. There was an apology from within. He felt the familiar embrace on his soul. The pain subsided quickly but could tell the darkness was still there. As usual, he was protecting Darrow from feeling anymore pain.

He could hear him lecture, though his words were distant. He needed to concentrate to hear what he had to say. His words were cut short when he felt his body sit up. He stood and he knew what was happening. Alder had taken over and he noticed the difference. He could feel his hatred. He could feel his thirst for revenge. The crazed man was in danger.

He felt the swift movement. He sprinted and it was faster than anything speed he had travelled. There was contact against another body. He heard the squeal of surprise followed by the curses. He heard the explosions and the sound of something whizzing past his ears. He wished he knew what was happening outside of his mind. He knew he was in conflict but with what.

Everything slowed down when his venomous fangs pieced flesh. It dispatched in great quantities. He had never allowed so much out before. It was overkill. A cut would paralyze most creatures. A bite would mortally wound it. The way he was holding on he was going for the kill and wanted to make sure whatever was grasped remained that way. He was shoved off and he was allowed out. He was finished with what he planned to do.

As Darrow's vision returned, he saw the deep wheezing from the leader of village. Baltazar was dressed in a black robe adorned with gold and violet trim with straight, long hair as black as night. He had reversed in age as the old man had gone and a young, slimy looking man stood before him. Alder had somehow found Baltazar and gotten close enough to bite him. His father was far in the distance running to catch up. He looked back to see him stand.

"I've come too far to let this end in your favor," Baltazar seethed. He wiped the wound on his shoulder and with his magic healed it. "So long as I kill you here before this poison gets to me, I won't die."

The magic from Emptharen gathered around the man. It was of pure darkness as a black orb surrounded him. Magic cast from his father hit the sphere. It was absorbed at impact and not affected. It only strengthened it. He growled. He had seen it before when the village was first attacked. There was no defeating it, he remembered that much.

Even though he knew how deadly it was, it was strangely pretty. It's black and violet hues swirled around as who knew what sort of monstrosity lay within. It gave him an idea. "It's a sparkling orb, Baltazar. I've really only seen girls do parlor tricks with shiny jewels and here you are encased in it. I guess what they say is true. You really must be a girl inside a poor man's body."

The magic paused before it shot directly at him. He could feel Alder burst forward and sprint off, cackling madly. He enjoyed the insults as it caused the enemy to react foolishly. He spun around and was allowed out again. Darrow watched as Baltazar descended and kneeled on a rock. He held a black rod in his hand as he tried to stand. It was cruel to insult others and it was beneath him to do it but it worked perfectly.

Darrow had to do it again. "You know, after all these years, I grew very tired of your lectures. I see now why you used words. You've made all of us use swords while you twirl a baton like a cheerleader."

Baltazar howled in rage as he charged forward. His moves were sluggish, and Darrow quickly deflected his attack.

They clashed again and again. He knew his power was failing but he could feel his strength leave as well. Frustration flared in his darkened eyes. "When I'm through with you, I'll make sure that whore pays for your treachery," he roared.

His words caused the fury again. No longer thinking logically, they both allowed the pole to pierce the shoulder as they plunged Learthdelsea's Grace into his heart. He saw the question burn as the darkness spread into his body once more. The impulse was unexpected. The sudden pain was not calculated. He knew Baltazar wanted to know why the calm and collected warrior allowed the hit to happen.

He pulled him closer, hearing the ringing of the blade. It sang the same sad song as when it was first pulled from its sheath. It was done, though he wasn't. He still had business with the monster. He hissed angrily as he felt more venom in his fangs. "No one insults Eve in front of us," he whispered darkly as it was mutual with the other.

He let the body fall as it engulfed in black flames. The sword rang out in its same sad song as it shook violently. The rod dispersed, but the dull thumping continued. He would need a healer as the darkness remained. They would have to lure it out with their magic. That was if any healer would help him in the village. He had just killed their leader. There was no doubt in his mind that no one would touch him. They never did.

Darrow sat, hoping he could return home soon. As the last of the ashes rose with the swirling winds, he caught the last words of the evil.

"Now the cycle begins. This battle was decided before you even began and I win," Baltazar cackled manically.

Darrow pondered his words. He hoped he hadn't unleashed an evil into the world that would kill everything.

The words bother him. He wanted to know why it was familiar. He closed his eyes and thought back. The images on the cavern walls returned to his memory. He had memorized the prophecy. He knew everything those walls held. He opened his eyes again. He knew what had happened. He had started the prophecy. His journey with Evelyn was the beginning. "Its corruption will travel to a time forgotten and change the destiny of Garlandon. Only those chosen by my hand will save us, and the cycle will begin and repeat until time's end. This is Creanni's prophecy and the destiny of the Gate of Life.

"Only when the ultimate child is born and the evil brought to its knees I will give them a choice. That choice will bring an end to the darkness but at a cost. What my children choose is up to them," he recited as he watched the sand storm dwindle to nothing. It was eerie to see how calm and how quiet Emptharen was without battle. He wondered if the ultimate child was her as the spiraney was the ultimate mage. He could faintly remember that Baltazar was searching for it as he was kept in the dungeon.

Her time period had forgotten his culture. No one he had met resembled his people in any form. None had the telltale ears or vibrant eyes. None held magic and he could tell that any slight resemblance to magic was counted off as a fluke or well-prepared stunt. It made him wonder if the time forgotten was his own. Baltazar had corrupted his peaceful village, he came from a future time and many had heard him muttering about a lord higher than him. Being a guardian and a spiraney, according to his culture's scriptures, they were both handpicked by The Mother. Everything pointed towards they were the first. It also raised a question as to who would be the last.

A hand touched his shoulder and took him from his thoughts. He turned around as he heard his father's breathlessness. It was clear he was happy as he had a smile that had spread to both ears. He pulled him into a tight hug as he turned around to face him. He could feel the release of tension within himself. It had been too long since he felt the embrace of his father.

He pulled him away and saw his tears of joy. "I'm so proud of you. You have defeated the evil and in doing so have saved us all," Arron congratulated. He frowned. It wasn't the case. He held his shoulders. "I know what the prophecy states, but he didn't have the key piece of the prophecy," he explained. He looked at him confused. He continued to smile. "It was a secret guarded by our family, passed down from the first guardian of Learthdelsea.

"You see, there was always going to be a battle here. Baltazar and the evil he worshiped, the creature Devren, knew of the cycle and are now planning to try and foil the next generation of heroes." Alder tried to tear out in fury at the new name mentioned. Something about the name Devren caused him great anguish, embarrassment, disappointment and anger. He felt his lips at his ear. "They do not know that this battle decided it all. The ending that begins the cycle is the ending that will always happen, no matter the story. Each time they face the guardians in Emptharen, they will always lose."

Darrow pulled away and looked skeptically at the man. He had truly lost it. Even through his thoughts he could feel the sadness and pity coming from the other. It was as if he didn't want the evil to suffer such a fate even though they brought it onto themselves. It made him question more who he really was.

It also raised the question on what he should do. If he were to return to Evelyn, there would be no one to confine what lingered in his village. With their new teachings, they would actively spread out and try to conquer the continent. They were all filled with malice and violence and, without guidance from the leader, they would run wild. Nothing could stop them. There were only a handful who believed in the old ways and they were only kept alive as they followed the command of the strongest. Those few were also not safe.

His heart ached at the thought. He would have to leave the only person who made him happy. He would have to leave his new found family and friends. He would have to leave the life he was shown. Everything he ever wanted, he would have to leave behind. With his thoughts, he knew Alder felt the same as his emotions of desire only amplified his own.

"I see in your expression that you have a hard choice ahead of you," Arron stated. He nodded as he closed his eyes. He didn't want to make the choice. He wished he could have both. With the gate, it would probably be possible. "It's probably the one that I must ask you. Just know now that whatever choice you make, your mother and I have always been proud of you." He watched as his tears trickled down his proud, soiled cheeks. "As it is written that The Mother will give her children a choice, each before the ultimate child must make a choice that will change the destiny of the future.

"Which will you choose, Darrow," he asked. He held up his hands and pointed to both Gates of Life that had appeared. They were healthy again with their bright, comforting glow. Everything was green and lush. He wondered why he had never noticed two but knew that the complexities of Emptharen would only confuse him. "Will you choose to return to your time and potentially lead your brethren to peaceful lives, or live in the future where your influence will be removed and the future you saw may not be the outcome when you return?

"Now choose…"

Chapter 26

And So It Goes

Months had passed since he had placed a spell to force her to sleep. Evelyn knew him fully and, even through her struggle to go with him, he would do something to make her stay. She fought feeling the small glimmer of hope that she could sneak away. It all was crushed when she was woken by her younger cousins. He was gone and there was no way for her to follow.

The seasons had changed since his absence. The winter melted into spring, then bloomed into a warm summer. Everything happened in a fog. People would ask where Darrow had gone. She couldn't answer them truthfully. No one would believe he was from the distant past and was of a people long since extinct. She would be taken away if she were to mention anything about a great war that was happening, especially since it was in a place no one knew about. No, everything she had seen and done had to be kept a secret. The rumors they spread could never be disputed as she couldn't say anything about the truth.

They could all feel her worry and gloom. She would catch them looking at her pitifully as she sat at work. They were nicer for quite some time and offered support. As time progressed, she could tell they were trying to give their condolences without directly saying it. They all thought he had died by some accident in the forest as his body was never found and no ports had record of his departure. For all she knew, it could have very well happened.

Despite her deep loneliness and worry, she tried going on with her life. She had to live and care for herself. If he ever were to come back, she would be in trouble. He had always put her health first. He would worry if he caught her doing anything but living her life.

She also had to live for the child forming in her womb. It was strange when her monthly cycle had not come. Then she remembered the last night with him. How she agreed to finish his wedding ritual and bare him a child. As he was the guardian of Learthdelsea, the life god, there was no doubt in either of their minds that pregnancy would surely follow. She took the test anyways and it only confirmed their suspicions. With the news, she devoted her energy and focus on it.

When word had reached Celthric, she wasn't surprised to find him at her doorstep. She could see the fury in his features. She worried that he would go look for Darrow and force him to return. She was surprised, however, to find that his wife wasn't at his side. She always went with him if it was to visit Evelyn, the few times that he did since their wedding. She had to make sure her competition wouldn't get any ideas. Evelyn could only roll her eyes and ignore her. Even after she had explained to her hundreds of times that he was a brother and she had no interest, the woman still pressed that one day she would try.

Celthric sat at her kitchen table. She served some cookies and milk that she had just made. She watched as his anger faded and was replaced with a smile. He ate one and sighed happily as he reclined in the chair. "I never tire of your cookies. No matter where I go, I still say your cooking is the best, Eve," he complemented.

She giggled as she sat next to him. "I should feel proud considering you have tasted food from the best chefs in the world." He nodded as he ate another.

"I worry about you," he mumbled.

She nodded and petted her stomach. The bump had more than appeared. She had a few months to go and some tasks were becoming difficult. She would smile as she felt the energetic presence stretch and kick. It would be a handful whenever it arrived. She could already see it running around the farm as soon as walking was discovered.

"I wish I never told him he should go back, though I know what would happen if he didn't. Knowing how sad it's made you."

She nodded and shifted her empty plate. "I know what you are, Celthric," she said. He looked surprised. She smiled and looked away. "I've known since that incident what you are. They said they were also after you and I heard you two argue in my hospital room. It all confirmed the feelings I had about you so long ago. Your family is also one of the chosen, isn't it?"

Celthric took in a breath and let it out slowly. He shook his head. "So even as a kid, you knew but never said anything." She continued to smile and looked at him mischievously. He chuckled and shifted in his chair. "Seems like we're both in this now, so there no point hiding it anymore," he sighed.

He stretched and stood. He looked at the plants hanging in the windows. "Yes, my family is one of the guardian families and my ancestors are the second and third heroes. We were also the only ones permitted to keep our magic, though we never use it. I know the true history of Garlandon but there are a few crucial pieces missing." He looked at her with sadness. "The first is, where did the evil come from?" He turned back to the window and watched the plants blow in the summer breeze. "The second is what happened to the first hero after his battle in Emptharen? Records indicate he returned to his home, but then he vanishes from history.

"You know who I'm talking about don't you," he questioned.

She frowned and nodded. Darrow had mentioned that no wars occurred in his time yet the prophecy stated that great battles would arise. It led her to believe that the calling was due to the first battle. He may have been the first hero.

"He never comes back for me," she whispered sadly. She had a feeling that it would be so. As was pointed out by her friend, he was from the past and her from the future. Their meeting set a course for an unending war. She wouldn't be surprised that if they were to stay together the world would fall apart. It had to be that way. She should have seen it from the start.

She felt him hold her hands. "If your love for each other meant anything, then I'm sure he'll come back to at least say goodbye. I can't see him just leaving." He smiled and patted her hands. "If the care I saw in his eyes was true, he will return. It helps that he's a stubborn fool." He chuckled as he sat beside her. "I tried to convince him to leave for a good a week after your incident. He refused to listen and I swear he tried to bite me the one time."

She could only smile. It was probably Alder that tried to bite him. He had a way to show his anger, they never promoted it. It quickly turned into a frown when memories about him returned to her. She wondered how many nights she had spent crying, wishing for them both to come home. How many hours she had spent wondering if he was alright. She found herself a few times thinking if he was really ever there, that perhaps she was still in a waking dream from a coma she suffered from the cold.

Celthric patted her shoulder and headed for the door. "I must be off, Evelyn. I lied to my wife saying I would be at the office," he explained.

She shrugged her shoulders and smirked. "Didn't I mention something about being bad news," she teased.

He snorted and tied up his shoes and jacket. "Yeah, and here I was calling Darrow the stubborn fool. Guess I'm in no position in calling the kettle black," he chuckled.

As he stood she could feel the love for the man. If she hadn't been so close to him, perhaps they would've been together in the end. She remembered they tried dating but found it awkward. The chemistry wasn't there for either party. She could still remember the awkward night they spent after school. They decided then it would be best if they remained simply friends and proceeded to play board games.

He opened the door and closed it again. He looked at her and she wondered why the sudden sadness. He walked back to her and pulled an envelope from his inside jacket pocket. He handed it to her and she noticed Darrow's name written on it. She looked back to him confused. He smiled and kissed her forehead lightly. "I'm breaking the rules but I've never been able to stand you being so lonely." He pulled her into a tight hug. He was definitely her older brother in every way. He always took care of her and looked out for her, just as she would for him. "When you see him, give it to him. I have an idea what happened all those years ago. I'm hoping this will help. It's all I can do."

For days after she wondered what it was. It was addressed to Darrow, so she couldn't open it. Her morals were too strong for that sort of thing. It had to do with the prophecy. It held some sort of secret that might change something in the past. Her only problem was she couldn't fathom what it was.

One day during the summer, she was restless. It didn't matter what she did in the house she wanted more. She looked outside and felt the cool summer's breeze blow in the open windows. She wanted to be outside. She had been cooped up in the house under her grandparent's orders for too long. Since Darrow's leaving, her grandfather had been overprotective. She wanted to rebel. She wanted one of her careless walks to clear her mind. She took a deep breath of the pure air and knew what she had to do.

She changed into one of her newer dresses and slipped on some socks and shoes. She made sure her grandparents were sound asleep for their afternoon nap. They had noticed that her migraines had returned and were worse than ever. Many times she would feint and would wake in the hospital. It worried all that were around her and soon she was forced to take early maternity leave. She took a radio just in case anything was to happen. She left quietly with a small pack containing a snack, the envelope and water.

The breeze cooled her skin from the hot rays of the sun. She listened to the songs of the birds. They were happy as they twittered by. She smiled and followed them onto the old path. The long blades of grass proved it was no longer used. They would tickle her calves as she walked through them. It saddened her as she would always walk along it with them. All those memories were distant. She wondered if the strain of constant worry and feinting spells were affecting her memory.

She walked along lazily as the gap between her and society grew. It was no secret that she preferred the company of the trees. They were quiet and listened well. She was more at home with them; it was one of the reasons she never left her grandparents. She knew that forest nearly as well as her grandfather. After all the years she had spent within their loving gaze, she had grown to feel it was a part of her.

Her mind had wandered and she was startled to find The Gate of Life. She smiled as she saw the lush green covering it. It was healthy, unlike the last time. She placed her hand on the moss and felt the moisture soak her hand as she applied pressure. She pulled it away leaving a hand print. She smiled as she watched it fade away while playing with the vines. They were strong, and she had no doubt she could climb up.

The windows intrigued her. She looked into their diamond shape. The glass was cool as she leaned on it. There was nothing but light on the inside. It wasn't blinding, yet there was nothing but yellowish glow. It was hard to keep looking in as she had to stand on her tiptoes. She felt them tingle from the pressure and lowered herself down.

She heard a snapping twig nearby. She carefully looked around while keeping close to the door. She had no weapons for defense. What made it worse was no one knew she had gone in there. She inwardly groaned as she felt her grandfather's lectures flood her mind. She hoped he would never find out she went exploring. She had made a promise since she returned with Darrow that she would never go in alone again. If anything were to attack her, she would be gone without a trace.

She watched as a shadow emerged from the trees. Her heart palpitated and she leaned on the doors for support. She was seeing a ghost. She never expected to see his leather gloves, belt and boots, green tunic and worn brown pants again. She smiled as she took in the fabled sword and realised how much she missed its glow. Her eyes traced his soft features and long pointed ears. They rested on his always sad and longing, grey eyes.

She felt she couldn't believe she saw him standing there. She cautiously stepped forward as she couldn't risk falling. If it was simply a hallucination, she couldn't rush to meet him. Meeting something that wasn't truly there could result in her falling and hurting the baby. The thought led her to believe that another hospital visit may have been a good idea. Her loneliness and worry was starting to affect her more than they thought.

As she touched his cheek, she saw him smile. She tried holding back her tears as relief washed over her. It was truly him. He was standing with her in the forest. She hugged him tightly. His strong arms enveloped her, filling her with the loving she had missed. She never wanted to let him go. She should have tried harder to stay with him when he left.

She could feel his tears moisten her neck as he breathed in deeply. It was followed by hungry kisses as he made his way from there to her lips where he slowed to caress them tenderly. He pulled away only to hold her tightly again. "I know I should say hi and ask how you've been but it's been too long since I've last held you," he whispered breathlessly. She sighed and assured him it was fine.

He let her go and sat beneath the nearest tree. She followed him and sat, with some effort, next to him. He wasn't pleased with it as he moved around her and held her from behind. She leaned back and enjoyed his presence. She heard him sigh as he placed his hands on her stomach, releasing the tension in his body. Soon she caught him snoring and knew that he was sleeping.

She watched the clouds float by as she felt the safety and joy in her surroundings. It was as it should be. He should have never left. The war her grandfather explained to her never happened. Everything was as it should have been.

She couldn't leave it be. She had been standing there, looking at the gate, for some time and never once did it open. It meant that he had been watching her. He had come earlier. It made no sense why he didn't walk to the house. What made him linger back?

"Darrow?" she questioned. She heard him startle and felt him shift but he remained silent. His snoring stopped. "What happened when you left?" He tensed and held her tightly. His hand rubbed her stomach as they trembled slightly. She could feel it squirm and then stretch to the new touch. He shushed and mumbled something in his tongue. By his words she felt it relax and sleep again.

"Darrow," she questioned again. He moved from behind her and walked towards the gate. He mumbled frantically and reached for the handles. She stood up quickly and felt nauseated from the action. She leaned against the tree and looked at him. He cried as he argued with himself. It only worried her more and made curiosity grow.

He breathed deeply and leaned his head against the mossy door. He pounded it but it barely made a sound. "I should have never come back here. I'm not supposed to come back here." He looked over to her and she saw the pain. He was conflicted as he always was. The peace he had found had gone. He reverted back to the turmoil though it wasn't the same. It was different but tormented him still. "I made a promise and out of everything, I will at least keep this one."

He stood up straight, though she saw his posture slouch again. "I fought a battle, Eve. One that I hope neither of you will ever witness. It changed me as I fought among the dead, including my father." She had difficulty believing what she had heard. His father was dead. He had seen it and she lived through his soul and also witnessed it through her nightmares.

"We won but I was given a choice. One that I wished that I didn't have to make alone," he continued. The sadness and pain only intensified as he continued to watch her. If it was something that life altering, how much time did it take for him to choose. "I had to choose between our happiness or your safety and potential to having a better life. I had to make that choice before I left Emptharen and the longer I stayed the more my mind faded."

He turned away as she saw him tremble again. He took deep breath and looked back. "Eve, I meant what I said last summer. I would rather lose you, knowing that for one night I had made the lasting connection with someone I loved so dearly, than finding a second-rate wife who could never replace you."

She stared at him. Though he didn't say it outright, she knew his meaning. "You can't go! You have a life here, with me. You have a job, a father and a mother, and soon you'll have a baby. You were so happy here. Why would you leave all that," she asked loudly. He looked away and more tears fell. "I don't but I have to. As all those things… I want to protect them. I want to be the husband and father my own father was."

"You still can't go. I don't want you to go. I don't want to be alone again," she cried. She couldn't lose him. After all that they had done together. After how deeply she fell in love with him. He couldn't leave.

He smiled weakly. "You're an Engardonian. Unlike me, you can find another partner. Your life won't end here like mine. I can never give myself to anyone else; I will always remain faithful to you.

"I want you to live life happily and safely which will be here. My village is no longer the City of Light, it never was. It is filled with darkness and hatred and it will be felt in this time if someone doesn't stop it." His intensity made her desperation wane. "I won't let them hurt you and I will do everything to make sure that they can't. If I have to screen and kill every last one of them, I will; but I can only do that if I remain there."

His features softened and he breathed deeply. He had aged since he left. She could tell that something had worn him down. He was showing signs of fatigue, which was rare for him. "I will always watch over you, Eve, even if you can't see me. It's what I've always done and it's what I always will do. I will protect you from your past while guaranteeing your future."

She rubbed her stomach again and felt the baby squirm. "What about our baby? It won't know its father. I thought you didn't want that," she questioned. He had said he wanted to be a good father. He wanted to be able to protect and raise his child as his father had started with him. It was the only desire he cherished throughout everything.

He walked over and placed his hand on her stomach. His touched caused a reaction in the child and it wiggled more. He spoke to it, and she swore it felt as if it wanted to reach out to him. He rubbed it again and it settled just as quickly. He smiled and brushed her cheek caringly. "He will be fine. If he turns out to be anything like me, he will be a handful. I can feel it already," he whispered tenderly.

She watched as he pulled a molar from his mouth and a hand full of hair. He held it in his hand as it glowed with golden light. She watched it transform into a golden leaf hanging from a golden string. He placed it in her hand as she saw his eyes tear. "Tell him to wear it and I will protect him from anything evil like those insects. It's my second one; I wouldn't be surprised if my first tooth was given to you all those years ago."

She nodded and stifled her tears. She reached quickly into her small pack and took out the letter. She handed it to him and he looked at it confused. "Celthric said he's breaking the rules with whatever is written in it. He said it will help with whatever is going to happen in your future," she explained, trying to contain the quivering in her voice. He nodded and slipped it within his shirt.

The gate creaked open and she grabbed his hand and held tight. She refused to let him go. He couldn't leave. She had spent all those months worrying and it was for nothing. He kissed her forehead like he always did and his lips trembled. "Neither of us wants to leave, Eve, we'd rather stay here with you. If we could guarantee this future if we stayed here, we would stay in a heartbeat. We can't, so we must go." He looked to the light within and looked back. She could see the pain as his tears stained his proud cheeks. "I'd wait hundreds of lifetimes if it meant seeing you again," he whispered.

He forced her to let go of his hand and held her wrists. She couldn't do anything to stop him. He'd tie her to a tree if it meant keeping her there. He placed his lips next to her ear and felt him tremble. "E lonfi ku," he whispered tenderly.

She began to cry and nuzzled his neck, knowing it would be the last. "I love you too."

He let her go and ran for the light. It engulfed him as soon as he was past the door frame, leaving nothing but the shadow of a still hand. In that instant, he was gone and the door slammed quickly behind him. She jumped at the sound after it soon locked with its loud clunk. It would never open again, as the light in the beautiful windows dimmed before going dark. It only opened the first time because of him, same with every other time. She only saw him for a brief instant and he was gone.

She sat on the path and cried. She could feel it in her soul that she would never see him again. The child who then slept soundly within her would never know that man. That strange man who marked her for death and then decided to save her because of her innocence. That man who grew to love her by finding who he was meant to be. The same man who taught her how to trust again. The one that had just given up everything he loved to protect them from their past.

She stood slowly and watched the trees. She would have to raise the child without him. She would have stay on that farm like her grandfather and protect the gate. No one else should have access to it. She couldn't send another evil to the past. It would not do, and she refused to let it happen.

She looked at the path. It was old and had seen time flow. She would have to learn how to use her strange power of the spiraney on her own. She had to. It was the only way to protect the child. She had to learn the ways of magic of what little she could do by trusting her instincts. As she stood watching the world about her, she couldn't let it die. She walked forward and felt her heart clench. She stopped and looked back at the gate.

She walked back and placed her hand where the shadow hand had been. She could feel his warmth through the moss and smiled. She remembered her grandfather's tale of the little boy. The young child filled with life and happiness. How his smile warmed his heart. How her grandfather's soul touched his and he trusted him with his life. She could only imagine it was the same warmth she felt in her hand. "I will wait my lifetime here, because I know I will never find another man like you," she whispered.

She turned and left back down the trail feeling that all was not over. She smiled. The instinctual push pounded in her mind. She massaged her temples as the pain was returning. As she pushed back, she felt it wasn't meant for defense. She breathed deeply and felt the words of the first spiraney speak from her lips. "I will teach you if you are ready to listen, because you were the beginning, Evelyn, and, in time, you will be the end."

The End

Glossary of Terms and Pronunciations

Zakulnea [zaa-cull-nee-ah] – term for the white insects
Doolkfaerian [do-olk-fair-ian] – a race in Doolkfae
Engardonian [en-guard-doe-nian] – a race migrated to Doolkfae
Sacrilan [za-cree-lan] - sacrifice
Kul [cull] – soul
Runder [run-door] - hunter
Moma [moe-mah] – mom/mother
Lonfi [low-fee] - love
E [ee] – I/me
Ku [koo] – you
Keflen [kee-flan] – different
Kulpsylin [cul-zi-lyn] – split animal personality term

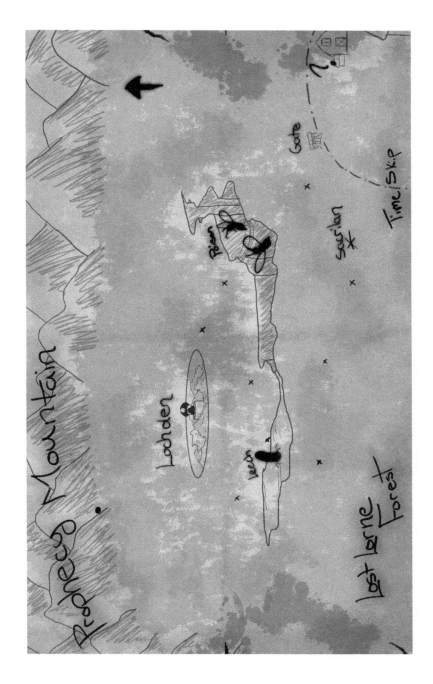

Lightning Source UK Ltd.
Milton Keynes UK
UKHW030359141020
371533UK00006B/51